Burke's Gamble

Bob Burke Suspense Thriller #2

a novel by

William F. Brown

CHAPTER ONE

Atlantic City, New Jersey, 12:30 a.m.

To paraphrase the Russian writer Leo Tolstoy, "All winning gamblers are alike; each losing gambler is unhappy in his own way." If US Army Sergeant First Class Vinnie Pastorini had ever read Tolstoy or had even heard of him, he probably would have agreed, but Vinnie knew nothing about Russian literature. What he did know a lot about was Special Operations, "asymmetrical" warfare, weapons, fighting, drinking, gambling, and losing.

Vinnie had spent countless hours at the tables in Las Vegas, Monte Carlo, Biloxi, the Indian casinos in North Carolina and northern California, even here in Atlantic City. Along the way, he had experienced his share of long winning streaks and even longer losing streaks, but the past few months were his all-time worst. As they say, bullets can miss, hand grenades are fickle bitches, life's short, sometimes the wrong guy gets killed, and sometimes "shit happens." For all that, Vinnie knew his luck was about to change. He knew it! What goes up must come down, and what goes down must always come back up. One hand! One big hand was all he needed for his luck to snap back and get the juices flowing again. It was going to happen, here and now, in Atlantic City. He could *feel* it!

On his previous trips to Atlantic City, Vinnie had played in most of the casinos, but he had never played at Caesars down on the Boardwalk before. When he walked inside, it was almost midnight and he immediately liked what he saw. The big action never got going in any of them until at least 11:00 p.m., when the heavy hitters came out and a guy could win some serious money. Vinnie hoped that was the case, because he was in dire need of winning some very serious money, and they said Caesars was the classiest casino with the best-heeled clientèle on the Boardwalk. The Bimini Bay, the Tuscany Towers, and the Siesta Cove casinos up in northeast Atlantic City were newer and nicer, but they were owned by Boardwalk Investments and he couldn't go back there until he recouped at least a major down-payment on what he owed them. The Borgata and Harrah's were nicer too. He didn't owe them anything, but they were too close to the Bimini Bay for comfort. They would be the first places that Shaka Corliss and his goons would look for him, and that was far too risky. No, he had to try the casinos on the south side along the Boardwalk and win his stake back before they caught up with him. If not, he'd be a dead man walking.

Strolling casually through the front doors of Caesars, he glanced at the gambling tables. The maximums were higher here than at Resorts or Bally's, and that was good. Even so, they weren't high enough. He put his hand in his pants pocket and felt what was left of his cash. No need to count. He knew he had a shade over $7,000 left, which meant he had already lost the $100,000 he brought back from North Carolina earlier that day, plus another $100,000 he had conned two other casinos out of. Vinnie shook his head and laughed at himself. Somehow, he'd managed to blow $218,000 in a little over seven hours. That was a record even by his standards, and now he owed a lot of money to the wrong people.

So what, he thought. Oh, Patsy was going to be super pissed at him, and Shaka Corliss and his goons would talk tough and shove him around a bit. In the end, however, they wanted their money back, and a dead man couldn't do that. Oh, he'd have to sell the new house and sign some promissory notes, but that would only put him back where he started three months before. The Army? What could they do? Bust him a grade? "Send him to Iraq?" as the old running Army joke had gone since Vietnam. Iraq? Afghanistan? He'd been there and done that too many times to count, and he was still on the right side of the grass looking down at all of them.

Vinnie's slide began two weeks before, when he and Patsy came up here for a little R&R. They had just bought the new house, paid cash, and had $30,000 left over. That was the perfect number for an insane weekend in Atlantic City, he thought, so they hit the road. Insane? You might say that, as Vinnie knew better than most. In two days, he blew through the $30,000 plus two $50,000 advances he talked the casino out of. It never ceased to amaze him what people would do for a Vet, if he flashed a big smile and an Army ID card. Unfortunately, that bill come due like any other; and when you owe the money to New Jersey casino operators, they came collecting with a baseball bat. So, he and Patsy drove back down to Fort Bragg, saw the Credit Union, and took out a $100,000 loan on the house to get them off his back before the Army heard about it.

A week later, they drove back up to Atlantic City with the best of intentions of getting a nice room for the night, paying off the loan sharks, having a good meal, and driving back south, suitably chastened and chagrined the next morning. And it almost worked. The Bimini Bay even comped him a room. After all, he'd racked up enough Gold Club Points for a top-floor suite with a nice view of the marina. Then, he took Patsy to Ruth's Chris for a great steak and told her there was no need for her to go down to the casino office with him. It would only take a minute for him to drop off the money and return to the room. Unfortunately, the guys in the Unit didn't call him "double-down Vinnie" for nothing, but he knew his luck had changed. He could feel it, and there was no sense in giving all that money to those clowns when he *knew* he could win it back. That was seven hours ago.

Vinnie wasn't stupid. When he left Patsy up in the room, he didn't run straight to the tables downstairs at the Bimini Bay. Instead, he drove south to the Boardwalk and began at The Trump Taj Mahal. He then tried his hand at Resorts, Bally's, the Tropicana, and finally at Caesars. Of the large, mainline casinos, this was the end of the line. By the time he left the Taj and Resorts, the $100,000 from North Carolina was gone. With his patented smile, Army ID, and a signature, they gave him lines of credit for another $50,000 at Bally's, plus two $25,000 advances at the Tropicana. Now he was at Caesars with his remaining $7,000.

There was no time to waste. Vinnie quickly walked around the table groupings and saw most of the usual games — craps and roulette on the ends, and a long, double line of semi-circular card tables in between. Each table had its own dealer, tabletop graphics, and an illuminated glass sign, which named the game being played — Three Card Poker, Blackjack, Caribbean Stud, Texas Hold 'em, Crisscross, Let it Ride, Spanish 21, even Casino War. They had them all, and he had enjoyed playing most of them on his last few trips here, winning and losing a pile at each. Tonight, those games were tempting, but their stakes were far too low and he did not have all night. Maybe he had two or three hours at best. By then, Shaka Corliss and the goons would track him down, and he had better have enough cash to buy that bastard off. Patsy was sitting in that hotel room back at the Bimini Bay, *their* Bimini Bay, and the two of them would be in deep trouble if he didn't.

Vinnie's eyes finally came to rest on the Texas Hold 'em Parlor on the back wall of the casino. It wasn't his favorite game, but they had unlimited stakes tables there, and that was what he desperately needed. He walked over and stepped inside and saw that it was a big room with dozens of tables, most of which were already full. Giving it no further thought, Vinnie stepped over to the control desk and told the man what he was looking for.

"You sure you want 'no limit,' young man?" the man asked.

Vinnie nodded, so the man pointed down the side wall. "A seat just opened up at table 22. But I'll tell ya, that's a fast crowd down there, so good luck."

Vinnie smiled, walked down to the table, and took his seat. Fast crowd? Looking around at the nine other players, all he saw was the usual collection of *World Series of Poker* wannabes: seven men and two women. Most of the men wore the usual de rigueur combination of black sunglasses, "Beats" earphones, layers of gold chains around their necks, and backward baseball hats. The others wore western shirts, bolo ties, and cowboy hats. The former stared at him with blank expressions, while the cowboys at least said, "Howdy." The women were another matter. One was bright-eyed and straight out of a Dolly Parton look-alike contest, while the other had dark, dead, "shark" eyes. She had body art up and down both arms and her neck, big loop earrings, studs, and about anything else that could be stuck through her nose, lips, tongue, ears, and probably a few uncomfortable places he couldn't see. Vinnie never could figure out what any of that had to do with the luck of the draw, much less beauty; but if that was "normal," then the world was in big trouble.

The next hour went about as he had learned to expect. He started winning big early and got his $7,000 up to $35,000, before it all slowly went to hell again and he found himself staring at the small pile of $2,200 in front of him. The dealer button was Vinnie's, not that it mattered. The house dealer was a woman for this set, and she seemed to know what she was doing when she opened a new deck and shuffled. The "blinds" were posted, the chips were down, and Vinnie was staring vacantly at the table as she began to deal the first-hand. She got halfway around the table when she froze in mid card. That never happened. Vinnie looked up and saw the pit boss and one of their big, uniformed security guards standing to her right and left. Surprisingly, they weren't looking at Vinnie or anyone else at the table. They were looking behind Vinnie, over his shoulder.

That was when he felt a not-so-gentle tap on his shoulder. He turned his head and looked up to see two more beefy Caesars security guys flanking him. Behind them were Shaka Corliss and his twin goons. They were hard to miss. Corliss was black, with a gleaming, shaved head, white-capped teeth, wraparound Oakley sunglasses, a huge chrome-plated revolver in a shoulder holster, and a terminal case of arrogance and anger. Little more than average height, he rippled with the kind of phony muscles you get from too many hours lifting weights at a gym.

Between him and Vinnie, it had been mutual dislike at first glance. Maybe Corliss didn't like white people, or Army sergeants, or just losers, but Vinnie doubted Corliss got along with anyone. The two look-alike, baby-faced goons standing on each side of him looked like they ran six foot six and around 270 pounds each, like football players from some small town in Nebraska. Corliss got off by ordering them around and being rude, arrogant, and insulting whenever he could. Vinnie guessed he must pay them a ton of money to put up with that crap, because they towered over him and either one of them could break him in half.

The Caesars security guy was nothing but polite. "I hate to interrupt, Sir, but if you'd come with us, please?" he asked Vinnie.

"You're kidding, I'm in the middle of a hand here," he complained.

"We'll hold your seat and your chips. It'll just be a minute."

"Like hell it will!" Corliss shoved the Caesars guy aside. "Tha's *our* chips and *our* money, Sucker, and you already burned through all you're gonna burn through!"

Vinnie looked up at Corliss and thought about it as he slowly got to his feet. Obviously, the game was over, and he wasn't recouping any of the money he owed them. However, "in for a penny, in for a pound," he thought as his right

6

hand shot up in a perfect uppercut — compact, explosive, and straight to the ceiling. It caught Corliss under his chin and sent him flying back into his twin goons. All things considered, other than the Ruth's Chris steak, the surprised, open-mouthed, stupid expression on Corliss's face was the most satisfying highlight of the evening.

At six foot two and a solid, athletic 200 pounds, Vinnie was no small man himself, but after he got in that first punch, all he remembered was a blur of more punches, counter punches, kicks, and a good bit of pain. He had fought his way through six combat tours in two different official wars, and a lot more unofficial ones as an Army Ranger and Delta Force upper-level NCO Operator, although membership in that elite fraternity would always be top secret and never to be acknowledged. He was considered an expert with most weapons in the Army inventory and just as good in no-holds-barred, hand-to-hand combat, and had been in more than his share of old-fashioned bar fights at one Army post after another. Tonight, he was able to get in a dozen good shots at one goon after another. He even tossed one security guard onto a nearby poker table, breaking it in half, and tossed one of Corliss's goons upside down into the wall. In the end, however, six to one, almost all of whom were bigger than he was, usually won. When someone broke a chair over his head and he went down for the count, that was all she wrote.

CHAPTER TWO

Arlington Heights, Illinois, 3:30 a.m.

Bob and Linda Burke lay naked in the center of their new king-sized bed, sound asleep in a tangle of arms, legs, and random body parts. He had bought the big bed three weeks before, just prior to their wedding, because he thought it would provide more mattress space than his old double bed had. Navigating the new bed frame and mattress set up the steep stairs and then pushing and pulling them around several sharp corners into the rear, second-floor master bedroom of his townhouse proved to be a job and a half. All of his old Army pals from Fort Bragg had come up for a monster two-day blowout bachelor party, followed by the big nuptial bash itself. After enough beer and brats, it was amazing how six big men could levitate a king-sized bed up a tight staircase, and all he had to do was watch.

As it turned out, all that effort proved unnecessary. Linda needed no extra mattress space, because she had no territorial respect whatsoever. Left side, right side, top edge, or bottom meant absolutely nothing to the woman. Her normal nocturnal preference was for full-body contact and she would wrap herself around him like a boa constrictor wherever he retreated to on the bed. So, it could be king-sized, a twin, a narrow army cot, or the rear seat of a Volkswagen. Any of those would have provided more than enough space for her, as long as he was there. Like everything else with second marriages, he realized this bed geography thing would take some getting used to.

That night, he finally fell into a deep, REM sleep, when the loud ring of the bedside telephone jarred him awake. Back in the day, Bob had ample experience with rude noises in the night, such as exploding Russian 107-millimeter rockets, 82-millimeter Chinese mortars, the crack of a rifle bullet, or the panicky shout of "Incoming!" However, in the three years since he left the Army, he managed to wean himself from the worst of those reactions. He no longer dove onto the sidewalk when he heard a car backfire, crawled under the bed when the alarm went off, or jumped into the bathtub if a door slammed. Now, all a telephone call in the middle of the night did was to snap him out of his usual recurring dream, which was a good thing.

It was always the same. He was under heavy fire, running down a narrow mountain trail in Afghanistan, with Gramps, Ace, Vinnie, Koz, Chester, The Batman, Bulldog, Lonzo, and the rest of his sergeants close behind. Bullets zipped past their heads and ricocheted off the rocks as they leapfrogged from boulder to boulder, returning fire at every turn, but being chased by a hundred screaming, turbaned, bearded Taliban tribesmen. The nine crack American riflemen were more than holding their own, even against the stiff odds. However, no matter how many Taliban they killed, the bastards just kept coming and coming, like ducks flying over an Iowa cornfield. The bad dream kept coming too, but he guessed that was the price one paid for fifteen years in the Army. He fought in a mechanized infantry battalion in the rock-strewn deserts of Iraq during the Second Gulf War, followed by savage counter-insurgency warfare in the mountains and high plateaus of Afghanistan, serving in the Rangers and ultimately in the Army's elite Delta Force. Win or lose, regardless of the war, fighting at the side of good soldiers and better friends like those men were the things that rattled around inside a man's head for years to come. So did the bad dreams. This time, however, the insistent ring of the bedside telephone broke in to save him.

"That had better not be your mother again," he mumbled into the top of Linda's head.

"I doubt it," she answered. "I told her the last time that you'd wring her neck if she wakes us up in the middle of the night again. I think she finally believed me."

"Your mother? Come on, she loves me."

"Bob, you're a warm body with a steady job and a big paycheck, who took in her daughter and granddaughter. What mother-in-law wouldn't?" With her face buried in the crook of his neck, somehow she managed to press even closer, throwing her leg over him as she began to rub his stomach with her free hand.

"Girl, you are insatiable."

"Are you complaining?"

"Me? Never. But let me take care of the phone call first," he answered, trying not to smile. Somehow, he managed to twist and turn his head far enough around to see the display on the dimly lit telephone console. The caller's Area Code read 910. That was Fort Bragg, North Carolina, his former playpen and home away from home, and he immediately recognized the phone number as Vinnie Pastorini's, one of his former Delta team leaders. Stretching back even further, he managed to get two fingers on the handset and bring it to his ear. "It's 3:30, Vinnie. What's up?"

"It's... it's not Vinnie," he heard a young woman's hesitant voice say. "It's me... Patsy."

"Patsy? Hey, girl, how's everything going down there in God's country? I heard a vicious rumor that Vinnie threw you over his shoulder and carried you down there after the wedding. Just remember, when you get tired of him, I'll always have a job for you up here."

"I appreciate that, Major, but that's not why I'm calling."

9

"It's not 'Major' anymore, Patsy. Those days are long gone. It's just plain old, decrepit civilian 'Bob' now."

"I'm… I'm not down at Fort Bragg; I'm up in Atlantic City. Vinnie and I came here yesterday."

"Atlantic City? And you two can't figure out something better to do at this hour than to phone me?"

"Vinnie's in trouble… Bob," she finally blurted out. "No, we're both in trouble, and I didn't know who else to call."

"Don't tell me, not the poker tables again?" he groaned.

"At the time, it didn't seem like such a bad idea. We bought that new house, you know; and we had some money left over, $30,000, I guess. Since he was going on another deployment, Vinnie decided we deserved what he called an insane weekend."

"Insane? Figures."

"It was a spur of the moment thing. We flew up, got a room at the Bimini Bay Casino, and he hit the tables."

"How much?"

"How much? Well, he started out winning, but by the end of the second day…"

"His luck changed? That's what casinos do, Patsy; they suck you in. How much?"

There was a long pause before she answered. "Well, for starters, he lost the $30,000; but you know Vinnie. He wasn't about to quit after that. We went up to the Gold Club office, where this cute little blonde with a big smile named Eva gave him another $50,000, after he signed a note and a bunch of papers, of course."

"Casinos are nothing if not accommodating."

"I told him not to take the money, but he wouldn't listen. The more I argued, the angrier he got at me; so I finally shut up."

"I take it he lost that $50,000 too?"

"Of course, but this time there was no cute blonde to go see. They cut him off, and two big gorillas took us by the arms and walked us down this long corridor to the business office — both of us — where we ended up in front of the desk of a man named Martijn Van Gries. He's Dutch, I think, pleasant enough, but a real smart-ass. I wanted to cut our losses and leave right then. Hell, I wanted to leave after the first $30,000, but you know Vinnie. He talked Van Gries into giving him *another* $50,000, if you can believe it! Well, by the end of the third night…"

"He'd lost that too?"

"You got it. So we ended up back in the business office again with that

Dutch jerk Van Gries. The bottom line is that he gave Vinnie ten days to come back and pay off the markers. If he didn't, they'd go down to North Carolina and take the $100,000 out of our hides... his and mine."

"Well, I'm glad you called me."

"Vinnie didn't want me to call *anyone*, especially you. He is so embarrassed that he made me promise, 'Don't call the major,' he told me, over and over again. 'You can call Ace, but don't call the major!' Anyway, he swore up and down that he'd learned his lesson."

"Vinnie?" Bob shook his head in dismay. "That'll be the day."

"So, we flew back home, took out a loan from the credit union on the house, and came back up here yesterday with $100,000 in cash to pay them off. This time, I didn't go to the business office with him. I couldn't stand the thought of seeing that man again."

"A wise choice."

"Vinnie had an appointment with Van Gries, and he said he wanted to do it himself, so he took the cash and left. He said it shouldn't take more than a couple of minutes. However, when seven hours passed, and he hadn't returned..."

"Don't tell me," Bob said in frustration. "He went back and doubled down?"

"More or less. He went to four or five other casinos down on the Boardwalk, where the genius figured they wouldn't know him, determined to win it back. And since he was using cash, at least in the beginning..."

"He lost all of that money too?"

"Worse. He lost that $100,000, plus another $100,000 he managed to talk those other casinos out of... and there were damages, too."

"$200,000?"

"That isn't even counting the $130,000 of *our* money he blew!"

"What was he thinking?"

"I don't have a clue; you know him better than I do."

"I doubt it, but that's why the guys call him 'Double-Down' Vinnie."

"And to top it all off, he got in a big fight at Caesars with some of their security people and the ones who went down from the Bimini Bay to pick him up. Anyway, I had given up and gone to bed. The first thing I knew about it was when two big gorillas came to the room, woke me up, and dragged me down to the Risk Management Office. I think that's what they call Security now. Some big joke if you ask me! Anyway, Vinnie was there, and he looked like he'd been worked over pretty good. So did two of their Risk Management Associates."

"Knowing Vinnie, that comes as no surprise. Look, Patsy, I'll call Van Gries first thing in the morning. I'm sure I can work something out..."

"It was a different guy the second time. Van Gries was there, but so was a musclebound black psycho named Shaka Corliss."

"He must be their enforcer."

"Well, if he is, it looked like he had a fresh bruise on his chin. Anyway, he was really rude and pushy, and he said Vinnie owes them $275,000. That's for the markers at their casino, plus the others, the damages, the 'vig,' and for being a general pain in the ass."

"Well, I'd say they have a point."

"No question, and they also have *us*… but what's the vig?"

"The 'vig' is the vigorish. That's the daily interest on the principal; but with them, it's usually pretty steep, probably loan shark rates," he answered. "But what did he damage?"

"Two gambling tables and a bank of slot machines at Caesars, and the medical bills for four or five security people, two of whom he said Vinnie put in the hospital."

"That's my boy, all right."

"Corliss said the tab is growing by $10,000 per day, and he wasn't very pleasant about it. He says they want their money, all of it, in cash, or they'll start breaking body parts."

"Well, I can't blame him for that, but where are you?"

"Back in our room at the Bimini Bay. I told Corliss I had to call some people to raise that kind of money. He gave me Vinnie's cell phone and said that was a really good idea, if I wanted him back in one piece," she sobbed. "I… I didn't know who else to call, Bob."

"You did the right thing calling me, Patsy. Where's Vinnie?"

"Van Gries told me they locked him up in the basement storeroom, so Vinnie 'won't hurt himself anymore,' he said. And Corliss said he's staying there until I 'come through' with the money… that is, unless 'a cute little thing' like me wants to 'work it off' in one of their 'escort services' all winter… God, they scare me, Bob. I'm afraid they're going to kill him, and they already told me what they're going to do with me."

"None of that's going to happen, Patsy. I'll get with Van Gries and work something out. Don't worry, they don't want Vinnie or you; they want the money he owes."

"It's $275,000, Bob! We don't have that kind of money."

"I'll take care of it, Patsy."

"I'm really sorry about all this, but…"

"Look, I owe Vinnie, Ace, and all the other guys in the Unit a lot more than that — you, too. When Linda and I had our problem up here in Chicago, everyone came, no questions asked. I have the money, and it's the least I can do. So try to get some sleep. I'll call you when I know more."

Bob reached back, stretching as far as he could to hang up the phone, and then rolled back with every intention of going back to sleep. By the time he did, however, Linda had already scooched over and taken up half the area he vacated.

"$275,000? Who we gonna kill this time?" she asked.

"Probably Vinnie. And forget that 'we' stuff. I don't want you involved this time."

"Patsy is. And it's Atlantic City. How come she gets all the fun?"

"I doubt she's having any fun. Now go to sleep."

"Sure," she said as she threw her leg across him.

"Hey, you gonna leave me some room here?"

"Not unless I have to," she mumbled into his chest and pressed even closer.

Bob was ten years older than Linda, but they had both been married before and were no longer kids. It had been so very different with his first wife, "the fierce and dreaded" Angie. While Linda was soft and cuddly, the late, great Angie Toler was nothing but sharp edges, hard muscles, and knees and elbows like ball-peen hammers. Her father gave them the family's big English Tudor mansion on the lakeshore up in Winnetka, a white Cadillac Escalade, a Porsche, a Harley Davidson motorcycle, and three country club memberships. A spoiled brat? No doubt about it. After all, she was the one who talked Daddy into hiring Bob in the first place. She knew her father was looking for someone to succeed him and bypass her. When she and some of her friends met Bob and his friends on a long weekend in Hilton Head, it was "lust at first sight," as they both admitted later. But the more she learned about this career Army officer, the more she saw him as the missing link in her master plan to block her father's plan to freeze her out. Getting her father to hire him would be easy. Convincing Bob to get out of the Army would be the hard part.

He was a third generation Army brat. His father put in 30 years, retiring as an infantry colonel after three tours in Vietnam. His grandfather had been a hard-as-nails sergeant major, who rose through the ranks fighting Germans in WWII, and later in Korea. He grew up on a dozen Army bases around the world, followed by four years at that exclusive government school for wayward youth up the Hudson River Valley called West Point, where he instinctively gravitated to *his* family business, the infantry, spending fifteen years on the Fort Benning, Fort Bragg, Iraq, and Afghanistan carousel, serving in turn in the 82nd Airborne Division, the elite 75th Ranger Regiment, and the 1st Special Forces Operational Detachment or Delta Force, as it is called in the movies, or simply "the Unit" by its members. In the end, while Bob still believed passionately in the men he fought with, he no longer believed in political wars run by idiots in Washington who knew nothing about those places, but who kept sending a long line of young men to die in them anyway.

That was the weak moment when Ed Toler offered Bob a top job in his rapidly growing telecommunications company in Chicago. At the time, Bob thought the man was out of his mind. He knew next to nothing about business and even less about the high-tech, high-security telecommunications equipment that Toler TeleCom built on exclusive contracts for the Defense Department. Technically, Bob was a Signal Corps officer, which was the Army's communication branch, but he had been "detailed" to the Infantry for most of his career. While the Signal Corps made a great cover story for a guy who never looked like Special Ops to begin with, all he knew about communications was what they taught him fifteen years before in the Signal Officer Basic Course. By the time he got out, that stuff was as obsolete as a flip phone. When Ed Toler made his offer, Bob politely but firmly turned him down. He had no intention of becoming one more "beltway bandit" lobbyist who sold his integrity back to an Army he had served so honorably and for so long. That was never going to happen. Slowly, however, Ed Toler convinced him that wasn't what he wanted either; and in the end, the opportunity was far too good for Bob to let pass by.

Ed later admitted that when Angie brought Bob home the first time and introduced him, he assumed this was one more of his daughter's moronic jokes. Bob looked so very ordinary. He was on the short side, with a slight build and not exactly rippling with muscles like Angie's usual gym-rat boyfriends. But a West Point career officer with short hair? Battle scars instead of tats? No nose ring or body piercings? A man who actually shook your hand, looked you in the eye, and said "sir." Ed quickly glanced around, trying to find the hidden camera, but there wasn't one.

It was a closely guarded secret, but Ed's health was failing. Not even Angie knew, but he was desperate to find someone who could take over the company when he was gone. To Ed, that was a sacred obligation that he owed to his employees. So instead of another bozo she could control, Angie had inadvertently brought Ed exactly what he had been looking for — a dynamic leader who commanded respect and knew how to manage people. Ed wasn't stupid, though. He didn't give Bob a desk next to his and introduce him as the boss's new son-in-law. Instead, he started him at the bottom in customer service, manufacturing, installation, sales, distribution, and technical systems design.

Unfortunately, the company would never be more than a big cookie jar to Angie, something she could dip her hands into any time she wanted; and something she could cash out to the highest bidder when Ed was finally gone. Fortunately, Ed understood her better than she knew, and crafted a diabolical succession plan that left controlling interest of the company to his new son-in-law, instead of his daughter. When she realized she stood no chance of controlling Bob or her father, that iced whatever was left between them. She would have the houses and expensive cars, including the big mansion, a minority stake in the company, and more than enough money to support her exorbitant lifestyle; but she would never get her hands on the cookie jar.

Angie's reaction was to act out with any tennis or golf pro she could get her hands on, but Bob wasn't one to dwell on mistakes, or on people or things he couldn't change. He threw himself into the job, and in less than a year, the dynamic Delta Force major had morphed into what was occasionally mistaken for the "telephone guy."

CHAPTER THREE

Sherwood Forest

The next morning, with the aftershocks of Patsy's phone call still rattling around in his head, and the press of Linda's body against his, he had been unable to go back to sleep. Dressed in his usual "business casual" outfit — blue jeans, a button-down white Oxford cloth shirt, tweed sports coat, and Asics running shoes — he was sitting at his desk in the President's office at Toler TeleCom long before the sun came up. He was banging away on his computer when he heard Maryanne Simpson, his executive assistant, rattling around in the outer office. When she saw the lights on in his office, she stuck her head around the doorframe, looked at her watch, the steaming mug of coffee sitting on his desk, and gave him a puzzled frown.

"What's the matter, Stud, the honeymoon over already?" she asked. "I haven't seen you here this early since Linda moved in."

"No, no, nothing like that, Maryanne," he laughed as he looked up at her. "Just trying to help an old army buddy with a problem."

"And you even made your own coffee? Sheesh, I didn't know you knew how."

"Oh, you'd be surprised to learn all the things I can do."

"A man of many parts."

"Unfortunately, most of them are getting old and creaky sitting behind this damned thing," he said as he patted the desk. "I think I've put on five pounds since Ed died and I agreed to take this crazy job."

"Five pounds? Oh, give me a break! After what you used to do, it ought to be fifteen like the rest of us mere mortals."

"Tell me, how much cash do we have in the office right now — petty cash, purchasing? How much could you scrape together, if you had to?"

She frowned. "Off the top of my head, I'd say the better part of $65,000, but let me check." In less than five minutes, she was back at the door and told him, "I make it more like $75,000. Why?"

"Let's just say I need it, all of it and then some, to bail someone out. George Grierson, our attorney, usually gets in early doesn't he?" Maryanne nodded, so Bob continued, "Give him a call and tell him I need another $200,000 in cash... No, he'd better make it $225,000. Have him call the bank. They'll probably listen to him a lot faster than they'll listen to me, but I need it pronto. I'm headed for the airport later this morning, so see if he can arrange for me to pick it up at the local branch on Mannheim Road by ten o'clock."

"$225,000?" she asked with a frown. "This isn't another of your little… 'adventures,' is it? George's gonna crap when I hit him with a number like that."

"He's a lawyer. They teach them how to hold it in in law school."

"And you wouldn't rather deal with him yourself?"

"Nice try. That's why I pay you the big bucks, Maryanne."

"If it involves lawyers, not nearly enough," she grumbled.

An old army buddy with a problem? Like that would be a first. Bob leaned back in his desk chair and found himself staring at the gallery of photographs and plaques that took up the far wall of his office. Most were standard company PR stuff that Ed put up when he sat behind the big desk. There were full-color shots of their biggest projects, of Ed shaking hands with customers, group shots of the key company staff, various shiny metallic plaques and awards that he and the company received over the years, and that kind of stuff. Almost lost in the sea of bright Kodachrome were two framed photographs on the far right edge of the pictorial array. Angie had hung them on the wall, not him, and she used those big drywall butterfly screws, so he couldn't take them down without tearing the wall apart.

Both scenes were beige on dull, dusty beige and showed Bob back in his Army days. The lower shot dated from the Second Gulf War. Like a posed class photograph, it showed a platoon of four dozen laughing, grinning American soldiers dressed in their field uniforms. They knelt and stood in four neat rows with their company pennant and regimental flag front and center. Behind it knelt a young, smiling Lieutenant Robert T. Burke and his platoon sergeants and squad leaders, backed by two M-113 Armored Personnel Carriers and an Abrams M1A1 Main Battle Tank, with its gun barrel pointed at the camera. Behind them lay an empty, rock-strewn desert that could have been on the moon or Mars, but it was Iraq.

The second photograph looked to be an informal shot of eight heavily armed men set against a craggy, snowcapped mountain range. These were older men, not boys, and the only discernible uniform parts they wore were beige U.S. Army desert combat boots on their feet. They had thick, unkempt beards, shoulder-length hair, baggy civilian pants, shawls, and flat Afghan pakol hats. None of them wore nametags, insignias of rank, or unit patches. They didn't need them. They knew exactly who they were. The guy near the center wore the same Afghan pakol hat, shaggy beard, and mustache as the others, but he didn't seem to fit. At five foot eight inches tall and 150 pounds, he was by far the smallest in the group, looking like a supply clerk who gave the real soldiers a case of beer so he could get in their photograph and scarf some free drinks at the local VFW when he got back home. He leaned on a long-barreled Barrett M-107 sniper rifle that made him look even smaller. Still, if you leaned closer and studied those hard, black eyes, you would realize they belonged to Major Robert T. Burke, and that they were the eyes of a stone-cold killer.

On Burke's right stood his Executive Officer, Captain Randy "Gramps" Benson, and on his left Master Sergeant Harold "Ace" Randall. The others were Sergeant First Class Vincent "Vinnie" Pastorini, the currently out-of-luck gambler, destroyer of New Jersey casinos, and best shot in the Unit other than Ace or Bob Burke. In the background were Staff Sergeant Frederick "Chester" Blackledge, Sergeants Rudy "Koz" Kozlowski, Joseph "The Batman" Hendrix, and Freddie "Bulldog" Peterson.

Burke was a West Point graduate, a major, and their commanding officer, but none of that mattered in the field, where everyone was addressed by their radio handle. His was "the Ghost," because he could seemingly disappear any time he wanted. To a man, though, the others would readily admit that with a gun, a knife, or his bare hands, it was that little runt in the middle that you wouldn't want to run into in a dark alley.

Since he got out, Bob had stayed in touch with all the others, except Gramps Benson. In the Unit, assignments were always top secret, but the jungle drums told him Benson got out sometime after he had. Perhaps Gramps went into some deep cover assignment with the Army or the CIA, as often happened; but by all accounts, he simply disappeared. He had always been somewhat cold and distant around the others, especially after Burke arrived, so nothing he did would have come as a surprise, Bob thought.

However, Benson was a fellow officer. Losing track of him should have bothered Burke, but it didn't. Benson was two years older and more experienced, but he got his commission through ROTC. He wasn't part of the West Point "ring knocker" fraternity. In the Army, that mattered; and no doubt, it rankled. They fast-tracked Bob to major and appointed him as commanding officer, not Benson. Rank or not, the enlisted men understood leadership and knew who the leader was. They also knew Benson was older, which was why they tagged him "Gramps." As his Exec, Benson was a quiet and effective #2 man, but Bob felt Benson was always hanging back, biding his time, and working all the angles. Being passed over twice for major and command time was the kiss of death for a career, not that it was any of Bob's doing. After Bob got out of the Army, he was too busy learning his new job to give much thought to Randy Benson. Later, when Bob needed help in Chicago, it was Ace, Vinnie, and his other sergeants who came running. If he had known where Benson was, he would have called him too; but as they said, the man had vanished.

With a fresh mug of hot, strong coffee in hand, Bob turned away from the photographs and back to his computer. Time to conduct a little "cyber research," as his former Vice President of Finance, Charlie Newcomb used to call it. An experienced combat commander like Bob Burke would call it old-fashioned recon with a monitor and mouse, but the target today was the Bimini Bay Casino and Atlantic City, and it was time to see what he was up against.

Bob graduated number three in his class at West Point, with what was essentially an engineering degree. Despite all that technical education, none of it prepared him for business analysis, online snooping, or dirty tricks. He received that training by looking over the shoulder of his former CFO Charlie Newcomb. While Bob was studying Army 101 and advanced infantry tactics, Charlie was at the University of Chicago and Northwestern's Kellogg School of Business, where "Legal and Illegal Techno-Wizardry" must have been as much a part of the curriculum as the M4 automatic rifle and the M67 hand grenade were to Bob's.

Charlie had the forensic nose of a bloodhound. Watching his fingers flash on the keyboard, Bob would shake his head, knowing he could never hope to reach that level of competence. It was a gift. But after six months of his tutelage, Bob could drill down into corporate or government databases with the best of them — dissecting an annual report, sifting through online public records, checking local business license applications, and deciphering real estate records. Charlie also taught him how to track newspaper stories, hack into classified tax and bank records, and peel back the layers of corporate ownership to learn who owned what and who was really giving the orders to whom. Coupling that with what the Army taught him about planning, evaluating the opposition, finding their vulnerabilities, and learning where and how to attack, made him an expert tactician in both the business and military arenas.

Technology and Charlie aside, the simplest solution is usually the best. He typed "Atlantic City" into Google and got a quick-and-dirty, twenty-minute overview of the city's history in Wikipedia and Trip Advisor. The beach and the world-renowned hotels along the Boardwalk had been the foundation of the city's economy for fifty years, anchored by the Ambassador, the Breakers, the Mayflower, and the Ritz Carlton. However, gambling, prostitution, the mob, bootlegging, and smuggling were always there, just below the surface and at the heart of what Atlantic City was all about. In the early years, the mob dominance was so blatant that in 1929, "Lucky" Luciano convened the first summit of mob bosses at The Breakers, drawing characters such as Vito Genovese, Albert Anastasia, "Bugsy" Siegel, Dutch Schultz, Al Capone, Luigi DiGrigoria, and Santos Trafficante, to name but a few.

After gambling was legalized in 1976, the city exploded. A line of new casinos quickly went up along the Boardwalk in an attempt to compete with Las Vegas. The 1980s and 1990s were the city's high-water mark, drawing legions of tourists from New York and the other East Coast cities as fourteen big casinos were opened. Inevitably, however, cheap airfares to Las Vegas, the rise of Indian reservation casinos, and the recession led to an equally fast decline. Only half of the casinos were still open, and four of the fourteen closed in 2014 alone.

The Bimini Bay Hotel and Casino, where Vinnie lost most of his money, was owned by Boardwalk Investments, along with the Siesta Cove Hotel and Casino and the Tuscany Towers Casino and Shopping Mall, making them the largest single casino owner and developer in Atlantic City. The three properties were located in the northeast quadrant away from the Boardwalk, and the Bimini Bay was by far the largest single complex in the city. It had twenty-five hundred rooms, a 100,000 square-foot casino, ballrooms, and a conference center. Its buildings were stunning, featuring gleaming aquamarine glass and stainless steel. Ranging from two stories to six, they formed a horseshoe along the water, wrapping around its own large boat marina. To everyone's surprise, even the current slowdown did not appear to have a major effect upon Boardwalk Investments.

According to the *Philadelphia Inquirer,* if one patiently peeled away the many layers of corporate ownership, all you'd find inside were lawyers, more corporations, and still more lawyers. However, deed or not, everyone in Philadelphia knew that Atlantic City's Carbonari crime family owned Boardwalk Investments. The money to build their hotels and casinos came from the Genoveses and Luccheses in New York, from Angelo Bruno, the mob boss of Philadelphia, and from loans from the Teamsters and other Metro-New York union pension funds. It was a long-standing "front" to launder mob money from the big cities, which may be why Boardwalk Investments remained healthy regardless of the economy.

"Goddammit," Bob Burke pounded his head on the front edge of his desk, which is about as demonstrative as he ever got. "More Gumbahs!"

Having recently been forced to deal with Chicago's infamous DiGrigoria mob, the last thing he wanted was to butt heads with their New York and Philadelphia cousins. Last time, they gave him no choice, and it didn't look like he would have much choice this time either, not if he wanted to get Vinnie out of his current fix.

Maryanne tapped on his door, interrupting his research, and said, "George has some good news and some bad news. Which do you want first?"

Bob rolled his eyes. "Okay, let's start with the bad," he answered. "It's been that kind of morning, anyway."

"He said he beat on the bank, but that kind of cash withdrawal has to be approved downtown. He went on and on about Treasury Department money laundering rules on anything over $10,000, how you would need a notarized and sealed Board Resolution, how the Feds require every such transaction to be reported, and... well, frankly, my eyes glazed over before he was half finished. But even if it was approved, it would take twenty-four hours to clear."

Bob grimaced and began to say something, but Maryanne held up her hand. "What they *can* do, since our deposits are fairly hefty, is to get you another $50,000 in cash, plus a certified Citibank cashier's check for the remaining $175,000. That should be almost as good, and you can pick it up at the Mannheim Road branch in an hour. That'll give you $225,000 plus our $75,000 for the $300,000 you wanted."

He shrugged. "Okay, that will have to do. Tell them I'll be right over."

"I'll let them know."

"And close the door. There might be some swearing going on in here."

Bob stared at the telephone for a few minutes, debating how to handle the call. However, not knowing what kind of reception he would receive, he realized he was only wasting time, so he picked up the receiver and began punching numbers.

"Bimini Bay Casino, the crown jewel of the Atlantic City Boardwalk, to whom may I direct you?" he heard an overly friendly female voice ask.

"Mr. Van Gries' office, please."

"That would be the Business Office. I'll connect you."

After a half-dozen rings, a softer, sexier female voice answered. "Business Office, Eva Pender speaking."

"Who else would it be, darlin' " Burke asked with a smile and his best dumbass rural North Carolina accent. "Tell me, is old Marty in?"

There was a momentary pause before she corrected him, "Well, if you're referring to Mr. Martijn Van Gries — that's Martijn with a 'J' — our Executive Vice President, I doubt he'll respond very well if you call him Marty... darlin' "

"My apologies, Evie. I do stand corrected. Is that pompous ass Martijn with a 'J' in?"

After a longer pause, she replied, "I'll have to see. Who may I say is calling?"

"Tell him it's Bobbie Burke, and I'm calling about my old pal Vinnie Pastorini."

"Ah! A 'pal' of Mr. Pastorini. Well, shut my mouth, why am I not surprised?"

"I wouldn't possibly know, Evie."

"It's *Eva*, and I'll put you right through... *darlin'!* "

A few long minutes later, a man's voice with a cultured Dutch accent came on the line. "Mr. Burke? This is Martijn Van Gries. To prevent any further aggravating of our staff, may I be of assistance? I understand you are calling about our special guest, Mr. Pastorini."

"I am indeed. Look, I hear my old pal Vinnie has been a bad boy. You know how hot headed these I-talians can get sometimes."

"Indeed, Mr. Burke, I work for one."

"So I understand, Marty, and I hear Vinnie owes you boys some money."

"He owes us a *lot* of money, Mr. Burke."

"$275,000? I'd think that was 'chump change' to a large operation like Boardwalk Investments."

"Chump change? I must admit, you have a vivid imagination, Mr. Burke. Unfortunately, if you add in today's 'vig,' that $275,000 totals $285,000... and counting."

"And counting? Gee, why am I not surprised?"

"I do not have the slightest." Van Gries added, "Now tell me what you want, Mr. Burke; I am a busy man."

"Too busy to take my $285,000?"

There was a brief pause before Van Gries said, "To be perfectly clear, you intend to pay off his markers? All $285,000? He must be quite a 'pal,' as you put it, Mr. Burke."

"I'll be in your office at 4:00 this afternoon with the money. If you would kindly have Vinnie and Patsy packed, smiling, and ready to go, there should be no problem."

"Not if you have the money, Mr. Burke. We shall see you at 4:00 p.m., then."

Since he had thirty minutes before he had to leave for the bank and the airport, Bob returned to his computer screen and read the rest of the article. Stefano "Stevie Boy" Carbonari was the patriarch of the family, passing through Ellis Island at the turn of the century. His youngest son, Giuseppe "Little Joey" Carbonari, abandoned the crowded New York City rackets for the wide-open turf of Philadelphia. He was a giant, tall and barrel-chested with big fists. They proved useful for a union enforcer on the Philly docks, a loan shark leg breaker, and a bootlegger during Prohibition. He enjoyed hurting people with a cut-down pool cue or his fists, especially anyone who didn't pay up. As his success grew, he loved to cruise down Market Street in his white, chauffeur-driven, Packard Phaeton wearing a dark-blue pinstripe suit with a bright red handkerchief in the breast pocket and a dapper bowler hat. Accompanying him were two beefy bodyguards, one in the front seat next to the driver and the other on the jump seat in back, each holding a Thomson submachine-gun across his knees.

His son, "Crazy Eddie," made "his bones" back in Brooklyn, but he saw the opportunity in Atlantic City, and grabbed it. One summer day in 1944, he and his "boys" left the Marine Basin marina in Brooklyn in Crazy Eddie's new boat for some deep-sea fishing in the Gulf Stream. They had rods, reels, and a full bucket of bait; but if there was no action and they got bored, Eddie would liven things up with hand grenades, his .45-caliber pistol, or the big Browning automatic rifle he kept below deck. As he later explained, "We wuz just doin' our patriotic duty, keepin' da freakin' Kraut U-boats out 'a da Delaware River."

On the return trip that day, the captain put in at Atlantic City for gas. Eddie liked what he saw and decided he wanted the territory. That put him on a collision course with Morrie "the Stump" Levine, who ran the city for the Genoveses in New York. It didn't take Crazy Eddie very long to convince Angelo Bruno and Vito Genovese that blood mattered, and they could do a lot better with a loyal Sicilian boy like him than an immigrant Jew from Poland, who everyone knew was really Meyer Lansky's stooge to begin with. Two weeks later, Levine vanished. While the police never closed the case, the smart money said The Stump became the first of many Carbonari rivals to end up in a 55-gallon drum a few miles off the picturesque town of Brigantine, just north of Atlantic City.

"Oh, cute," Bob mumbled, another 'piece of cake.' "

CHAPTER FOUR

Atlantic City, New Jersey

With only a carry-on brown leather briefcase for luggage and that morning's *Chicago Tribune* tucked under his arm, Bob Burke took his window seat in the third row of First Class on the 11:35 United flight from O'Hare to Philadelphia. He always had an aversion to flying up in First, but on such short notice you took what you could get. Despite what was inside the briefcase, he tried to look nonchalant as he slid it under the seat in front of him. With $125,000 in neat stacks of one hundred dollar bills and a Citibank cashier's check for $175,000 in an embossed bank envelope inside, the briefcase would make anyone nervous, even him. It also contained a Board Resolution and a letter on Toler TeleCom stationery, both signed by himself as President and Maryanne Simpson as Corporate Secretary saying it was all perfectly legal in the event TSA stopped him. Everyone knew that they never hassled the big spenders in First Class, but you never could tell.

While he waited for the other passengers to finish boarding, he opened the *Tribune* to the sports section and leaned back. He was in the middle of a story about the Cubs new trades, when some smart-ass flicked the corner of his newspaper, "Hey sailor, is this seat taken?"

He shook his head, immediately recognizing Linda's voice. "No, and you aren't here."

"Guess again."

He lowered the paper a few inches and looked over the top at her. "I was serious when I told you I didn't want you involved in this."

"I'm sure you were, but I owe Patsy even more than you owe Vinnie," Linda answered as she plopped down in the seat next to him. "You may not remember, but I do."

One look into her eyes told him he wasn't going to win this one. "Speaking of which, where exactly did you ditch our darling daughter?" he asked.

"I didn't 'ditch her.' I left her in the loving care of my sister up in Prospect Heights."

"And I suppose it was Maryanne who told you where I was going?" He glowered at her, none too happy.

"My sources shall remain anonymous."

"You're not a reporter, a lawyer, and certainly not a priest…"

"You noticed?" Linda looked up at him with an angelic expression.

"Several times last night, but who's counting?"

"But if you're getting too old for a young, extremely affectionate wife…"

"No, no, but I'm going to wring Maryanne's neck when I get back."

"No you won't. Without her, that place would collapse. Besides, you and I are a team. I distract 'em with my rampant sexuality, while you… do whatever it is you do."

He looked over and thought she wasn't far from wrong. She wore just the right amount of makeup, and the stunning, very expensive casual dress he'd bought her on their honeymoon in Paris. "Yeah, well, I guess you have a point, but I'm still not very happy about it."

"Well, get used to it," she said as she wrapped herself around his arm and snuggled in close. "I guess I'll just have to think of some new ways to make you all happy again." She looked up and fluttered her long eyelashes at him.

Linda had been curled around his right arm since they took off, like a sweet-smelling boa constrictor taking a long nap. The quiet time gave him the opportunity to study the Atlantic City map and some online articles and photos he had printed before he left the office. Ever since the Army, maps were something he could never get enough of. How did that old line go? 'There is nothing more dangerous than a general with a radio or a second lieutenant with a map.' He had been to Atlantic City once before, but that was for a long, drunken weekend almost ten years ago, and those memories were little more than a blur now.

From the maps and photos, he saw that water surrounded and crisscrossed the city, from the oceanfront with its line of protecting dunes, to the tidal bays and broad wetlands that wrapped around it and spread inland to the north and east. There was a toll road and two highways that came down from Philly along a wide neck of land and a thin chain of islands that extended down the coast to the southwest. Basically, all that water turned the city into a cul-de-sac, which any good infantryman knew to avoid. He turned to some online aerial photos he had printed back in the office and took a close look at the Bimini Bay. It had its own large boat marina that fronted on one of the inland bays, and he saw a freshly painted helipad on the roof of the tallest hotel tower. Those were worth noting.

Turning to the online articles he had been reading, Crazy Eddie's Atlantic City turf was "small potatoes" compared to New York, Chicago, or even Philly. Still, he was careful to build alliances with the larger "families" through personal relationships, avoiding making enemies, and passing generous cuts "up the food chain." As he reportedly told his son Donatello, "Remember, kid, pigs get fat, hogs get slaughtered, and everybody loves a freakin' cash cow." Perhaps he picked up animal husbandry doing three to five at Dannemora, Bob wondered.

To protect his growing operations, he also became actively involved in local politics, paying particular attention to the city council, the county board, the local judges, and the sheriff, making generous campaign contributions to ensure only the "right" people got elected, or hired as police chief. As he told Donatello, "I don't give a rat's ass if da moke's a Democrat or Republican. He's either a friend of ours, or he ain't." That's why they all came to see Crazy Eddie, hat in hand, and why his "associates" from New York, Philly, and Chicago could come down on a vacation, knowing they could enjoy themselves with no police to worry about. As the custodian of one of the mob's "playgrounds," Eddy maintained Atlantic City as an "open" territory, like Las Vegas, where they all could party or invest. If they did, he always earned them a handsome rate of return, further cementing his usefulness.

Unfortunately, his little world could not continue forever. With wiretaps, informers, and a relentless full-court press, the Feds took down one New York crime family after another, putting a legion of "wise guys" in the federal pen. As the dominoes fell, they ratted each other out, putting an end to the old mob credo of "*Omerta*." Eventually, the Feds even reached down to the second and third tier cities like Atlantic City, and Crazy Eddie found himself in a Federal Supermax prison. That left Atlantic City to his then thirty-two-year-old son, Donatello. While he was very young to be handed such a responsibility, he was the fourth generation of this quintessential American mob family, and it was "in the blood."

"Isn't that nice," Bob thought as he leaned back in his seat. "It's in his blood."

Linda finally woke when the 737 bounced a time or two on the runway.

"Are we in the air yet?" Linda mumbled and snuggled closer.

"No, we just landed."

"Must have dozed off," she added as she sat up with a glassy-eyed stare.

"Yeah, something like that," he chuckled, wiggling his fingers to get the circulation back in his arm.

"When's the next flight?"

"There isn't one. We're renting a car and driving. With all that cash in the briefcase, I'd rather not take another chance with a TSA security check. Besides, Atlantic City is only an hour away, and it would take a lot longer than that to deal with two airports."

Being recently acquainted with car chases, while that was extremely unlikely, he chose a full-size, six-cylinder Buick at the rental car counter.

Hands on hips, Linda took one look at the big, gas-guzzling road hog and turned up her nose. "If the Sierra Club sees me in a thing like this, they'll burn my membership card. Don't they have a Prius?"

He laughed. "The first time you get in trouble out there, you're gonna want something big and powerful underneath you when you need it."

She turned toward him, let her sunglasses drop to the bridge of her nose, and looked over the top at him. "God, I love it when you talk dirty... but I still hate the car."

They were on the road and headed south toward the toll road in twenty minutes. An hour and fifteen minutes later, the toll road ended in Atlantic City and he turned northeast on Atlantic Avenue. Better safe than sorry, he thought as he used the opportunity to examine the battleground up close and personal. Tactics might only be a hobby or a habit to him now, but he always viewed new ground as an infantryman would — topography, obstacles, cover, fields of fire, and distances. He never thought he'd need to resurrect those old skills when he put away the uniform, but the three days of going head-to-head against the DiGrigorias taught him otherwise.

The Bimini Bay Casino, "the crown jewel of the Boardwalk," as the receptionist had called it, was located on a low hill at the northeast end of the island facing Absecon Bay. He continued to the end of Atlantic Avenue, where it reached the water. Rather than head for the tall buildings of the casino complex, perhaps a mile away, he turned away and headed south to Pacific Avenue. He then turned southwest, passing the former Revel and Showboat casinos, now closed, and the Trump Taj Mahal, Resorts, Bally's, Caesars, the Wild West, the closed Trump Plaza, and finally the Tropicana. Pink, blue, white, or gray, they all showed their age.

He turned back north and then east again, slowly circling the area, familiarizing himself with what it looked like on the ground. As he did, he passed streets named Maryland, Virginia, Vermont, Indiana, Pennsylvania, and Mediterranean and thought he'd been dropped onto a Monopoly game board, which he guessed he had. The old board game was based on an Atlantic City street map. As he continued northeast, he passed block after block of older three-story houses, liquor stores, 7-11s, bodegas, T-shirt shops, and pawn shops, demonstrating that the city's long slide hadn't ended yet.

"Depressing," Linda commented. "Where'd all the money go?"

"Probably to the tax collectors in Trenton, and the Luccheses, and the Genoveses in New York."

"Well, none of it stuck here," she commented as he continued to circle. "Are you headed anywhere specific, or just driving around aimlessly?"

"Tryin' to tell me how to do my job, again?" he asked. "Actually, I'm looking for a good place to stash you, before I go to the Bimini Bay."

"Haven't you learned that I don't 'stash' very well? Just take me to the casino and I'll camp out in the slot room and blend in. No one will even know I'm there."

"Blend in? Looking like that?" he laughed. "You'd need a walker, an oxygen bottle, and a few less teeth to pull that off."

She stared at him for a moment. "Is there a compliment hiding in there somewhere?"

"Of course, but I really didn't want you anywhere near that place."

"I'll be fine. You're giving them the money. Why would there be a problem?"

"There shouldn't be, but it's their turf, not ours. Until I have it figured out, I'd prefer you keep a very low profile."

Satisfied with his preliminary reconnaissance, he finally headed back north toward the Bimini Bay. It was hard to miss. The four- and six-story turquoise and chrome buildings stood out like a mountain peak and towered over the northeast corner of the city. The tallest building in the group was the main hotel tower, sitting on a low hill with the other buildings kneeling around it like a nativity scene. When you add the glittering palm trees and bright red letters on the neon rooftop sign, it was hard to miss. To the right, they passed the old black-and-white spire of the Absecon Lighthouse. It was a historic tourist attraction now, not that a lighthouse was necessary here any longer. The gaudy, flashing neon palm trees atop the Bimini Bay could probably be seen halfway to Boston or Miami, safely marking the boat channel and even serving as an outer beacon for Philadelphia International Airport.

The Bimini Bay was surrounded by large surface parking lots containing the majority of the healthy trees left in the city, or so it seemed. In front and to the right stood a new forest of tall sailboat masts in the Bimini Bay's marina on Absecon Inlet. Continuing along the curved entry road to the casino, he noted the security cameras on the buildings and light poles, so he turned his face away and followed the signs to the main casino entrance.

"I'm dropping you at the front doors," he said. Work your way back to the Self Park exit, find a slot machine you like, and wait for us there. Here," he said as he opened the briefcase, took out $15,000, and handed it to her, decreasing the amount in the briefcase to the $285,000 that Van Gries wanted. "That's to hold, not to use. We may need it later."

"Gotcha boss," she said. As the car rolled to a stop, she opened the door, kept her hand over her face, and was gone.

He quickly drove away toward the entrance to the Self Park ramp. Once inside, he circled the half-empty garage and found an empty space near the casino entry doors. They were hard to miss, ringed with flashing lights and a big neon sign that read "CASINO" in red, white, and blue. He backed the rental car into the parking space, in the event he had to make a sudden departure later. That was highly unlikely, but when you're dealing with "wise guys," it's a smart idea to be prepared for anything really stupid.

Bob looked at his watch. It was 4:10 p.m., just about right, he thought, roughly on time, but sufficiently late to demonstrate he really didn't give a damn.

Briefcase firmly in hand, he walked through those big double doors and onto the casino's main floor where he was assaulted by flashing lights, loud rap music from a nearby bar, and the irritating jingle of 4,000 slot machines. The décor was a tasteless blend of Jimmy Buffett "Margaritaville" and schlock, Bob Marley Caribbean done in turquoise and flashing chrome. The high ceiling had been painted a rich medium blue, with gold stars and billowing white clouds rotating and changing shapes as he watched. Clever, he thought. They make everything seem so make-believe, you might think your money is make-believe, too. The colors and flashing lights also distracted attention from the security cameras and beefy guards posted discreetly around the casino floor. The cameras were hidden inside small, upside-down black-plastic domes mounted on the ceiling above the entrances and above every bank of slot machines, gaming tables, the doors to the restaurants and restrooms, the ticket cashing machines, and the cashier cages. Bob walked to the closest one and smiled at the bored young woman leaning on her elbow behind the wrought iron bars.

"Hey, darlin'," he asked, "can you tell me where I can find the casino's administrative office?"

The girl leaned forward, pointed to her right, and snapped her gum. "Down that corridor over there, you can't miss it."

"Second star to the right and straight on till morning?"

"Yeah, something like that," she shrugged and turned away. The corridor took a dogleg right. At the far end, he saw a wooden door with "Business Office" stenciled on it in gold. More significantly, there were two barrel-chested, baby-faced "Hulks" in blue blazers and gray slacks, flanking the door. They had their hands clasped in front of them, eyeing him as he approached. Must be Hulk One and Hulk Two, Bob thought. Too much time in the weight room, and too many steroids, but he now knew where the old offensive linemen from Rutgers ended up after they flunked out or blew a knee. Looking at them, he noted that one had a black eye, and the other one had bruises on his cheek and ear. You might as well put out a sign that said, "Vinnie was here," he thought.

"Can we help you, sir?" Hulk One on the right asked with a frown.

"The name's Burke," Bob answered. "I have an appointment with Mr. Van Gries."

"Raise your arms, please," Hulk Two said as he quickly patted Bob down, not really caring what his answer would be, or how hard he patted. "And what's in the briefcase, sir?"

"A really big bomb," Bob replied. "See, I'm a suicide gambler and I'm going to blow this damned casino halfway to Delaware," he added, trying to keep a straight face. Hulk Two blinked and retreated a step until Bob said, "Just kidding. The briefcase is full of money. What else would I be bringing up here?"

"Uh, yeah, well, mind opening it?" Hulk One finally asked, still not sure.

Bob shook his head, raised the briefcase, and popped the top open. Hulk One leaned forward and poked his finger between several stacks of $100 bills. "Thank you, sir," he finally said as he opened the office door behind him and stepped back. Bob snapped the briefcase shut and the Hulk said, "Have a nice day, sir," as Bob walked past. The two Hulks then followed him inside and posted themselves on each side of the doorway, arms crossed, with smug expressions.

CHAPTER FIVE

Martijn Van Grice's Office

Bob strode to the center of the office. To his right, against the wall, stood two conference room chairs. Vinnie sat in one, his right wrist handcuffed to the chair arm, and Patsy sat in the other, crying. Vinnie's face appeared bruised, and he had dried blood on one ear and his cheek. His polo shirt was torn and it had dirt marks on the shoulder. Clearly, he had ended up on the wrong end of a fight, which was very unusual, not that Vinnie didn't get in fights, but he rarely lost them. Must have been really long odds, Bob thought as he nodded at them.

"Major," Vinnie mumbled, too embarrassed to look Bob in the eyes.

"Tell me you didn't let the football team get the best of you," Bob asked him.

"I got sucker punched... and they had a lot of help."

Bob was already on high alert. His eyes narrowed ever so slightly, he felt his face flush, his breathing slow, and his muscles tighten, ready and waiting, not that anyone else in the room would notice except Vinnie, who had seen him go into action more times than either of them could remember. For the moment, though, he did nothing.

Straight ahead of him was a large mahogany desk. Behind it sat a thin man with red-framed glasses, trendy, spiked hair, and a Harris Tweed jacket with the sleeves pushed up to the elbows. He was leaning back in his leather desk chair with his feet propped up on the corner of his desk, his hands clasped behind his head, and a smug expression. Standing to his left beyond the desk stood a stocky black man with a shaved head, dark Oakley sunglasses, and a ton of gold chains. That pretty much matched Patsy's description of Shaka Corliss.

"Major?" the man behind the desk asked in a high, grating voice as he sat up. "Why did he call you that?"

"I was his commanding officer. He was one of my sergeants," Bob answered as he glanced back at Hulk One and Hulk Two. "What do the boys call you, Marty? Coach?"

"No, simply Martijn," Van Gries answered with a thin smile. "However, my younger brother was a lieutenant in the Royal Dutch Marines, the Korps of Mariniers."

"The Black Devils? They're an excellent unit."

"Yes, I wondered if your paths might have crossed over there, trudging across one trackless desert or another.

"We worked with Dutch and other NATO troops on several occasions and did my share of trudging, but there was a lot of desert over there and the name doesn't ring a bell."

"Well, I wondered, since you career military types run to form," Van Gries said with obvious distaste.

Bob had enough of Van Gries and looked over at Corliss and the twin Hulks. "Looks like you should've hired your brother instead of these clowns. They might be okay to chase a few drunks out of the bar on a Saturday night; but if only one of my guys did that much damage, Marty, they'll end up getting your ass kicked."

Van Gries glanced at the two beefy 'Risk Management Associates.' From his expression, he got it and probably agreed, but they didn't.

Shaka finally spoke up. "Wait a minute, who you callin' clown?" He turned and glared at Bob. "A major? Well, kiss my ass. You sure ain't no Marine. Must'a been the goddamn Army," he snorted and put his hands on his hips. "Figures!"

Bob slowly looked him over. Corliss wasn't much taller than he was, but the black man was broad, musclebound, and probably had him by sixty or seventy pounds. "Don't tell me, another Marine Corps washout?" Bob asked. "I guess that figures, too."

Corliss's eyes flared and he started toward Burke, until Van Gries raised his hand and stopped him. "Not now."

"Enough games, Marty," Bob turned back toward the Dutchman. "Time's short and we have some business to conclude," he said as he put his briefcase on the desk. "Or would you rather we stand here and keep pissing on each other's shoes?"

Van Gries smiled as he leaned forward, pulled the briefcase across the desk, and opened the top. He looked inside and poked his finger around between the stacks of money. "The count looks a tad light... Major," he said as he looked up and leaned back in his chair.

"There's $110,000 in cash in there."

"Unfortunately, your friend owes us $285,000, not $110,000; and the former is what you told me you were bringing."

Bob reached into the briefcase, pulled out the envelope, and laid it on the desk. "This is from Citibank — it's a certified cashier's check for the rest with one of my business cards inside. That's all the cash I could raise on short notice."

Van Gries picked up the business card and studied it for a moment. "Toler TeleCom? What is that? A Chicago telephone company?"

"Hi-tech telecommunications, mostly for the government. I'm good for it."

"Like he was?" Shaka snorted. "And you can shove that 'cashier's check.' Any Nigerian with a color printer can make 'em a whole lot better lookin' than that."

"The check's good. You can call them."

"We ain't callin' nobody. If it's good, then you go cash it and bring us the green," Shaka shot back and leaned closer. As he did, his jacket fell open, revealing a large, chrome-plated .44-magnum Smith and Wesson Model 29 revolver, the famous "Dirty Harry" cannon, hanging in a shoulder holster under his arm. As if the size of a well-aimed bullet mattered, Bob laughed to himself. Another goddamn amateur.

"Shaka may be blunt, Major, but he has a point," Van Gries said as he glanced at his watch. "There is a Citibank branch down on Atlantic Avenue, and they are open for another hour. You can't miss it. We shall still be here... and so will they, he nodded at Vinnie and Patsy.

"If the branch will cooperate that quickly, I have no problem with that. You know how banks are, however, and I want to get this thing done today."

"Point taken," Van Gries conceded. "So, to show you what 'nice' people we really are, I'll call the branch manager personally, and tell him to expect you."

" 'Cause we want our money, boy; else we start cutting off body parts, startin' with him," Shaka added as he gave Vinnie a tap to the side of the head. "Then, I'll be moving on to that cute squeeze of his, and then on to you."

Bob saw Vinnie grimace. Obviously, he was in pain, probably a lot of it.

"I wouldn't recommend that," Burke turned and made several subtle adjustments to his stance and weight distribution, which only another martial arts expert might notice, and focused all of his attention on the stocky black man.

Corliss smacked his fist into the palm of his other hand. "You know, fo' such a little dude, you sho got a big mouth."

"Yeah, I do, and I usually back it up," Bob answered nonchalantly. "I should be back here in an hour with the rest of the money, if your branch manager cooperates. Meanwhile, I'm taking Vinnie to the hospital. He needs a doctor."

"He ain't goin' nowhere, least wise not until we see the rest of the green, and his tab be going up 'ten large' a day." Corliss was rippling with "gym" muscles, but during his fifteen years in the Army, Bob had become highly proficient in many fighting disciplines, from Judo to Karate, Aikido, and Tae Kwon Do. His current favorite, however, was the specialized and highly lethal techniques called Krav Maga or "contact combat," which the Israelis developed. While the other disciplines were primarily for self-defense, Krav Maga was a brutal, attacking form of street fighting intended to "neutralize threats," as the Israelis so delicately put it. For a small man like Bob Burke, it was particularly useful to end fights before they began.

Corliss stepped forward and tried to intimidate Burke, strutting and puffing as he saw the heavyweight boxers do on TV before a big pay-per-view fight. He scowled and glared into Bob's eyes, and then made the mistake of poking Bob in the chest with his index finger.

Bob took a step back and looked at Van Gries. "I only give one warning, Marty. Call him off, or he's going to get seriously hurt."

Enraged, Shaka poked him in the chest a second time, harder, which was when push did come to shove. Bob was never known for "playing well with others," and only had one rule when it came to fighting — strike first and end it before it began. His hands were a blur as they flashed out. One grabbed Shaka Corliss by the offending finger, twisted, and pulled him forward, off balance; as he did, he stepped in closer and his other hand reached inside Shaka's jacket and pulled the big .44 hog leg from its holster. Unfortunately for Corliss, the two blond Hulks standing behind him on either side of the office door had more muscle and even less brains than he did. By the time they reacted, Bob had Shaka bent over and running around in a tight, painful circle. With a leg sweep to get him off his feet, Bob sent him flying into the two Hulks like a shaved-headed bowling ball going for a 7 – 10 split.

Shaka's dark sunglasses went flying in one direction and the two bodybuilders in the other, as they landed in a heap of arms and legs in the doorway. Burke then spun around and pointed Corliss's big, chrome-plated revolver at Martijn Van Gries's head. Bob knew from first-hand experience that staring cross-eyed down the barrel of a large caliber gun could be a "religious experience" for the uninitiated. With a .44-magnum, it was more like falling off a horse on the road to Damascus.

"Marty," Bob warned as he picked up the briefcase and dumped the stacks of money on Van Gries's desk. "Before someone else gets stupid, the cash is yours, all of it, like I told you; and I'll be back here with the rest of it in an hour. When I do, these three clowns had better not get in my way, or they're going to the hospital. All of them. You got that? And those two are coming with me," he motioned toward Vinnie and Patsy.

"No, I'm afraid they aren't," Bob heard a new, authoritative voice speak to him from the doorway. He turned his head, and from the photographs online, he immediately recognized Donatello Carbonari. Tall and muscular, with olive skin and dark, wavy hair and a well-tailored, three-piece suit, the big Mafioso more than filled the doorframe and the role. He paused to look down at his three goons lying in a disjointed heap at his feet as if they were something stuck to the bottom of his shoe.

"Are they yours?" Bob asked as he backed up, so he could cover the entire room with the .44 Smith and Wesson.

"Unfortunately, they are," Carbonari said disgustedly as he focused his dark brown eyes on the small man standing in the middle of the room with the big revolver.

"You know," Bob warned, "incompetent help is worse than no help at all. Keep them on a short leash, or I'll really hurt them next time."

"You must be Mr. Burke. Is that the name I heard? Well done, but you might pay attention as to where you are. This is my business, *my* city, and your friend and the young woman are collateral on a very large debt they ran up, nothing more and nothing less. If you don't like that, I suggest you start shooting; but you're not going to do that, are you?"

"It's okay, Major," Vinnie said. "You take Patsy. I'll stay here until you get back."

Burke looked at Vinnie for a moment and then back at the big Italian. "The girl had nothing to do with this," Burke told him.

Carbonari looked at him for a moment and then shrugged. "All right, she may go with you," he said as he glanced at his expensive Phillipe Patek watch. "Consider it a peace offering, since you're the one holding the gun at the moment; but you're 'on the clock,' as they say. If you aren't back here by 5:00 o'clock, sharp, I'll let these three have some fun with your friend. Understood?"

Burke nodded as he lowered the chrome revolver, picked up the business card he had placed on Van Gries' desk, and handed it to Carbonari. The mob boss studied it for a moment and said, "Chicago? Interesting, I had some friends back there."

"Had? Probably the DiGrigorias," Bob said, trying to sound nonchalant, but watching the big Italian's eyes for a reaction. Carbonari did not disappoint. He quickly looked up from the business card, then focused on Bob Burke, surprised to hear that name spoken so indifferently. "Yeah," Bob went on, sensing Carbonari was taking him more seriously now. "The *Chicago Tribune* was filled with stories about that big shoot-out in the suburbs. And that office building in Evanston that got bombed? The TV stuff went on for weeks."

"So I understand," Carbonari said as he looked at the business card again. "So what do I call you? Is it Mister Burke? President Burke? Or did I hear Shaka call you Major?"

"That was a long time ago. I'm retired from all that Army stuff now," he told him with a cold smile. "I'm just 'the telephone guy' now."

Carbonari looked at him for a moment longer and then turned toward Van Gries. "Take the handcuffs off her," he ordered. The Dutchman opened his desk drawer, pulled out a set of keys, and tossed them to Burke. "Time is getting short, and you should be going, Mister Burke. My men will escort your sergeant back to his room and help him pack, but don't take too long. As Shaka put it somewhat crudely, the vig on the remaining $185,000 is ten grand a day and the clock is running."

"Ten grand? That sounds a bit steep, don't you think?"

"Not when you consider the damage he caused and the injuries to my security people." Carbonari then turned toward the twin Hulks and a thoroughly chagrined Shaka Corliss. "Got that? All three of you?" he asked, not too pleasantly.

Burke motioned toward Vinnie. "He needs a doctor."

Carbonari eyed Vinnie for a moment "All right, I'll have our house doctor check him out. Will that make you happy, Mr. Burke?"

"No, but it will do. And I expect him to be in no worse shape when I get back."

"That's fine with me, as long as he doesn't prove disruptive again."

"He won't," Burke said as he glared at Vinnie, and Van Gries opened Patsy's handcuffs and helped her to her feet. Bob snapped the big Smith and Wesson open at the breech, tipped it up, and let a half dozen big .44-magnum slugs drop onto the carpet with heavy thumps. He then released the cylinder and tossed the revolver and the cylinder into the far corner. Motioning for Patsy to follow, he headed for the office door.

"I'll give you one thing," Carbonari said with a thin smile on his lips as Bob walked by. "You've got balls."

"Don't worry, Donnie, I'll be back," Bob answered as he turned away and walked down the hallway. "And I'm always up for a rematch."

"Ah'm counting on it, sucka'," Corliss countered from behind his boss.

As Bob and Patsy reached the end of the hallway, rounded the corner, and entered the casino, Patsy slowed and looked nervously back toward the office corridor. "But what about Vinnie, Bob? And our things?" she asked.

"They won't hurt him," he told her. "They want their money. Now, let's get you out of here before they change their minds."

Carbonari followed them into the hallway and then stopped. He was seething inside as he watched Burke and the woman walk to the end of the corridor, turn to the left, and disappear. He watched, but he wouldn't allow himself to show any emotion, not yet.

Shaka came up next to him, smacked his right fist into the palm of his left hand and said, "You ain't gonna let that little bastard walk out of here like that, are you, Boss?"

Carbonari's head snapped around and he looked down on the shorter black man, his thin plastic smile slowly fading. "Help me out here, Shaka. Why exactly did I hire you? I know there must have been a reason, but I'm drawing a complete blank at the moment."

Shaka had been in trouble before, but he could see he was in big trouble this time. The two Hulks knew it too and began to slowly back away. Shaka did not have that option. He had to stand there and take it, knowing never to argue back when Donatello Carbonari was in one of these "moods" of his. Finally, Shaka dared to speak up. "Look, you let me go after him, and I'll…"

The corridor was only five feet wide. For a moment, Carbonari was content to merely glare down at the shorter, muscular black man. "You just don't know when to shut up, do you?" he asked as his eyes flared and he slammed Shaka Corliss in the chest with both fists, lifting him off the floor and bouncing him off the office wall.

Corliss found himself on the floor, looking up into the harsh fluorescent lights and the figure of Donatello Carbonari looming over him. Corliss's signature pair of black, wraparound Oakley sunglasses must have flown off his head and were now lying somewhere on the floor in Martijn Van Gries's office. Without them, Carbonari and the entire world could look into his eyes, leaving Shaka Corliss feeling oddly mortal, like Sampson, the moment he discovered his hair was gone. The street thug wasn't accustomed to being talked to or cuffed about like that by anyone. However, as he looked up at Carbonari and saw the crazy anger in his boss's eyes, he knew to stay down.

"I… I don't know what happened, Boss. I swear it. That little bastard was quicker than I thought, but he won't…"

"That's the first halfway intelligent thing you've said today, Shaka," Carbonari turned and vented some of his anger on the two Hulks. Finally, he strode back into Martijn Van Gries's office, pointed at Vinnie still cuffed to the chair, and looked back at Corliss. "Take this one back up to his room, and help him pack up their stuff. And by the way, Shaka, are you a good swimmer? How long can you hold your breath underwater?"

Shaka paused, confused by the question. "I don't know, Boss. Maybe a minute or two. I ain't real good at it. Why?"

"Why? If this one disappears, or you screw anything else up today, I've got a 55-gallon oil drum down on the pier, and we may just find out." Shaka looked across at him and blinked as Carbonari's words sunk in. "Burke will be back here in an hour and we'll take care of him then. You can make book on it. Then, we'll take care of all of them — maybe you, too. So, get the hell out of my sight!"

Shaka unlocked Vinnie's handcuffs and he and the two goons grabbed the sergeant by his arms. Half dragging him, they were out the door as quickly as they could move. That left Carbonari and Van Gries alone in the office. That was when Carbonari discovered he still had Burke's business card in his hand. He held it up and gave it a closer examination.

"Chicago…" Carbonari mused for a moment, and then flicked the card at the Dutchman. "Make some calls. Check this guy out before he gets back."

Van Gries picked up the card and looked at it. "You think he's trouble?"

"Oh, I think the 'Major' has already established that fact, don't you agree, Martijn? One of the things that separates me from those cretins in New York is that I don't sit around waiting for someone to get the jump on me. I squash them before they get the chance."

Van Gries shrugged. "Some bugs are easier to squash than others, you know, and I'm not sure about this one."

Carbonari glared at him. "Get your sweet little ass out from behind that desk, and follow me," he said. "There's some 'maintenance' work that needs our attention in the basement." That said, he quickly turned, walked out of the office and headed for the rear service corridor.

CHAPTER SIX

The Bimini Bay Basement

As soon as Bob and Patsy disappeared around the corner, he took her lightly by the elbow. "Keep your head down," he told her as he picked up speed, and headed for the casino's Self Park exit, avoiding the overhead security cameras and blending into the crowd. From the moment his jet landed at the Philly airport, his old infantryman's antennae had ratcheted up to a higher level. When he entered the casino, they went on high alert, his eyes sweeping the room and his ears listening for any sound. Patsy wasn't aware of it, but after he met Corliss and Carbonari, his lethal hands and feet went into full combat mode, ready to make or counter any attack in a split second.

When they strode through the casino and neared the Self Park ramp, he saw three tall rows of slot machines near the exit doors, and Linda. She sat on a high-back stool at the end machine on the aisle, the tip of her tongue sticking out of the corner of her mouth, totally absorbed in Wheel of Fortune. It featured a large rotating multicolored wheel and perhaps the highest concentration of flashing lights on the casino floor. Linda was so engrossed in the game that she hadn't seen them coming until Bob tapped on her shoulder.

"Jeez, you scared the hell out of me, Bob," she said as she almost fell off the chair.

"Let's go," he said quietly as he continued to look around.

"Go? But I'm up eighty-seven bucks," she pointed at the screen and pleaded. That was when she finally saw a badly frazzled Patsy Evans standing next to him. "Oh, God, what am I thinking?" She gave herself a dopey-slap on the forehead, stood, and threw her arms around the younger woman. "Are you all right, honey? Where's Vinnie? Isn't he coming?"

Bob let them have a three second hug before he broke the clinch with, "We need to go now, Linda. They're keeping him until we get back."

"Keeping him? Didn't you give them the money?"

"I'll explain in the car," he told her as he handed her the empty briefcase so he could keep his hands free, and herded the two women toward the exit.

Donatello Carbonari could not have been more different from his father, his grandfather, or the other members of the family. Smart, tall, sophisticated, and olive-skinned handsome, he graduated Summa Cum Laude from Yale with a degree in finance, followed by an MBA from the Stanford Graduate School of Business. However, underneath that three-piece suit, Phi Beta Kappa key, and good looks, he had inherited his "freakin' old man's" violent temper and flashes of irrationality. It made for a very lethal combination in a career criminal. With his education and intelligence, the rackets were not what his father had in mind for him. He intended for him to stay on the outside, squeaky clean, so he could run the legitimate businesses and money laundering for the big New York families.

From the moment the feds locked up "Crazy Eddie" in the Supermax, ignoring his father's wishes, Donatello jumped into the family business with both feet, working hard to make himself invaluable to the New York City crime families. He squeezed his operations and immediately produced more profits. In ever-larger steps, he got them to increase their investments in his expanding casino, hotel, and real estate empire. As those projects spun off more and more cash, his reputation for making money, a lot of money, for his partners grew, and it became easier and easier to pull in still more partners and still more cash. He soon added labor unions and mob bosses in Boston, Chicago, Detroit, and New Orleans, helping to counterbalance the heavy New York interests. As his operations grew, however, the "low-hanging fruit" became harder and harder to find. Profits finally stagnated, but the appetites of his partners for still more profits never abated. That was when he met Martijn Van Gries, who taught him a few badly needed and very complicated tricks to shift money around and make it happen anyway.

"Marty, I'm not stupid. This is brilliant, but it's a Ponzi scheme," Donatello finally told him. "They're going to kill us."

"Would you rather tell them you are out of money?"

"No, but they're going to figure this out, we can't keep..."

"Why not? You and I are smarter than all of their bookkeepers put together. As long as more money keeps coming in, I would not worry. Play to their greed. Give them their checks, and they will not give a damn how you are doing it."

With Martijn's "creative accounting," the operation appeared to be awash in cash. Considered one of New Jersey's most eligible bachelors, Donatello Carbonari lived in an opulent penthouse on the top floor of the Bimini Bay hotel. It gave him an unsurpassed view of the oceanfront, the city, and most of south Jersey. Like Donatello himself, his rooftop perch was unassailable. He even became a licensed helicopter pilot and bought a Sikorsky S76C helicopter, which he parked on his new helipad next to the pool and the penthouse. It was the very expensive commercial version of the Army's Blackhawk. Donatello loved to fly it from the Bimini Bay to his new Park Avenue condominium in New York, where he polished his public image by being seen in the city's most exclusive clubs and restaurants and serving on the boards of a number of museums and high-profile charities. Life was good.

Never one for pasta, open collar shirts, sharkskin jackets, or gold chains, Donatello's preferences ran to the best London-tailored suits, gourmet food and wine, and athletic, delicate young men. Like good food and good wine, they were a "taste" he acquired in the bars and coffee houses in the Castro District of San Francisco, while he attended Stanford. Now back on the East Coast, he knew to be more circumspect. He only "hooked up" with his "special friends" at several very private, very discreet men's clubs in SoHo or Greenwich Village, or in his penthouse. The time might be long past when young men in most professions were hesitant to come out of the closet, but that was hardly the case for a young, ambitious Mafioso. "Our thing" remained a very conservative fraternity with rigid, nineteenth-century traditions and taboos, and he knew his rivals and numerous enemies would jump on the slightest hint that he was gay like a flock of vultures. With beaks and talons flashing, they would tear him to pieces.

When he took over, he considered most of his father's contemporaries to be cretins and beneath his intelligence. Perhaps it was that disdain that allowed him to become even more arrogant and vicious than the worst of them. He never asked for approval or the blessing of anyone, especially not the Commission in New York, before he "whacked some moke," as his old man would have put it. Like any smart CEO, he began by cleaning out the unproductive deadwood and anyone who had their hand too deep in his till. Rumor was, he personally added nine new oil drums to his father's underwater collection off Brigantine Beach north of Atlantic City. If any of the dons in New York had any objections, he simply increased their monthly take, and the objections vanished.

Success soon followed success, making him more powerful than his father ever dreamt of becoming. The New York City bosses even began calling him The Chinaman, because no one could launder things better than Donatello Carbonari. He even thought he had become bullet-proof, and he no longer saw himself merely as the Don of Atlantic City, a niche player in a second-tier city. Being a student of the mob history, he understood that the power "Lucky" Luciano and Meyer Lansky were able to consolidate in the 1930s was based on their ability to make money for others. He also understood the others had never allowed another crime boss to become that powerful ever since. The center of that power was the five families in New York City and the Commission, which they controlled. For now, Donatello's goal was a chair at that table. Eventually, he wanted the center chair, and then the entire table. He wanted to be the *Capo tuti Capo* — the Big Don.

Aspirations such as that had gotten many young, ambitious Mafiosi dumped in the East River. As they said back in the day, "If you go for the king, you better not miss; or you're a dead man." Still, Donatello wasn't worried. Time was on his side. He was twenty or thirty years younger than any of them, and he had two secret weapons. First, he had a brilliant computer expert named Martijn Van Gries.

Second, he let Van Gries bring in the most sophisticated data analysis video and security system north of the Pentagon or the CIA headquarters in Langley, which produced the most elaborate blackmail, extortion, identity theft, and computer fraud scheme anyone ever dreamed of, and few knew about. It was the real cash cow that kept the operation afloat and lined his pockets and Martijn's.

Ironically enough, Donatello got the idea from a comment his father once made to him. "Hey, college boy, you know why J. Edgar Hoover stuck around Washington so long? It wasn't 'cause he was smarter or a harder worker than anybody else. No. Nobody could touch dat old bastard, 'cause he kept freakin' files on everyone, and he knew how to use them. Dat's what power's all about, Donnie: havin' it, and knowin' how to use it."

His father was dumb as a doorknob on most things, but he understood power.

The Bimini Bay's Self Park ramp posed a more difficult security challenge than the casino. The area around the entry doors was well lit, but the rest of the garage was dimly lit and had far too many shadows between the rows of parked cars where someone could hide. As soon as they left the casino, he motioned for the girls to stop.

"You two stay here," he told them as he scanned the garage. "I'll get the car."

"Aren't we becoming a little paranoid?" Linda joked.

Before he could answer, Patsy did. "You didn't see them, Linda; you don't know what they're like. They're animals."

He jogged off toward his car. When he got there, he checked the doors and even dropped to his knees to look under the car; but he saw nothing suspicious. Finally, he got in, drove back, and picked up the girls. He wasted no time racing down the switchback ramps to ground level and out onto Maryland Avenue, turning south toward the Boardwalk.

"Where are we going?" Linda asked.

"They wouldn't take the cashier's check. I have to get the Citicorp branch to do it."

"What about Vinnie?"

"They let me take Patsy, but they're keeping Vinnie as 'collateral' on his notes."

"You don't trust them, do you?"

"About as much as I trust Vinnie not to do something really stupid before we get back." As he drove, he kept one eye on the road and one eye on the rearview mirror. By the time he reached Mediterranean Avenue, a black Lincoln Town Car had come up behind and started tailing them. It remained a hundred yards back, but it was definitely following them. When he reached Atlantic Avenue, he turned right and said, "Let's face it, our boy didn't do himself any favors. Those aren't the kind of people you want to owe money to, much less double down on, lose even more, and then get in a fight with."

When Linda saw him looking into the rearview mirror again, she turned and looked back too. "Sheesh, not another Lincoln Town Car?" she moaned. "Those guys have zero originality. It's like somebody requisitioned Gumbahs from central casting."

"Except those are the real ones and they have Vinnie," Patsy moaned.

"Don't worry, we'll get him back," Bob reassured her as he saw the sign for the Citicorp branch bank up ahead. When he slowed and turned into its parking lot, the black Lincoln also slowed, but did not turn in. It passed the parking lot entrance and continued down Atlantic. As it did, he saw two men in dark suits and sunglasses sitting in the front seat, looking in his direction. "And you're right, central casting."

He circled the lot and found a parking space near the bank's front door, opened the car door, and grabbed his empty briefcase. "Come on, let's get this done."

With Martijn Van Gries in tow, Donatello Carbonari walked to the rear of the casino, along the long service corridor, through a fire door, and down the emergency stairs to the basement. At the bottom stood a recessed, gray steel door with a small sign that read "Maintenance." However, this was no ordinary service door. The panels were made of quarter-inch steel plates secured to the doorframe by four large industrial-grade hinges and a pair of sophisticated magnetic locks, one at the upper and one at the lower corner of the door, each powerful enough to hold back a bull elephant. To the right of the door was a digital keypad with a fingerprint reader. Other than Donatello Carbonari, Martijn Van Gries, and a handful of Martijn's data technicians, no one else ever got inside.

From the outside, the small maintenance building appeared to be little more than a cheap, one-story, cinderblock addition on the rear of the casino. Inside, the building actually had two floors. The lower, basement level held a sophisticated array of computers, servers, and telecommunications equipment. The upper floor, at ground level, contained a ring of windowless offices, secure storerooms, and a conference room, which fronted on a central atrium. Outside, two unusually large cooling compressors sat in the center of the maintenance building's roof, operating independently from the hotel and casino's main air conditioning system. Anyone vaguely familiar with commercial air conditioning would know that even one of those monsters could cool a space several times as large as the Maintenance Building appeared to be. That made no sense, unless you were one of a handful of people who knew that the maintenance building was in fact a state-of-the-art data center for the Bimini Bay, its sister casinos, and Donatello Carbonari's criminal activities.

The building stood at the corner of the casino's loading dock. It was blocked from view from the driveways and parking lots by a retaining wall and a huge, industrial-sized trash compactor, all of which was covered by four high-resolution security cameras. Carbonari also owned the city's only trash hauling business and was the sole operator of the city's landfill, located ten miles inland. Those were lucrative in their own right, and the strong trash compactor proved useful to get rid of all sorts of unwanted trash.

The maintenance building was the exclusive domain of Martijn Van Gries, who had managed to integrate the Gold Club membership and gambling records with hotel history and reservations, and the video and audio systems he had installed in a dozen of the hotel suites. As Martijn later explained to Donatello, it was truly amazing what personal and financial information people would voluntarily enter on the application form for a casino Gold Club Card, if you gave them $50 in free play, entry to the Gold Room, or some other silly perk or bonus. That information allowed him to create thousands of personal dossiers containing names, employment, addresses, phone numbers, email addresses, credit card numbers, social security numbers, and photographs.

Using their bank account numbers and dozens of public and private databases, he could glean everything there was to know about them, steal their identities, and make fraudulent charges or withdrawals. Coupling that with the hotel and casino's gambling records, his system instantly recognized "high rollers" and people with large incomes and assets, politicians, executives of large corporations, bank loan officers, account managers at investment houses, and many other useful clients, invite them down for free stays, and automatically "comp" them for free food, rooms, and women. When the "right" guest stayed at the Bimini Bay a second time, the system immediately assigned him to one of a dozen "special" fifth floor rooms, which contained hidden video cameras and microphones, making Van Gries's integrated intelligence system the ultimate blackmail and extortion tool.

In the end, this elaborate system only worked because Donatello and Martijn were perfect complements for each other. Both men were scary smart. Donatello Carbonari was uniquely positioned to satisfy Van Gries's cravings for various illicit or exotic chemicals and white powders. On the other hand, in addition to his technical expertise, Van Gries knew how to satisfy Carbonari's far-ranging sexual appetites. As the Dutchman quipped late one night as they sat naked in Carbonari's rooftop hot tub finishing another bottle of Crystal champagne and line of cocaine, "Ours is a match made in Heaven, isn't it, Donatello?"

"Or in Hell," Carbonari answered with a sly grin.

"Hell, you say?" Van Gries laughed as he switched on his elaborate data and audiovisual system, running the feed to a 60-inch HD TV monitor adjacent to the hot tub. Sometimes he ran Donatello's favorite gay porn. Other times, he ran his own "special" videos from the rooms.

"You've seen those ads that say, 'What happens in Vegas stays in Vegas.' With my system, what happens in Atlantic City can go viral anytime we choose." With that, he turned on a theater-quality video of a sweating, grunting, sixty-year-old Federal Appeals Court judge in bed with an underage prostitute. The "action" was shown split screen, with feeds from four separate video cameras and surround-sound audio.

"I have two more disks that I can show you from last weekend, which are way hotter," Van Gries laughed. "One features that investment analyst from Goldman who you comp'd. The other has that US senator and his 'nephew' doing a couple of lines of coke and some wonderfully athletic sex, complete with leather, handcuffs, and toys."

"Really?" Carbonari beamed. "Show me that one."

"I was afraid that would be the one you would chose."

"Why?" he turned toward the Dutchman and asked.

"Because I did not want you to get any 'new' ideas. I am getting too old for moves like that, Donnie… and so are you."

"We'll see, Sweet Cakes. Now, cue the video, if you please," Carbonari said as he ran his fingers through Van Gries's hair. "I'm feeling randy."

CHAPTER SEVEN

Banks and Parking Lots

There was nothing special about this Citibank branch. See one, you've seen them all, Bob quickly concluded, as he ushered the two girls inside. There were glass-walled offices along the front and right side for the junior-assistant managers, a long counter along the far wall that opened onto a set of automated drive-through lanes, and a big vault in the corner held safe deposit boxes. The vault had a massive stainless steel door with huge hinges and six-inch locking pins. Bob smiled, wondering why they even bothered to close the damned thing, given that all the average suburban family kept in their boxes were legal documents and other useless crap. The lobby contained homey groupings of early American furniture that would do Ethan Allen proud, a bright red, serve-yourself popcorn wagon, and a half dozen ceiling-mounted security cameras. John Dillinger was long gone now, and robbing bank branches had been dumbed down to the crime *du jour* of a kid in a hoodie with his finger in his pocket, who grabbed the cash from a teller's drawer and ran like hell. As a return on investment, the popcorn machine was more valuable than the security cameras or that big steel vault door.

When Linda stepped into the branch lobby and saw the bright-red wagon, she made a quick detour and grabbed a heaping bag for herself and Patsy. Bob smiled.

"Don't look at me in that tone of voice, Robert Burke," Linda told him. "I haven't had anything to eat since that bag of stale pretzels on the airplane."

"I'll buy you a big dinner."

"That's then, now's now. I'm starved, and you know how 'love machines' like me need to carb-up for peak performance."

He rolled his eyes and turned toward the row of glass-fronted offices on his right. As he did, a nervous young man hurried out of the corner office, still pulling on his suit jacket. "Mister Burke?" the man asked, "I didn't expect you here this soon. I'm Henry Stern, the branch manager. Mister Van Gries from the Bimini Bay phoned and said you had a cashier's check from our Chicago division, which you need cashed. Please step over to my office here, and we'll see what we can do."

Bob began to follow, but then turned back to Linda and Patsy. "You two stay here and graze on the popcorn. This shouldn't take very long."

"Good idea," Linda answered as she held up the bag. "Besides, I really need a potty break. I had my legs crossed the whole time I was sitting at that slot machine."

He shook his head. "You could've gotten up any time you wanted. There was a restroom right around the corner from where you were."

"And leave a winning slot? Break the mojo, the karma? You gotta be kidding. Get the money; Patsy and I will be back in a minute," she said as she grabbed the younger woman by her arm and headed for the restroom sign.

Bob followed the branch manager into his office and handed him the certified check along with one of his business cards. Stern looked the check over carefully, front and back, and held it up to the light to check the paper and watermarks.

"It appears perfectly legitimate, Mister Burke; but $170,000 dollars is a lot of money, even here, and you wouldn't believe the forgeries floating around out there."

"Do you keep that much cash on hand in a small branch like this? When Van Gries told me to come here, I was a little concerned."

"I doubt there are many bank branches anywhere that do, but this is Atlantic City. Like our offices in Las Vegas, we do handle a lot of cash and try to support the gaming industry wherever possible. So yes, we can cover it, but it will pretty much clean me out for the day."

"Thanks, I appreciate the help."

"I'm going to have one of my associates go into the vault and begin counting it out, while I call Chicago and verify the serial numbers. I'm sure you can understand."

"Of course," Bob said as he handed Stern the briefcase. "I guess you can put the cash in here."

Stern laughed. "I think you're underestimating how much room that much cash will take. We may need to give you one of our canvas bank bags as well, depending on how the denominations work out. But we'll see."

Five minutes later, Linda and Patsy had returned from the restroom, grabbed three more bags of popcorn, and handed one to Bob as they joined him in Stern's office. "It's an anniversary present," Linda said solemnly.

Not being a novice at this husband thing and having no intention of being sandbagged again, he quickly replied, "Yours is in a little box in my desk drawer back in Chicago. It isn't on the insurance yet, so I didn't want to bring it on the plane."

"In a little box in your desk?" she smiled. "Well played, Burke."

Ten minutes later, the branch manager returned carrying Bob's briefcase and a white canvas "Citibank" bank bag. "Here you go, Mister Burke. I got about half of the cash in your briefcase, but I'm sure you'll want to count it all."

"No need. I'm sure you and your people did that several times. Besides, if the count's wrong, I'll just have Shaka Corliss come over and straighten it out."

Stern's eyes went wide at the mention of the muscular black man's name. "That won't be necessary," he stuttered. "If there are questions, ask Mister Van Gries to telephone me directly," he said, as he laid several bank and government forms on the desk. "These are from Citibank and the US Treasury. We are required to report all cash transactions over ten thousand dollars. I will also need to photocopy your driver's license."

Bob took the forms and began to fill them out. "Doesn't bother me in the least, Henry, but you're telling me that all of Van Gries's customers comply with this stuff?"

Stern shrugged, and gave him a thin smile. "The ones I handle do. We get regular visits from the Comptroller of the Currency, Federal Reserve, Treasury, the IRS, FDIC, the FBI, you name it. We aren't state-chartered, but even the New Jersey State Police's Organized Crime Task Force drops by from time to time."

"Impressive," Bob said. "That must keep you on your toes."

"Most of the bank managers in this town are young, like me," he said with a fragile smile. "When we are posted to Atlantic City, before we even get unpacked, the FBI agents in Philadelphia bring us in for a chat and a tour of the Federal High Security Penitentiary in Lewisburg. They make a point of introducing us to all the bankers doing time up there for money laundering and RICO violations. *That's* what keeps us on our toes."

"And I imagine getting squeezed between the FBI and a character like Shaka Corliss isn't fun either. Do the Feds have a big crew here?"

"Not really. With all the real-time electronics at their disposal, 'face time' here isn't necessary. They could be in Boise for all the difference it makes. Most of them are up in Philly or New York; but the FBI has a small field office in Northfield, over on the mainland."

"I bet they stay busy," Bob replied as he signed the last page. "You wouldn't have the name of any FBI people you met up there, would you?"

Stern gave him an odd look as he opened his desk drawer, pulled out a stark white business card and pushed it across the desk. "Here, keep it." Bob picked it up and read the name Philip T. Henderson, Resident Agent, Federal Bureau of Investigation, with an address and phone number. "I'm not sure what you're up to, Mister Burke," Stern said with a thin smile, "but this is Atlantic City. Anybody who reads the newspaper knows who Van Gries and Corliss are, and who really runs this town. So keep me out of it."

"Who, me?" Bob replied with an innocent smile. "I'm just paying off a friend's gambling debt." He picked up the briefcase and the bank bag, and headed for the door. "And thanks for your help, Henry. I'll try not to make things any more difficult for you."

As they got back in the rental car, Linda looked at her watch. "It's almost five o'clock. We need to get back before Vinnie gets himself into any more trouble."

"He'd better not," Bob answered. "I've got my limits, and I'm sure that casino crowd does, too." As he drove out of the parking lot and turned back east on Atlantic Avenue, the black Lincoln Town Car was parked across the street, waiting like a chrome-plated shark.

"The Gumbahs are back," Linda said as she stuck out her tongue at them.

"They make me so angry," Patsy added. "They act like they own the place."

"That's because they do," Bob corrected her.

"Then I suppose mooning them is out of the question?" Linda asked.

"How about we just pick up Vinnie and get the hell out of here," Bob said.

Linda shook her head. "You're getting middle-aged, Burke."

"Sad, but true," he sighed as he accelerated and left the big Lincoln behind in the dust. At Maryland, he turned north toward the Bimini Bay, clearly visible on a low hill a mile away. The street they were on dead-ended at the long, curving, casino entry road. As they turned, he suddenly saw flashing red and blue lights and a half dozen emergency vehicles up ahead. There were five black and white Atlantic City police cars, two casino security cars, and a large, boxy, red and white fire department ambulance parked at odd angles near the base of the six-story tower with their flashers going. But Bob was still too far away to see through the screen of trees and shrubs as brake lights came on and the inbound line of cars began to slow and stop. The road appeared to be blocked by yet another Atlantic City police car. With exaggerated arm motions and whistles, two of the "city's finest" and one of the white-shirted casino security guards directed the incoming cars onto a side road that took them around to the rear side of the building.

With all the visual clutter, Bob still couldn't see much, until the last car ahead of him turned up the side road and he reached the head of the line. Instead of following them, he stopped in the middle of the intersection, ignoring the whistles and animated arm motions of the cops. Further ahead, he saw four more city cops standing with Shaka Corliss, his twin Hulks, and the dominating figure of Donatello Carbonari at the base of the big hotel tower near the ambulance. They were smoking, talking, and laughing. A short distance away, three paramedics knelt in a semi-circle around what appeared to be a body lying on the edge of the pavement, where the parking lot met the sidewalk. The paramedics had their medical bags open, but from the lack of any frantic activity, Bob got a sick feeling in the pit of his stomach.

He ignored the two traffic cops directing him to turn with the other cars.

Instead, he pulled up next to the closest cop and rolled down his window. The officer stepped over and glared in at him through the open window. "Where the hell you think you're going, Sport? When I signal you to…"

"I have business with Mr. Carbonari," Bob cut him off. To no surprise, that was all it took. The cop turned his head and looked at the Don. The big man looked back and nodded.

"Oh, all right, all right!" the angry cop stepped away from the car and waved him through. "Pull over there to the right and stay the hell out of their way."

This time, Bob did what he was told, parked, and got out of the car. When Linda and Patsy opened their doors and began to follow, he motioned them back inside. "No, you two stay here with the money until I figure out what's going on."

Linda began to argue, until she saw the angry look on Bob's face and got back inside. He turned and walked toward Carbonari, but his eyes focused on the body lying in a large pool of blood on the curb. The paramedics were kneeling over it, blocking Bob's view of the dead man's face, but his gut told him he didn't want to see it, even if he could. The man wore the same shirt and slacks Vinnie wore when Bob last saw him handcuffed to the chair in Carbonari's office an hour before, and he had a pretty good idea what that meant.

"Mister Burke," Carbonari called out and walked toward him with an exaggerated expression of concern. "It appears we have a problem," he said, extending his hand.

Bob looked down at his hand for a moment. No doubt, it was some kind of peace offering, but Bob wasn't about to accept. Instead, he turned toward the paramedics as they unfolded a thick, black-plastic body bag. Working together, they lifted the man, rolled him over on his back, and carefully placed him inside. It was Vinnie. His head and face had borne the brunt of the fall, but it was him, all right. No doubt about it. Burke turned and walked toward the paramedics until two of the city cops who had been talking to Carbonari stepped forward and attempted to block his way.

The two cops directing traffic behind him wore plain, unadorned blue slacks and shirts, with tactical equipment harnesses. That marked them as low-ranking patrolmen, while these two were dressed as if they were headed to a cop convention or a Chamber of Commerce banquet, with gold braid on their hats, colorful ribbons on their chests, gold stripes and pins on their shirts, and big Glock 9-millimeter cannons on their hips. The one on the left wore colonel's eagles on his collar tabs and the one on the right had four big silver stars on his. Bob shook his head, wondering why every small town cop and hick sheriff felt he had to wear as much rank as George Patton or Creighton Abrams.

The "colonel" blocked Bob's way, with his legs spread as he had probably seen in some cop movie, while the 'general' reached his hand toward Bob's chest. In the mood Bob was in, that was a very dangerous thing for any man to do; but flattening the local Police Chief or breaking his arm might bring a few complications that Bob didn't need just then. Rather than force his way through, he stopped and glared at Carbonari. He said nothing, but as his eyes locked on Carbonari's, it was as if the doors of a Pittsburgh blast furnace had swung open in the big Italian's face. Burke might be slight of build and Carbonari much taller and heavier, but the power that radiated from Burke's eyes hit the big Italian like a slap in the face.

"Uh, that's okay all right," Carbonari quickly told the two cops. "Let him go."

The colonel and the general looked at each other, but quickly stepped aside and let Bob pass through. When he reached the paramedics, he looked down at Vinnie's badly broken body, at the pavement around him, and at the nearby hotel building. His eyes ran up the wall until they reached the roof, trying to figure out what happened here. Like any officer who had spent time in combat, he had lost his share of men. He had lost good ones, bad ones, brave ones, stupid ones, some amazingly skilled ones, and even a few cowards, but mostly he'd lost unlucky ones. Despite their training, equipment, tactics, and whatever leadership he could provide, sometimes that was how a war went. Nonetheless, every man who served under him was his responsibility and he took each loss personally.

This was different, however. Sergeant First Class Vincent Pastorini had served with him since he joined the 75th Ranger Regiment at Fort Benning nine years before. His weakness for gambling aside, Vinnie was a highly skilled, highly decorated, and very deadly "operator" who served his country honorably, working his way up the Army's special operations ladder one step at a time, and he deserved better than to end his days lying in the gutter next to a garish New Jersey gambling casino. His eyes were half-open. His mouth was open too, only a half inch or so, but enough to make it look as if he had been trying to say something before he died. Bob reached out, put his hand lightly on Vinnie's forehead, and closed his eyes.

"Farewell, old friend," he said quietly, and then stood. He looked back at Carbonari, Corliss, and the Atlantic City police brass, and felt like taking them apart. From the self-satisfied expressions on their faces, it looked as if there wasn't anything they couldn't get away with in the city. Well, not this time, Bob told himself. This time, they'd pay, but it wouldn't be now. It would be at a time and place of *his* choosing, not theirs.

Carbonari took a few steps toward Bob. "Your friend was very foolish, Mr. Burke," he said as he straightened his suit jacket and tugged lightly on his French cuffs. Finally, he glanced back at Corliss. "My head of security and his two men escorted Sergeant Pastorini back to his room on the fifth floor, as I told you they would. But while they were helping him pack, he went into the bathroom, supposedly to clean himself up. The next thing they knew, he had climbed out the bathroom window and was working his way across a narrow ledge, trying to escape, when he fell."

Bob looked back at the building and let his eyes run up the façade to the fifth floor windows high above him. "You're telling me he climbed out the bathroom window? One of those little ones?" Burke asked, even more skeptical. "And he *fell*."

"That's right. They couldn't tell whether he was trying to get to the hallway window or climb on up to the roof," Carbonari added. "They went out on the balcony and tried to talk him back in, but the damned fool wouldn't listen. He gave Shaka the finger and began to climb. As you see, that ledge is only a few inches wide; and, well... that's the result. He must have lost his balance and slipped off."

Bob looked up at the bathroom window, the ledge, and the balcony, and then down at Vinnie. Carbonari said he flipped Shaka the bird and kept on climbing? Bob smiled, knowing at least that part of Carbonari's story rang true. Bob looked back down at Vinnie's body. It lay on the parking lot curb, fifteen feet out from the base of the building. Bob looked up again at the ledge and then back down at the body, and his gut told him the geometry didn't work the way Carbonari was telling it. If Vinnie had slipped off the ledge or on the climb up to the roof, he would have dropped almost straight down and landed on the grass much closer to the wall.

"You say he fell and landed here?" Bob asked as he pointed to the body. "That's hard to do, 'Donnie.' In fact, it's damned near impossible to slip off that ledge, fall, and manage to land way out here, this far away from the building."

Carbonari shrugged. "If you say so."

"Oh, I do," Bob answered as his eyes bored in on the big Italian and then on Shaka Corliss. "I think someone threw him out the window or off the balcony."

Shaka frowned, and then grew indignant. "Whadjou lookin' at me for, man? I never touched the dude. He got out there all by hisself, and he fell, like he said. I ain't lyin.' "

"Why would I believe you, Shaka?" Bob asked.

"Why?" Shaka looked confused. " 'Cause it's the truth," he said, surprising himself with the answer. Slowly, he regained his old form and bluster. "You Army paratroop-types crack me up, man. Y'all think you can fly. Guess he couldn't after all, could he?"

Behind him, Bob heard Patsy scream. He looked and saw Linda trying to stop her, but the younger woman broke free and ran toward the body. Bob managed to stop her halfway, knowing it wasn't something anyone should see, especially not Vinnie's young lover. Bob wrapped his arms around her and turned her away, trying to block her view of the bloody corpse, but he was only partially successful. Patsy screamed again and went limp. She dropped to her knees as the paramedics zipped the thick plastic bag closed over Vinnie.

"No, no," she moaned as Bob led her back to Linda and the car.

Behind him, he heard Carbonari say, "Look, your friend owed us a lot of money. We're the last ones who would want this to happen. He was just a hothead."

"Really?" Bob replied as he turned and walked back. "Vinnie was impulsive, but he wasn't stupid. You know as well as I do, the only way he could've landed this far out from the wall was if he was thrown."

"I know you believe that," Carbonari answered, "but it's illogical. I'm in the money business, Mr. Burke, and dead men don't pay their gambling debts."

Bob turned, put his hands on his hips, and glared at the two senior Atlantic City police commanders. "This was murder. I know it and you'd know it too, if all the dirty money sloshing around in this town hadn't dumbed you two down to a couple of 'rent-a-cops.' "

"Now wait just a damned minute here," the 'general' stepped forward with feigned indignation, until a black, extended station wagon backed up the driveway between him and Burke. It had darkened side windows and simple white lettering on the doors that read New Jersey State Medical Examiner.

Bob's anger was up. He wanted to take Carbonari apart, but he stopped and backed away before he did anything as stupid as Vinnie had. Two black-uniformed, assistant medical examiners got out of the station wagon, looked at the angry faces around them, and realized they might not have picked the best timing. The one who had been in the passenger seat carried a clipboard and appeared to be in charge.

"Where are you taking him?" Bob asked him.

"Uh, we're from the State ME's regional office in Woodbine, southwest of here. Are you the deceased's next of kin?"

"His name is Sergeant First Class Vincent Pastorini. He is active duty U.S. Army and a highly decorated war veteran, so the Armed Forces Medical Examiner's Office in Dover, Delaware will be in touch with your office before you're halfway to Woodbine, as will the Army CID and the FBI. When they do, they'll want to talk to you," Bob said as he turned his steely eyes on the General. "You can bet your sweet ass there will be a real investigation of what happened here, so I'd make damned sure I preserved the evidence and your notes."

"Son, I seen plenty of people take a nosedive off the hotels in town," the Police Chief offered, trying to calm Bob down, and actually beginning to sound concerned.

"I'm not your son," Bob cut him off with a sweep of his hand, "and this wasn't an accident or a suicide. It was murder. You can see that as well as I can."

"That's the second time you accused me of somethin,' boy, and it could be real bad for yo' health." Corliss glared at him and took another step forward. "Besides, who the hell you trying to kid? This is freakin' New Jersey. This ain't no goddamned Army post, and you don't count for shit here. So, where's the rest of that money you went to fetch?"

"Oh, you want your money?" Bob asked. "Come over here and get it, Shaka."

Corliss flared. Instinctively, his hand reached inside his jacket for the .44-magnum revolver, but his shoulder holster was empty. He forgot that his hog-leg Smith & Wesson was lying in the corner of Martijn Van Gries's office in pieces. Corliss growled and took two more quick steps toward Burke anyway.

"Not now, you damned fool!" Carbonari lashed out at him as he looked around at the cops and the other witnesses who were staring at them.

"Let 'em watch, I don't give no damn. Ah had enough 'a him," Shaka said as he scowled at Burke and then at the general, showing no fear of either of them. "You got lucky back there in the office. You sucker punched me, but you ain't gonna get lucky this time," he said as he took two quick steps and threw a sweeping right hook at Burke's head.

Shaka was strong and bulked up, but that doesn't make a man quick. Part of his problem was too many muscles. Part was he was accustomed to beating up smaller people who had no fighting skills and were easily intimidated by a brash thug like him. Bob Burke was none of those. Watching Shaka's eyes and shoulders as he telegraphed the punch, Bob leaned back far enough for Shaka's big fist to pass harmlessly by, a few well-measured inches in front of Bob's nose. As it did, Bob's left hand swept in and struck the back of Shaka's right elbow and pushed. With all his weight behind the punch, the added momentum caused Shaka to turn even harder to his left, stumble, and fall to his knees, completely off-balance.

"I didn't start this," Bob told Carbonari and the general. "But if he comes at me again, I'm going to put him down, hard; and that's the only warning you're going to get."

Enraged, Corliss got to his feet and shouted, "I'm goin' kill you, you bastard!" as he lunged toward Burke and took another wild swing at him. This time, Bob didn't back away. He stepped inside, chopped Shaka across the front of his throat with the edge of his hand and followed through with a hard elbow to the bridge of his nose. For a small man, Bob Burke's various appendages were quick, precise, and lethal. The two shots dropped the shaved-headed black man to his knees as if he had been hit in the forehead by a brick. He coughed, gasped, and turned pale, as his eyes bulged out and his fingers grabbed at his throat. With the vision of Vinnie's broken body dancing in front of him, Bob wound up and planted his size nine shoe in Corliss's crotch. That ended the flight. Corliss toppled over into the grass, moaning.

Burke looked back at the two cops, and then at Donatello Carbonari. "I told you to keep him on a short leash, but you didn't listen."

The general's mouth dropped open as he looked down at Shaka Corliss. From reflex more than brains, the Police Chief's hand went for the butt of the Glock in his holster until Burke raised his hand in warning and the Police Chief stopped. Burke looked at him and Carbonari and said, "That's the second time he attacked me today. Punks like him need a good thumping every now and then, and he just got his."

The police chief paused and looked at Carbonari, not sure what he wanted him to do. Finally, Carbonari motioned for the police chief to back off, which he gladly did.

"I guess you're right, Burke," Carbonari finally said. "Shaka has been looking to get his ass kicked, and no doubt he deserved it. But I'd be very careful if I were you. Antagonizing a man like that isn't a smart thing to do."

Corliss lay on the ground between them, moaning. His nose looked flattened and blood ran down the front of his shirt when Carbonari turned to the Hulks. "Get your thumbs out of your asses and get him out of here," he said in disgust. The two security guards quickly grabbed Shaka under his shoulders and dragged him toward the casino's front doors. "Not that way, you morons!" Carbonari shouted. "The back door, where all the other trash goes."

"You haven't heard the end of this," Burke said as he glared at Carbonari. "Or of me."

"Good. I was hoping you'd say that," Carbonari answered. "Because you haven't heard the end of us, either."

Bob turned and walked quickly back to the Buick, got in the driver's seat, and threw the car in reverse. He did a tight, tire-screeching, backward "donut" around the small parking lot, kicking a cloud of dust, stones and dirt toward Carbonari, the general, and the colonel, and then floored it, sending the two cops at the roadblock scrambling into the grass to get out of the way, as he flashed past and raced away downhill.

Behind him, in the rear seat, Linda attempted to console Patsy without much success. "You aren't going to let them get away with this, are you, Bob?" Linda demanded to know.

"Of course not, but this isn't the time or place."

"Then where are we going?"

"Back to the Philly airport, and then some place safe."

CHAPTER EIGHT

Saying Goodbye to Atlantic City

As Bob sped away from the hotel, he saw the black Lincoln Town Car parked at the bottom of the hill waiting for them. As he drove past, he glanced into the driver's seat of the big car and saw the Gumbah fumbling with his cell phone. Apparently, Bob's sudden retreat down the hill left the two men inside without any instructions, but that didn't take long for Carbonari to correct. By the time they reached Maryland and crossed Mediterranean, he looked back and saw the Lincoln coming after them.

"Buckle up, girls," Bob warned Linda and Patsy, expecting trouble, but after the Lincoln caught up, they slowed and remained their usual hundred yards behind. Were they only an escort out of town? Hard to say. Bob continued south to Atlantic, with the Lincoln still filling the center of his rearview mirror. Bob took a sharp right on Atlantic and accelerated, crossing North Carolina and Martin Luther King Boulevard until he finally saw the sign for the Atlantic City Expressway ahead on the right. He fully expected to see the black car remain on Atlantic and not follow them any further, as it had done earlier in the afternoon. This time, however the Lincoln took the ramp behind them, and remained in his rearview mirror as he merged into the northbound Expressway lanes toward Philadelphia.

The Atlantic City Expressway was 44 miles long, ending in Philly, where they could cross the Delaware River and turn south on I-95 to the Philadelphia airport. Five miles after they got on the Expressway, they came to the first of two toll plazas. Bob headed for the cash lanes, and as they approached the tollbooth, the Lincoln cruised through the outer, E-ZPass Lane and continued north, as if the two men in the car hadn't even noticed the Buick. By the time he paid the toll and drove away, the Lincoln was nowhere to be seen. He considered getting off at the Egg Harbor exit, or even crossing the median, making a U-turn, and heading back south to get away from the Lincoln, but his top priority now was to get out of town.

Bob pulled out his cell phone, scanned through his Favorites, and found a number he knew all too well. It rang six times, but no one answered, which was what he expected. However, when the call rolled to voicemail, rather than the usual short, blunt, male recording, he heard a very sexy female voice and some heavy breathing. "This is the *new* Ace Storm Door and Window Company. *We* are really busy right now, doing what you think we're doing; since you don't want to interrupt, leave us a message."

That was followed by three quick beeps, so Bob said, "Hey, this is the Ghost," wondering who Ace had make the recording for him. "Give me a call. We have a problem."

Ten seconds later, Bob's cell phone rang. "Who's the woman?" he asked.

"Oh, that's my new pal Dorothy. Since I'm 'getting on in years,' as you keep reminding me, I thought I could use a little image makeover."

"Like Bruce Jenner?"

"Not quite that drastic," Ace laughed. "Dorothy's an Air Force captain, a fighter pilot actually, who I met at the rodeo."

"Don't tell me you started riding again?"

"Me? Are you kidding? With my back and leg? Dorothy says the horses can smell the shrapnel and pins, and it spooks them. No, I was there watching her ride. She took second in Barrel Riding and first in Tie-Down Calf Roping."

"Wow! A soulmate at your age. She should be a big help at the Old Soldiers Home."

"And a captain. Much better retirement checks."

"Fraternizing with an officer and a gentlewoman? Who'd 'a thunk?"

"All right, Major," Ace sighed. "That's enough bullshit for one afternoon. What's the problem we have? What did you get into now?"

"Not me. This time it was one of your senior sergeants."

"Let me guess. That dumbass, Vinnie?"

There was no easy way to do this, so he just let it out. "He's dead."

For the better part of a minute, there was silence at the other end of the line. Bob had been close to Vinnie, but Ace had been closer, much closer than an officer ever could be. The two sergeants had put up with boring stateside assignments, firefights in a dozen godforsaken places, bullet wounds, divorces, good deployments and bad ones, car wrecks, bar fights, and too much bad food. In the process, they buried a lot of good men, but those soldiers died on the battlefield, not like this.

Finally, he heard Ace cough and then say, "A couple of days ago, he took leave and said he was taking Patsy up to Atlantic City. It was their second trip up there in the last few weeks, but I didn't think much about it. He had the time coming, so why not? He was supposed to report back in here by 0800 today, but he never showed. I've been covering for him, figuring he'd walk in the door any minute now."

"Not this time."

"What happened?"

"He fell out a fifth floor window at the hotel."

"He fell?"

"That's what they're telling me."

"Doesn't sound like you believe them."

"I don't, but I can't prove it, not yet."

Ace grew quiet for a few moments, and then asked, "Is Patsy okay?"

"Physically, but emotionally she's a basket case."

"I can imagine. And you're still there? You want me to come up?"

"No, we're headed for the Philly airport — me, Patsy, and Linda — then we're going back to Chicago, as soon as I can get us a flight out."

"If he didn't 'fall,' I assume you know who did it."

"Probably. He was dealing with the same kind of morons we dealt with the last time, only a different branch of the family."

"And I assume they were more than you could handle at the time."

"Yep, but they claim they didn't do it."

"There's a surprise. I assume you're not gonna let it rest there, are you?"

"You're full of assumptions today, aren't you, Master Sergeant."

"Vinnie was one of ours. Whatever you're planning, count me in, and I won't be the only one," Ace grunted. "That was Dorothy jabbing me in the ribs. She says to count her in, too. But don't worry. She might be Air Force and an officer, but the lady can shoot, and she can kick your ass — mine too."

"Let's not get ahead of ourselves, not yet anyway, not until I'm sure."

"Doesn't sound like you, Ghost. If they killed one of our men..."

"*If...* Vinnie lost a lot of money up here — their money — and then he tried to fight his way out. Yeah, I hold them responsible, but I don't know if they killed him."

"When did the fine print start to matter? He was one of us."

"I know that, but I want to be certain who did what, before we go charging in there. That's why I called. You need to report this up the chain of command, ASAP. Call Colonel Jeffers and see if you can reach General Stansky over at the Joint Special Operations Command. Use my name and tell them what I told you. It happened about thirty minutes ago, and the New Jersey State Medical Examiner's office in Woodbine has his body. Somebody needs to call the Armed Forces Medical Examiner's Office in Dover, the Army CID, and the FBI. Stansky has the clout to make that happen."

"Roger that. So tell me what happened."

"Vinnie came up here and blew a lot of money in the casino."

"No surprise there."

"Nope. He started out with $30,000 of his own money, lost that, borrowed $100,000 of theirs, and lost that too. So he went back home, took out a mortgage on the new house, and came back here, but instead of paying off the markers like he said he was going to do..."

"Don't tell me," Ace groaned. "He went back to the tables and doubled down?"

"You got it. Pretty soon, he owed them almost $300,000."

"Christ! What an idiot."

"And these aren't people you want to owe money to."

"Still, they shouldn't have tossed him out a window."

"I'm not sure they did, Ace, but he got in a fight with their security people, busted a couple of them up pretty good, and did a lot of damage to the casino; so who knows?"

"No surprise there, either. He always was a bad loser."

There was silence for a moment or two, until Bob said, "Patsy called me last night."

"Too bad he got her involved in this… and you."

"No big deal. I flew in with some cash and a cashier's check to pay off his markers, but they wouldn't take the check. They sent me to a bank to get it cashed, while they took Vinnie up to his room to pack. By the time I got back, he was lying in the parking lot below, dead."

"No witnesses, I assume," Ace asked.

"Plenty, but none I'd believe. Their hotel security claims he climbed out the bathroom window onto a ledge and slipped off trying to get away, but it didn't look right to me. Unfortunately, I had the girls, and was in no position to push it at the time."

"But there's going to be a next time, isn't there?"

"Too early to tell, Ace, really. If they didn't do it… well, we've got to let it play out." All Bob heard was silence at the other end of the phone, so he tried to change the subject. "You're still down at Bragg, Master Sergeant Randall?"

"Roger that, sir! So is Koz and the Batman. Lonzo just got back from the desert and he's still highly pissed he wasn't around last time. Chester and Bulldog are here, too. Off the top of my head, there's probably ten or twenty more of our top operators down here now, and they'll all want a piece of this when they hear what happened to Vinnie."

"Good to hear, but don't do anything yet. Keep it quiet for the moment."

"Wilco. The last time you had one of your little reunions, up in Chicago, there were only four of us. This time, you won't have any problem staffing up. Vinnie had a lot of friends down here, and nobody does that to one of us and gets away with it. Nobody."

"I hear you, but I have to get the girls back to Chicago first, where they'll be safe. Your job is to talk to Jeffers and Stansky. Tell them I'll phone them tomorrow, and I'll come back down to Bragg in a couple of days. I'm sure there will be a big funeral. We can get together then, reassess the situation, and make some decisions."

"Sounds like another Gumbah hunt to me."

"Maybe... Wasn't exactly fair last time, was it?" Bob said with a grim smile.

"Wasn't supposed to be, and it won't be this time, either, if that's the way they want to play it. You and I both know only suckers want a fair fight."

After Burke drove away down the entrance drive, Donatello Carbonari pulled out his cell phone and made a quick call. Then, he turned and headed for the casino, ignoring the city police, the paramedics, and everyone else. With long, angry strides, he walked down the main aisle to the rear service corridor to the Risk Management office. He kicked the door open, stormed across the room, and vented his pent-up rage on Shaka Corliss. The black man lay in near collapse in his desk chair, legs splayed out, staring up vacantly at the ceiling. He held a large bag of ice against his crotch and another one against his face as Carbonari grabbed him by the lapels of his jacket and yanked him out of the chair. That sent ice cubes scattering around the room as he raised the stocky black man up to his level, face to face, with Corliss's feet dangling in mid-air. "You moron!" Carbonari began. "What happened in that room? What did you do?"

"Nuthin', I swear, Boss. I didn't do nuthin'."

"My ass! Burke's right. Any fool can see his friend didn't slip and 'fall' off that ledge. You threw him off, and even those stupid Atlantic City clowns could see it. Pretty soon we're gonna be up to our eyeballs in state and federal cops."

"I didn't do it, Boss! Ask them," he pleaded, pointing at the twin Hulks. They were about the same size — two big white guys in their mid-twenties with round, pink faces and blond buzz cuts. Corliss could never tell them apart; but who cares, he would laugh. "We wuz in his room, pullin' their stuff out of the dresser drawers and the closet, and jammin' it in their suitcases, like you told us to do. Ain't that right, boys?" Corliss tried to explain as he looked at the two goons for help. They nodded in agreement like two bobble heads; but it was obvious they were afraid of Corliss and didn't know what to say.

"That dude Pastrami went into the bathroom to take a piss," the black man went on. "The next thing we knew, he was gone."

"His name was Pastorini, you dumb ass, not Pastrami!" Carbonari shouted at him.

"Yeah, yeah Boss, Pastorini," Corliss quickly corrected himself. "Anyway, I heard something and went and looked. The bathroom window was up, so I ran over and looked out. These two opened the balcony door and looked out too. That was when we saw him on the ledge. We shouted for him to come back in, but he kept going and slipped and fell."

Carbonari looked away from Corliss and glared at the twins. Corliss may not know their names, but he did. He knew the name of everybody who worked for him. One of the twins was named Gerald and the other Phil; but like Corliss, he couldn't tell them apart either. "Gerald, Phil, is that what really happened up there? I swear to God; if you're lying to me, I'll castrate the both of you!" He knew the two big blond guards didn't know how to lie to a man like him. Their heads were hanging down and he saw them glance at each other. "Look at me!" he screamed again. When they wouldn't look him in the eyes, that was when Carbonari knew someone was bullshiting him. "I want the goddamned truth, now!"

"We don't know what happened, Boss," Gerald answered.

"What do you mean you don't know?" Carbonari asked, and then turned his rage back on Shaka Corliss. "You're a dead man, Shaka. You threw him out the window, didn't you?"

"No, no, Boss. I never touched him. We wuz nowhere near him. He climbed out the bathroom window, just like I said. We saw him on the ledge, but by then he was all the way at the far end. He pried the hallway window open. You know, that's where the elevators and stairs are, and we saw him climb inside. Anyway, the next thing we knew, not a half minute later, he comes flying back out, headfirst, arms and legs swinging around like he was trying to swim or something, and he landed in the parking lot."

Carbonari stared at him for a moment in disbelief. "You're telling me he 'came flying back out the window?' Out the hallway window? All on his own?" Carbonari stared at Corliss and then at the twins. "You saw him climb inside, and then he came 'flying back out'…? How stupid do you think I am?"

"It's the God's truth man," Corliss begged. "I told them two to shut up and back me up when I said he slipped off the ledge, 'cause I knew nobody'd ever believe us."

"Well, you got that right!"

"But that's what happened, man. We didn't believe it, either."

"Did you look in the elevator lobby?"

"Yeah, yeah. After he landed, we ran out of the room and down the hall. The elevators were all on different floors, and we looked in the emergency stairs, but we couldn't find nobody there. They wuz empty."

Carbonari looked at the twins. "And you're backing him up on a crazy story like this?"

"It's what happened, boss, we swear," Gerald pleaded and Phil quickly nodded his agreement. This time, Carbonari could tell they were telling him the truth. Finally, he dropped Corliss back in his chair, considering what they had just told him, but none of it made any sense. If these three didn't do it, and Burke and the two women were halfway across town at the bank, then who the hell would have done something like that? And why?

"All right, all right," Carbonari finally said. "Just remember, when Pastorini flew out that window, $175,000 of *my* money flew out the window with him."

Corliss frowned. "He didn't have no money on him, Boss. No way."

"You imbecile," Carbonari shook his head. "I'm talking about the money Burke got from the bank. He drove away from here with *my* money in his briefcase, Corliss. I *need* it, and I want it back!"

"Lemme go after him, Boss, I'll get it back for you, I swear," Corliss said as he managed to get to his feet. "I know I screwed up but give me another chance. I'll…"

"You're too late. I already sent Lenny and Gino after him," Carbonari dismissed the thought. "He's heading back to the Philly airport, but I'm going to have them stop him on the Expressway once they get out of town." Carbonari turned away and walked to the door, paused, and looked back at him again.

"I'll tell you what, Shaka," Carbonari said. "If they miss him or screw up, I'll let you go after him; because I want that damned money, all of it! But if you screw up again, go get yourself a shovel and start digging a big hole out back and save me the trouble."

CHAPTER NINE

On the Causeway

As they drove north through the flat farmland of southeast New Jersey, rush hour was at its height, and traffic was thick in both directions on the Atlantic City Expressway. The ever-hopeful evening gamblers raced south to the casinos in their cars, pickup trucks, motorcycles, and charter buses, eager to hit the tables; while the day-trippers retreated back to Philly and I-95 north with empty wallets and their tails between their legs.

Bob drove in silence, thinking of Charlie Newcomb, his late, great, friend, bean counter, and head of finance. Over the past three years, no one knew Bob better than Charlie. Observing Bob in one of these dark, tactical planning moods, Charlie compared him to an expert diamond cutter hiding away in a backroom workshop in the Diamond District on 47th Street in midtown Manhattan. They spend their days hunched over a workbench underneath a bright desk lamp studying raw, uncut stones through powerful jeweler's loupes. Every so often, they hold the stone up and turn it around under the bright light, until they see every flaw and imperfection hidden inside. Finally, with a precise plan in mind, they strike, betting it all on one swift, precise blow. They'd create a flawless gem, or shatter the gemstone into dust.

When he left Chicago that morning, all he wanted was to get Vinnie and Patsy out of that casino and back home. Now Vinnie was dead. Someone would answer for that, but Bob had no interest in going to war with another Mafia family, especially when Vinnie was a major contributor to his own problems, maybe even to his own death. Still, someone must answer. As much as he despised Carbonari, Shaka Corliss, and that toad Van Gries, he would wait for the FBI, the Army CID, and the Army medical examiners to investigate, determine the facts, and put whoever was responsible in jail, so he would not have to deal with it. The last time, he had nothing to lose and it was easy to do stupid, dangerous things. This time, things were different.

In the Buick's back seat, Linda continued to console Patsy Evans without much success. Finally, she looked up and caught Bob's eyes in the rearview mirror. "I heard what you said to Ace. You can try to convince him that you're going to wait and let the cops handle it, but I don't believe you. Neither did Ace. You're going after them; I know you are."

"Then you know something I don't know."

"I saw the smug expressions on their faces, and I know you. You won't wait; it's just that you don't do anything without a plan. What does the Army call it? An Ops Order? That's what you're doing, you're drawing one up in your head."

"If you say so."

"I *do* say so, because I know you, and if you think you're going to take us back to Chicago — Patsy and me — and find some excuse to dump us there, it won't work. We're coming. So, what's the plan, Major?"

"I don't have one yet!" he fumed. He turned his head and looked at her in the rearview mirror. "You don't seem to know who we're dealing with, do you? Carbonari and the rest of them? They're the Atlantic City mob, and they're tied to the Merlinos in Philadelphia and the Genovese and Lucchese mobs in New York City. That's serious trouble, Linda."

"I don't care who they are. I saw that look in your eye and I know you're not going to sit this one out. So, kindly tell the troops what the plan is."

"There isn't one, except not getting more of my friends killed. That's not going to bring Vinnie back." Bob shook his head. "I don't know what the hell happened in that fifth floor hotel room, and neither do you. Vinnie owed Carbonari a lot of money, and Carbonari wouldn't have touched him until he got it, which he never did. That isn't to say I don't blame Carbonari, Shaka Corliss, and even that prissy Dutchman Van Gries for his death, because I do, and I want justice; but Vinnie was at least partly at fault back there. A lot or a little, I don't know; but if he had stayed in that hotel room and waited for us to come back, he wouldn't be dead."

"But he *is* dead!" Patsy sat up and shouted angrily.

"And after I see the Army and FBI reports, I might change my mind. But Carbonari was right about one thing, none of this makes any sense; and I have too many responsibilities to charge in there on some maybes."

"Responsibilities? When did you become middle-aged?"

"I have a hundred employees who depend on me for their livelihoods now, Linda. Add to that a lovely new wife and a new stepdaughter I'd like to get to know better, and a squad of Army guys whom I have no right to keep putting in harm's way, and I'm not being fair to any of them, if I don't give them the benefit of the doubt and wait for some proof."

"The benefit of the doubt? That's their choice, not yours."

"No, it's mine, and the smart play is to walk away from this before I get more people killed, which is exactly what will happen if I turn the dogs loose before I'm absolutely certain what happened and who was responsible."

They were seven miles beyond the Egg Harbor tollbooths, driving in silence, when they passed the big, black Lincoln parked on the road shoulder. Bob looked back and saw it peel out, kick up a cloud of dust and dirt, as it came after them. Not wanting a problem with the local cops, Bob had been trying to keep the Buick near the speed limit, but the Lincoln in the rearview mirror changed all that. When you have "friends in high places," like the wise guys always seemed to have, speed limits might not be much of a problem, he guessed. Still, any expressway in rush hour wasn't a good place for a road race. He accelerated, trying to put as much distance between them and the Lincoln as he could, but the late afternoon traffic was getting thicker. Bobbing and weaving between the other cars, Bob kept one eye on the road ahead and one on the rearview mirror. As he expected, the black car was gaining on them. They had to be doing well over a hundred miles per hour, maybe a lot more, as he urged the Buick on.

"Buckle 'em tighter," he shouted to the two women in the backseat over the roar of Buick's powerful engine. Like two awkward heavyweights, the Buick and the Lincoln were powerful in the straightaways, but sluggish and hard to maneuver when things got tight. After finally catching up, the Lincoln swung into the left lane and began to pass them. Bob guessed they wanted to get the front of the Buick, suddenly turn, and force him off the road. That was something he couldn't let them do, but the Lincoln was faster, and Bob's options were few. As the Lincoln slipped ahead, in his side mirror he saw their passenger side window roll down and the stubby barrel of a sawed-off, 20-gauge shotgun suddenly appear, pointed at them.

"Get down!" he screamed at the girls as he swerved to his left into the Lincoln, door panel to door panel. The Buick bounced off the Lincoln, but it threw off the gunman's aim and nearly took off his arm. Still, he managed to get off a shot. The shotgun roared as a load of buckshot shattered the Buick's rear passenger window.

"You two, okay?" Bob shouted.

"Yeah, yeah, if you don't mind sitting on broken glass," Linda answered.

"Then get on the floor and hang on!" he answered, as he swung left again, bashing the Lincoln as he pulled up on his emergency brake. That put the big sedan into a controlled, 360° spinout, which bled off some of his own speed. As the Buick swung back around, Bob saw he was far behind the big black car, so he pressed his own gas pedal to the floor and went after them.

One moment, the man at the wheel of the Lincoln thought he was about to shove the Buick off the right side of the road; the next moment the Buick wasn't there. Like a heavyweight boxer who threw a roundhouse right at his opponent's head and braced himself for the impact when his fist struck, the driver hit nothing but thin air and found himself careening across the pavement toward the road shoulder and the deep drainage ditch beyond. Now in a panic, the driver suddenly spun the steering wheel back the other way, to the left; but all that accomplished was to send the heavy Lincoln fishtailing back across the road.

This wasn't the plan; the driver must be telling himself. He had to get the Lincoln back under control. Without thinking, he slammed on his brakes, which was precisely the wrong thing to do, making the skid and fishtail even worse. That was precisely when the Buick came racing up behind, and Bob drove the right corner of his front bumper into the left rear of the Lincoln. It didn't take much. Even a small tap would cause the Lincoln's driver to lose his remaining control and send the big car to go into a "death spiral" to the right. Bob didn't give him a small tap. He hit the Lincoln hard and it spun sideways out of control, flipped over, and flew off the road, landing upside down on its roof on the road shoulder, some fifty feet away. Bob watched it bounce, flip twice more, and finally land in the deep drainage ditch, which ran along the side of the road. It plowed a long furrow through the mud before it finally came to a stop upside down, half submerged in the water.

"Amateurs," he concluded as he swung into the left lane, raced away, and quickly blended into traffic.

Wide-eyed, Linda sat up and looked back through the rear window. A dozen or more cars on both side of the Expressway had pulled over onto the road shoulders. Brake lights came on, a few brave souls ran across the median to try to help, while most stayed back out of trouble and gawked at the upside-down car in the ditch.

"Jeez," Linda said. "I sure hope you took the good insurance on this thing. Where'd you learn to drive like that? Bubba Gump's Demolition Derby School?"

"Not quite," he smiled. "A defensive driving class in one of the CIA training schools in Virginia. It's just some high school geometry, a little physics, plus a dash of mechanical engineering."

"*Defensive driving,* my sweet patootie! That was a sawed-off shotgun he pointed at us," Linda glared at him. "Well? How's your 'benefit of the doubt' doing now? Do you still think what happened to Vinnie was an accident, or do you want some more proof?"

As they continued north up the Expressway toward Philly, one by one, the Lincoln, the drainage ditch, and the memories of the Atlantic City casinos faded from his rearview mirror. As they did, he got more and more angry and more and more certain of what he should do. That was when Linda chimed in.

"I don't know if they were after the money or if they just wanted to shut us up," Linda stated. "But whatever they did, they did it because Carbonari told them to. That changes everything and you know it."

"You can't let them get away with this," Patsy leaned forward and joined in.

"I'm not letting anyone get away with anything," he said, but one glance in the rearview mirror told him the girls weren't happy with him.

It was Linda who finally spoke up and said, "What you're telling us is that you aren't really backing off, you just want to see if someone else will do it for you?"

"Really?" Patsy glared at him. "How is that different from waiting?"

"Look," Bob tried to reason with them. "I'd love to walk in there and kick Carbonari's ass from one side of Atlantic City to the other, and then toss him, Corliss, and that four-star police chief off his own roof..."

"That wouldn't be a bad start."

"No, but that casino complex is a fortress. It has tall buildings commanding the high ground, surrounded by water, and with limited access. On top of that, the place's knee deep in private security guards and city cops now, with a top-quality, state-of-the-art camera and alarm systems inside and out."

"You weren't in that place more than twenty minutes and you figured all that out?"

"It's what I do, Patsy... no, it's what I *used to* do," he corrected himself, "but some things never change. It'll take a lot more than a couple of guys with sniper rifles and Ghillie suits to bring that place down."

"A handful of guys and two women," Linda reminded him.

"Both of whom I almost got killed a few minutes ago, because I got careless."

"It wouldn't have been your fault," Patsy told him. "We're here because we want to be, and when you go after them, we want to be there too."

He shook his head, knowing it was hopeless. "I might as well say yes, because I know I can't stop you."

"Good. Glad to see we got that out of the way," Linda said with a big smile. "I didn't want to keep fighting over it either, since we both know you weren't going to win."

Sad, but true, he consoled himself. "By the way, there will be three women in this, not just two. Ace has a new girlfriend. You'll meet her when we go down to Fort Bragg."

"Great," she said. "We already had you outnumbered; that will make it overkill."

CHAPTER TEN

Phily and Arlington Heights

They returned the rent-a-car at Philadelphia International somewhat the worse for wear and waited for the airport shuttle bus back to the main terminal. "Aren't you glad I took full coverage on that thing?" Bob said as the rental car personnel circled the Buick, crying.

"I'd try a different car company next time," Linda answered. "Those guys aren't going to want to see you again."

When they reached the terminal, they rode the escalators up one level to the shopping concourse, where Bob led them into one of those ubiquitous book, e-toy, and gift shops you can find at most metropolitan airports these days. They stocked about everything a traveler could conceivably want from computer accessories to luggage and carrying cases. When Bob saw a large, canvas carry-on bag with yellow and orange van Gogh sunflowers set against a bright blue sky, he grabbed it.

"That thing is hideous!" Linda announced. "You don't expect me to carry it, do you?"

"It's perfect," Bob corrected her as he headed for the cashier and paid for the bag. "In fact, since I'm not likely to find anything nicer, I was going to make it your anniversary present; but I knew you'd want it now." He had been carrying the canvas bank bag under his arm, rolled up to hide the bank logo and name since they got out of the rental car. Two doors down, he stepped into an alcove where a store had been closed for remodeling. Turning his back on the concourse, he tore the tags off the new shopping bag, stuffed the canvas Citicorp money bank bag inside, and handed it to Linda.

"Who do you think that's going to fool?" she asked petulantly. "It doesn't even begin to go with my dress or shoes. Ugh!" But he wasn't listening. He hung it over her shoulder, undid the top button on her dress, and slipped his index finger inside to pull out on the next button and her bra to expose even more cleavage.

"You're getting a little personal in there, aren't you?"

"Nowhere I haven't been before."

"And you may never go again, the way this day's been. What are you doing?"

"Giving the TSA something nicer to look at than the shopping bag."

"Want me to take the bra off, too?" she asked, exasperated.

He took a quick look around the concourse. "No, I don't want to start a full-fledged riot at the gate. I'm just trying to distract their attention a little."

"A *little*? Nice try, but you're only digging yourself in deeper," Linda said as Patsy began to laugh at both of them. Linda turned toward her and asked, "You want to carry this thing? A perky little thing like you? One peek and I'm sure you'd drive the guards crazy."

"No, no." Patsy quickly shook her head and backed up a step, glancing at Linda's chest and then down at her own, still laughing. "You're perfect. I... couldn't hope to compete."

"Oh, thanks! Looks like you've gone over to the 'dark side' with him, girl."

"Linda, there's $100,000 in that bag. Which would you rather try to stroll through the TSA checkpoint with? A canvas Citicorp cash bag or the ugly one with the sunflowers?"

"I suppose you want a dreamy bedroom smile to go with it?" she asked.

"Great idea," Bob answered. "But remember, if those million-dollar lips of yours don't work, you could be looking at six hours with the FBI and a body cavity search or two."

"Well, since those areas are reserved exclusively for you now, I guess I'll opt for the sunflowers."

"Somehow, I thought you might."

They walked back to the United Airlines counter. Bob was able to book first-class seats on a flight to Chicago using the company credit card. The airplane wasn't leaving for three hours, but with their First Class tickets and Linda's cleavage, they sailed through the TSA checkpoint without a ripple.

"Some security," Linda grumbled as they headed for their gate. "If I unbuttoned the next button and leaned forward, I could've walked through leading an elephant."

The wait proved longer than the flight.

"God, I want out of here. My butt's gone numb," Linda grumbled as they finally boarded the 737. "People who complain about O'Hare should try a long layover in Philly with those hard plastic seats and horrid food."

"You know what W. C. Fields put on his headstone? 'Better here than Philadelphia.' "

"Well, at least we're up in First," Patsy added.

"Free booze, free pretzels, and a free movie for three times the price of coach."

"With your position and all the business travel you do, I can't believe you don't buy a company jet. The new G-5 would do wonders for your image."

"And our bank account?" Bob shook his head. "You're forgetting, I spent a career in small aircraft with my own personal pilots."

"Yeah, but they had bullet holes in them and machine guns hanging out the doors. I meant the ones with a bar and soft Corinthian leather."

With time to kill, Bob pulled out his cell phone and pressed the speed dial phone number for an unlisted cell phone in Area 312 in Chicago. After five rings, he heard a muffled voice answer, "Yeah... Travers."

"You sound tired."

"That's because I'm tired. Is that you, Burke?"

"Who else? I heard you got promoted to captain and called to congratulate you, but from your voice, it sounds like they're already working you too hard."

"You have no idea, and the really stupid part is that I let them pull me out of the best damned job in the entire Chicago Police Department. I was drawing lieutenant's pay — not exactly shabby — ran my own little office out at O'Hare and was sliding gently down that slippery slope to retirement. Nobody bothered me. I was my own boss. I could come in late, leave early, and eat all the donuts I wanted... and then you had to take *that* goddamned flight from Washington and land on *my* doorstep."

"Bitch, bitch, bitch..."

"It was perfect," Ernie continued, completely ignoring him. "I didn't have to deal with department politics, nobody was shooting at me, hell, nobody who was anybody even knew I was out there. Now look at me. The donuts are stale, the coffee's cold, and I can't even see the top of my desk anymore."

"What did I read they made you? Vice Chief of the Organized Crime Division? And on a captain's pay. Wow! All that power and the big bucks too."

"Big bucks? Power? They moved me down to the 'Head Shed' at 35th and South Michigan. You know where that is? The gangbanger capital of the world — hookers and twelve-year-olds with crooked baseball hats, their pants falling down to their knees, and 9-mils jammed in their waistbands. I've got the brass in my shorts every time I turn around, I can't get a parking space in the damned garage, and I need a SWAT team escort to get to my car in the surface lot. Some favor you did me."

Burke smiled. "Well, yeah, we did put a few dents in their operation."

"Yeah, but it's like Whack-a-Mole. Whether it's the Black P. Stone Nation, the Gangster Disciples, the Latin Kings, the Russians, the Jamaicans, or the Italian mob, you knock one of them down and two new faces pop up to take his place. But it's been that way in Chicago since Al Capone, Frank Nitti, and Tony Accardo. It'll never change."

"Cute."

"Hey, I haven't talked to you since the wedding. How's life out in the 'burbs? Linda doing okay?"

"She's fine, Ernie."

"You don't deserve her, you know."

"I know."

"So what's up? You didn't call me to get an update on the Chicago mob, did you?"

"No, I'm calling the Vice Chief of Organized Crime for the Chicago Police Department to get a little intelligence information. You ever hear of the Carbonaris, in Atlantic City?"

"Oh, Christ!" Ernie groaned. "What'd you step in now?"

"Not me. You remember Vinnie?"

"Deadeye Vinnie? He was a fantastic shot with that sniper rifle."

"Well, now he's just dead."

"Dead? Whoa! What happened?"

"Donatello Carbonari says he fell off a fifth-floor ledge trying to climb out a window in the Bimini Bay casino, but I'm not buying it. I think they threw him out."

Ernie was silent for a moment, thinking it over. "Am I to assume he owed them a lot of money? That's usually the last thing a bookie or a casino would do. They might break his leg or throw him out a window *later*, but it's hard to squeeze money out of a dead man."

"That's what they said, too," Bob paused and reluctantly agreed. "I was at the scene right after it happened, and I can't figure it out. Vinnie's body landed too far out from the building for him to have slipped and fallen. That geometry just doesn't work. He had to have been pushed or thrown out."

"When did this happen?"

"About an hour and a half ago."

"And you're still in Atlantic City?"

"No, we're at the Philly airport."

"Who's we?"

"Me, Linda, and Patsy Evans."

"God, this is horrible. I assume there will be a service. Did he have any family?"

"Yeah, half of Fort Bragg. I'm sure there will be a service down there after the New Jersey State Medical Examiner's Office and the Army forensic people get finished."

"That sounds like a lot of investigators."

"Yeah, but they won't find anything. He fell five stories onto concrete. The rest is supposition. What we don't know, and we'll never know, is the why and the who."

"Sounds like you should be the detective captain, not me. Let me know when the service is and I'll be there."

"Thanks, Ernie, the guys will appreciate that, and it'll give me a chance to introduce you to a lot of people you've never met."

"Even though I was only with your guys for a couple of hours that night, I felt I really got to know them — Vinnie, Ace, Koz, and Chester — they were good men, all of them. In Iraq, I was only a Reserve MP Colonel running a POW stockade and trying to keep up with you guys, but I worked with a lot of other infantry and special ops guys, too, and they were all straight shooters. I became a big fan."

"Thanks, Ernie, but before you go down to Bragg, I have a couple of favors to ask."

"Tell me you're not thinking of taking on the Carbonaris, are you?"

"I hope not, but do you know anybody with the FBI in New Jersey? One of the bankers down here gave me a name — Philip T. Henderson in the FBI field office in Woodbine."

"I'll check, but like most cops, we avoid the 'Feebs' whenever we can. They always seem to have an agenda of their own when they're dealing with regular cops," Ernie told him. "But I attended a conference in Detroit a couple months ago and traded drinks with the number two man in the New Jersey State Police Organized Crime Task Force, a big guy named Carmine Bonafacio. You'd like him."

"An Irish boy?" Bob asked, surprised.

"Trust me, nobody hates the Mafia worse than an Italian cop. The mob runs Hoboken, Jersey City, Newark, Atlantic City, and most of the rest of the place. Keeps the cops hopping. I'll give him a call and see what I can learn."

"Okay, I'll leave that up to you. Just be careful."

"Me? *You're* telling *me* to be careful? Oh, that's rich."

When their flight was finally called for boarding, they quickly took their seats in the First Class section of the 737, with Bob by the window and Linda and Patsy next to him in aisle seats across. Linda closed her eyes and melted into the soft cushions. "Much better," she said with a contented smile. "No broken glass, no shotgun, no demolition derby."

Bob slipped his briefcase under the seat in front of him and stuffed the sunflower print bag under the seat in front of hers as a graying, middle-aged flight attendant elbowed her way through the line of boarding passengers to take their drink orders. "Oh, that sunflower bag is so cute," she gushed. "I'm from Kansas, and I've been looking for something just like that."

"Well, Christmas is coming," Linda said as she opened one eye and looked up at her. "If you're a *really* bad girl, maybe Santa will bring you one, too."

"Is that how you got yours?" the flight attendant shot back with an alligator smile.

"You have *no* idea," Linda retorted as she ran her hand down Bob's inner thigh. He jumped, and she asked, "How about a double martini for me and one for my friend across the aisle. You want one too, Stud? After all, you're paying."

"None for me," Bob replied. "I promised the Fraternal Sisterhood of Flight Attendants that I'll never drink on one of their flights again, not ever."

The flight attendant shrugged. "To each his own," she said and then scurried back to the galley to fill the girls' drink orders.

Two hours and fifteen minutes later the airplane landed at O'Hare. Without any luggage and sitting up in First Class, they were out of the plane, down the concourse, and onto the parking lot shuttle bus in twenty minutes.

"We need to pick up Ellie and her new cat before it gets any later," Linda reminded him as they got into Bob's old Saturn. "Patsy, we have an extra room, and you haven't been home in weeks. Come stay with us for a couple of days. This isn't something you should go through alone. Besides, Ellie really misses you."

"Okay," Patsy reluctantly agreed. "Normally, I'd insist on going home, but I haven't slept for two days and I'm too tired to argue with anyone right now."

Bob was brain-dead too, and it took a few moments for Linda's words to sink in. "Did I hear you say 'Ellie's new cat'?" he asked with a puzzled frown. "You know cats don't like me."

"That's not true. *You* don't like *them,* and cats are very sensitive. They can tell."

Bob turned his head and eyed her suspiciously.

"The cat's a present to Ellie from my sister," Linda tried to explain, "and she absolutely loves him. The therapist at her school says she's very fragile right now after all that happened, so we can't say no."

"Fragile? If Ellie was here, she'd be the most mature and well-adjusted female in this car," he said as he shifted his forearm, anticipating a sharp elbow to the ribs.

Linda saw the arm block too. "You're learning, Burke, but time is on my side and I can wait. I have a lot more of it left than you do, you know."

"But it won't be half as much fun," he quipped. "You know, there's two kinds of people in this world — cat people and dog people."

"Every kid needs a pet, Bob," Patsy chimed in. "And little girls just love cute little kittens, especially a girl like Ellie, after everything she's been through."

Linda began to fidget in her seat. "Well, uh… this isn't exactly a cute little kitten," she said as she went into "escape and evasion" mode.

Bob finally got it. "Oh, no! Not that big, ugly tomcat of your sister's? She isn't trying to foist that beast off on us again, is she? A kitten? He's the size of a Thanksgiving turkey, arrogant, ornery, and what does he weigh? Twenty? Twenty-five pounds?"

"Yes, he needs to go on a diet, but Ellie has really bonded with him," Linda explained.

"I can see it now, cat hair everywhere, scratched furniture… scratched me!"

"You really need to see them together, Bob."

"…and I hate to think of how many times he'll set off my alarm system."

"You will absolutely break her heart if you make her send him back."

"What's his name, Godzilla?" Bob asked as he turned in the seat and glared at her, knowing full well he was trapped, which was exactly what her sister had in mind.

"No, she named him Crookshanks. Besides," Linda added, grabbing the last stake to pound into his heart. "If you're nice, I'll try *extra special* to make it up to you."

He glanced back at her again. "*Extra special*, huh?"

"*Extra, extra special*," she said with a knowing smile as she blew him a kiss.

Patsy started laughing. "Boy, are you whipped."

"Tell me about it," he muttered.

"You two aren't gonna keep me up all night with that noise again, are you?"

"Only if she starts screaming," Bob answered. "Usually, she just moans."

"He is so lying! …But we'll put you at the end of the hall, just in case."

Bob and Linda's modest townhouse in Arlington Heights dated to his bachelor days after he and Angie separated. It was different from the Toler family "mansion" up on the lake shore in Winnetka, which he recently put up for sale. No way was he ever going to move into that house again. After he and Linda got comfortable with each other, he would find them a new place; but for now, the townhouse suited them just fine. It was a tall, narrow, two-story middle unit sandwiched between two end units. Each contained three bedrooms, with two baths up, a large living room and kitchen down, a rear yard surrounded by an eight-foot-high board fence, and an attached, two-car garage that opened onto a rear alley. It came with standard builder finishes and cheap, disposable furniture. He added large-screen HD TVs in the living room and the other bedrooms, a good Onkyo CD player, Tyler Acoustics speakers, and two standing racks for his prized collection of jazz CDs. Other than an occasional weekend football game, the TVs were a waste of money. His schedule rarely afforded him time to watch much of anything unless he recorded it and fast-forwarded through the commercials.

Bob had no interest in remodeling or tinkering with any of the furniture or finishes before he met Linda, and even less now. After they moved on to a real house, she could do those things to her heart's content. Other than the TV and audio system, the only other thing he spent much money on was a state-of-the-art, integrated security system. Old enemies can be the most persistent, especially Middle Eastern ones, and he had made them by the dozens during his fifteen years in the Army. With the help of some "black ops" pals from Fort Bragg, they installed the system one weekend without getting permits or posting any of those cute little stickers on his doors or windows. He wired the doors and windows with sensors, and installed motion detectors and miniature video and infrared cameras in all the first floor rooms and the garage. The wiring, contacts, and motion sensors were almost invisible. Finally, they hid the control panel and video recorder on a high shelf in his closet behind a box. They were easily accessible for him, but the last place anyone else would think of looking to disable the system.

If a sensor tripped when he was away from home, it would activate the cameras and the interior and exterior lights on the house, the garage, and the yard, and then send an alarm and live camera feed to his cell phone. He knew from experience that bright lights were usually all it took to send an intruder running. On the other hand, when he was home, the sensors would only activate a series of small flashing lights, codes, and faint beeps on his phones. They would not activate any of the inside or outside lights, but he could quickly stream a rotating set of camera feeds to his phone or bedroom television. That way, he could keep his options open, determine the extent of the threat, and decide which countermeasures to employ.

It was almost 11:00 p.m. before they got home. They picked up Ellie at Linda's sister's, and she and Patsy were sound asleep, arm in arm in the backseat with the cat lying on his back, paws up in the air, between them. As he turned off the main road into his townhouse complex and reached the rear alley behind his unit, he pulled out his cell phone and toggled the home security app, as he routinely did every time he came home. He looked at the screen and saw that none of the door or window sensors had been tripped. Neither had the garage door, so he reached up and pushed the button on the garage door opener. When the big double door began to tilt up, the bright exterior and interior garage lights came on. He continued to see nothing amiss, so he pulled his old Saturn inside the garage and turned the engine off.

Bob got out the driver's door, looked back inside, and saw he was the only one still awake. Linda and Patsy were easy to awaken, but Ellie and her big cat were down for the count. "I'll carry Ellie inside," he told Linda. "You grab the cat, and Patsy can bring the two bags with the money."

Linda reached inside and picked up the big cat in her arms. "Jeez, Godzilla really does weigh a ton, doesn't he?"

"His name isn't Godzilla, Mommy, it's Crookshanks," Ellie corrected her as she got out of the car by herself and immediately took the big cat from her mother.

"Crookshanks! That's Hermione's cat in *Harry Potter.*" Patsy nodded knowingly and smiled. "Excellent choice."

Bob shook his head and took several steps toward the alarm box to reset everything, when he heard an all-too-familiar voice call to him from the dark alley outside the garage.

"Well, lookie what we got here," Shaka Corliss said as he stepped into the pool of light outside the garage, grinning. "It's my smart-ass Army friend, *Major* Burke, two of his slot machine cuties, and a new little play pal. My, my, ain't we gonna have us some fun tonight!"

CHAPTER ELEVEN

Standing in the bright light directly behind Bob's old Saturn and perhaps fifteen feet away, Shaka Corliss grinned at Bob with his white-capped teeth flashing under the bright spotlights on the rear of the garage. His bald head, shades, and gold chains gave him the intended street thug appearance, but they weren't nearly as impressive as the chrome-plated .44-magnum in his hand. To Corliss's immediate left and right were the twin Hulks from the Bimini Bay, not that Corliss really needed any help. The big, hog-leg revolver was pointed at the center of Bob's chest. The two Hulks had garden-variety 9-millimeter Glocks pointed at the two women, but the expressions on their faces were no less murderous.

Bob knew he had to act, and fast. "Is that you hiding out there in the shadows, Shaka?" he asked, silently cussing himself out for allowing these three bozos to get the drop on him. They did, however, and maybe that was a blessing in disguise. He could deny it all he wanted, but marriage and corporate life had left him soft and fat. The combat awareness and lightning-quick reflexes he had depended upon for so many years had grown rusty and dull, like a fine Henry hunting knife left out in the rain. That could be fatal for a man who still thought of himself as a "lean mean fighting machine." From now on, he would need to be doubly diligent, if there was going to be a "from now on."

"I ain't hidin' nowhere," Corliss bristled. "But you gonna be dead, you don't shut up," he said as he pulled back the hammer on the big Smith & Wesson revolver with a loud Click!

Few things focus the mind better than the sound of a cocked pistol. Triangulating the bodies in the space around him, they had him trapped here inside the garage. Retreating or doing nothing was not an option, not with three armed gunmen standing in front of him and the three girls arrayed behind. No, when you are surprised, outgunned, and outflanked, the best choice was to strike first and attack. To paraphrase Chesty Puller when he and his Marines were surrounded by ten Chinese divisions, *"Those poor bastards. They've got us right where we want them."* And if the opposition was better at it than he was, he'd be no more dead than if he did nothing.

Bob held his hand up to shield his eyes as if he was having trouble seeing in the bright light, and he continued to walk slowly toward Shaka Corliss, closing the gap.

Patsy held Bob's briefcase and the brightly colored carry-on bag. Corliss turned to Hulk One and waved the revolver at her. "See what's in them bags that bitch is carryin,' dummy." Hulk One frowned, but he stuck his Glock in his belt, took the two bags from Patsy, and shoved her up against the car, trying to out-macho his boss.

"Touch her again and you'll walk with a permanent limp." Linda glared at him.

The Hulk turned on her, saw the expression on her face, and backed away, keeping one eye on her as he threw the two bags on the car trunk. Popping the top on the briefcase, he saw thick stacks of cash inside and poked his finger around to be sure. He then set the gaudy carry bag on the briefcase, pulled out the bank bag inside, and stuck his nose inside.

"That the money?" Shaka asked impatiently.

"Yeah," the Hulk answered. "They're both full of cash, and there is a lot of it."

Bob didn't like these odds, but while they were talking to each other and looking at the money, he continued to work himself closer. Now, all he had to do was to figure out a way to get them off-balance.

Corliss grinned at him and reached inside his jacket pocket. He pulled out his new iPhone 6s and pressed the top listing in Favorites. He put it on speaker and turned up the volume. After four rings, Donatello Carbonari answered. "Yeah, what have you got?"

"Well, I got that asshole Burke, his two girlfriends, and a couple of big bags of cash," Corliss crowed, his white-capped teeth flashing under the bright floodlight. "I ain't counted all it yet but…"

"Then get it done and stop bothering me!"

"Don't you want to watch me do him?" Shaka frowned, eager to please, and clearly disappointed. "I can turn on the cell phone video camera and…"

"No, you fool! I don't want to get tied into any of that! It's your job, now finish it," Carbonari ordered, and the line went dead.

Corliss tried to keep smiling, but Bob could see this was a major rebuke by his boss in front of his two white lackeys. From the angry look in his eyes, it was obvious that Corliss wasn't happy to be shown up like that, and it stung. Good, Bob thought. That should get him thinking about something else. The last time he saw Corliss, the two Hulks were carrying his prostrate form toward the back door of the Bimini Bay hotel. Bob remembered how solidly he caught him in the face with his elbow. He could still feel it and hear it and expected to see tape across the bridge of a badly flattened nose and a pair of big, black "raccoon" eyes on either side. It was hard to tell the extent of Shaka Corliss's damage, however. The alley was dark and he wore those silly, wraparound, black Oakley sunglasses. They would partially cover any bandage and the two black eyes. Nonetheless, Bob knew how hard he hit him, and still felt the crunch of cartilage as his elbow slammed into the bridge of Corliss's nose. The pain and likely concussion should leave Corliss woozy, seeing double, angry, and out for revenge. That was an edge, but he needed to be closer to use it.

While Corliss was stocky and musclebound, he was short; and the chrome "Dirty Harry" revolver made him appear even smaller, a point Burke immediately jumped on as he continued to step closer. "Jeez, can you turn off the 'bling'?" Burke laughed, holding up his left hand as if he were trying to shade his eyes, pointing at the gold chains hanging around Shaka's neck. "Between the light reflecting off your ugly bald head, the gold, and that flashy, chrome-plated cannon in your hand, I can't see a damn thing."

"You got a real smart mouth, boy! I'm gonna enjoy shuttin' it permanently." Corliss raised the revolver and pointed it at Burke's head.

"Seriously?" Burke smiled and asked. "A little guy like you might want to pack something a lot smaller than a chrome-plated hog-leg like that. The gun's so big, it makes you look like a shrimp."

"A shrimp? That so, Burke?" Shaka answered, clearly seething inside.

"Yeah, and I'd bet it knocks you on your fat ass when you fire it."

"I guess we'll see, after it blows big holes in you," Corliss said as he turned toward the two Hulks. "Grab them two hos. We'll do 'em all inside."

"Who you calling a ho?" Linda glared at him.

"Shut up," Hulk One ordered as he pushed his Glock in the back of his belt and stepped toward the two women, eager to show Corliss that he could be a bad ass too. He grabbed Linda and Patsy by their upper arms, thinking he was controlling them.

Control Linda? That was Big Mistake #1. Bob smiled as he edged closer to Corliss. "Besides, we both know you're not going to shoot me."

"No? Just you wait until we get inside, then you'll see what this thing can do," Corliss said angrily. "Let's go, get 'em inside."

"Like I said, you can't shoot me, Shaka. In front of your boys here? You'll lose all your 'street creds,' my man." Burke said with a smile. "I kicked your ass twice back at the casino and flattened your nose like a rotten cucumber." Burke continued moving toward him. "And I'm not some guy you and your two pals can toss off a balcony…"

"Ah told you, we didn't do that."

"No? Well, it's your turn. You gotta kick my ass now, just you and me, straight up and man-to-man. If you don't, these two crash test dummies are going back to New Jersey and telling the rest of the boys that you're a wimp — all hard-ass show and no go."

He had gotten within three feet of Corliss and glanced at the two Hulks. "Look at them, Shaka," he said. "Look at their eyes. They're already laughing at your sorry ass, thinking you're 'the short black man with no balls.' I think that's what I heard them call you when they carried you out of the parking lot.

"No, man!" Hulk Two quickly spoke up to deny it. "We didn't say nothing like that."

"Ask Carbonari. He heard what they said," Burke told him. "That's why he told them to drag you inside through the *back door*. He didn't want anybody to see you. Besides, you're just gonna end up in one of his oil drums off Brigantine after you get back there, anyway. That is, if he didn't tell these two to put one in the back of your head as soon as you're done here."

"That ain't true, we swear!" Hulk One joined in.

"He's lying, nobody told us to do nothing like that, Shaka," Hulk Two quickly agreed.

"Whadjou tell Carbonari?" Corliss took his eyes off Burke and glared at the two big white men, demanding to know.

"Nuttin', man. We never said nuttin' to him," Hulk One insisted.

"Of course that's what they'd say now," Bob continued as he took that one last step. "Look at them; they're laughin' at you, both of them, 'cause they know you're a dead man."

Corliss's eyes narrowed as he focused on Hulk One, trying to read his eyes. That was all the edge Bob needed. His left hand flashed out faster than a Bud Frog's tongue going for a fly. In close quarters like this, the long barrel on a big hog-leg revolver worked to the black man's disadvantage — it was easy to grab and even easier to get leverage on. Bob grabbed the end of the barrel, twisted, and bent it backward. With Shaka's index finger trapped inside the trigger guard, the big handgun went off with a deafening Boom! but the 240-grain hollow-point slug ripped harmlessly through the overhead door and into the ceiling.

Bob was just beginning. He continued to twist, forcing Corliss to his knees until Bob pulled the revolver from his grip as effortlessly as if he were taking a toy from a small child. At the same time, having a firm grip on the Smith & Wesson's heavy barrel, Bob swung it around and backhanded Corliss on the side of his head with the pistol butt. The black man's eyes rolled up in his head and he toppled over sideways onto the concrete pad outside the garage door, out cold.

Hulk One's eyes went as round as saucers as he watched his boss collapse onto the concrete. He stood between and behind the two women, his big hands gripping each of them by their upper arms. He had tucked his Glock in the rear waistband of his pants, where it was out of reach and of no use to him now. Not one for quick reactions to begin with, before he could even think of doing anything intelligent, Linda raised her foot and raked the hard, sharp-edged heel of her leather dress shoe down his shinbone. Few things in life can render more pain than a determined woman in a pair of hard, leather-heeled shoes. The Hulk screamed as his shin was suddenly wracked with pain. Without waiting, Linda raised her leg again and drove her heel down onto the instep of his foot, sending him hopping up and down on the other leg. As he did, she grabbed the Glock from the rear waistband of his pants, swung it around, and struck him on the back of his head with its steel butt plate. Like his boss, Hulk One was out cold before he hit the floor.

Apparently, things had been moving way too fast for Hulk Two's pea brain to absorb. Wide-eyed, he finally reacted by turning and trying to point his Glock at Burke. Ellie was holding the big, ugly cat in her arms. Before Hulk Two could think about what to do, Ellie whispered in the cat's ear, "Go get 'em, Crookshanks!" She stepped forward and threw the cat at the Hulk. She had become a pretty good basketball player, used both of her arms, and stepped into it, like a perfect two-handed "push" shot in gym class — out and up from the chest.

Even though Crookshanks had spent most of his pampered existence as a fat house cat, Linda's sister was one of those cat people who did not believe in declawing them. It wasn't fair to the cat, she said, which proved to have been an exceptionally good decision. Between the loud gunshot and being tossed around like a gym ball, Crookshanks was thoroughly pissed and ready to take it out on someone. He screeched and howled as he found himself flying through the air. Still, cats have a surprisingly well-developed sense of balance and excellent defensive instincts. With his paws out in front of him and claws fully extended, his legs were a blur as they clawed the air. Somehow, Crookshanks managed to right himself, just before he landed on the big goon's chest. Like a runaway chainsaw, his claws dug in and found traction as he ran up the Hulk's chest, across his face and over the top of his head, shredding everything in his path, and sending bits of shirt, blood, and skin flying in all directions.

The Hulk screamed and stood frozen in the garage doorway, in shock. Wide-eyed, with his hands out and shaking in fear, he gave no further thought to Shaka, Burke, or the gun in his hand. It dropped harmlessly on the concrete next to Corliss as he looked down at his chest, now covered with blood, and continued screaming. Apparently, the cat had enough as well. Rather than come back for a victory lap on the goon, Crookshanks landed on his feet behind the Hulk, howled, and took off running down the alley.

Bob turned toward Ellie and smiled. "Good job!" he told her and then looked at Linda. "You too! Oh, and you can forget about all those bad things I said about Godzilla... I mean Crookshanks. He can stay... assuming he'll ever want to come back." Finally, Bob glanced down at Hulk One, who Linda left lying unconscious on the garage floor at her feet. "And a big high-five to you," he said to Linda. "I guess you can stay, too."

"Really? What makes you think I'll want to, either?" she shot back.

"All right, all right, I'm sorry. But let's get you guys inside," he told Linda and Patsy. "Put Ellie to bed and try to relax for a few minutes. I'm going to call the cops, but they probably heard that big .44 go off in Wisconsin and are already on the way, so stay loose. They'll need to talk to you because they're never going to believe me."

"I'm not going to bed until we find Crookshanks," Ellie stated as she crossed her arms across her chest and scowled.

"I'll find him, Sweetie, just as soon as I get rid of this garbage out here. I promise."

"You promise?" she asked as her eyes narrowed suspiciously, still not certain.

"I promise, even if I have to go through the entire neighborhood and look in every garage and trashcan."

"All right," the little girl reluctantly agreed.

"Okay, where's the booze?" Linda demanded. "I'm not going to bed until I get a drink. Maybe a couple of tall ones."

"And I'll get you one," Bob promised, "but wait until the cops leave. I want you sober as a judge when you talk to them."

"All right, I'll go in and put Ellie to bed, but tell them to hurry, because I'm not waiting very long," she added as she followed Ellie and Patsy inside the house.

Bob picked up the three handguns and tucked them into his waistband. Shaka Corliss and Hulk One lay on the concrete apron in the garage doorway behind the car. Hulk Two was still standing, wobbling back and forth with his hands on his face, moaning, as he tried to stop the bleeding.

"Sit down or I'll call the cat back," Bob told him, ready to put him down if he didn't, but that proved unnecessary. The Hulk collapsed on the ground where he was. In any event, he was no longer a threat, so Bob turned away and stepped inside the garage. He remembered there was a box of rags under his workbench, and several shanks of clothesline hanging from hooks on a pegboard. He grabbed them and went back outside.

"Here," he told Hulk Two as he threw him the towel. "You're bleeding all over my alley." He then turned his attention to Corliss and Hulk One. Flipping them onto their stomachs, he quickly hog-tied them, pulling their arms and legs behind them and wrapping the clothesline around their wrists and ankles a half-dozen times. Only then did he begin to relax. He would have added Hulk Two to the pile, but one look told him that wasn't necessary.

It had been a long day, and Bob suddenly realized how truly bone tired he was. He pulled a canvas sports chair out of his garage, unfolded it in the middle of the alley under the light, and laid the three handguns on the concrete in front of him. This was a good spot, under the light. It gave him a clear view of the three goons, and the police would have a clear view of him when they arrived. After all, a dark alley wasn't the best of locations to surprise a bunch of heavily-armed, nervous cops. Finally, he walked over to Shaka Corliss, rifled through his pockets, and pulled out his new iPhone. The last entry under Recent Calls had a New Jersey Area Code. Bob pressed re-dial and didn't have to wait long.

"What now?" Donatello Carbonari's angry voice answered. "Can't you take care of this, Corliss, or do I have to spell it out for you? What's wrong now?"

"Oh, nothing's wrong, Donnie. I've just missed your pleasant voice."

There was dead silence at the other end of the line. "Burke? What the hell's going on?"

"Oh, nothing really, Shaka just decided to take a nap. So did your offensive line. Want me to send you a picture? Maybe a video? But don't worry, the Arlington Heights cops will be here in a couple minutes. When they arrive, I'll give them Shaka's phone. I'm sure they'll want to talk to you."

"You're a dead man!"

"Donnie, you sound like a broken record. You tried that earlier tonight on the Expressway. How'd that work out for you? Now, in your infinite stupidity, you sent Shaka and his two pet rocks out here to Chicago for another ass kicking. They got here quick, too. There's a nice company jet parked around here somewhere, isn't there? That should be easy to trace through FAA records, and the Feds have a nasty habit of confiscating things like that."

"You have no idea who you're messing with," Carbonari continued to vent.

"Yes, I do, but you made a big mistake tonight. I was almost willing to give you a walk on Vinnie. After all, he was a hothead, as you said. He probably started it, and he owed you a lot of money, didn't he? I get that. But the Expressway? I had 'civilians' in that car with me. Up 'til then, I figured it was just an accident and I'd let bygones be bygones, but that pissed me off, so I took those guys off the board. I wrecked their car and probably wrecked them too. Then you got *real* stupid and sent these three out here. Now it's your turn, Donnie, and I'm coming after you."

"Nobody talks to me like that, you little prick!"

"I do! The score's five to one now — the two in the Lincoln plus these three you sent here. And I'll tell you a little story. I just love to run up the score on perps like you."

"That's big talk."

"Oh, you haven't heard anything yet. I'm going to take your lunch money, break your toys, and then I'm going to sit you down in the mud, just like I did with the other bullies in third grade."

"Yeah? Well, I'm waiting for you," Carbonari screamed into the phone. "I'll even comp you a room, but pack a lunch. You may be here for a while."

Carbonari broke the connection, and maybe the phone, as the line went dead, leaving Bob staring at a blank screen. "That was rude," he muttered. "I didn't even get to any serious name calling or talk about his mother. Oh, well," he said as he dropped Shaka's iPhone on the ground next to the three handguns. "Well, at least I have your attention, now, Donnie, don't I?"

CHAPTER TWELVE

Bob pulled out his cell phone and dialed 911. It only took two rings for the emergency dispatcher to answer, "Arlington Heights EMS, how may I help you?"

"This is Bob Burke at 847 Poplar Drive…"

"Sir, we just had multiple reports of gunshots at that location."

"There was only one… but I guess it was pretty loud."

"There are multiple units responding to the scene. Are there any injuries?"

"None that I'll lose any sleep over, but tell your shift sergeant I'm sitting in a chair in the alley behind my garage with the three intruders whom I've disarmed and incapacitated."

"The three intruders you've…?"

"That's right. And mention the name Burke. I have a skosh of history with you folks. Again, I am unarmed, I'm in a chair in the alley, and I'm sure I'll see them soon."

"Uh… Yes, sir!" the 911 dispatcher replied as Bob hung up.

As he began to make a second call, he saw Godzilla the Cat stick his head around a trashcan across the alley. The cat looked over at him, still unsure, and then slowly walked across the alley toward him. His fur was standing up down the center of its back, and his head continued to rotate warily from side to side like a radar dish. Given all that had happened, the cat's attitude was understandable, Bob thought.

"Good boy," Bob called out and put his hand down out to welcome the cat back. "I'm glad you returned on your own, because I wasn't looking forward to an all-night cat hunt." Bob even wiggled his fingers, offering to pet the beast, but the cat would have none of it. Instead, it slowly walked over to Hulk Two, whom it had thoroughly mauled a few minutes before, and sat down four feet away from him, close enough, but just beyond the big man's reach. The cat then stared up at him and cocked its head, apparently studying him, as only a cat can do. When that got no reaction from the large, nearly comatose gunman, the cat began to mew. Finally tiring of the sport, the cat began to clean his paws, carefully licking off the blood, while keeping a watchful eye on the goon.

Between his own pathetic moans, Hulk Two finally lowered the towel far enough to see the big feline cleaning his paws and staring up at him. That did it. The goon began to tremble. "Keep that thing away from me!" he pleaded.

Bob shrugged. "He came back for another piece of you, so shut up or I'll sick him on you again," as if he had any control whatsoever over the beast. Well, to the victor belong the spoils, and the cat was staking out his new turf, which now included the alley and the dummy in the chair. Personally, Bob had always preferred dogs, like a German Shepherd or a Golden Retriever. If things ever got really dicey and your life was at stake, the dog would give it up for you, while a cat would turn and run away, thinking it was every feline for itself.

Hearing the first police sirens in the distance, he picked up his cell phone again and completed the call. On the third ring, Ernie Travers answered.

"Not you again?" the big Chicago police captain asked.

"Is that any way to treat a long-lost friend? You got caller ID, huh?"

"I finally get home, put dinner in the microwave, and... Don't tell me, who'd you kill?"

"No time for details. You got any friends in the Arlington Heights Police Department?"

"After your last escapade, I doubt I have friends anywhere anymore."

The sirens were getting closer now, and then they suddenly went silent. "Can you give them a quick call, Ernie? They're rolling to a 911 call at my townhouse. Maybe you can tell them I'm one of the good guys?"

"Oh, all right. But why'd you call 911?"

"Because I have three hitmen from New Jersey lying on the ground next to me and..."

"You didn't kill them, did you?"

"No, no, I just dented them a bit. Two of them are trussed up like Thanksgiving turkeys, and my cat's guarding the third one. Anyway, can you give them a call?"

"And you took all three of them down?"

"Not really," Bob answered as he saw a police car enter the alley to his left and another one enter from the right, with their lights off. "I bagged one, Linda coldcocked another with his pistol, and the cat took down the third."

"This I gotta see," Ernie laughed. "Don't go anywhere, I'll be right over."

That was when both squad cars turned on their headlights, bracketed him with their spotlights, and hit the loudspeaker. "You in the chair, put your hands in the air and remain where you are."

Bob gave the police his biggest smile as a half-dozen tactical officers in full body armor and automatic rifles closed in on him from both ends of the alley.

It took three more minutes for the Arlington Heights police chief and assistant chief to arrive, fifteen more for Ernie Travers, and another hour before they finished interviewing Bob, Linda, Patsy, Ellie, and the cat. Only then did they remove Bob's handcuffs. They made several attempts to interview Shaka Corliss and Hulk One but they "lawyered up" and refused to say anything. Hulk Two, on the other hand, never stopped talking, begging for a doctor and pleading for them to shoot the cat. By that time, Crookshanks was the picture of innocence, curled up asleep in Ellie's lap in a kitchen chair.

After the cops hauled Shaka and the Hulks away, Ernie introduced Bob to the Arlington Heights Police Chief. "This isn't the first time we've rolled our Tactical Units to this address, Mister Burke. You seem to attract some very dangerous company."

"I didn't invite them, Chief," Bob replied as he reached into his pants pocket and pulled out the wrinkled FBI business card that Henry Stern, the Citicorp branch bank manager gave him. "After you finish booking them, run their guns and fingerprints, and give this guy a call." The police chief looked down and saw the name Philip T. Henderson, FBI Resident Agent, Northfield, NJ. "I suspect he can give you some background on them."

"And I have a friend with the New Jersey State Police," Ernie added. "I'll have him give you a call too."

"This isn't our usual fare out here in Arlington Heights, Mister Burke," the Chief said with a wry smile. "Not to pry, but I read you inherited a beautiful house on the lake in Winnetka. Chief Novak runs a real fine department up there. You ever thought of relocating?"

"With all this unwanted attention from New Jersey, you never can tell."

"Well, when you do decide to move, give me a call." The Chief smiled politely. "I'm sure I can get a dozen volunteers to help load that truck."

Bob laughed. "I'm sure you can. Meanwhile, we've decided to take a little trip down to North Carolina, if that's okay. Captain Travers will know where we are if you need us."

"We're leaving again?" Linda whined. "But we just got home."

"Given what happened here, I think your husband's right, Mrs. Burke, you'd be safer someplace else. Our patrol units can keep an eye on the place while you're gone."

"Let's throw some stuff in a suitcase," Bob said. "Then we can swing by Patsy's and let her grab some stuff, too. We'll get some motel rooms for the night and fly out tomorrow. Call your sister and ask if Ellie can stay with her for a few days."

"Will she let me bring Crookshanks?" Ellie asked as she hugged the cat.

"Why not?" Bob answered. "Tell your sister we'll keep the cat. I think he earned the right to be part of the family now, and your sister can't argue about that deal."

Linda smiled as Ellie gave him a big hug.

At 10:30 the next morning, Martijn Van Gries knocked on Donatello Carbonari's office door and let himself in. The big man sat slumped in his desk chair, looking surprisingly unkempt. He hadn't shaved, his hair was mussed, and while he wore a white shirt, he was without a tie or jacket. For him, that was as bad as it got. Van Gries was halfway across the room before Carbonari made a halfhearted motion toward one of the empty armchairs in front of his desk.

"Sit," the big man glowered. "I've been up since 3:30. Know what I've been doing?"

Van Gries thought for a moment. "Deep-sea fishing? Duck hunting? Robbing a gas station? What else do people around here do at that hour?"

Carbonari's eyes narrowed. Clearly, he wasn't amused by Dutch humor this early. "I've been on the phone with lawyers, and you know how much I hate lawyers, especially in the middle of night. It started when I got a phone call from that moron Shaka Corliss asking me if I wanted to watch him '*do*' Burke. He was going to *video* it on his cell phone for me, if you can believe that, maybe take a goddamn '*selfie*' with his *body*!"

"Calm down," Martijn warned. "You'll pop a blood vessel. Did he get the money?"

"No! A few minutes later I got another call on Shaka's cell phone from Burke! He took out Corliss and those two dummies he took with him, and now he's coming after *me*. He says he also took out Lenny and Gino…"

"That accident on the Expressway? He did that?"

"Apparently it wasn't an accident. Then, he's got the balls to tell me he likes to 'run up the score' on guys like me."

"He killed Shaka and the other two?"

"No, much worse. They're locked up in the Cook County jail. They've been booked on a half-dozen charges from Assault with a Deadly Weapon to unregistered firearms, RICO violations, and the list goes on. I had to call that law firm in Chicago our 'friends' there use. By that time, the switchboard was lit up with calls from the Arlington Heights cops, wherever the hell that is, the newspapers, the New Jersey State cops, even the goddamned FBI! I ain't taking anymore. They can subpoena me if they want, but I ain't talkin' to nobody no more."

"I warned you that Burke could be a problem," Van Gries reminded him, knowing that when Carbonari waxed into New Jersey colloquialisms, he became exceedingly dangerous.

"You didn't tell me squat!" Carbonari leaned forward and glared at him.

"Can you get them out of jail?"

"The lawyers say probably. It's Cook County. It all depends on the judge we draw and how much money we want to pay him, but we can't leave them in there. The FBI's probably working on them already, trying to get them to flip on us."

"I see the problem. Anything you want me to do?"

"Yeah. Find out who this guy Burke really is. He said he was Army, and claims he's running some kind of phone company, but I don't believe any of it. The lawyer I talked to back in Chicago said he remembered that name from all the stuff that blew up with the DiGrigorias and Tony Scalese a few months ago. About two dozen of our guys got whacked back there. He thought it was some kind of turf fight between the DiGrigorias, but he didn't know much else."

"Do you think he's some kind of undercover cop or something?"

"I don't have the slightest idea."

"What if I phone our local congressman? We've given him enough money over the years. If Burke has any kind of an Army record…"

"No, I don't want that tracking back here to me." Carbonari thought for a moment. "But my father had a black congressman in Harlem on the payroll. Call him."

"Will do," Van Gries said as he stood up. "With the three of them in the can, what do we do about security?"

"I was going to call Philly, maybe Brooklyn, and have them send me some of their boys."

"Before you do that, give me the rest of the day to do some checking."

"Why?" Carbonari asked suspiciously.

"I doubt your friends from New York would be any better than what we had. If Burke is coming after you now, you need to ratchet things up."

"You know somebody?"

"Not me, but my brother knows people. Let me call him," Van Gries said as he stood and headed for the door. "What about Corliss and the other two?"

Carbonari looked up at him with the coldest, hardest eyes Van Gries had ever seen. "They're a problem we don't need. When they get out, take care of it."

At 4:30 p.m. the next afternoon, their connecting flight from Charlotte finally touched down at the small Fayetteville, North Carolina airport. It was located some fifteen miles southeast of Fort Bragg, and Linda and Patsy had spent most of that flight arguing whether or not Patsy should return to the house she and Vinnie had recently purchased east of the post.

"Honey, there's too many memories in that place. Come with us to the Embassy Suites," Linda told her.

"I'm tired of other people's beds. I'll be fine, and I need to start cleaning things out."

"You don't need to start right now."

"She'll be fine," Bob said. They were headed toward the rent-a-cars, while Patsy was picking up Vinnie's car in the express lot, where they had left it before their flight. "But, Patsy, if you change your mind or need to talk, give us a call at the hotel. Promise?"

"I promise," Patsy said as they parted company, "but you're treating me like a little kid. I'll be fine, honest."

At 2:00 a.m., the telephone on the end table in their hotel room rang. His hand groped about in the dark until he finally found it. "Burke here," he answered.

"Major Burke, this is Sergeant Iversen with the Fayetteville Police Department. Do you know a Patsy Evans?"

"I sure do, Sergeant. What's the problem?" he asked.

"There's been a shooting incident over here at 227 Maple Hill Drive..."

"A shooting? Is she all right?" he asked, at which point Linda was up, leaning over him and trying to hear.

"She's fine, although a little shaken up. Unfortunately, I can't say the same for the man she shot. Apparently he broke in the house and she put three 9-mils in the center of his chest."

"Nice shot grouping," Bob quipped.

"That sounds like Delta talk," Iversen quickly replied.

"Me? Oh, no, Signal Corps, and retired. Does she need a lawyer?"

"I doubt it. Two masked intruders cut the screen and entered her house through the dining room window. We have their muddy footprints down the hallway to the master bedroom from the flowerbed outside. When the first one opened the door, she took him out and the second one took off running. We found some blood on the dining room window frame, so she might have winged the second one too. Maybe the lab can figure out who it belongs to."

"My wife and I will be right over."

"That might be a good idea. The Glock she fired belongs to a Sergeant Vincent Pastorini. The house is registered in both their names. I believe he served with you?"

"That's correct. He was one of my senior sergeants. We're in town for his funeral tomorrow, and Patsy is a close friend of my wife and me. Can I speak with her?"

"We're still taking her statement, so I'd rather you wait until it's finished."

"We'll be there in about twenty minutes."

"Good. By the way, that three-shot grouping was excellent, but she got off seven rounds at them. Blew the hell out of the wall and doorframe. Since her husband worked for you, I guess he must have been Signal Corps too, 'cause four misses definitely wouldn't be up to Delta standards, would they?"

Maple Hill Drive was a short residential street on the north side of

Fayetteville. By the time Bob and Linda arrived, it was crowded with city police and sheriff's cars, an ambulance, a black coroner's wagon, and a large, white police lab van. Sergeant Iversen met them at the front door and led them inside. Patsy sat in the kitchen, and Linda made a mad dash to give her a big hug. Iversen motioned for Bob to accompany him toward the back of the house, where a body lay sprawled in the doorway to the master bedroom, covered with a black plastic sheet. Iversen knelt and pulled the sheet aside. The man wore black slacks, a black turtleneck sweater, and black leather utility shoes. The black balaclava he had worn was lying on the floor next to him.

"Recognize him?" the police sergeant asked.

"Nope, never seen him before," Bob replied as he knelt and studied the man's face.

"You've never seen him around Fort Bragg?"

"No, but I've been gone three years. Did you find anything on him?" Bob asked.

"Nothing, other than some disposable plastic wrist and ankle restraints and a knife," Iversen answered as he held up three plastic bags. "No IDs, no car keys, nothing."

Bob reached inside the rear collar of the man's sweater, looking for the manufacturer's tag, but it had been cut out too. Same for the pants. No tags. Bob looked at the plastic bag with the sleek, gunmetal black knife that Iversen was holding. "I'm no expert, but it looks like a Hill tactical knife, European manufacture, and pretty expensive."

"Is that a brand that Delta uses?"

"You keep hinting, but do I look like a Delta?" Bob laughed as he looked down at himself, knowing he was his own best camouflage.

The police sergeant looked at him too, and shrugged. "No, I guess not; but let me get to the nut of it, Major," Iversen said as he leaned in closer. "Two guys in black, with ski masks, plastic restraints, no IDs, no tags, and a knife like that…"

"They weren't amateurs, were they?"

"No, and I don't think this was a burglary gone wrong, or a sexual attack, either."

"The snap-cuffs? You think it was a kidnapping?" Bob asked, skeptical.

"Call it what you like, but she was the target."

"Patsy? But why? Have you asked her about this?"

"At length. But tell me about Sergeant Pastorini. You've come in for his funeral, was he a combat casualty somewhere?"

"Combat?" Bob shook his head. "He fell out the fifth-floor window of an Atlantic City casino."

"In Atlantic City? Was it an accident? Suicide?"

"Depends on who you ask. Look, I know what you're thinking, but where's the connection? Vinnie ran up a bunch of gambling debts in a casino up there and tried to get away by crawling out a window. Patsy had nothing to do with that."

"Well, she sure had something to do with this," Iversen nodded at the corpse.

"You're running fingerprints on this guy and tests on the blood on the front door?"

"Of course. Fingerprints clear pretty fast in the state and Federal databases, but don't hold your breath on the blood."

"Well, if you get a match, let me know." Bob said as he looked into the kitchen. "Can we get Patsy out of here now? I'd like to take her back to the Embassy Suites with us, maybe have my wife grab some of her stuff."

"Yeah, okay, but let me know where she'll be. That second guy is still out there."

As soon as they got Patsy in the car, she began to cry. "God, I can't tell you guys how much I appreciate this. I don't know what I'd have done... those two men..."

"It's been a rough few days for you," Bob commiserated. "But before we get to the hotel, let me ask you a couple of things. First, where'd you get the Glock?"

"It was Vinnie's. He took me to the range and taught me how to shoot."

"Looks like he taught you pretty well. But what woke you up? You must have been tired, and it looked like they were careful, creeping around in the house."

"I don't know. Something did. There's a couple of boards out in that hallway that aren't right. Vinnie complained to the builder two or three times that they need nailing down again. I'm a light sleeper, maybe that was it. Anyway, something woke me, so I pulled the gun out of the bedside table and waited. When the bedroom door opened and I saw someone standing in the doorway... I started pulling the trigger, like he told me to do."

"You did the right thing. They were after you."

"Me? But why? I didn't..."

"You never saw him before, maybe with Vinnie, or around the post?"

"No, I swear."

"Okay, okay, I believe you; but you need to be careful. They were here for a reason, and the other one is still out there."

CHAPTER THIRTEEN

Fort Bragg, North Carolina is one of the largest United States Army installations anywhere in the world. Sprawling across parts of four counties in the central North Carolina Piedmont, it covers 251 square miles, an area larger than the city of Chicago. As every infantry grunt knows, Fort Benning Georgia, two states to the south, is the home of the boring, old-fashioned, crawl-in-the-mud, "leg" infantry and the elite 75th Ranger Regiment, while Fort Bragg cornered the Army's fun jobs. It is home to the 82nd Airborne Division, the sky troopers who jump out of airplanes. It's also home to the John F. Kennedy Special Warfare School, and the men and women who wear those nifty green, maroon, and beige berets. Many of them belong to various hush-hush, "if-I-told-you-I'd-have-to-kill-you" Special Operations units, like the ultra-secret Delta Force, who work under the Joint Special Operations Command or JSOC as it's called. As such, it was home to 77,000 of Bob Burke's "close personal friends," each of whom takes it very personally when one of his fellow soldiers is murdered.

Three days after they left Chicago, Bob found himself slowly ascending the curved staircase to the elevated pulpit inside Fort Bragg's Main Post Chapel. It is a lovely, two-story white clapboard colonial building with a tall, red-shingled, bell tower. The chapel's interior is painted pure white, with stained-glass windows and balconies, a crimson carpet down the main aisle, and an elegant brass chandelier hanging high overhead.

The pulpit where Bob stood was no less impressive. Hung from the side wall, it looked down on the altar, the main floor, and the flag-draped casket at the head of the main aisle. He had been inside the chapel many times for weddings, ordinary church services, and funerals. Today was the third occasion when he had been asked to deliver the eulogy. The first two were when the Iraq and Afghanistan wars were at their peak, and post chapels were busy places everywhere. This time, it was different. The level of conflict around the world had slowed, and Washington was even pulling Special Operations troops out of many places, which only made a eulogy that much harder.

Vinnie served in many of the units at Bragg and at Benning, especially the elite ones, such as Delta and the 75th Ranger Regiment and all its components, with distinction. Any death among this elite fraternity of warriors was to be mourned, but Vinnie's death was anything but ordinary, and everyone in the room knew it. Perhaps that was why Bob found himself standing in front of an overflow crowd that morning.

In the front row sat Lieutenant General Arnold Stansky from JSOC and

Colonel Irving Jeffers from Delta, with Patsy and Linda sitting between them, accompanied by several other general officers and a phalanx of colonels, lieutenant colonels, and majors, all in uniform. To their immediate rear sat Master Sergeant Harold Ace Randall, several graying command sergeant majors, and Chester, Lonzo, The Batman, Koz, Bulldog, and countless other NCOs and warrant officers with whom Vinnie had served, or at least tipped a few beers over the years. Most wore their dress green uniforms, as Bob had done, complete with all the ribbons, special badges, and insignias. Sitting next to Linda was Ernie Travers, who arrived from Chicago minutes before the chapel service began. One of only a handful of men in dark business suits, at his size he was hard to miss.

From the serious expressions on everyone's face, it was obvious they wanted answers. Unfortunately, Bob knew if he told them the truth, a torch-lit mob would head north and storm Donatello Carbonari's New Jersey "castle," as the good citizens of Transylvania had marched on Count Frankenstein's. Looking down on the grim faces and the closed, flag-draped casket with Vinnie's many medals and his tan beret from the 75th Ranger Regiment lying on it, it would be hard for Bob to say they shouldn't.

"This is not a happy occasion for any of us," he began. "Today, we lay to rest Sergeant First Class Vincent Pastorini, a highly decorated veteran of fifteen years' service in two wars and many other conflicts, and the recipient of two Silver Stars, two Bronze Stars, four Purple Hearts, the Meritorious Service Medal and three Army Commendation Medals. Over the years, as many of you can attest, there are very few elite Army fighting units in which Vinnie did not serve. Those of us who fought and bled with him knew him as a warrior who left us far too soon. He was a good friend, a brave soldier, a loyal comrade-in-arms, and he'll be sorely missed. Someone once said that the only noble end for a soldier is to be killed by the last spear, or the last arrow, or the last bullet in the last battle of a war; and then be carried off the field on his shield by his fellow soldiers. I'm sure that's what Vinnie would have preferred, but it was not to be. Instead, he died in a tragic accident not of his making. However, rather than dwell on his sad ending, let us remember the man and the good times when he walked amongst us with a moment of silent prayer."

After a few minutes of absolute silence in the chapel, Bob looked up and said, "Following this service, Vinnie will be interred in the Main Post Cemetery, and I'd like to thank General Stansky for his help in making that happen. Finally, there will be an informal gathering of Vinnie's friends at the Conference Center at 4:00 p.m., and everyone is welcome to help send Vinnie off in the style I'm sure he would have wanted. Thank you for coming."

The "informal gathering" in the rear ballroom of the large, new

Conference Center was well underway and already elbow to elbow by the time the cemetery crowd arrived. Like the others, Bob headed for the bar, but from the moment he passed through the door, he couldn't walk five feet without a handshake, a backslap, or sharp questions about what the hell had happened and what was being done about it. Eventually, he persevered long enough to make it back to the bar, where Ernie Travers waited with a large bourbon on the rocks for him.

"I've got to admit, Army guys know how to throw a good Irish wake," Ernie said.

"We get a lot of practice," Bob answered.

"Still, if it wasn't for all those green uniforms, I'd think I was in O'Shaughnessy's or The Galway Arms on the north side of Chicago." Within moments, Ace, Chester, The Batman, Koz, and even Bulldog had gathered around, shaking hands with Bob, Ernie and each other. "Like any good Chicago cop, I'll drink with anyone regardless of race, creed, national origin, rank, or height."

"Same for Army sergeants," The Batman answered with a big grin. "We'll even drink with a Chicago cop." That was when the girls walked in — Linda, Patsy, and Ace's new friend Dorothy, whom they met at dinner the night before and immediately became fast friends. Dorothy was a tall, solidly-built blonde, perhaps in her early thirties and older than the other two women. She wore a simple black sheath dress and a striking string of pearls. As they approached the men, Bob asked her, "No uniform, Captain?"

"If I did, I'm not sure what would look more awkward," Dorothy answered as she latched onto Ace's arm, "having an Air Force captain put an occasional lip lock on this handsome Army master sergeant, or being the only blue uniform in a sea of green."

"It wouldn't be awkward for him, I assure you," Bob answered. "He'd love it."

As the group broke up into a number of side conversations, Ernie seized the opportunity to pull Bob aside. "Have you decided what you're going to do?" he asked.

"When we left Atlantic City, I figured I'd let it ride, and see what the coroner came up with; but after what happened on the Expressway, and then outside my garage, Carbonari crossed the line. I'm a simple guy, Ernie. I don't get mad, I get even."

"I understand completely, especially when family is involved. But what's with those people? Haven't any of them watched *The Godfather*, for Chris' sake? Don't they know the women are supposed to be off limits?"

"Yeah, where's Vito Corleone when you really need him? Anyway, I assume Shaka and his pals were arraigned the next morning."

"In the county court center in Rolling Meadows, just a few miles west of where you live, so I went up there myself to watch the show. It didn't take long. Black eyes, heads bandaged, and Corliss's arm in a sling — they made quite a sight when the deputies trooped them in," Ernie laughed. "You really beat the crap out of them, Bob."

"Hey! Linda and the cat did most of it. Besides, they got what they deserved."

"Well, somebody must've tipped somebody off, because the court room was full of reporters. The Chief Judge himself presided and the Deputy State's Attorney handled the prosecution. I know the FBI and the New Jersey state cops had been on the phone with the prosecutors all morning, because I called them too. Everybody wanted a piece of Corliss. We all expected the judge would set a high bail, or no bail at all, so the cops could sweat them in that hellhole they call Cook County Jail, and try to flip them. When their case was called, a big-time criminal defense attorney named Winston Jenkins from Ernst and Willie downtown stood up, complete with his $5,000 Savile Row suit and handmade Italian shoes, and told the judge he was representing them. That rattled the judge. He's up for reelection and Ernst and Willie are *big* contributors to all the Circuit Court races."

"Illinois politics: don't you just love it?"

"Well, to his credit, the judge didn't back off. He set bail for $1 million for Corliss and a half a million each for the other two. Ninety-nine times out of a hundred, that's going to keep a perp behind bars. Not that day. Jenkins posted the bonds without even blinking, and they were out the door in thirty minutes. We were floored, all of us."

Bob shook his head. "You'll never see them again."

"Well, if they don't show, it's gonna cost somebody a lot of money."

"Doesn't matter. Carbonari wasn't about to let those three spend another night in jail, where the cops can work on them. Next stop would be Witness Protection in Oregon or New Mexico, and the Federal Supermax prison for Donnie."

"You think he'll get rid of all three of them?"

"Wouldn't you?" Bob answered with a cynical laugh.

"My imagination doesn't stretch that far, but I see your point."

"The two Hulks are dime-a-dozen muscle," Bob said. "But Corliss isn't that stupid. When the judge offered bail, he should have jumped up and screamed, 'No thanks, man, lock me back up!' They're dead men walking, they just haven't figured it out yet."

As he and Ernie finished talking, Master Sergeant Harold "Ace" Randall squeezed in next to them. For Bob's last six years on active duty, Ace had been his senior NCO and alter ego. That included four deployments in Afghanistan, two in Iraq, and countless battles and firefights in between. Physically, the two men could not be more different. Ace was everyone's image of a soldier's soldier — six feet two inches tall, a muscular two hundred and ten pounds, and ruggedly handsome. With twenty-one years in, he was older than the other sergeants in the unit, almost Bob's age, and had the scars to prove it. On the other hand, at five feet nine and now one sixty-five, Bob was no one's image of a special ops officer.

The Army's Delta Force had three odd peculiarities that distinguished it from other units. First, membership in the Unit was top-secret. Other than wives, you told no one, not girlfriends, not even your mother, for their own protection. Second, like undercover cops, Delta Force "operators" were not required to adhere to the Army's normal physical appearance standards. Long hair, beards, and earrings were the norm, allowing them to blend more easily into civilian populations. In Ace's case, he wore a long, tightly braided ponytail, a Fu Manchu moustache, and a tattoo on each forearm. One read, "Been There, Done That," and the other said, "Kill 'em All, Let God Sort It Out." And, third, except in formal military settings with other soldiers around, they usually used their tactical radio names or "handles" when talking to each other, regardless of rank. It was a sign of unit cohesion, exclusivity, and even affection.

Ace smiled and extended his hand to Ernie. "Colonel-Captain Travers," he said, having fun with Ernie's twin status as a Reserve Military Police colonel and a Chicago Police Department detective captain. "I didn't expect to see you again soon."

Ernie laughed. "Funny how things like that go; how have you been?"

"Good, until a few days ago, anyway. I saw you and 'the Ghost' with your heads together over here. What's he decided? We going on another Gumbah hunt?"

"Sounds like you're up for it," Bob laughed.

"Locked and loaded, sir, as are half the guys in the room, if we asked."

"Sir? Did you hear that, Ernie?" Bob asked. "Now I know the man's desperate."

"Not desperate, just determined. This one's personal," Ace answered as his expression turned serious. "Somebody's gotta pay for Vinnie, but I get it. The Ghost just got married, and we're a long way from Chicago. But no need, I can pull a Barrett from the arms room, spend a few weekends up on the Jersey shore, and drive all their business away until they come clean."

The M107 Barrett was the most lethal sniper rifle in the world. In the hands of an expert, it can accurately hit targets up to a mile away and its .50-caliber bullets can punch large holes through the exterior brick and stucco walls of a hotel, a car body, a slot machine, or a hotel window. The best shot in the unit had been

Vinnie Pastorini, but the second best was Ace, and a close third was the Ghost.

Ace shrugged. "You guys know me. It ain't bragging if you can do it."

"We'll talk about that later," Bob told him as he looked around the room. "By the way, looks like all the old unit is here. Vinnie would have liked that."

"Guys came in from a lot of places," Ace told him. "Benning, Campbell, Eglin…"

"I see about everybody here except Gramps Benson," Bob said. "I heard he had some problems at the end, but somehow I still expected to see him walk in."

"You got me," Ace answered. "He disappeared about six months after you did. It was all hush-hush, and us lowly NCOs knew not to ask what was going on in your 'secret officer fraternity.' He must've really pissed somebody off, though. I heard there was a Board or something, but none of the guys were ever called to testify. He just disappeared."

"You don't think they sent him somewhere, maybe on a detached assignment?"

"Who knows. It felt more like he took a dump in the middle of the general's carpet, and they escorted him off the post, cut off his buttons, broke his sword, and sealed the files."

"Still, he was close to Vinnie, and I'm surprised he didn't come."

"Maybe couldn't," Ace shrugged, "or knew not to."

An awkward silence fell on the large room. Bob turned his head and saw Lieutenant General Stansky and Colonel Jeffers step inside the front door, followed by their top NCOs. Stansky's cold blue eyes could freeze a waterfall. He stood there a moment scanning the crowd until his eyes finally came to rest on Bob Burke. The room was packed, but as Stansky suddenly stepped forward and headed toward Burke, the crowd parted like the Red Sea did for Moses.

"Well, this should be interesting," Ace muttered as he and Ernie backed up a step or two to allow the circle to widen.

"General… Colonel," Bob nodded to both of them, while Stansky's Command Sergeant Major, Pat O'Connor, peeled off and marched double-time to the bar to grab drinks.

"Great speech, Bobby," Stansky began with no preliminaries. "As I always said, when I die, grab a West Point 'ring knocker' to give the eulogy. I hear they teach that touchy-feely crap up on the Hudson now, don't they?" he nudged Colonel Jeffers.

"Yes, sir, it's in the core curriculum, now," Jeffers answered as O'Connor returned with their drinks. "It's right up there with reading, writing, and knowing which fork to use."

The only man in the room who might be shorter than Bob Burke, Stansky was a blunt, soldier's soldier who had advanced through the ranks the hard way, starting as a highly decorated, twenty-year-old, 130-pound, Warrant Officer gunship and medevac helicopter pilot in the last years of the Vietnam War. After having four helicopters shot out from under him, Creighton Abrams personally awarded him the Distinguished Service Cross, the second highest award the Army gave for bravery under fire, pulled him out of the field over his vociferous objections, and packed him off to OCS. Always irascible and irreverent, Stansky had a special disdain for West Pointers, staff officers, and the occasional senior NCO who forgot where he came from. CSM Patrick O'Connor knew not to make a mistake like that. O'Connor was the only man in the room who looked as fit as Ace Randall and had almost as many medals on his jacket as Stansky or Bob Burke.

The general raised his tumbler and said, "To Sergeant First Class Vincent Pastorini, a good soldier, who we were all proud to serve with. God bless him."

"Hear, hear," the others seconded the sentiment and pulled in closer.

Stansky looked surprised as he raised his glass again, sniffed the double shot of bourbon, and smiled. "This is really good stuff, Bobby! I grew up in those hills, and I know it when I drink it. I hear we have you to thank?"

"My privilege, sir."

"Then, to good bourbon: God's gift to eastern Tennessee, 'cause he sure as hell didn't give it much else to work with," the general said as he led them in another drink.

"Vinnie would've appreciated it, too," Bob said.

"Vinnie? I don't recall his taste being all that cultivated. I thought he ran more to Old Crow and Early Times, but I won't argue," Stansky laughed as he looked at Burke and studied him for a moment. "I hear you've done well in the telephone business since you left us, Bobby. We do so appreciate you remembering us poor folk back here on the Piedmont. After three years of undisciplined civilian sloth, does this mean you are ready to come back in?"

"Not quite yet, sir," Bob laughed.

"Sounds like you're getting more action on the outside now than the Army can offer, at least from what I heard about that little dust-up in Chicago a few months ago," Stansky said as he cast a knowing eye around the small circle around him. "I don't miss much, you know."

"Oh, you can't believe all the crazy stories you hear these days," Bob answered.

Stansky ignored him and turned to Ernie. "You must be Detective Captain Travers of the Chicago Police Department. I understand you've been promoted to the Organized Crime unit. I'm sure that's a much better place for a reserve MP colonel, but be careful hanging around these Delta scoundrels. They'll have you on the other side of the bars, if you're not careful." Stansky stepped closer, chest to chest with Ernie. "By the way, I heard those three gunmen who assaulted Bobby and his young wife are out on bail already. Whether it's New Jersey, Chicago, or the hills of Tennessee, I guess money talks, doesn't it?

"No doubt about it, sir," Ernie had to agree.

Finally, he nodded at the others, and pulled Bob aside for a slow, head-down walk around the perimeter of the room. "I got a backdoor copy of the ME's Report from Dover and the CID's findings," he told him in a low voice.

"What did they conclude?" Bob asked, now acutely interested.

"The report pulls no punches. Vinnie didn't fall off that ledge; he was thrown out the hallway window. But who did it? No one knows? They don't know and the local cops don't either, but those three clowns who went after you in Chicago were the only ones up there. Still, it's impossible to prove anything, particularly when the local cops don't want to bother."

"Even if they aren't guilty, I intend to hold them accountable."

"I figured you would, but tread lightly," Stansky warned. "The last time, you had a clear case for self-defense, and everyone supported you. But if you let this thing become some kind of revenge killing for Pastorini, you'll lose all that. Understand?"

"Roger that, sir," he looked Stansky in the eyes, and both men nodded in agreement. "You seem very well informed, as usual."

"You bet your sweet ass I am!" Stansky said as they circled back around to the rest of the group. "There isn't much that goes on around here I'm not *well informed* about, or I'll have his ass," he threw a thumb over his shoulder towards CSM Pat O'Connor, who had been trailing behind. Then he cast his steely eyes on Bob Burke and Ace Randall again. "But what *really* pisses me off, *gentlemen*, is that I never get included in any of the fun anymore."

"The heavy responsibility of rank, sir," Bob commiserated with a smile.

"Spoken like a true civilian, Bobby," Stansky laughed as he turned toward O'Connor and snapped his fingers. "Give him a card, Pat." A white business card instantly appeared in the big CSM's hand, which he handed to Bob. "Look, I know you're going after them."

"With all due respect, sir, you know something I don't know."

"Oh, you will," Stansky corrected him. "Vinnie was one of ours, dammit! No gang of Sicilian street punks is going to get away with that."

"And the business card?"

"A phone number, in case you ever need it, 24–7. Got that?" Stansky told him, as he locked his eyes on Bob's, then Jeffers's, Ace's, and finally on Ernie's. "I expect you'll be in this, too, Colonel Travers."

"If he asks, like the rest of his men, sir."

"He's that kind of leader, isn't he?"

"The best I've ever seen, sir, and I've seen a few."

"Me, too, and the best combat officer I've ever had the pleasure to serve under me. Still, it pisses me off that we lost him so he can get rich… fixing telephones!"

"We design complex telecommunications software for…" Bob tried to correct him.

"Who's fixing telephones?" Linda suddenly appeared at Bob's elbow and pushed her way into their tight "man circle."

"That infuriating husband of yours, my dear," Stansky told her. "He's back there fixing telephones, when he should be *here*, doing the important work of a nation."

"Like rearranging the rubble in Syria or Libya? Or making peace between the Shia and the Sunni in Iraq?" Bob loved the old man, but sometimes you gotta say what you gotta say. "But what finally pisses me off, General, is that no one in the Pentagon ever reads history, much less understands it. Vietnam, Iraq and Iran… Oh, hell, Kipling would have told them everything they needed to know about Afghanistan."

"Then you should be here helping to change that, Bobby, not off somewhere fixing goddamn telephones!"

After the General continued on his rounds through the large room, Bob did the same, finding himself in one conversation with old friends after another. He had put his cell phone in his hip pocket on vibrate but was somewhat surprised to feel it ringing. He excused himself as he turned away and looked at the screen. The number was local, which surprised him, since almost everyone he knew in Fayetteville was here in the room.

"Burke," he answered, curious.

"Major Burke, this is Sergeant Iversen again, Fayetteville Police Department. I hope I'm not disturbing you, but you asked me to get back to you on those two assailants."

"Absolutely, and I appreciate it," Bob said as he began walking toward the side door to escape the noise. "Did you get any ID on them?"

"No, and that's the odd thing. We've come up with nothing, zip, zero. I expected that on the blood, but not on the fingerprints. Given all the things you and I discussed about how they entered the premises, the clothes, the zip locks, the knife, and all the rest, it just doesn't figure that the perp would have no prints on record anywhere, civilian or military."

Bob frowned. "No, I think I'm as surprised as you are."

"When I got absolutely nothing back from the Feds, I made a few phone calls to some people I know. I got nothing but denials, and my contacts didn't get anything either; but I began to sense it was more like no one would tell us anything, than that there was nothing to tell, like someone had put a block on those prints. You know what I mean?"

"I was hoping I didn't, but I guess I do."

"That's why I called you. Normally, I'd never discuss a case like this with a civilian, but in this town, I've been around enough to know when I run into some 'national security' stonewalling. Hell, we even get that on traffic tickets. But somehow, I have a sneaking suspicion that you know a couple of people too, and maybe you can help me out."

"Maybe. It's probably worth a call or two."

"I don't mind telling you that the people I called were fairly high up on the totem pole, but maybe you can do better."

Bob looked around the room and saw Stansky's head on the far side. "I'm not saying I do, but let me see what I can come up with. I'll call you back if I learn anything."

CHAPTER FOURTEEN

As the afternoon wore on, the liquor flowed and tongues loosened; but as Bob circulated around the room, he spent much more time holding his glass than drinking from it. As he moved from group to group, he also kept one eye on General Stansky. Bob had one more thing he wanted to ask the general, but neither this crowd nor the general's office were the places to do it. Finally, he saw Stansky and Command Sergeant Major O'Connor head for the door. It took a few moments for him to catch up, but as they stood outside waiting for the general's staff car to come up, Bob was able to close the gap.

The driver opened the rear passenger side door and as Stansky started to get in, Bob put his hand on the doorframe and asked, "Would you mind a quick question, sir?"

Stansky looked up at him and frowned. "It better be good. Get in. I'm late for a reception, and the general's wife will pound lumps on his head if I'm any later."

Bob hurried around to the other door and slipped inside. "I was surprised that my old Exec, Randy Benson didn't make it here today," Bob began. "He and Vinnie ran a number of ops together, even more than he did with me. I heard he left the Army shortly after I did, perhaps on some questionable terms, but nobody seems to know very much after that."

Stansky looked at him and sighed. "Okay... Larry, let's take a little drive. The ten-minute tour," he told his driver, pausing to light a cigarette. "Frankly, I'm surprised you heard that much. That sneaky bastard Benson did indeed leave under some 'questionable terms,' as you so delicately put it. It was hushed up, but gone is gone and he ain't coming back."

Bob looked puzzled, so Stansky leaned closer, "Maybe a year and a half ago, he was detached to one of those goddamned, 'independent' CIA operational units that everybody seems to know about, but nobody can control. That was when some very valuable stuff went missing from The Iraqi National Museum in Baghdad — about $13 million in gold, coins, jewelry, precious gems — mostly Babylonian and Assyrian stuff. I don't know a damned thing about ancient art, but that's what they said."

"I thought that museum got cleaned out back in '03?"

"It did. Most of what was taken back then were small items that could be carried, or even stuffed in somebody's pocket — call it your garden-variety looting. Those people didn't have a clue what they had or even what to do with it. Probably buried it in their backyards. But over the next few years, the Iraqis managed to get over half of it back. They used some US money and bought it from the dumb schleps who grabbed it in '03."

"Sounds like the typical Baghdad 'disorganized' crime."

"That's right, until your Captain Benson, some of his Langley playmates, and some shady characters from Iraqi Military Intelligence pulled their little caper. Benson was maybe the number two or three man in the unit, most of whom were international mercs and 'contractors.' Contractors! Goddamnit, we have an Army post full of the best light infantry in the world, and those bozos at Langley go out and hire contract mercenaries to do their work for them — foreigners, misfits, rejects, you name it. They aren't very particular who they hire. Do you know why?"

"Deniability," Bob answered. "It's all off book."

"No, it's because they can find men who will do things our regular troops are told we *don't* do. Have you ever talked to any of our people after they came back from one of those off book, CIA assignments? They're ruined. They no longer have any concept of right or wrong, or what the American Army stands for. That's why we'll never win those wars. I was a twenty-year-old helicopter pilot in the Central Highlands, and believe me, I know. When an army loses its moral compass, it's all over," Stansky said, staring vacantly out the window.

"You're beginning to sound like me, sir."

"I know, and it scares the hell out of me. Anyway, Benson and his playmates were smart. The theft at the Baghdad museum happened late one Thursday night. Friday was the Muslim holy day, so when it reopened Saturday morning, they found the bodies of two museum guards, three dead Iraqi Military Intelligence agents, a bunch of empty display cases, and two empty safes. No one keeps a secret like that in a place like Iraq for very long. Obviously, it was an inside job, and sooner or later, a lot of fingers began pointing at Iraqi Military Intelligence, a Kurdish general, and a CIA contractor group in Mosul, which included our very own Captain Benson. There was an investigation, of course, but the CID couldn't prove a damned thing. The people involved claimed they never left Mosul, and no one ever saw them in Baghdad."

"Sounds like a well-planned op, and a better-planned cover-up."

"You may have trained him too damn well. Anyway, three quiet months later, Benson rotated back here, put in his papers, and walked out the gate. So did most of the CIA contract people. The Army CID still wanted to hold them for questioning, but they had nothing. Besides, it had taken too long, and there were a lot of people in Washington and Baghdad who wanted the whole thing swept under the rug. You know how that goes."

"Any idea where he went or what he's doing?"

"As I understand it, he and the others are still in the Middle East, peddling their services to the highest bidder," Stansky said as he turned and looked at him. "And you might as well know the really sick part. Vinnie Pastorini was assigned to that same unit at roughly the same time Benson was. To give him the benefit of the doubt, Vinnie's alibi checked out a whole lot better than Benson's or the others did, so I hate to cast aspersions on the honored dead, especially one I liked, but who knows?"

Bob leaned back in the seat and shook his head, wondering.

Stansky picked up his briefcase from the floor of the car and opened it. "Here's the CID's report and the ME's findings," he said as he handed Bob the envelope. "They probably raise more questions than they answer, but you were there. Let me know what you think."

"Corliss kept telling me he didn't do it."

"What would you expect him to say?"

"I know, but he didn't have to say anything. And I hate to say it, but the guy's too stupid and arrogant to lie very well."

"All right, but if he didn't do it... ?" Stansky shrugged. The two men stared at each other for a long moment, but neither of them came up with an answer. "By the way," Stansky added. "You tend to pick up enemies like a Tennessee bloodhound picks up fleas. Who did you piss off up in Harlem?"

"Harlem?" Bob laughed. "That's a new one on me."

"This morning, I got a phone call from a black congressman up there who tried to squeeze me for some background information on you. He's been on the House Armed Services Committee for decades. He rarely attends any meetings, and when he does, he sits at the far end in the back row and sleeps. I don't think we've exchanged ten words over the years and he never supports us, but I guess he thinks he's got some clout with me. Anyway, some fool in Washington gave him my direct line. When he told me what he wanted, I referred him back to Army personnel in Washington and told him to ask for your 201 file. He said he already did that, but almost everything was blacked out and redacted."

"I've heard that one before," Bob laughed.

"Imagine that?" Stansky laughed along with him. "Anyway, I told him you were a fine, upstanding officer. Then, I asked him who wanted to know. He hemmed and hawed, and finally told me some contributors of his in New Jersey who were considering your company for a big contract. Does that make any sense to you?" Stansky asked as his sedan pulled up at the front door of the conference center.

"The only business interests I know up there don't do any kind of *contract* I would want."

"You think it's that bunch in Atlantic City?"

"Probably."

"That's what I thought, too."

"While I've got you," Bob said as he leaned closer. "There was a break-in last night at Vinnie's house. Patsy was there. Two masked men broke in…"

"I heard," Stansky said, stone faced.

"Somehow I thought you might. She put three bullets in one of them. He was DOA. She might have winged the second one, but no one's sure. I saw the dead guy. These weren't amateurs. It was Patsy they were after. To everyone's surprise, the local cops can find absolutely nothing on the dead guy. Civilian, military, there's no record of his fingerprints anywhere. They're trying a DNA match on the blood from the other guy, but that isn't getting them anywhere either. They think they're getting stonewalled."

"And you want me to see if I can do better?"

"Can you?"

Stansky looked at O'Connor who was sitting in the front seat and nodded. "Perhaps. I don't like it when someone messes with one of our women any more than you do, so we'll see. I'm a little bit harder to bullshit than the Fayetteville Police Department."

By that time, the sedan had swung back around to the front door of the conference center and Bob knew his time had expired. As he opened the door and started to get out, Stansky said to him, "You be careful up there, Bobby, and remember what I told you about hound dogs and fleas. Pretty soon, they'll take a bite out of your ass."

After the General's sedan dropped him off and pulled away from the conference center, Bob reflected on how much Stansky could cram into a ten-minute meeting. Obviously, he had a lot of experience with these base tours of his, Bob thought. But what was he to make of what Stansky told him about Randy Benson? Obviously, thirteen million dollars was a lot of temptation for anyone; and as the man said, "Who knows?" He turned back toward the building's front door and saw Linda and Patsy stroll out, arm in arm with their new pal Dorothy. Ace and Ernie followed close behind, and the rest of the "rat pack" — Chester, Koz, The Batman, Lonzo, Bulldog, and a few other of the "old hands" — took up the rear.

Linda took the lead. "All right, Stud, what now? Inquiring minds want to know."

"Tell them I'm working on it."

"What was it you once said? The only two places that teach leadership are the U.S. Army and the Boy Scouts?" she pressed, her hands on hips. "Well, I've got all the merit badges I want; so lead, follow, or get out of the way."

He shook his head and smiled. "Impressive. Something must have rubbed off."

"You and I can discuss close-body contact later. What are we going to do?"

"For the moment, we're going to go back inside and get back to some serious partying," he answered her. "But if you want to take Donatello Carbonari on, we have a lot of work to do; and the parking lot of the Fort Bragg Conference Center isn't the place to do it. How about the group reconvenes at the hotel for lunch, noon tomorrow? I'll get a room."

"Lunch?" Ace laughed. "What happened to Ops meetings at 06:00?"

"06:00? I'll be lucky if you've even stopped drinking by then, much less gotten sober. That's why I said noon, after everyone's had some sleep. Ya'll got that?" he asked as he looked around from face to face, took Linda by the arm, and turned back toward the conference center's front door.

"That casino complex in Atlantic City has a wicked security system — cameras, alarms, motion sensors, guards, the whole nine yards," he said. "So, we'll need some *really* good tech people to pop it open," he told her. "Last time, I had Charlie. He could crack any digital system anywhere, any time; but with him gone, I wouldn't even know where to begin. Do you know any contractors who are good at that kind of stuff?"

Linda thought for a moment and then chuckled. "This may come as a surprise to you, but we have a couple of incredibly sharp new hires of our own in the tech department."

"You don't mean those two kids Charlie talked me into hiring?" Bob frowned. "Barker and Talmadge? One looks like he's fifteen and the other looks like his younger brother."

Linda laughed. "You really are an idiot, you know."

"What? Coke-bottle-bottom glasses with taped frames, superhero T-shirts, and Garfield calendars. I thought they were summer interns from Schaumburg High School."

"Haven't you learned by now that when you really have a serious computer problem, you call in the youngest, geekiest nerd in the smallest cubicle in the back corner of the tech department? Charlie knew exactly what he was getting when he hired them. And I hate to tell you, but for the last six to eight months, they were doing most of his work for him."

"Those two? You're kidding me? How old are they eighteen? Nineteen?"

"More like twenty, twenty-one, with advanced degrees from Berkeley. Every big firm in town wanted them."

"Really? The only thing missing was a shirt-pocket full of Bic pens."

"Bic pens? I doubt they know how one works. Today, everything uses a joystick, stylus, audio dictation, the tip of the finger, or a virtual reality helmet."

"Hmmm, I can think of two or three things *their* joysticks can't do," Bob mumbled as he patted her on the butt.

"Promises, promises, but do you know how Charlie got them? It wasn't the salary or the benefits — they don't have a clue what a benefit is to begin with. No, he promised to buy them the hottest, latest, fastest, biggest gaming computers on the market."

"Gaming computers?"

Patsy stared at him. "You have no idea what kids like that do, do you?"

"Well... no," he admitted, "but I saw them drag themselves in on Monday mornings. I've watched enough enlisted men do the same thing over the years, and I figured tech kids were party animals just like the others."

"Boy, are you wrong. From the time they get home on Friday until the crack of dawn Monday morning, they're online playing in massive, roll-playing, simulation games."

"Role-playing? With their 'joysticks'?"

"You are incorrigible."

"If I knew what that was, I'd probably be insulted, wouldn't I?"

"Probably, but they're another generation. They have the day jobs to pay for new weekend toys. And on the weekends, they wouldn't know The Chicago Bears from the ones in the Lincoln Park Zoo. You just don't understand them."

"*Them?* I barely understand *you.*"

"You really are Neanderthal, aren't you?" she said as she squeezed his arm. "So tell me what you want them to do, and I'll give them a call."

"For the moment, I need some serious research on that Bimini Bay building complex."

"Do you want them to fly out here?"

"Sure, but I figure they need to be near those big computers Charlie bought."

"You dolt. These days, really big is really small, which is why Charlie bought them laptops. They can work anywhere."

"All right. The meeting's at noon. Get them out here."

Casinos work 24-7, and so do the people who run them. At 10:15 that night, Martijn Van Gries was at his "other" desk, below the Bimini Bay Casino in the "Maintenance Building," when he picked up his cell phone and speed-dialed Shaka Corliss.

Corliss could see who the call was from, so he let it ring half a dozen times before he answered. "Yeah? Wuz up?" he asked brusquely. The Dutchman outranked him in the casino pecking order, but neither of them was a member of the Sicilian brotherhood and Corliss didn't work for him. They both worked directly for Donatello Carbonari, which forced Corliss to cooperate with Van

Gries, but he didn't have to act as if he liked it. In fact, he could be as rude as he wanted, knowing the Dutchman wouldn't dare run to Papa.

"The boss has a job for us, for *both* of us," Van Gries began. "Meet me on the loading dock and bring the 'muscle twins,' Gerald and Phil, with you."

"They're busy. Whadaya want 'em for?"

"Some heavy lifting, so stop arguing with me, Shaka. Ten minutes... unless you'd rather do it yourself," he shot back and hung up. "Damn that black bastard," Van Gries muttered between clenched teeth. He opened his desk drawer and pulled out his .380-caliber Walther PPK automatic. It was the iconic James Bond model and Martijn loved it. He screwed on an SSG silencer, slipped its 7-round magazine into the butt, and seated it with a firm blow from the heel of his hand. He jacked a round into the chamber, slipped the Walther into his rear waistband, and headed for the door.

The Bimini Bay's loading dock sat on the rear facade of the building, well screened from the casino's driveways and parking lots by a tall retaining wall and by the complex's large trash compactor. For security reasons, all the perimeter and parking lot lights remained on all night long, including three spotlights high on the building's rear exterior. It was also covered by overlapping video cameras. Van Gries knew he would have to deal with the cameras later, but that would be no problem for him. The video recordings were his exclusive domain.

This late at night, the loading dock was always deserted. Tonight, however, a white, unmarked panel truck was parked at the far end, with its rear door rolled up. Van Gries had been there for twenty minutes, pacing back and forth, but Corliss still hadn't arrived. He knew Corliss was late on purpose, trying to provoke him, as usual. The Dutchman grinned. This time, there would be retribution. Finally, the door at the far end of the dock opened and Corliss sauntered out, followed by his blond muscle. Van Gries was convinced that he hired those two precisely because they were big, blond, pink-faced, and dumber than he was. He probably carried their photos on his cell phone, so he could show his street pals that he could slap these two dumb farm boys around anytime he wanted.

"You're late," Van Gries seethed. "I told you ten minutes."

"Like I give a shit. I don't work for you, and neither do they."

Van Gries bit his tongue. "There are four file cabinets full of accounting reports that Carbonari sent over from Tuscany Towers. He wants them locked up in the basement here."

"What? They're too heavy for you and your 'little pals' in bookkeeping?"

"No, *he* wants Risk Management to do it. The auditors are coming, and those reports would be bad news if they fell in the wrong hands. For some strange reason, he trusts your people more than mine. Is that good enough? Of course, he can call Philly and ask them to send some people down; but if he did, he wouldn't have much use for your insolent ass, would he?"

Shaka glared at him, not sure if he had been complimented or insulted. "Yeah, yeah, okay. Just checkin'. All right, show these two dummies what you want moved."

Van Gries led them into the dark cargo compartment of the truck. There was a small light bulb in the ceiling. He turned it on and pointed toward the file cabinets along the front wall. To the side stood two 55-gallon chemical drums, a pile of concrete blocks, some iron pipe, steel chains, and a large dolly. "Just the file cabinets," Van Gries said. "They weigh a ton. Once you get one on the dolly you can walk it to the elevator."

As the two big white men bent over and grabbed the first of the heavy cabinets, Van Gries stepped behind them. He pulled out his Walther PPK from his rear waistband and shot Phil in the back of his head, and then turned and did the same to Gerald. With the silencer attached, all that could be heard inside the truck was a soft "Phap, Phap!" and the two security guards were dead before they hit the floor.

Corliss took a step back, wide-eyed, stunned. "What? Whatchu doin,' man?" he screamed as the Dutchman leaned forward and shot each of them in the head a second time. The second bullet wasn't necessary, but Van Gries did what he was told. He then turned around and faced Corliss. The big black man must have thought he was next, and was trying to draw his big .44-caliber revolver from his shoulder holster, but it slipped out of his sweating hands and clattered on the floor.

To Van Gries, the terrified expression on Shaka's face was worth it all. Corliss looked down at his big revolver, but before he could bend over and pick it up, Van Gries pulled out his cell phone, speed dialed a number, and pushed it in the black man's face.

"Here!" Van Gries snapped. "Shut up and listen!"

Corliss wasn't the brightest bulb in the pack. It took a long moment for him to understand what Van Gries said. His hand shook as he took the phone and raised it to his ear.

"Hey, Shaka, is that you?" he heard Donatello Carbonari speaking to him.

"Uh, yeah, yeah, Boss. Uh, he…" Corliss stammered.

"I told Martijn to do that. Do you know why?"

"Uh, yeah, yeah, I… uh, no, I…"

"Those two knew too much," Carbonari said. "Our lawyers called me. The Illinois cops are headed here with more warrants, and those two were headed back to jail. I couldn't have that because they aren't like you or Martijn. They'd flip on us as soon as they got behind bars again, so they had to be eliminated. You

111

understand now, don't you?"

"Uh, yeah, Boss. I do, but if you'd 'a told me, I…"

"No. You might have said something or done something without thinking, and tipped them off. That's why I told Martijn to keep you out of the loop. That's how it had to be."

"Uh, yeah, I guess I see that now, I…"

"Good! Now go with Martijn and do what he tells you to do. My old man's fishing boat is up at Brigantine, and you two are going to make them disappear. Understand?"

"Sure, sure, Boss," Shaka answered as he felt his old confidence beginning to return. "Sure, I'll go with…" he started to say, until he realized Carbonari had already hung up. Slowly, he handed the phone back to Van Gries. "I, uh, well…" he tried to explain, his hand still shaking as he bent over and picked up his .44 revolver.

"Come on," Van Gries told him as he put his automatic away, led him back out onto the dock, and rolled down the rear truck door. They went around and got in the truck's front seat, with Van Gries behind the wheel, and drove slowly away.

CHAPTER FIFTEEN

The small town of Brigantine is located five minutes northeast of Atlantic City via a long, elevated boulevard that spanned Absecon Inlet and its surrounding marshes. While Atlantic City had captured all the casinos and pawnshops, Brigantine took pride in having the nice new beach houses and townhouses. It also had a police department that might actually stop an old, beat-up, white van driving through their town in the middle of the night. Donatello had docked his father's old thirty-five-foot wooden fishing trawler in Brigantine after the Feds packed "Crazy Eddie" off to the Federal pen a few years before. He found a cheap slip on one of the older, run-down piers at the far, landward side of the small island, and left it there.

"We gonna jam them boys in them oil drums?" Corliss finally asked.

"If they'll fit, but I doubt it," Van Gries answered.

"You got that right. They didn't miss too damned many meals, did they?" Corliss offered with a nervous laugh. "I gotta tell ya, I never did get rid of no body like this. We'd bury 'em out in the Pine Barrens. I heard the Philly and New York boys use oil drums like this, but they bust up the legs or cut 'em into pieces. Whadjou think? We gonna chop 'em up?"

"Jeezus, Shaka! Do you have any idea how much blood a human body holds, especially big ones like those two? Maybe you'd like to clean out that truck tomorrow and hose down the boss's boat, but not me. No, we'll get most of them in the drums, weigh them down with those concrete blocks, and tie them in with some chain. That should do."

"Yeah, and now I see why you needed me. Them boys is all beef."

"Don't flatter yourself. After that screw up in Chicago, there could have been three drums back there; but I told the Boss we needed to keep you around."

Shaka looked over at the Dutchman, surprised. "You told him that?" he asked.

"Yeah, because there's no way I can lift these two bastards."

Shaka laughed loud and hard. "You okay, Van Gries. You know, you okay."

The private dock where Carbonari kept the old boat was at the end of a short, dark road on the north side of the island. There was only one dim light at the foot of the dock, so Corliss got out and directed as Van Gries backed the truck to the boat. Pausing to be certain they were alone, Van Gries walked around to the rear, climbed onto the tailgate, and rolled the rear door up. "Let's get them in the drums, then we'll roll the drums to the boat."

113

Corliss joined him inside. They grabbed Gerald under his arms and dragged him over to one of the barrels. "Jeez, he heavy," Shaka groaned as they shoved his head and arms inside. "Grab dat other leg, and we'll bof lift." Together, lifting, pulling, and pushing, they got Gerald's gut over the rim and pushed him in head-first. As his heavy body crumpled inside, his legs buckled at the knees, but they still stuck out the top of the drum.

The two men backed away to survey their work. "It sho ain't no thing of beauty," Corliss huffed as he leaned his elbows on the drum.

"No, but it will do," Van Gries answered.

"You want me to bust his legs and get them in too?"

"No, no." The Dutchman cringed, bending down to take a closer look at the drum. "There are two holes up here near the top. We'll throw a couple of those concrete blocks inside with him and run the chain through. That should hold him in." Fortunately, the rear tailgate had a power lift. Corliss got the drum onto the dolly and lowered it to the dock. Together they rolled and muscled the first drum onto the aft deck of Carbonari's boat.

"Ah could use a beer, man," Corliss said, as they paused for a moment.

"There's a whole case in the galley. After we're done you can drink your fill."

They went back inside the truck, stuffed Phil in the other drum, and muscled it onto the deck of the boat next to the first one. "Tell you what," Van Gries said. "You go down to the galley and grab a couple of beers for us, while I move the truck."

When he got back on board a few minutes later, the big black man was sprawled on the bare-wood side bench in the small cabin, finishing his third beer. He looked around the dilapidated boat and asked, "This thing gonna make it? 'Cause ah cain't swim so well."

"It'll make it. It's never sunk before," the Dutchman answered as he struggled under the weight of two more concrete blocks, a gallon of bleach, and a long length of the heavy steel chain that he finally dumped on the deck near the drums.

"Whadjou bring them for?" Corliss sat up and frowned.

"Those two are big and fat," Van Gries answered, breathing hard. "Sometimes a body can float back up after they've been in the water for a while, so I decided to add some more weight, just in case."

"Yeah, yeah, I guess I can see that." Corliss leaned back on the bench and relaxed.

Van Gries grabbed one of the beers that Corliss had brought up and headed for the wheelhouse. Soon, the boat's two big diesel engines started up with a few coughs and a stutter. The Dutchman steered the boat through the twisting channels between the marshes and headed toward the harbor entrance and the ocean beyond. With a quarter moon, the bright lights of Atlantic City, Brigantine, and the rest of the Jersey coast slowly faded away behind them.

"None 'a dat GPS stuff, huh?" Corliss asked, looking around the spartan cockpit.

"No, we navigate the old fashioned way, by eyeballs." Twenty-five minutes later, Van Gries powered back and set the boat engines to idle. "We're here," he said as he walked back to the stern. "Let's get this done and get out of here."

"Dis boat's a piece of crap, man," Corliss said as he looked around and grabbed the first drum. "Ah didn't even know Carbonari had it."

"It was his old man's. He hates it."

"Why don't he sell it, then?"

"I have no idea. For some reason, he'd rather leave it over there and watch it rot."

They tipped the first barrel on edge and rolled it to the aft railing. Both men then bent down, one to each side, and tipped it forward to get a good grip. Looking Corliss in the eyes, Van Gries said, "All right, on three — one, two, three, lift!" With grunts and groans, they got the heavy barrel up far enough to tip it over the aft rail and topple it over into the ocean. It made a big splash, floated for a moment or two as it filled with water, and promptly went to the bottom. "Good," Van Gries puffed. "My worst fear was that it would just float there."

"What about them other blocks and that chain?" Corliss asked suspiciously.

"Damn! I forgot. Ah, screw it! That first one went straight down, and I'm tired."

The second barrel was no easier, but they got it to the rail and over the side too. "Jeez, them boys is heavy," Corliss said, as it also dropped over the stern and went straight down, too. Breathing heavily, the stocky black man leaned against the railing and watched a line of bubbles come back up to the surface from the drum. "Lookie that," he laughed as he looked back over his shoulder at Van Gries. That was when he saw the Walther PPK in the Dutchman's hand. He had taken off the silencer, but the barrel was pointed straight at him.

"Put your hands behind your back," Van Gries ordered.

"Now, wait just a damn minute," Corliss tried to bluster, until the .380 automatic barked, and a bullet dug a deep gouge along the side of Corliss's head. "Ah!" he screamed, as the bullet knocked the fight right out of him.

Van Gries quickly turned Corliss around, bent him over the stern rail, and snapped a pair of handcuffs on his wrists.

"Damn, man," Corliss groaned as he felt blood run down the side of his head. "Why'd you go and..." he asked as he turned his head and looked back again. Before he could finish, however, Van Gries had threaded the thick chain through the handcuffs and around his wrists. He then picked up one of the heavy concrete blocks and dropped it in the center of Corliss's back. "Ah, shit, man," the black man groaned as he tried to straighten up, but Van Gries jammed the Walther in the back of his neck.

"Come on, man," Corliss pleaded as Van Gries quickly dropped a second concrete block on his back, ran the chain through its openings too, and back around his arms and wrists. Finally, he tied the ends off in a square knot. "Why you doin' me like this?"

"You are one heavy bugger, I'll give you that," Van Gries groaned as he bent over and wrapped his arms around Corliss's knees, "but this is going to be pure pleasure."

Corliss screamed as Martijn raised his legs and then let the weight of the concrete blocks do the rest. They tipped the black man over the railing, dragged him down, head first, and flipped him onto his back even before he struck the water. For a fleeting second, Van Gries saw Corliss's terrified eyes looking up at him before the two concrete blocks pulled him under. He went straight down, just as the two oil drums had done.

Van Gries smiled and dusted off his hands, thinking he could not remember the last time he had enjoyed a late-night boat ride as much as this one. He reached in his belt, pulled out his Walther PPK again, and looked at it for a long, fond moment, before he wound up and threw it into the ocean. It was a lovely pistol, but he could always get another in Virginia or North Carolina for a few hundred dollars. He then threw the silencer as far as he could in the other direction. If the police ever found Shaka Corliss's body, they would find his chrome-plated Smith & Wesson .44 in his shoulder holster. That would close more than a few open murder cases. However, the cops would never catch Martijn Van Gries with any incriminating evidence on him.

He rummaged around the boat until he found a coiled rubber hose in one of the storage lockers, connected it to the freshwater spigot near the stairs to the galley, and turned it on. This had been hot work, he concluded, as he put his head under the stream of water and luxuriated in it for a long moment. Cooled off, he hosed down the aft deck, grabbed an old brush from the galley, the gallon of bleach, and scrubbed away at the scrapes and smeared blood on the deck and aft railing until they looked like their grimy selves again. Only then did he pull out his cell phone and punch redial.

Donatello quickly answered. "Is it done?" he asked.

"Our problems sleep with the fishes."

"Stop with *The Godfather* crap, already! I hate that goddamned movie."

At the stroke of noon the next day, Bob Burke entered the small conference room in the Marriott Courtyard halfway between Fort Bragg and Fayetteville and hung a sign on the outside of the door, which read, "Private Meeting in Progress." Several ten-foot-long tables had been arranged in a large square in the center of the room, with tablecloths, glasses, water pitchers, pens, and pads of paper.

"Master Sergeant Randall says I should begin promptly," he said. "But before I do, slide all of those pads of paper down to Linda at the far end. No notes. No doodling. If you can't remember what we decide to do, you shouldn't be here to begin with."

Looking around at the faces, Bob quickly concluded this was the strangest operations meeting he had ever convened. There were three women, two of whom were formerly office clerks and receptionists and one tall, blonde female Air Force captain. The rest included a burly Chicago police detective captain, and six of the Army's most highly-skilled and deadly Delta Force operatives — Ace, Koz, The Batman, Chester, Lonzo, and Bulldog. Two of the chairs at the table were still empty, waiting for the computer wizards from Chicago to arrive.

"Let's start with the obvious," Bob said as he unrolled a 36-inch by 36-inch aerial photo that he had blown up and printed at Staples that morning. He laid it in the center of the table, allowing the others to lean forward and view it for a moment. "This is the Bimini Bay Hotel and Casino in Atlantic City and the surrounding parts of the town. Linda, Patsy and I had an opportunity to check it out last week. Have any of you been up there before?" he asked as he looked around. Dorothy's hand went up, but the others shook their heads no. "Good. The rest of you can look at it with fresh eyes, and their video cameras won't have seen you yet, either. Did you get a Gold Club card?" Bob turned and asked Dorothy.

"Of course, but that was maybe five years ago," she said as she shrank down in her seat, embarrassed.

"Good. In the last year or so they've added facial recognition software to their system, but you were there before all that."

"In a casino?" Several of the men looked surprised. "Facial recognition?" Koz asked.

"I doubt they use it on everyone, but the Bimini Bay and its two sister properties have some of the most sophisticated electronic and security systems in the business," Bob said as he looked directly at Ace. "Taking down a complex like that is going to take more than a couple of guys with sniper rifles."

"And three women," Linda interjected.

"Three or a hundred and three, only the Marines would try a frontal assault on a place like that. We have three targets: Donatello Carbonari, Martijn Van Gries, and Shaka Corliss. They're the ones responsible for Vinnie. I'm not counting the two blond Hulk security guards who work for Corliss, but if they get dented and their paint scraped a bit, that's fine. They're too dumb to know any better but getting our hands on those other three will take some serious stealth and guile."

"By the way," Ernie spoke up, "I had a phone call this morning from a friend in the Cook County State's Attorney's office. They've filed more charges on Corliss and his two beefy pals yesterday, and two of their deputies arrived in Atlantic City to take them into custody this morning. They went around with two local deputies from Atlantic County, but they couldn't find them at the casinos or in their apartments. The casino says they were terminated but their cars are still parked at Bimini Bay and their stuff is still in their apartments. So who knows?"

"Terminated?" Linda chuckled.

"Even the Atlantic County deputies thought that was funny, almost as funny as two Chicago cops trying to serve papers on Mafia gunmen in New Jersey."

"Maybe." Ernie shrugged. "But Corliss and the other two aren't Sicilian. Neither is Van Gries. That makes them throw-aways, whether they know it or not."

"Look," The Batman asked, "if they've already started 'disappearing' their own people, why can't we just grab Carbonari and Van Gries and do them a favor? We've done a few of those 'black hood' rendition snatches, back in the day."

"That's always an option," Bob quickly agreed. "But remember who they are and where they are. There's a lot of human and electronic security around those buildings, and snatching one of them without setting it off would be hard. We'd need to grab all three of them at the same time. That would be even more difficult, and we'd only get one try. If it ends up an open battle with Carbonari, that'll bring in the Philly mob, and then the Genoveses and the Luccheses from New York City. That's a war we can't win."

"No shooting?" Ace bristled. "What do you need us for?"

"I never said there might not be shooting, but we have to be careful. There are way too many civilians running around the casinos and the parking garages, who would be in the line of fire. But if I come across someone in serious need of shooting, I know I can always call on you and your Barrett to punch big holes in them. How's that sound?" Bob asked.

"Maybe that won't be necessary," Ernie offered. "Maybe we can get someone else to do the heavy lifting for us."

"You mean his underworld pals in New York?" Dorothy asked.

"Exactly," Bob answered. "But to pull that off, we'll need to get into their computers and security systems — no noise, no footprints, and no one even knowing we were there."

"What fun would that be?" The Batman countered.

The hallway door opened and two very young men stuck their heads inside the meeting room. Tentative and uncertain, they looked at the bearded, long-haired group sitting around the table and began to back away, until they saw Linda and Patsy and finally smiled.

"Those the bus boys?" Koz asked. "We need more coffee."

"Ignore him. Come on in, guys." Linda hurried to the door, threw her arms around them and pulled them into the room like a Den Mother with two new Cub Scouts.

"We've been looking in every room," the taller of the two apologized. He was rail thin and looked to be about fifteen years old. The other one was short, thicker, and looked like his younger brother. He wore glasses with heavy black frames and a thick glob of white adhesive tape holding the nose bridge together. They threw their overnight bags in the corner, grabbed their laptop computers, and took their seats.

"Must be Navy." Bulldog looked them over and sighed.

"Nah, the Coast Guard," Chester corrected him.

"You two behave!" Linda chided them. "This is Jimmy Barker and Ronald Talmadge from our Tech Department at Toler TeleCom back in Schaumburg."

"Civilians. Even worse," The Batman added.

Linda gave him her evil eye and continued anyway. "Jimmy, Ronald, you know Bob and Patsy, and I might introduce you to the others later… or not."

The two Geeks glanced nervously at the hard faces around the table as they opened their laptops. "I didn't know you sold us to the pirates, Mrs. B.," Jimmy said. His chair happened to be across from Patsy's, and Bob saw her look up at him and smile.

"I know Linda briefed you on the problem we are trying to solve. With your tech and computer backgrounds, particularly the tricks you picked up from Charlie, I want to turn you two loose on Van Gries's accounting and security systems. At the end of the day, your mission is to get into his financial system and find his books, the real ones. Got that?"

The two geeks looked at each other. "Our mission?" Ronald nudged Jimmy and giggled. "Just like Tom Cruise in *Mission Impossible*."

"Yeah, and *you'll* self-destruct if you screw it up." Ace gave him his fiercest scowl.

"Don't worry, Mister B.," Jimmy quickly replied, not the least bit intimidated. "Ronald and I are a one-stop shop. There isn't much we can't crack."

"Yeah," Ronald giggled. "But no sweat. We already went online and peeked under that casino's hood. That guy Carbonari was Yale undergrad and Stanford for his MBA. Pretty smart, in a business kinda way. But his tech guy, Van Gries was MIT, middle of his class at best," he said with a dismissive sneer. "No contest."

Bob looked down the table at them, puzzled.

"We're both Berkeley," Jimmy explained nonchalantly. "We ate those MIT derbs for breakfast in all the software competitions. Trust me, we'll scorch his butt so bad, he'll have to dunk it in the Charles River to cool off."

"Tell you what," Bob told him. "You do that, and I'll owe you guys, big time."

They glanced at each other out of the corners of their eyes. "Owe? Big time?" Jimmy smiled like the Cheshire Cat. "Well, if that's the case, before we really start bustin' on 'em, Ronald and I could both use some upgraded battle hardware, some new weapons."

"I thought Charlie just got you new laptops?" Bob looked at Linda, confused.

Ronald shrugged and leaned forward. "Here's the thing, Mister B. There's new, and then again, there's bigger, faster, warp speed, seriously new."

"Yeah." Jimmy patted at his laptop. "Charlie got us these boogers like, six months ago, and that's Stone Age now. If you want us to really kick butt…"

"Enough. Don't tell me, tell Linda. She'll run you over to Charlotte, or you can get an express order online. Whatever you need, get it done, because we need to get into Carbonari's books — not the ones he shows the State gambling and tax people, or the IRS, or even his partners in New York, but the real cash flow before he skims off the top. That's what will put him in jail, or get him whacked by his fellow hoods."

"Speaking of which," Ernie jumped in, "I spoke to my New Jersey State Police pal, Carmine Bonafacio. In fact, I have him on hold on my cell phone. Instead of repeating what he said, I'd like to put him on speaker, and you can hear it for yourself." Ernie pushed the speaker button. "Inspector, tell my friends what you told me."

"The Carbonaris aren't one of the front-line families but they go back two or three generations in Atlantic City and to Philly and New York before that. Those casinos spin off a lot of cash, but it's mostly Lucchese and Genovese money. That's a dangerous crowd to work for. While Donatello might look like a Mafia big shot to us dummies, he's bought and paid for by the New York City families, like his father."

"Carmine, this is Ernie's pal Bob. How do you think Carbonari's doing?"

"The hotel and casino business is bad everywhere, but especially in Atlantic City — recession, Indian casinos, cheap flights to Las Vegas, and a ton of online gaming, you name it. Nobody knows what his real numbers are, and whenever he talks to the press, he keeps saying everything's great, but he's gotta be stretched thin."

"I read a lot of the newspaper stories on him and I saw his quotes," Bob said. "Isn't it a little strange for one of those guys to talk to reporters to begin with?"

"One of those guys? You mean Italian? Or New Jersey?" Carmine laughed.

"I mean the mob."

"Yeah, it's more than strange. I know the bosses in New York don't like it, but that's Donnie — he hates that name, by the way — and he's the goose who lays their golden eggs."

"With half dozen casinos in town closed, how's he have any eggs at all?" Ernie asked. "You told me he has a big 'nut' he owes the Genoveses and Luccheses every month."

"That's the question. They put up with all his 'Prince Donnie' crap, but our New York contacts say the goose better not run out of golden eggs or he's going to be cooked."

"Maybe that was why he was pressing so hard to get the money Vinnie owed them," Ace said. "At the time, I figured it was just chump change for a big operation like that."

"Nothing's chump change for any of them anymore," Bonafacio corrected him. "Donatello enjoys a lavish lifestyle, flying back and forth to the city in his new helicopter. His new Park Avenue condo has already been featured in a half-dozen architectural magazines. The one on the top of the Bimini Bay isn't too shabby, either. It has over 3,000 square feet and takes up half the rooftop of that six-story tower, along with an outdoor pool, gardens, and a helipad, plus he has a million-dollar sailboat in the marina. They don't like it when a guy flaunts it and draws attention to himself. He's been getting away with it, but if he falls behind. Well, the bigger they think they are..."

"So, those casinos aren't really his?" Chester asked.

"Oh, no. Boardwalk Investments owns them. It was founded by his grandfather. Donatello is Chairman of the Board and CEO, but the New York mob families are the real owners. Hey, that's about all I got for the moment. I've got a meeting I've got to run to but let me know if I can help with anything."

"Thanks, Carmine, we'll give you a call," Bob told him as he hung up.

"If he's already on thin ice with his pals in New York..." Ace began to ask.

"Maybe we can give him a push?" Koz finished the thought.

"My thoughts exactly," Bob answered. "We also need to dig into Martijn Van Gries, our talented Dutchman. He's closest to Carbonari, and we need to find out everything there is to know about him — where he's from, where else he's worked, if he has a police record anywhere, and what his weaknesses are. The same holds true for the missing Shaka Corliss. I'm confident he has one as long as my arm, but let's find out.

"For those who'd like to tag along, plan on leaving in forty-eight hours.

That means start putting together lists of anything you think you'll need." Bob looked around the room and made eye contact with each of them. "Great, let's plan on getting together here at 08:00 and noon each day until we leave. Now let's get to it."

CHAPTER SIXTEEN

It was 3:30 that afternoon when Martijn Van Gries's administrative assistant, Eva Pender, called back to his desk. "I have a Congressman Jepperson from Harlem on line three. All those DC people ever want is comps. Want me to get rid of him, or let him die on hold?"

"No, no, he is returning my call. I shall take it." Van Gries told her as he raised his finger to punch the lit button for line three, and then he stopped. "Dinner later on the boat, Eva?"

"I've been thinking of nothing else all afternoon."

"How utterly delicious. The gangplank will be out at 7:00."

"Yours or the boat's?" she asked in a husky voice as she hung up.

Martijn tried to refocus as he pressed line #3 and said, "Congressman, how nice to talk to you again. Did you learn anything about our friend?"

"Yeah, well, anything for Donnie. You know, I been callin' him Donnie since he was a little kid playin' under his father's big desk in that cracker box office behind the bar over on Pacific, where he kept book. Yeah, we used to go down there all the time. He always showed us a good time. You never meet Donnie's old man, Crazy Eddie did you?"

"No, regrettably, I never had the pleasure."

"Weren't never no pleasure," Jefferson laughed and coughed. "He was one ornery old son of a bitch."

"Ah, the good old days."

"Some, but I'd be lyin' if'n I said they wuz all good."

"Congressman, as much as I enjoyed reminiscing, did you learn anything?"

"Frankly, not a whole hell of a lot, Marty. You know, I'm on the House Armed Services Committee. Been on it for... oh, hell, maybe since George Washington, but I couldn't get squat out of the Pentagon, or outta that damned bunch down at Fort Bragg, neither. Gotta tell you, I ain't used to being treated like that, and there'll be hell to pay in the next budget."

"What did you learn? Anything?"

"They let one of my staffers take a look at his 201 File. That's his army personnel file. Says he was a top graduate from West Point and served fifteen years in the Signal Corps. That's bullshit! He got most every medal they can give a man, which is real pe-cu-liar for the Signal Corps. Anyway, most of his file was 'redacted,' which is a fancy word for sayin' somebody crossed everything out with a thick black marking pen, so you cain't read it. That's 'national security' stuff. Means he musta been Special Operations, Delta Force, Green Berets, or maybe even the damned CIA. So, you ain't gonna learn much about what he really did."

Van Gries thought it over for a minute. "I understand. My younger brother performed similar duties in the Royal Dutch Marines."

"Well, I don't know nuthin' about them Dutch Marines, but I called a colonel I know in G-2 at the Pentagon, and all he'd tell me was this fella' Burke was 'a real bad ass,' very lethal. So you can take that for what it's worth, 'cause it's all you're gonna get."

Martijn leaned back in his desk chair for a moment, thinking. Finally, he got up and took the executive elevator to the penthouse. Martijn's technicians swept the offices every day for bugs, and he had recently installed white noise and jamming gear; but in their business, one can never be too careful. He sat down across from Donatello and said, "With the departure of some key members of our Risk Management staff we need to find some new people, some good people, to replace them."

"Okay, I'll call Philly, or maybe Angelo in Brooklyn, and see who's available."

"Are you sure that is the direction you want to go?" Van Gries asked, sounding pointedly skeptical. "I heard back from that Harlem congressman you told me to call."

"Jepperson? Did he learn anything?"

"Not much, which speaks volumes in itself."

"I'm tired of your goddamn Dutch riddles. What did he say?"

"Burke's file is mostly top-secret. All the good parts are redacted, crossed out, so you cannot read them."

"What's that mean? Is he some kind of spy, or something?"

"Perhaps, or the Army version anyway. He attended West Point and worked in special operations, where he was referred to as 'a real bad ass.' His words, not mine."

"I've known a few bad asses, myself."

"Not with his skill set. Remember how easily he took Corliss and the twins down with his bare hands? I saw him do it once and you saw him do it the second time. I hate to think of what he could do with a pistol or a rifle."

Carbonari frowned and thought it over. "Yeah, maybe you're right, he is different."

"If we bring in more clowns like the last bunch, he'll go right through them, too."

"All right, smart guy, who then?" Carbonari asked, frustrated.

"Give me until tomorrow morning. My brother was in the Dutch Royal Marines, *their* Special Forces. He has fought all over the world with many of the same type people as Burke. I shall call him. I think we need to fight fire with fire."

"Your brother?" Carbonari mused. "How yummy. Is he... like you?"

"No, the complete opposite, I am afraid — cold, clear eyed, and deadly as Cleopatra's asp. He and some of his men operate a private security company to handle protection for 'high net-worth individuals' throughout the Middle East. On occasion, they get called upon to 'eliminate pests,' some of whom were just as difficult as the one confronting us."

"But your brother? Isn't that nepotism?"

"Nepotism? Your Sicilian 'fraternity' was founded on nepotism, wasn't it?"

"All right, give him a call, but we need to put an end to this thing."

As their meeting took a ten-minute break, Bob motioned for Patsy and Linda to come up front and talk to him. "I need someone in charge of logistics — travel, hotel rooms, rental cars, meeting places, supplies, cell phones, a boat, all that stuff. You two would be perfect."

"Sounds awfully sexist to me." Linda folded her arms across her chest and scowled.

"Process of elimination," he countered. "Look, it's what you two used to do for a living, and you can't go anywhere near the casino, anyway. Besides, I don't want either of you shooting anybody again... or getting shot at. We need to find an operational base in Atlantic City. I was thinking of that old Holiday Inn on Atlantic Avenue. It's only a few miles from the Bimini Bay, and not flashy. We also need plane tickets to Philly, and some cars. We can pick them up at the Philly airport — different car agencies, different credit cards, you get the idea.

"While we're doing all the drudge work, what are you going to be doing?" Linda asked.

"Me? I'm going to be renting us a really big boat that I found online."

"A boat? Why is it you get all the fun?" Linda glared at him.

"Our company lawyer, George Grierson, is finalizing the arrangements. If you get your work done and you're nice to me, I might even take you down to Cape May when I go to pick it up. You too, Patsy."

"Oh, no, I know you two. It'll get way too noisy below deck for my innocent ears — all that moaning and screaming. You might even capsize the boat."

"That's all him," Linda answered, straight faced. "I just lie there."

"Uh, it's not *his* voice I hear." Patsy shook her head. "If it's just the same to you, I'll stay behind, so you two can have your fun without any inhibitions... and without me getting jealous."

"That's not why you want to stay behind, and you know it, girl," Linda said as she looked up at Bob. "She thinks Jimmy Barker is cute, so cute in fact..."

"Barker? You mean the skinny Geek?" Bob asked.

"Linda! I can't say anything around you, can I?" Patsy glared at her.

"None of my business," Bob raised his hands in mock surrender. "But I'm not sure how much experience Jimmy's had with the fairer sex."

"I doubt he's had experience with any sex at all," Linda clucked as Patsy turned red.

Bob looked at her. "I hate to get personal, but you just spent three months with Vinnie. I know this has been a pretty bad week for you, but Jimmy? You're sure you're not jumping into something? He might be a... change of pace for you."

Patsy looked down at the floor for a moment, carefully composing what she was about to say. "Don't get me wrong, major; I liked Vinnie, I liked him a lot. He was fun, but everything's been kind of a blur since Chicago. He talked me into coming down here with him, and there was the money, and the house, and he put me on his insurance, which I *did not* want; but... it all kind of happened. I had just turned twenty-one, and he was... how can I put this? He was a real man, with a lot more experience, as you call it, than I had. Anyway, we had a lot of fun... a *lot* of fun. But with his age and what he did in the Army, it was never going to be permanent between us. He knew that, and so did I. We were both out to have a good time, and we did, but... well, Jimmy's *my* age. We like the same kind of music, and he's so smart... and, well, so cuddly."

"Vinnie was a lot of things, but cuddly was not one of them," Linda conceded.

"Look," Bob told her, "when this is over, we'll all go back down to Bragg. You have a house and that insurance to take care of. After that, you can stay down there or come back to Chicago with us, whatever you want. So don't worry."

Linda gave her a big hug. "So have that fun and get all the 'cuddling,' you want. You've earned it."

"And if Jimmy doesn't take the hint, Linda will throw him in your room some night and lock the door," Bob added.

"Oh, he doesn't need any hints," Patsy said as her face turned red.

"Just don't hurt the poor thing," Linda told her.

When the group reconvened, Bob told them, "I was checking the online employment ads in the *Press of Atlantic City*. The Bimini Bay has a big ad in there almost every day for janitors and cleaning staff. That would be a great way to get a couple of our guys inside. Master Sergeant Randall, who are the biggest neat freaks in the outfit?"

Ace's eyes narrowed as he looked around the table at face after face that looked away and wouldn't return his stare. "Well, major, it's a very close race. But after considerable thought, I think it would have to be Lonzo and Chester."

Those two groaned, while the other three clapped and grinned.

"When we get to Atlantic City, I want you two guys to go in and apply. Tell them you cleaned office buildings in… Boston. The odds are they don't know anybody up there."

"What's it pay?" Chester asked.

"With experience, I thought I saw twelve dollars an hour."

"That's more than we're making now," Lonzo told Chester. "Maybe we should stay."

"See, a whole new career field has opened up for you guys," Bob laughed.

"What about a background check? Won't that blow the whole thing?" Dorothy asked.

The Delta guys around the table shook their heads and snickered; and she heard them say things like, "Noob," "Newbie," "Background check?" and, "Where'd you get her?"

Bob smiled. "JSOC has a document staff section that does nothing but build phony 'legends,' or ID packages for our guys. They always have four or five ready to go for the operators, so I'll take advantage of General Stansky's offer," Bob said as he pulled the business card the general gave him. "I'll make a call and get some made up."

"It's that easy, huh?" Linda asked.

"Yep, it's that easy," Bob told her. "Everybody who works on the casino floor has to be certified by the State Gambling Commission, but that takes a couple of weeks. Everybody wants to be a dealer; but they're so short on semi-skilled labor at all the casinos that they'll jump on two men with cleaning experience who speak English and are ready to start. They'll probably put you to work cleaning the offices, since that doesn't fall under the Commission rules, and that's exactly where I want you. It'll get you inside the Business Office, maybe even Van Gries's."

Finally, Bob smiled as he turned towards Dorothy. "I don't want us to fly commercial. A Gulfstream G-550 is pretty nice, isn't it? Can you fly one of those?"

"Are you kidding?" she grinned. "It's the gold standard for civilian aviation; and yes, I can fly one. I can also fly an F-16 Eagle, an F-22 Raptor, and I've even put some time on the new F-35 Lightning," she said with an embarrassed smile. "I can also fly most helicopters, but I don't usually count them."

Ace patted her hand and said, "She's mine, and she's taken."

"I can see why," Bob laughed. "I don't think I can get any of the others, but I'll rent the jet for a week or two and you can fly us up. Let's figure wheels up at 18:00, folks. That's 6:00 p.m. for you civilians." he said, looking straight at Linda and Patsy.

"Smart-ass. I know what 18:00 is," Linda told him. "I watch NCIS."

"Good to know. Well, between reruns, get Ace and Koz rooms at the Tuscany Towers and Siesta Cove," he said as he turned to the two Deltas. "Their roofs look to be the right height and distance from the Bimini Bay for a nest or two, if we need them."

"A nest...?" Linda asked as the men all turned and looked at her again. "Okay, okay, don't ask, right?"

Bob rolled his eyes and finally looked over at Ace. "We need some good tactical communications. If you can, get us one of those new PRC 154A Rifleman systems and a dozen of the headsets. And stop by the arms room and check out some of your favorite toys."

"A couple of Barrett .50-calibers?" Ace asked hopefully.

"That works for me," Bob said as he watched Ace smile. "And take the guys to the 'Haberdashery' for an assortment of costumes that might be useful — Otis Elevator, Direct TV, Trane Air Conditioning, you know," he said as he looked around the table. "That should do. See you all at Windermere Airport at 18:00."

When Linda called the Holiday Inn, she went into her full "executive assistant" mode, telling the manager they were doing some very sensitive analytical work for the casinos and did not negotiate his hugely inflated rack rates. She insisted on six top-floor rooms and the 'Presidential' suite. It featured two large bedrooms, where she put the Geeks, a living room, and a large dining room table, where they could spread out their computers, maps and papers. She rented them for a week, in return for which, they were to have total privacy, doing their own room cleaning and eating their meals in the hotel restaurant or through room service. It was the sweetest piece of business the manager had seen in over a year. Giddy, he even allowed them to install small satellite dishes and an antenna array on the balcony. To the geeks, those were worth any price, because they provided a secure, ultra-high-speed, satellite connection to the Toler TeleCom corporate data and telephone network.

By 9:00 p.m., they had landed at the small Atlantic City "International" Airport and driven into the city, ten miles to the south. Jimmy and Ronald were busily setting up the data and communications dishes and equipment on the balcony. Lonzo and Chester had left to recon the Siesta Cove, while Koz and Bulldog took the Tuscany Towers. Because the Bimini Bay was the biggest and had central administrative offices and presumably the central computers, Bob sent two teams — Ace and Dorothy, and Ernie Travers and The Batman.

The crews were casually dressed in blue jeans, windbreakers, sports team gear, and NASCAR jackets, and indistinguishable from the rest of the middle-aged, long-haired tourists inside. The assignment was to check out the slots, table games, sports book, hotel lobby and common areas, bars, and restaurants, observing the guards, the security cameras, and the closed-circuit television feeds. Are the guards stationary, did they circulate, and were they armed? If possible they were to gain entrance to some of the rear service corridors, administrative offices, building roofs, and the basements, as well. Outside, Bob also wanted information on the doors, utility pads, parking garage, surface parking lots, telephone lines, switch boxes, perimeter lighting, satellite dishes, and the Bimini Bay boat marina.

Bob was the last to arrive. When he did, he found the Geeks already busily at work. Ronald lay on the plush living room carpet furiously typing on his laptop, while Jimmy sat in one of the overstuffed leather armchairs typing away on his. A smiling Patsy Evans sat behind him in the chair, giving Jimmy a vigorous shoulder and neck rub. From the expression on his face, Jimmy was in heaven as Bob walked over and asked, "How's it coming guys?"

"Not as well as we expected," Ronald answered, embarrassed, as he looked up and suddenly began to run his fingertips across his scalp like a wild man.

"Don't mind him," Jimmy said. "That's the way he gets when he is working."

"When we hack a system, we use a step-by-step process with a lot of trial and error," Ronald ignored him and went on. "We've already blown through the easy options and grabbed at the 'low hanging fruit,' if you will."

"And no luck?" Bob asked.

"Not much, but if it was easy, you wouldn't need us, would you?" Jimmy laughed.

"The people who put this security system together weren't complete dweebs," Ronald conceded. "They've set up some good countermeasures and took away our usual paths, but we'll get in. They're just making it more of a challenge."

"Can you do it without setting off any alarms or tripwires?" Bob asked.

"We aren't total virgins, you know, Mister B.," Jimmy laughed.

"Not anymore," Bob heard Ronald mumble as he turned back to his computer.

Patsy kissed Jimmy on the side of his neck, and he grinned.

Over the next two hours, the recon teams began returning to the Holiday Inn, grabbing a beer in the kitchen and flopping on one of the couches. By and large, they all told the same story about the building security and physical layout.

"The personnel office was closed, as we expected," Lonzo reported. "But Chester and I will go there first thing and get the job applications going."

"Dorothy got one of those new Gold Cards," Ace said as he flipped it to Talmadge. "Maybe you guys can find some codes in there we can use. We walked up the service corridor and tried the office doors, but they've got cameras everywhere and one of the Risk Management goons chased us out of there."

"Our room is on the top floor in the big tower," Dorothy said. "The guest elevators only go to the guest floors, 1 through 6; and there's a separate express elevator in the service corridor that goes all the way to the penthouse on the roof. We couldn't tell if it goes to the basement or any other floors, since we couldn't get inside."

"However, the emergency stairs do go to all the floors," Ace added. "That's required by the fire code. You can always pretend to be walking up and down for exercise, so Dorothy and I walked up to the sixth floor. Fortunately, they went cheap and didn't put any cameras in the stairwells."

"That could be useful to know," Bob said.

"The stairs go to a mechanical room on the roof, but they have big magnetic locks on the fire door, and a card reader. Same thing down on the basement doors."

"Same at Tuscany Towers," Bulldog said, "and those mag locks are big suckers. No way you'll get them open without the key card or some C-4."

"Ditto for the Siesta Cove," Chester added. "A rogue elephant couldn't pull that mag lock open."

"When we get the cleaning jobs, I'm sure they'll give us cards that provide access to a lot of areas, but I doubt that'll include Carbonari's penthouse at the Bimini Bay. Maybe we can get into the basement, if that's where they keep their cleaning compounds."

"When you get the cards, let us scan them," Ronald said. "Maybe we can adapt them to give generic access to all the doors."

"That could work," Ace said. "And for future reference, our room on the top floor at the Bimini Bay looks straight across to Tuscany Towers, so without actually getting up there, it looks like the Tuscany Towers roof has a clear view of the Bimini Bay penthouse and helipad. Using my rangefinder from our balcony, it's right at 2,000 meters. Piece of cake."

"Piece of what cake?" Linda frowned and asked suspiciously.

"One other thing," Bob said as he handed Linda a piece of paper. "Here's the deal on the boat rental. It will be ready tomorrow afternoon, so you and I can drive down to Cape May and pick it up."

Linda looked down at the piece of paper and her eyes bulged out. "Wow!" she said. "$75,000, plus a $100,000 deposit? What is it, the *Queen Mary?*"

"Just about," he laughed. "You'll understand when you see it."

CHAPTER SEVENTEEN

Martijn Van Gries waited until midnight to phone his brother. There was a seven-hour time difference between Atlantic City and Kuwait, but as a former Royal Dutch Marine Corps officer, Theo had always been an early riser. He could also be anywhere in the world, but Kuwait was where he was working the last time Martijn called. Theo kept trying to get Martijn to relocate to the Gulf. It was tempting, but he had not yet succeeded.

"Money really does grow on trees over here," Theo kept telling him. There were several high-end resorts in the region that would pay Martijn three or four times what Carbonari paid him; and despite their conservative rhetoric, the Arabs were more than tolerant of wealthy foreign men with "unusual" sexual proclivities. So far, Martijn had resisted the temptation. The heat and the dust of the Middle East always seemed a bit off putting to him, but so was working for the rude louts in the American Mafia.

After five rings, he heard the familiar, accented voice answer, "Van Gries here."

"Have you had your morning coffee yet, brother?" Martijn asked in Dutch, and the two men began conversing in their native tongue with little fear of anyone listening in. Dutch was difficult enough, but theirs was a colloquial, guttural dialect only found in the ethnically mixed Asian and Middle Eastern neighborhoods around the docks in Rotterdam, where they grew up. It was incomprehensible to anyone but another native.

"Actually, I just returned from my morning run and am sitting on my balcony, looking north across the city and the bay before the heat comes up, enjoying that first cup."

"How nice. But you are up on the twenty-seventh floor, and I bet the stench and the flies of the city never get much higher than ten."

"Ah! I forgot you have been here, but money does have its advantages."

"No taxes, no government interference, and no questions. I doubt you miss the Marines very much.

"That depends on the day, Martijn, but why are you calling? Are you coming to visit me again?"

"Actually I would like to have you and some of your men come visit me — perhaps for a week — it should not take much more than that."

"Work, then? We are not inexpensive, you know. What is it you need?"

"Let us say, we have a bothersome pest that needs to be eliminated."

"When it comes to the Russians, the Corsicans, the Sicilians, or the

American underworld, I have always tried to avoid your intra-family spats."

"This is not intra-family, Theo. It involves an outsider, an American Army commando of some type, who blames my boss for the death of one of his men."

"Ah! I see your problem. Those groups are very tightly knit. If they think Donatello was responsible... well, they can indeed be difficult. What is this fellow's name?"

"Burke. He is a former American Army major."

Theo paused, thinking. "I may have heard the name, but their special operations people typically operate under a nom de guerre. I'll have to do some checking. There is a fellow I employ from time to time who was in Delta. Perhaps he knows him."

"Excellent, but I need you over here. How much for the week?"

"Well, we would need to drop several other things we are working on..."

"I can hear the wheels turning, Theo. How much?"

"To employ me and seven of my men for a week, I would require €300,000, say $400,000 of your dollars, plus expenses. We can usually bring in our own weapons and equipment, but there are costs associated with doing that."

"Understood. Send me a list of anything else you need, and when you will arrive."

"Meanwhile, I shall see what I can learn regarding this pest of yours."

Donatello rarely got up before nine o'clock. The next morning, Martijn gave him an extra five minutes before he took the elevator up, opened Carbonari's office door and slipped confidently into one of the armchairs in front of his desk. "Do you remember that better idea I had about security?" he began.

"You mean that I should hire your brother?"

"I called him, and he and seven of his men are available."

"That seems like a lot, this isn't the Middle East. Does he know what he's doing?"

"He is a gun for hire, Donatello, and the coldest and deadliest man I have ever met. If you want to get rid of Burke, Theo is who you need."

"Corliss was a Marine, you know."

Van Gries shook his head. "To the same extent a used Ford Fiesta and a Maserati are both automobiles. The Royal Dutch Marines, the 'Black Devils,' as the Germans called them in the Second World War, are an elite commando unit." Van Gries paused, determined not to let this stupid Italian get under his skin. Italians! They are as incompetent in warfare as the French. "With the wind-down of the Iraq and Afghanistan wars and the breakup of the Soviet Union, Europe and the Middle East are full of special operations soldiers from many countries who are willing to contract their services to the highest bidder."

"Like those samurais, after their lords are dead. Yeah, I saw that movie," Carbonari grunted. "So what's that mean in English? Is he a merc, or a hitman, or what?"

"A bit of both, I expect. More importantly, he has worked with the American Rangers, the SEALs, and even the Delta Force in Iraq and Afghanistan. He thinks Burke might have been one of those. If that is true, he is exceedingly dangerous."

"And what will he cost me?"

"$400,000, plus expenses, for a week."

"Jesus Christ! Four hundred grand? Are you kidding me?"

"It is a lot, but much less than your funeral would run."

Carbonari glared at him. "All right," he reluctantly agreed. "But I'm calling Brooklyn and see if I can get some of their men too."

"You know what they say about letting the camel get his nose under your tent, you'll have hell to pay getting him out."

After Martijn Van Gries left, Carbonari sat back in his desk chair, debating some really bad choices. Reluctantly, he picked up his telephone and made the call he knew he must make to Brooklyn. When a familiar female voice answered, he said in his smarmiest voice, "Barbara, my dear, this is Donatello Carbonari. Is Angelo in?"

"Nice to hear from you again, Mr. Carbonari. It's been a while. Let me see."

He fully expected to be left on hold for a few minutes. It was the little game Angelo Roselli played to remind him who was boss. When the wait continued to a full five minutes, he knew the conversation was going to be a ball buster.

"Yeah," the big man finally answered. "Dat you, 'Donnie?' What the hell's going on down dere? I been hearin' stories."

"Stories? What kind of stories?" Carbonari asked, trying to sound confident.

"Cops, ambulances, guys falling off freakin' roofs..."

"That was an accident. A man climbed out on a ledge and fell, that's all."

"What? Suicide by casino? Dat ain't the way I heard it. Anyway, how'd the weekend go? Business startin' to pick up?"

"Some," Carbonari answered, shaken that Roselli seemed to know everything that was happening. "The slots have picked up, but that's a lot of local trade. The rooms and shows are holding their own, but the tables are still way off. Those discount flights to Vegas out of LaGuardia are killing us."

"Yeah, well, we all got problems that are killing us, don't we?" Roselli replied, his voice devoid of any sympathy or humor. "Speakin' 'a problems, wit dat guy takin' a header off da Bimini Bay, and now dis business in Chicago, I told you months ago you shoulda brought in some of our Brooklyn guys to help you wit security. Dat gorilla Corliss thinks he's freakin' Mister T, and those football players he hired are useless."

"They were useful, given the clientèle we get down here."

"Dey ain't good for shit, you ask me, Donnie. And you can't trust 'em. You're running a serious business down dere; you need some serious help. And if those three chamokes end up back in jail in Chicago and start talkin'…"

"That won't happen. The problem has been taken care of."

"Taken care of?" Angelo paused for a minute, knowing how *he* interpreted that answer, and wanting to verify what he just heard. "Taken *care* of? All of 'em, *permanently*, you mean?"

"All of them. Permanently. That's why I called you, to let you know and to tell you that you were right. And I would like to get a couple of your men down here, temporarily, perhaps two or three for a week or so, until I can get Corliss and the others replaced."

Angelo grunted. "Smart move, Donnie. You're finally catchin' on. I like a man who can admit he made a mistake, so long as he don't make too many more of 'em. You know what I'm sayin'?"

Carbonari bit his tongue and said, "Yes, I guess we all live and learn."

"No, you got dat ass backwards, kid. We *learn* and we *live*," Roselli laughed. "But I'll tell you what, I'll call Cheech and tell him to take a few of his boys down dere and help you out for the next week or so."

"Cheech?" Carbonari cringed. "Good, he'll be perfect," knowing that Roselli could not have possibly made a worse choice, at least for him. Cheech Mazoulli was a crude lout who was one hundred percent loyal to Angelo Roselli. He wouldn't stop to piss on Carbonari if he were on fire.

"I have plenty of private security guards, the guys in the blue blazers who keep an eye on the floor and handle drunks. But with three casinos and three hotels to look out for, I need some guys to keep an eye on them. As I said, two or three guys should be plenty. Have them call me when they get here, and I'll meet them in the lobby."

"They'll be down dere tonight. Normally, I'd charge you two hundred large a week for a crew like that; but to show how understanding your partners up here in Brooklyn can be, I'll even pay half. All you gotta do is pick up their room and meal charges."

"Whatever you say, Angelo," Donatello answered, trying to sound happy, but knowing full well how much the food and bar bill for Roselli's men would run.

"Good," Roselli said. "By the way, how much you wirin' up here tomorrow?"

"I haven't seen the final numbers. Let me talk to Van Gries and I'll call you back."

"No need. We been gettin' eight, sometimes eight and a quarter. That's the size 'a golden eggs da boys are expectin' to see up here — call 'em extra-large eggs! — and you don't want to disappoint, do you, Donnie?"

Angelo Roselli's office was at the back of his large Italian restaurant located on Cristoforo Columbo Boulevard, or 18th Avenue to the ethnically challenged, and 70th Street in the center of Bensonhurst's "Little Italy" neighborhood on the southwest side of Brooklyn. The decor inside harked back to the 1950s and 1960s, but so did Bensonhurst and most of his clientèle. Back then, the area used to be a lot nicer and a lot more Italian, Roselli lamented, but he guessed everything had to change, even those chickens down the coast in Atlantic City. They'd laid gold for a lot of years. Unfortunately, as his Sicilian grandfather used to say, "Even da best hen's gonna stop layin' sooner or later. Dat's what Sunday dinner's for."

Angelo put out a marvelous plate of veal scaloppini, and everyone in Brooklyn knew his cannoli were to die for. He usually spent his evenings in the kitchen, making his signature dishes himself, giving rise to his mob nickname, "The Baker." Cooking was only a hobby for him, however, because Angelo Roselli was the underboss of the Lucchese crime family in Brooklyn, one of the original five Mafia families that still ruled New York.

Like the vast majority of the other bosses and underbosses, he had been in and out of one state or federal prison after another for most of the past fifty years. He did time in Sing Sing, Attica, Dannemora, Lewisburg, and Allenwood, for labor racketeering, loan sharking, illegal gambling, extortion, soliciting bribes, bribery, bid rigging, corrupting union officials, prostitution, bookmaking, hijacking, and bank fraud. Those serious charges aside, 'going inside' as a renowned cook and baker always got him assigned to the prison kitchens. Everyone inside liked to eat, including the baddest Latin, Black, and White Supremacist gangs, the guards, and the wardens; and providing good food and desserts was better protection than any bulletproof vest. "Soft time" or not, prison had made an old man out of him. Angelo had no intention of ever going back inside again, which was why he became very cautious in all of his dealings and very circumspect with everyone he spoke to.

Roselli had his key people closely watched, and he even had the watchers watched. His secretary, Barbara, was his sister, and undoubtedly the largest single purchaser of one-time, "burner" cell phones in Brooklyn or the Bronx. She would spend one entire day each month driving around Long Island, Manhattan, Brooklyn, and even New Jersey visiting discount stores and drugstores to purchase dozens of cheap cell phones with pre-loaded minutes for him and his key people.

Angelo had a desk drawer full of them, and his cardinal rule was to use them only once. Before Barbara left each day, she picked up his used ones, took them down to the restaurant basement, and personally tossed them in the furnace.

After he hung up on Carbonari, Roselli reached in his bottom desk drawer, pulled out a new cell phone, and tapped in a number.

"It's me... yeah... Listen, I need you to take six of your best men down da coast for a little while. You're going to help dat guy with some security at his three places... No, should be routine stuff. Dat other guy, da one you had da beef with, he ain't around no more. When you get dere, call da guy. He'll make the arrangements. It's on his tab, but I want you to take da right guys with you. No broads, no booze, no gambling. All business. And I want your guys to make nice with him, chat him up and be friendly, but remember dey work for me... Yeah, I been hearin' a lotta stuff too, and I want to know what's going on down there."

After his conversation with Roselli, Donatello Carbonari found himself in a funk, staring absently out his office window. He was usually over-confident to a fault, but getting grilled by "the boys" up in Brooklyn drove him crazy. If anybody dared to call him Donnie again, he'd cap one in their ear. God, he hated that name!

Finally, he picked up the telephone and almost punched Van Gries's extension number through the other side of the dial. "How much are we wiring up to Brooklyn tonight?" Carbonari demanded to know, without any preliminaries or social niceties.

"Tonight?" Van Gries asked, surprised by the suddenness of the question and the angry tone in Carbonari's voice. He rustled some papers on his desk, as if he was looking for a report, trying to sidestep the question. "It has been a bad week, you know."

"It's been a freakin' bad year, Martijn, so stop bullshitting me!"

"I understand, Donatello, but occupancy's down, we had some unusual losses at the tables, and there's no holiday weekend this month..."

"I know the goddamn problems; give me the goddamn number!"

"All right! I can do six million, maybe six and a half if I really stretch things."

"It's got to be eight and a quarter."

"Jesus!" Van Gries answered as he spun around in his chair and faced the window. He cupped his hand over the receiver and said, "You know we don't have that kind of free cash, not with the taxes coming up and all the rest."

"You aren't hearing me," Carbonari fumed. "I need to send those bastards eight and a quarter. If I don't, Brooklyn's gonna crap all over me, and then they're gonna come down here and crap all over you. You get the picture?"

"Yes, and it's not a very pretty one," Van Gries told him as he realized where this conversation was headed.

"Do what you did last time."

"And what I did a couple of times before that. Now you want even more. If I take another two million out of the tax reserve and escrow accounts, we're going to be light by over nine million by the end of the next quarter. What do I do then?"

"Then you take it from someplace else! Hey, didn't Detroit and New Orleans just send us some new investment money for that addition I pitched them for Tuscany Towers? How much was that? Three million? Use that."

Van Gries was quiet for a moment. "You know, your people were the ones who invented the Ponzi scheme in the first place. One of these days, they're gonna wake up and realize what we're doing down here."

"Bullshit! This town's gone through bad times before. You wouldn't believe all the tricks my father and grandfather used to pull. Talk about creative accounting. But it'll come back, it always does," Carbonari said, lying even to himself. "And if they do wake up, at least it won't be tomorrow. So, unless you got a better idea, do what I told you."

Martijn wanted to keep arguing, but he found himself holding a dead telephone. Carbonari had hung up on him. As the Dutchman well knew, the problem wasn't just the tax escrows or Detroit, or New Orleans. The problem was he had also skimmed over ten million for himself, and the skimming was beginning to trip over the skimming.

The Geeks were sprawled on the living room floor, with Patsy Evans lying on the floor next to Jimmy, feeding him Doritos. Jimmy and Ronald were doing a duet, banging away on the keyboard of the new laptops Linda had bought them. From the intense expressions on their faces, they weren't having much success. Bob had come in some twenty minutes before and sat at the dining room table with Ace and Linda, drinking coffee and observing Jimmy and Ronald much as one might watch some rare species in the zoo. As they watched, Ronald began to furiously scratch the top of his head, in some nervous release of energy.

"How are the new machines working out?" Bob finally asked.

That was when Jimmy and Ronald looked up and saw the three adults watching them.

"Oh, I didn't see you guys come in," Jimmy began to explain, and then changed direction. "The new machines are totally radacious, Mr. B., but I'm glad you're here. I hate to admit this, but we seem to have encountered a significant problem. Last night, our first attempts to penetrate their system failed. The deeper we probed, trying to get into the important financial areas you said you wanted…"

"Penetrate… the deeper he probed… I bet Patsy loves it when he talks dirty like that, don't ya think?" Linda whispered.

"…the more we run into some very clever firewalls," Jimmy continued, either not hearing the snickers or not caring. "Ordinarily, we would push on, but you said you didn't want to trigger any alarms."

Ace looked down at them, took another sip of coffee, and asked, "Don't I remember something about a middle-of-the-class, MIT derb, and how you'd scorch his butt so bad, he'd have to dunk it in the Charles River to cool off… Did I get that about right?"

"Well, yeah, but he cheated," Ronald quickly answered.

"He cheated?" Bob coughed, almost spilling what was left of his coffee into his lap.

"It's really quite simple," Jimmy bristled. "There's no way a clunk from MIT could have designed a sophisticated data security system like this. He had to have outsourced it. All we need to do is figure out who he went to."

"Aren't there like a bazillion software shops up and down Route 128?" Ace asked.

"Chock full of still more MIT derbs, building still more firewalls?" Bob added.

"Firewalls?" Ace quickly sat up. "I've got my Barrett out in the trunk. Point me in the right direction, and I'll punch a bunch of holes through that wall in no time."

The two Geeks looked at each other, open-mouthed, wondering who invited the Neanderthal to the party.

"He's only joking guys," Bob laughed. "But he could. Anyway, keep at it, we have no choice. Linda and I are going down this afternoon and picking up the boat. We should be back after dark. It's big and fast and should give us a closer base to operate from than sitting down here at the Holiday Inn."

"You gonna park it in the Bimini Bay marina?" Koz asked.

"No, there's another marina on the south side of the little harbor, a small one, but we can watch the Bimini Bay from there. Anyway, we'll reconvene on the boat later."

As the group broke up, Bob motioned for Ace and Dorothy to come closer. "We need a set of building plans for the Bimini Bay."

"The architects are never going to let you see the plans," Ace told him, "but the city might. Dorothy and I will go over to the City Building Department. We'll pretend we have a job over at the hotel. My father was an electrical contractor, and I can still talk the game."

"See if you can get a look at them this afternoon, while we're gone. Oh, one other thing. Hey, Jimmy, unhand the young maiden and come here a minute," Bob called to him.

"Maiden?" Linda looked away and snickered. "You gotta be kidding."

"Just trying to get the boy's attention," Bob replied as Jimmy walked over. "You too, Ace. It seems to me that almost everyone going into the hotel or casino uses the parking garage or the front doors, right? Is there some way we could rig a couple of video cameras over there, so we could monitor them back here?"

"Or can we tap into theirs?" Jimmy suggested.

Ace shrugged. "Putting up a set of our own would take a lot of time and be hard to pull off without being noticed. But there's nothing particularly special about their equipment. The cameras are probably hardwired into junction boxes, and I assume the junction boxes feed into their servers and in turn into their computers. If we pirated the feed... but where would we get power?"

Jimmy thought about the problem for a minute. "The junction boxes must have power. We could tap their line with a modem, a small one."

"But would it be strong enough to get a signal to the marina?" Ace asked.

"No way," Jimmy thought some more, "but we could park a car in the garage and a second one at the south corner of the parking lot with a couple of big signal boosters in their trunks. We could power them with a car battery and a transformer. Then, the signal would reach."

"Okay. It's worth a try. Thanks, Jimmy," Bob said. "Ace, see if you can get it done this afternoon. We need to know what's going on over there."

"Roger that. I'll get on it as soon as we get back from the city with the plans. They might give me some ideas on how to bootleg a signal."

"One other thing, when Linda and I get back with the boat, we'll need to post a watch, 24-7. It has a flying bridge up top. That's the highest spot on the boat and will provide 360-degree visibility."

"I assume you only want our guys, and put them on two-hour shifts?"

"That's what I thought. One man per shift should do. Add me and Ernie to the rotation but leave the Geeks and the girls out. You can put Lonzo and Chester in, but only on the day shift. They'll need some sleep when they get back from cleaning, but they can cover the morning and early afternoon."

"Not having seen the marina, I assume we'll be most vulnerable after dark."

"I took a look. The dock is reasonably lit."

"But the water won't be," Ace told him. "We'll put some rifles, handguns, grenades, and flares up on the bridge."

"Good idea. And I saw a set of Zeiss binoculars on the boat inventory, so the guys on watch can scan the buildings and keep an eye on the Bimini Bay marina from time to time."

"Will do."

CHAPTER EIGHTEEN

It took an hour and a half to drive the fifty miles from Atlantic City to Cape May at the far southern tip of the New Jersey coast. Rather than head west and take the fast Garden State Parkway south, Bob opted for the much slower and more scenic coast road that wound through the laid-back beach communities from Atlantic City through Ocean City, Strathmere, Avalon, Stone Harbor, and Wildwood, to Cape May at the far tip of the narrow island where the Delaware River and the Atlantic Ocean met. Known for its beaches, colorful Victorian gingerbread houses, and boat marinas, it provided a wonderful emotional break for them.

"I don't want to leave," Linda said as they looped through the small town.

"We can come back after Atlantic City is finished. Looks like it would be a great place to unwind." Bob drove the full length of Washington Street before he checked his GPS and headed to the boat marina. He pulled into a visitor's space in front of the office and followed Linda inside, where a friendly young receptionist greeted them.

"Is Mr. Marble here?" Bob asked her.

"Sam's down on Pier 6 giving the final check to one of the rentals."

"My name's Bob Burke, he said to meet him here at..."

"That's where he is, on your boat. You can go on down, and I'll get the papers ready."

They walked through the busy boatyard and found the sign to Pier 6, where they tied up the larger yachts and sailboats.

"What's the name of ours?" Linda asked.

"*The Enchantress.*"

"Oh, great name! They must've known I was coming."

"No doubt about it. There it is, parked over there," he said as he pointed to a huge, sleek white yacht moored in Slip 9.

Linda's mouth fell open and she stopped in her tracks as she looked at the boat from the bow to the stern. "Holy crap! Are you kidding me?"

"Well, I thought we needed something with some size and speed."

"You couldn't talk the Navy out of a battleship?"

"Oh, it's big, but it's not *that* big. It's a Ferrenti 750 — that means it's seventy-five feet long — and Italian. It's the Maserati of motor yachts, so powerful it purrs."

"It's a boat, Burke! I purr, the boat doesn't."

"It comes with every bell and whistle you could want, from two big diesel engines to a hot tub on the upper deck."

"A hot tub? On the upper deck? Margaritas and baby oil in the sun?" She looked up in awe as they approached the big boat. "Maybe you have a point after all."

"I knew you'd like that, but more important to me is the CRRC on the aft deck."

"The what?"

"A Combat Rubber Raiding Craft, that's what the military calls them. It's a rubber life raft with a big outboard motor. I figure we can use it to scoot across to the Bimini Bay if we need to. The military ones are black, of course, and this one's white."

"I'll bet they call it a white rubber life raft down here."

He stared at her for a moment. "But that takes all the fun out of it."

"That boat is huge!" she said as they got closer. "Are you going to be able to handle it?"

Just then, a short, barrel-chested man in a white shirt leaned over the upper railing and called down to them, "Mister Burke? Hey, I'm Sam Marble, come on up, and I'll show you around this sweet beauty."

"Should I take my shoes off? Cover my head?" Linda whispered.

Bob ignored her, walked across the gangplank and shook hands with Marble. "Did you get the check and the rest of the papers you wanted from my attorney in Chicago?" Bob asked.

"Sure did, and the insurance and corporate guarantees checked out just fine. But before you take off in this thing, I thought I should take a few minutes and show you around," Marble said as he led them up to the flying bridge. "Normally, a boat like this goes out with a professional crew of three. You didn't ask us to provide any hired help, and that concerns me a little. This ain't no bass boat you haul out to the lake on Saturday morning. It's a Ferrenti, sleek, fast, maneuverable, and she can run at thirty knots all day long."

"Is that fast?" Linda asked.

"Fast? Yes, that's fast, very fast," Marble warned. "Are you two sure you can handle something like this?"

"We'll be fine, Mr. Marble. I've driven my share of big boats and fast ones," Bob smiled, "as have the half dozen friends of mine who are going out with us."

"Navy?" Marble asked.

"Something like that," he looked at him and smiled. "Together, there isn't much that flies or floats that we haven't taken out." He looked around and concluded that the Ferrenti was even better than he expected. The windows in the lounges and cabins were tinted black, so passengers could look out, but no one could look in. The dining room and galley could easily sit ten and the four cabins up front, plus the crew quarters, were more than adequate for the number of people he wanted to have on board. "Besides, I'm taking it up to Atlantic City this afternoon, where it will remain for perhaps a week as a base for my friends to enjoy the casinos. I'm not sure if we'll be going very far after that until we come back here. I left the keys to our rental car in your office."

"No problem. You have the boat rented for two weeks. If you decide that's too long, just give me a call and we'll drive your car up and pick up the boat."

"Or, my wife and I might decide it's not nearly long enough, dump the rest of them and work our way down the coast by ourselves."

Linda beamed as Marble said, "Whatever floats your boat, as they say. Just let me know and we can work something out."

"Linda, why don't you take the car back to that supermarket we passed and stock up on food for the guys," he told her as he took out his wallet and pulled out five one-hundred dollar bills.

"We've already stocked the galley with some snacks and drinks to get you going. It sounds like you'll be loading up with a lot more, so let me send my maintenance man Ernesto to the store with your wife. He can carry things, while I walk you around the engines, navigational equipment, and communications gear. It's pretty complicated stuff."

Bob handed him one of his Toler TeleCom corporate business cards. "Don't worry, that stuff's in my wheelhouse. And if I don't understand it, I'll have a couple of techies with me, who will."

It took almost an hour for Sam Marble to show Bob through the complex machinery in engine room, and for Linda to stow the last of the food, booze, and beer in the galley and the two bars. Finally, Bob and Linda waved goodbye as Charlie walked down the pier to his office.

Bob looked at his watch and saw it was only 4:30 p.m. "Well, it's a little early, but we could go ahead and head back north," he told Linda. "My plan was not to get there until dark. You want to go ashore and get something to eat before we leave?"

"I have a much better plan," she said as she grabbed his arm and pulled him down the stairs, through the lounge and galley, and toward the cabins. "We don't need to go out. The boat's stocked with enough food for a week, but you're not going to believe this master stateroom. They even have a mirror on the ceiling, Robert. A mirror! And I haven't had you alone for some quality time in days."

"Quality time? Is that what they're calling it now?"

She glanced up at him. "I can hurt you, you know."

Bob finally sat up and looked out the large, oblong porthole next to the bed. The shadows were beginning to lengthen around the harbor. He bent down and gave her a kiss and attempted to pull away without much success. "Linda, dearest," he gave her another kiss and pleaded. "The sun will be down in about a half an hour, and I don't trust myself with all that navigational equipment yet. I'd like to be out of the harbor and into open water while we still have some daylight to work by."

"I am a love kitten. I purr, remember, I don't work," she said as she reached up and tried to pull him down on top of her again.

"How about, you've worn me out."

She looked up at him and finally sighed. "I wore you out? All right. I guess that's what I get for marrying an old man."

"You got that right. Now get up and get dressed, because I'll need you to untie the lines and go up to the bow and keep watch while I steer this thing out into the channel."

"He rejects me, and then he wants to put me to work. The honeymoon is over."

"I'll get the engines and equipment going. You pull up the gangplank and untie all the lines, throw them up on the deck, and then get back on board."

"Get back on board? With no gangplank? What if I fall in the water?"

"You won't fall in the water. The boat shouldn't move... just don't waste any time."

"As I just said, 'if I fall in the water,' I will *not* be happy, Burke."

Bob threw the switches and started the big, twin MTU 2000 diesel engines, turned on the GPS navigation, the running lights, the satellite communications, the radar, and the depth finder. As night fell, he was taking no chances. Finally, he remembered the most important thing, and walked to the railing to see how Linda was doing. She had cast off the lines and stood on the pier, hands on hips, looking down at the gap between the pier and the aft deck of the boat, and then up at the bridge, glaring at him.

Quickly, he ran down to the rear deck, pushed the gangplank back out to the pier, and waited for her to walk back up. "Sorry," he said as he pulled up the gangplank. "I guess that was farther than I thought for someone with short legs."

"Short legs? Nice try," she brushed past him and headed for the bow. "Let's get out of here before you get yourself in worse trouble than you already are."

Thirty minutes later and ten miles up the coast, they sat in the captain and mate's chairs on the flying bridge as they neared the small town of Avalon, New Jersey, when Bob's cell phone rang. He pulled it out of his pocket, looked at the screen, and saw a 910 Area Code.

"Burke, here," he quickly answered.

"Major Burke," he immediately recognized the gruff, no-nonsense voice of Command Sergeant Major Patrick O'Connor, General Stansky's lead NCO. "Hate to disturb you during the cocktail hour," O'Connor began, "but the general asked me to call you."

"Never a problem, Command Sergeant Major."

"It appears that there's been another break-in at Sergeant Pastorini's house over in Fayetteville. We haven't been able to locate Miss Evans, so the general was worried and asked me to give you a call."

"She's traveling with my wife and me. We thought it best to get her out of there."

"Looks like that was a good idea. The Fayetteville Police told us they had been checking on the house; but on their last visit this afternoon, they found it thoroughly ransacked. All the drawers, boxes, and containers were dumped out, the cushions and upholstered furniture had been sliced open, even the mattresses. The ladder to the attic had been left down, some boxes up there dumped out. Downstairs, a few floorboards had been torn up, and even a couple of holes were punched in the walls."

"Sounds like someone was looking for something."

"That's what the Fayetteville PD and our own CID think. No one saw anything, but it looks like it happened sometime within the past eighteen hours. With the previous questions that surrounded Sergeant Pastorini's last tour in Afghanistan, the general immediately brought them in."

"Good idea," Bob quickly agreed.

"Do you know when Miss Evans will be returning here?"

"In a few days, probably not much more than that, but she needed to get away."

"Understood, but please advise her that the CID needs to talk to her as soon as she does return here."

"Will do. I'll bring her by as soon as we get back, and let the general know," Bob said as he rang off and began to think.

"What's that all about?" Linda asked.

"I'm not sure, but I don't think I like it."

Ace's father owned a small electric contracting business in suburban Pittsburgh. When Ace was in high school, he helped on small jobs and played general go-fer after school, spending much of that time driving around to the town halls in McKeesport, West Mifflin, North Braddock, and the other small suburbs to the south and west of the city. He filed construction plans and picked up building permits, so he had a good idea how to get his hands on the construction drawings for the Bimini Bay complex in the Atlantic City municipal offices.

As numerous undercover assignments with Delta had taught him, the secret to any good disguise was to talk and look the part. He and Dorothy wore blue jeans. He added a red plaid flannel shirt with the sleeves rolled halfway up to his elbows, while she wore a baggy gray sweatshirt, a pencil tucked behind her ear, and a clipboard. Rather than drive straight to the city offices, they made a side trip to the Bimini Bay hotel. On his recon the night before, he remembered seeing a section of meeting rooms on the second floor that were closed for remodeling. A temporary plywood wall blocked access, and a contractor sign and row of city building permits were posted outside. Those documents provided a wealth of information on the contractors and subcontractors already working the site, which was all Ace needed, as he pulled out his cell phone and took a few pictures.

There was a makeshift man-door in the plywood wall, which closed off the construction area from the hallway. Workers in hard hats had been going in and out carrying tools and construction supplies, so Ace walked over, pulled the door open, and stuck his head inside for a quick look to see what materials and equipment they were using. Dorothy stuck her head under his arm and also glanced around. "See those?" she asked as she nodded toward a long plywood table sitting to the right of the doorway. On top of the table, she saw a recharger station that held a dozen two-way commercial radios, construction drawings, and a tall stack of white hardhats. "Just what we need to complete our outfits, don't you think?" she whispered.

"Very sneaky, oh Captain, my Captain," he replied as he reached inside, grabbed two, and quickly backed out again. He put one hardhat on his head and the other on hers, raised the clipboard as if he was studying something, and set off toward the escalators.

The city's Licensing and Inspection Division reviews construction plans, issues building permits, and performs the subsequent structural, plumbing, electrical, mechanical, and related inspections while the work is in progress. They were located off Atlantic Avenue on Bacharach Boulevard in the center of the city, not far from the Holiday Inn. Ace had learned from his father that most of the people who staffed city building departments were old carpenters and plumbers who had spent too many winters on cold building sites, or who had hit themselves on the thumb with a hammer once too often. The rest had been tradesmen who went through one too many recessions, or small-time contractors who couldn't run a successful business to save their lives. The net result was to opt for the lower-paying certainty of a city job, where the New Jersey public employees unions would prevent them from firing anyone for at least a month or two, even after they found his dead body propped up behind his desk, as long as he had a pencil in his hand.

Ace also learned that the best times to go to any city office was in the middle of their lunch hour or at 4:15, just before closing. That was usually when the counters were staffed by low-ranking clerks, who either were in a hurry, or didn't care much to begin with. That's what made it the best time of the day to get what you want, particularly if you came bearing gifts.

Ace and Dorothy entered the Licensing and Inspection Division at 12:30 p.m., purposely in the middle of lunch hour, wearing their new hardhats and carrying a large Donato's carry-out pizza box. Behind the counter stood a bored, middle-aged clerk with thinning hair, a beer gut, and a large pin-on city nametag on his shirt pocket that read, "Hi! I'm Larry!" As they approached the counter, Ace would have liked to think that the clerk's eyes were on him, but he knew they were split between the gorgeous blonde standing at his side and the pizza box.

"Hi, Larry," Ace began with a big smile as he set the pizza box down on the counter. "I'm Jerry with Consolidated Electric. We're bidding some electrical work over at the Bimini Bay. You suppose we can take a quick look at the building and electrical plans?"

"Sure. All the city file copies are digitized now. You've got to order them, and that usually takes 48 hours. But there's always work going on over at the Bimini, so we keep a hard copy of the full set in the conference room next door."

"Hey, thanks, man," Ace replied as he turned and began to walk away.

"Uh, the pizza, we can't accept gifts."

"Gift? Oh, no, that's just trash," Ace told him as he lifted the cover and let Larry see the fresh, hot pie inside. "We were going to throw it in the dumpster outside, but maybe you can do that for me... since it's trash... and therefore not worth anything. So it's not a gift, is it?" Ace smiled as he turned away, watched Larry raise the top of the pizza box, peek inside again, and slip it under the counter.

"That should keep him out of our hair for a while," Ace said as they stepped out and walked down the hall to the conference room. There was a large stack of bound blueprints strewn across the long table.

"Where do we start?" Dorothy asked him.

"I'm looking for the set with the roof, the penthouse, and the helipad, the basement level, and the first floor admin area. We'll start with those — the structural and electrical plans in particular. Let me look at them. We'll photograph anything interesting with our cell phones, but I'd like to be out of here in twenty, maybe thirty minutes."

It took them closer to forty minutes, but in the end, Ace had most of what he wanted.

"Learn anything?" Dorothy asked as they stacked the plans in the center of the table.

"Yeah, the major is right. That place is a fortress. If we want in, it'll take some serious stealth and guile."

When they walked back through the office, Larry the code clerk was still standing behind the counter where they left him, his mouth full of pizza, and several fresh tomato stains on his white shirt.

"Thanks, man," Ace smiled and waved. Larry waved back, smiled, and mumbled something, but Ace couldn't understand the words.

"Did you get what he said?" Dorothy asked as they went out the door.

"Yeah, something about putting more anchovies on the trash next time."

"Okay, where now, back to the Holiday Inn? We need to grab our stuff."

"No, there's an electronics store I found just west of the city, off the toll road," Ace said. "The major wants me to see if we can tap into the hotel's security camera feeds and Wi-Fi the video over to the boat."

"Can you do that?" she questioned.

"I think so. If I can get my hands on the right kind of modem, a couple of power packs, and two signal boosters, we'll go ahead and do it right after dark."

CHAPTER NINETEEN

At 8:50 that evening, Bob slowly maneuvered the big Ferrenti yacht through the dark water and into its reserved slip in the small marina across the harbor, taking the time to turn the boat around so the bow pointed at the flashing neon palm trees on the Bimini Bay hotel tower. With some delicate back and forth, he finally managed to get the big boat pressed against the line of tires that lined the pier, where the others were waiting to come aboard.

"Linda, go down and toss them the lines, before this big beast moves again," he yelled to tell her, but she had already run down the stairs to the lower deck and was chattering excitedly with Dorothy and Patsy about the boat as the three women finally tied it off.

Each boat slip had one of those cutesy, four-foot-tall, white fiberglass lighthouses into which a boat can connect all its utilities. The larger slips like this one had three of them, each with a working light on top to illuminate the dock. Looking down on the pier, he saw Ace, Dorothy, Ernie, Patsy, the Geeks and their bags. Most of them were looking up at the boat with their mouths hanging open. He went down to the aft deck and ran out the gangplank.

"Throw your stuff below," he told them, "and grab a beer. The boat can hold eleven, and we'll figure out sleeping arrangements for those of you who aren't staying at the hotels."

Looking at the faces as they paired off and came on board, he knew rank would have its privileges, as it inevitably did. He and Linda kept the front stateroom, while Ace and Dorothy took the other. Ernie and Koz could have one of the two side cabins. Patsy and Jimmy came aboard with their arms wrapped around each other's waists and her head leaning against his shoulder. Given the inevitability of that situation, he gave them the other side cabin. That left Ronald, The Batman, and Bulldog with the three bunks in the crew's quarters aft. Even that small cabin would seem luxurious for the two Army guys, and he doubted Ronald's experience was much different. Since Chester and Lonzo were cleaning at night and still had rooms at the Siesta Cove, the numbers worked, at least until things blew up here in Atlantic City and they all bailed. By that time, the extra bodies could sleep on the floor in the lounge, because it wouldn't matter.

The group assembled in the main lounge and paused, marveling at the gorgeous interior. It was airy and open, featuring a large, C-shaped, white leather couch along the port bulkhead, a large galley set beyond that, and refrigerators and coolers down the starboard side. While the others got settled in their cabins, he grabbed a beer and sat down at the boat's dining room table with Ace. The big

Master Sergeant pulled out his cell phone and showed him the photographs he had taken of the Bimini Bay building plans.

"The only way up to the roof is the private elevator to the penthouse, or the emergency stairs with those big mag-locks at the top and bottom."

"Or rappel down from a helicopter?" Bob asked.

"Rappel?" Ace laughed. "When we were all younger and a hell of a lot dumber. But the big thing I discovered looking at the plans is that there's something really odd about that Maintenance Building addition on the back of the building near the loading dock."

"You mean that rinky-dink cinder block thing?" Bob asked as Jimmy came in.

Ace motioned him over. "Hey, take a look at this, Jimmy. There's an entire second floor under this addition with major redundant power, a raised-floor on the lower level, and big cooling loads. The only thing that could possibly be for is a huge server array."

"That's a lot more data capacity than three hotels need," Jimmy agreed.

"And the door from the loading dock is reinforced steel, if it opens at all," Ace said. "So, the only way in might be through the basement, with more steel doors and mag-locks."

"What could they possibly want that much data storage for?"

"Well, if we can't physically get in, we can try 'virtual' access," Jimmy smiled. "Ronald and I have been working our buns off all afternoon…"

Bob looked at him and then at Patsy, who had her head on his chest, both arms wrapped around his waist and enough of "that" sleepy glow left to force a skeptical response. "Really?" Bob asked.

"Well, most of the afternoon," Jimmy blushed, trying to keep his composure. "But we couldn't get into the really good stuff. We need some passwords or their programming codes. Without those, we're afraid we might set off some alarm bells in their system."

"We don't want to do that yet, so hold off. How did the janitor thing work out?" Bob turned and asked Koz, while motioning for Ronald to join them. "I've got to think that's our best shot at getting the passwords and the key cards Jimmy wants."

"Chester and Lonzo got hired, just as you thought they would," Koz told him. "They started at 4:00 p.m. on the evening shift, cleaning the back offices at the Tuscany Tower and the Bimini Bay. Ronald and Jimmy have a lot more experience with what goes on in an office than any of us do. They told Lonzo and Chester that a lot of the secretaries get lazy and leave their passwords pinned to the walls of their cubicles, taped to the underside of their keyboards, or just sitting loose in their top desk drawers. They should be back by midnight, then we'll see what they were able to find in the personnel, security, and finance offices."

"Clever," Bob said.

"Actually, it isn't," Ronald corrected him. "Convincing someone to give you their passwords and employee numbers with a telephone con, or simply finding them laying around in an office is how most hacking and data theft is done these days. Even the best security system breaks down when someone is dumb enough to hand you the keys."

"In a few hours we'll see what they were able to come up with and how useful it will be," Jimmy added. "Most data's segregated by department, so even if they were able to get a few passwords, they might only let us into part of the system."

"You know, while we're waiting..." Ronald began to fidget.

"We thought it might be useful if Ronald and I went in and took a quick look around the hotel and casino, in the flesh, so to speak," Jimmy explained. "You know, if we can see the setup, the cameras, the alarms, the slots and gambling tables, and all the rest, it might make more sense later, when we try to get into their computers."

"Maybe play a little, like the rest of the tourists," Ronald said under his breath.

"You two are critical to the mission, I don't want you..." Bob tried to explain.

"Neither do we. We'll be careful," Jimmy answered.

Ace looked at Bob and said, "What would it harm? Nobody's seen them. Dorothy and I can tag along and keep an eye out."

"Stay low key, and if you're going to gamble, don't lose too much."

Jimmy looked at Ronald and they both giggled. "Lose? Mister B., we don't lose at all, at least not at blackjack or some of the other card games."

"Jimmy, everybody loses," Ace corrected them. "That's how the casinos stay in business."

"Not us. We never lose, not unless we want to. Ronald and I are card counters," Jimmy looked around at the group and announced proudly. "It's how we paid for graduate school."

Bob stared at him. "I thought the casinos all went to a six-deck system, with mechanical shuffling, intelligent shoes, and all that stuff, just to stop those systems."

"They did," Jimmy replied, "but it doesn't matter."

"You mean you can keep six decks of cards in your head?" Linda asked, skeptical.

"Well, *I* can, but most counters use a plus and minus system to keep track of the values that are played. It's not nearly as good, but it does improve the odds somewhat. Unfortunately, if the casino has implemented the security systems you mentioned, it becomes more difficult."

"Then, how do you do it?" Bob asked.

"Me? Well..." Jimmy sounded embarrassed, "I can actually remember all the cards that are played — four decks, six decks, eight decks, it really doesn't matter. It's a little 'gift' I have, and none of the casino countermeasures can stop that. But we did get caught a couple of times," Jimmy admitted, shrugging it off.

"Yeah, like at the Sun Casino in Connecticut," Ronald added.

"That Indian joint?" Ace asked.

"And out in Vegas, at the Venetian, the Bellagio, and Harrah's. We kind of got a little... carried away, and we weren't too careful. We won too much, but those were the first times we tried it."

"You guys have expensive tastes," Bob laughed. "You like to get beat up by the best."

"It was a long time ago, when we were freshmen out at Berkeley," Jimmy said.

"Young and dumb, who'd 'a guessed?" Ace smiled.

"But you're right, in Vegas, we thought they were going to beat the crap out of us, and the Indians almost did. They said they could do anything they wanted with us, since we were on the Res, and it's a foreign country. They even had some hanks of hair hanging on the wall in their security office and they threatened us with some big hunting knives. They said they could scalp us, and nobody could do anything about it."

"But we knew they were just trying to scare us... and I guess they did," Ronald said.

"With the Indians, we weren't really sure," Jimmy added. "They kept all of our money, which is the same thing they did out in Vegas, but in the end they all just tossed us into the parking lot."

"That isn't all they did. I'll bet they also took your pictures," Bob warned them. "The casinos have a national database on cheaters, and I'm pretty sure you guys are in it now."

"That was in our long-haired, geeky days, Mister B.," Jimmy smiled. "We don't look anything like that anymore."

"Great! That makes me feel a whole lot better," Bob said, trying to keep a straight face.

"Don't worry, that's when we learned we've got to intentionally lose a lot of hands," Ronald added. "That way, they don't notice all the big ones we're winning. But tonight we'll only break even. Promise."

Bob stared up at them and tried not to smile. "Okay, but I'm sending The Batman and Bulldog with you. Ace and Dorothy will catch up when we're done here," Bob told them. "I don't want you getting grabbed by Carbonari's security people. So no winning, you got that!"

"Telling a gambler not to win?" Linda chirped. "Oh, lots of luck with that."

"Can I go too?" Patsy pleaded.

"Absolutely not!" Bob told her. "After our last trip, your pretty face is all over their security cameras and computers — Linda's and mine, too — so you stay here with us. But Jimmy, make sure you're back by 12:30. Chester and Lonzo should be here by then."

The Geeks couldn't wait to get off the boat. Batman and Bulldog followed closely behind, glancing back long enough to give Bob and Ace an amused look. As they disappeared down the pier, Bob saw Patsy going forward toward her cabin and called out to her, "Hey, girl, can you come here for a minute."

She turned around and gave him a frown, still pouting, but she slowly walked back. "You aren't going to lecture me about Jimmy again, are you? Because…"

"Nope, no lecture, not this time. Unlike my wife, I pick my battles." That put a big smile on her face, until Bob told her the rest of the news. "I got a call from North Carolina when we were on the way up here. It seems somebody broke into your house in Fayetteville again and really tore the place apart. The police and the Army CID people think it wasn't just vandalism. The burglars were looking for something. Do you have any idea what that might be?"

"Me? No," she answered. "Maybe they just saw an empty house. I'm not sure if I left any lights on, and we barely got to meet any of the neighbors."

"Okay, but if you think of anything, let me know. There were questions after Vinnie's last tour in Afghanistan, and the CID's going to want to talk to you when we get back."

"The CID? What did I do?" she asked, sounding afraid.

"Nobody's saying *you* did anything; but you own the house with Vinnie, and he's the one they would have really liked to talk to."

"All he left me is that big mortgage he took out a week ago to pay off the casino, but you said they tore the place apart?"

"Yes, and if you think of anything, have any questions, just want to talk, or want me to get you a lawyer, let me know, okay?"

"Yeah, sure," she said as she turned and walked away, suddenly looking shaken.

Ace shook his head. "Double-down Vinnie strikes again."

"God, I hope not. Did you get anywhere with the video feeds?" Bob asked him.

"Oh, yeah," Ace smiled. "Operation Bootleg is up and running; and as it turns out, it wasn't all that hard. Dorothy and I played electrical contractors again, complete with the hard hats we stole from the conference wing. Jimmy told me what to look for at the store, what to get, and how to install it. He's smart, real smart. Too bad the Army can't figure out how to get kids like that and keep them," Ace said as he shook his head. "Ah, hell, I guess it wouldn't be practical, anyway, would it? Two different worlds."

"More like two different universes."

"Point taken. Anyway, we hit the hotel around 7:00 when all the regular staff was gone. The junction boxes were tucked behind some bushes, but easy to get at. That let us work out of sight and hide our modem behind their boxes. We were in and out in five minutes. We put the booster in my rental car and powered it off one of the car batteries I bought."

"And it works?"

"Five-by-five, but come up to the bridge for a moment. I have something you need to see." Ace said. "You too, Ernie. I think we could use your expertise."

"This should be good," Bob said as the three men and Dorothy walked the two flights of narrow stairs up to the dark flying bridge, where Koz sat in the captain's chair with an M110 sniper rifle with night vision scope lying across his thighs. In his hands were a pair of Zeiss 8x56 binoculars, which Bob had found in the master suite and they were using to scan the Bimini Bay and its boat marina.

"How's it going?" Bob asked. "See anything?"

"No, just your normal gambling and stuff-yourself-at-the-buffet crowd, plus the new gunmen Ace spotted."

"The new gunmen?" Bob's head snapped around.

"Here, I'll show you," Ace answered as he opened the notebook computer and hit replay. "I have the video feeds from both cameras going to DVD. One camera covers the door into the casino from the parking garage, while the other covers the big front door under the portico. Wait one. Let me find the time marker on the disk."

Dorothy stepped in and continued, "Right after we finished hooking it all up and turned on the modem, we drove down the parking ramp and stopped at the garage exit. Two dark-blue Mercedes limos zipped past us heading for the main hotel entrance."

"We followed them. I'm not sure why," Ace went on. "Sure enough, they pulled under the portico and seven guys got out. They stretched, as if they'd been in the cars for a while, which was when your friend Carbonari came out and greeted them. All smiles and hugs. I watched them, and they reminded me of the clowns we ran into in those woods outside Chicago — same cars, same ugly sports coats and gold chains, and the same beer guts."

"Reinforcements," Bob quickly concluded.

"You got it. Here, watch the video, I'll slow it down."

Bob and Ernie leaned in closer and saw four Gumbahs get out of the lead car. As they did, it was easy to make out the shoulder and waist holsters they were wearing. The drivers popped open the car trunks and flipped their keys to the valets. At first, Carbonari was smiling, but as the Don saw three more men pile out of the second car, Bob thought he appeared much less enthusiastic. Still, they all exchanged handshakes and back slaps as they headed for the front doors.

"The license plates on the cars are from New York. If you can zoom in on the numbers, I can run a trace on them," Ernie said.

"I figured you'd say that, already done," Ace said as he handed him a slip of paper.

"I'll do it now," Ernie said as he pulled out his cell phone and pressed a speed-dial number. "Gladys, this is Captain Travis over in Organized Crime. Can you run two plates for me...? Great. They're New York State, numbers BSW-7522 and BSW-7523... Yes, I'll wait," he told her. "It shouldn't take too long," he said to the others as they watched the video recording again, carefully examining the faces. "Yes, what was that...?" Ernie said as Gladys came back on the line. "Okay, thanks." Ernie hung up and turned toward the others and told them, "They are both registered to 'Brooklyn Solid Waste,' probably another mob front, but there are no 'wants or warrants' out on them."

Bob leaned in and watched the video a second time, and a third. "Yep, reinforcements, but that raises an interesting question. Who don't you see?"

The others leaned in, but they all shook their heads, not getting it.

"Shaka Corliss and the two Hulks. Think about it — reinforcements arrive from Brooklyn, Carbonari comes out to greet them, and his head of security and two muscle men are nowhere to be seen?"

"Another sign that we'll never see them again," Ernie agreed.

It was almost 1:00 a.m. when the Geeks and their entourage managed to find their way back to the marina from the casino. Jimmy and Ronald were giggly and amped-up as they came aboard the big boat, still dressed in their "incognito casino outfits," as Jimmy called them. He wore a black porkpie hat with dark sunglasses and a loud flower-print Hawaiian shirt, while Ronald opted for a flat-brim New York Yankees baseball hat, dark sunglasses, and a black turtleneck. Patsy met them like a new puppy who had been locked up alone all evening, which was pretty much the case, as she jumped up and down and giggled right along with them. Ace, Dorothy, the Batman, and Bulldog took up the rear, and headed for the refrigerator for beers.

The two Geeks bounced over to the couch where Bob, Linda, Ernie, and Koz sat. They pulled several large wads of crumpled-up cash from their pockets and dropped it on the coffee table. "Almost $5,300," Ronald said. "I can't believe how hot we were."

"I thought you weren't going to win, only break even," Bob glared at him.

"We tried!" Jimmy pleaded. "We only played maybe ten or fifteen hands of blackjack, just a taste, and I'm not even sure we won there. Most of that's from craps, Caribbean stud, some slots, and even the roulette table. We kept moving around, but we just kept winning."

Bob stared at him. "Well, I'm glad you had fun."

"And I'm glad you didn't get your legs broken," Ace said.

"Or get scalped," Linda added.

That was when Lonzo and Chester came aboard, still wearing their blue work pants and shirt with a large "Boardwalk Services" embroidered patch across the back. They paused in the middle of the stairs and saw the others laughing and drinking beer. "I don't know, about you Lonzo," Chester said, "but I think we got the short end of this deal."

"Somebody get those guys a beer too," Bob laughed. "It looks like they earned one."

"It really wasn't all that bad, just boring," Lonzo said as Ace handed them both a cold Bud. "And I wouldn't want to do it for a living. The Army's bad enough."

"Did you have any luck finding passwords?" Bob asked.

"Jimmy was right; it wasn't hard at all. Somebody spends all that money on complicated systems and passwords with all sorts of random letters and numbers, and then the worker bees leave them out in plain sight."

"And nobody saw you?"

"I don't think so," Chester answered. "There are a couple of cameras in each office, mostly in the corners. They cover the room, but from a high angle; and they can't see below the desktops. As we went around sweeping, dusting, and picking up trash, it was pretty easy to bend over and look around the computers, and grab the pieces of paper they wrote the passwords on. When we found one, we wrote the name down, too."

"Okay, give all those to Jimmy and Ronald. And Jimmy," Bob turned and told him, "Get on these first thing in the morning. Now let's get some sleep."

"Before we all disappear," Ernie turned to Bob and asked, "Ace said you need a key card to get up to the roof and into the basement?"

"We hoped Jimmy and Ronald might be able to work with the ones they gave the janitors, but those might not cover the really secure areas."

"Their security guards would have those, wouldn't they?" Ernie asked.

"Corliss and Van Gries certainly would," Bob answered. "And maybe the supervisors and the Gumbahs, but probably not the ordinary, blue-coat rent-a-cops."

"Then why don't we steal one?" Ernie asked. Bob stared at him and began to ask something, but Ernie continued. "Those same guys, wouldn't their cell phones also be useful?"

"Uh, yeah, they'd have all sorts of stuff on them — calls, numbers, and probably e-mail access, server information, and a lot of other things... but steal one? Who, you?"

"No, no," Ernie smiled and shook his head. "I mean a professional pickpocket. Look, there's this guy named Dimitri Karides, whom I arrested at O'Hare just before your escapade up there. If I hadn't been checking some other stuff on video, and started watching him for four or five days, I'd have never caught him. Even using slow motion, only rarely could I figure out what he was doing. The guy's that good. Turns out there's an international pickpocket school in Columbia. He said they wanted him to stay and teach, but they couldn't afford him."

"Can we?" Bob asked.

"Oh, he's cheap now," Ernie laughed. "He's sitting in Cook County Jail."

"And you think you can get him out to come here to steal something for us?"

"Are you kidding? Oh, I can come up with one reason or another to 'badge him out;' and if I promise him a good steak, he'd do anything to get out of that place for a few days. The odd thing is, he's really a nice guy. Short, fat, thick glasses, with a big smile: he looks like a middle-aged bookkeeper. If Dorothy can fly me up there tomorrow in that Gulfstream, I can have him back here by mid-afternoon. Getting Dimi to steal something is the easy part; getting him to stop will be the problem."

CHAPTER TWENTY

At 8:30 the next morning, Bob was on the flying bridge with Ace, trying to stay awake as he stared at the video feeds from the casino entrances on his notebook computer, when his cell phone rang.

"Burke," he answered.

"Bobbie, Arnold Stansky here," he heard and immediately sat up at attention.

"Yes, sir, what can I..." he started to ask, but Stansky didn't wait.

"No time for that. Look, normally, I'd have O'Connor call you, but I wanted you to hear this from me, direct. It's about those fingerprints and the blood."

"Yes, sir. What did you learn?"

"Too damned much. For starters, any time you scratch a problem around here, you find the goddamn CIA underneath. They kept pulling that national security crap with *me*, if you can believe it! As if they thought *that* was gonna fly. I had to raise hell with the Deputy DCI himself out at Langley to get a straight story. And I only got that after I threatened to take the whole thing to the Chief of Staff and the Sec-Def, if they didn't come clean."

"How could they argue with prints and a dead body, sir?"

"You think? Anyway, the stiff is an ex-Navy SEAL named Peter Kowalski."

"A SEAL? What the hell was he..."

"I bypassed the CIA. I went to the DoD database, which chained the prints to the Navy; and then I personally called the CNO. No one likes to air their dirty linen to another service, but when they learned the CIA was behind this, they were as pissed as I was. After seven years on active duty, Kowalski was court martialed and given a General Discharge 'for the good of the service.' Seems like there were a number of allegations regarding brutality and mistreatment of prisoners, which are notoriously hard to prove, a similar rape charge, and then one against a female Marine, eighteen months ago. Guess where he popped back up?"

"Oh, don't tell me," Bob said in disgust. "Not that same rogue Ops group in Mosul, the one they think hit the Baghdad Museum?"

"Bingo!"

"But what was he doing in Fayetteville?"

"You're slow this morning, Ghost. The museum gold, two break-ins at that house, Vinnie Pastorini — why else would they ignore a KIA and go right back in to search the place again? It has to be the gold. They think it's inside the house, or that the girl knows where it is."

Bob thought about it for a moment. "But they tore the whole house apart, all of it. If they found the gold, wouldn't they have stopped and left?"

"I don't know if they found it or not, but I haven't told you the worst part. The blood on the doorframe was Benson's."

"Benson's?"

"The Army blood-types every recruit who comes in. But six or seven years ago, we also began recording DNA profiles on the blood samples of all of our special ops troops in case we ever needed to make post-mortem IDs. The blood on that door was a DNA match to Benson."

"Too bad Patsy didn't aim a bit further right," Bob told him.

"No," Stansky replied. "That would be too easy. I want him to answer for what he's done."

At the same time, Dorothy waited while the ground crew topped off the Gulfstream G-550's fuel tanks with some fresh Jet-A, and then taxied to the flight line at Atlantic City International Airport. After she finished her pre-flight check and filed her flight plan with the tower, she turned and looked back into the main cabin at Ernie. He had settled into one of the plush leather-upholstered swivel chairs and opened the morning's *Philadelphia Inquirer*.

"Hey, Ernie," she called out. "Why don't you come up here and sit with me?"

"Isn't there some FAA rule against pretending to be a co-pilot?"

"Oh, maybe in the big commercial airliners," she said as he came forward and wedged himself into the other seat. "Not one of these."

He looked down at the complicated array of screens and controls and said, "I hope you're not expecting me to fly this thing."

"Don't worry. We'll be on autopilot. It flies itself. All you have to do is look out the windows for other airplanes and bring me coffee."

"That assumes I can ever get out of this seat again," Ernie said as he buckled the harness and looked around the cockpit. "I'm 6'4" tall and 240 pounds. They don't make machines like this for guys my size. I guess that's why I went into the Army."

"You could have ended up in a tank, you know."

"Worse, I ended up an Army cop. I never liked small jail cells, either."

When they finished laughing, she got her clearance, rolled to the end of the taxiway, turned right, and stopped at the end of the runway. "They have an incoming flight. As soon as it lands, they'll clear us to take off." In less than a minute, another sleek long-range corporate jet touched down and rolled toward the terminal. "That's a Dassault Falcon," Dorothy told him as she pushed the stick forward. "It's French. You don't see too many of them over here."

The twin Rolls-Royce BR-710 turbo fan engines roared and pressed Ernie back in his padded chair. "Wow! That's a kick in the chest" he said.

As they raced down the runway, Ernie looked over at the Dassault. It had parked in a transient space at the side of the runway. As they passed, he saw that its stairs were down and the cargo compartment in its belly was open. Five men were unloading equipment bags and metal gun cases onto the tarmac. As they did, two black stretch limos drove in the airport's service gate and pulled up next to the airplane. On their doors, he saw the name "Bimini Bay" with the bright casino logo below.

"Can you call the tower and find out where that airplane came from?" Ernie asked. "I'd like to know if it was New York or Philadelphia."

Dorothy keyed her chin mic and said, "ACA tower, this is Gulf Stream 795. That Dassault that just landed, can you tell me where it came from?"

"Gulfstream 795, ACA tower. From the Middle East, I think. Yeah, make it Bahrain, via Alexandria, the Azores, and LaGuardia. Long trip."

"Thanks, ACA tower. See you later this afternoon," Dorothy said, and signed off. "Why the question, Ernie?" she asked as the sleek Gulfstream continued to gain altitude and turned west.

"Maybe nothing, but dark sunglasses, short hair, suntans, nylon equipment bags, and gun cases — none of those guys looked like duck hunters to me."

"And the two Bimini Bay limos? They drove right through the gate and never stopped, like they own the place."

"I ran the Chicago police detachment at O'Hare for four years," Ernie told her, "and you can't drive an unauthorized vehicle out onto one of *our* flight lines, by-passing TSA and customs without a lot of bells going off."

"Looks like this isn't O'Hare."

"Neither is LaGuardia, I'm afraid."

"Want me to let the boat know?

"Yeah. It might just be old cop nerves, but it looks to me that they're bringing in more reinforcements, and I think Bob and Ace should know about it."

"Roger that," she said, reaching for her microphone again.

Ernie was right when he said that New York's LaGuardia Airport wasn't like Chicago's O'Hare. If you put enough money in a white envelope and handed it to the right people at LaGuardia's small general aviation terminal, no one gave a damn who you were or what you were bringing in. As long as the right wise guy make the arrangements and you were in transit to another airport, they'd stamp your passport and clear you through customs while you and your luggage sat on the airplane. All in all, it was a most civilized system, Theo Van Gries thought, especially when you want to bring a number of highly specialized and unique pieces of equipment with you.

Theo had lost track of how many hours they had been in the air since they took off from Bahrain the day before, or perhaps it was the day before that. All he did know was that they were on their third aircrew, and the six passengers in back had done little other than sleep, play cards, and clean their weapons since they took off. Three of the men were former Dutch Marines like him, one was a German from the Bundeswehr KSK, and one was a Brit who had spent nine years in the SAS. Like soldiers the world over, they were bored, randy, and more than ready to kick someone's ass.

When the Dassault took off from LaGuardia, Theo asked the pilot to call ahead to his brother. "Tell him we will be there at 8:30, and we would appreciate a van to pick us up."

He and his men had just come down the stairs from the plush passenger compartment and were unloading their luggage and equipment onto the tarmac when the automatic gate near the terminal rolled open and two long black cars raced in. As they screeched to a halt next to the Dassault, Theo's right hand reached inside his jacket for the 9-millimeter Walther automatic he kept in a shoulder holster. The FBI? INS? But instead of trouble, the limo drivers alighted from the cars and quickly opened the rear doors. Out jumped six scantily clad casino cocktail waitresses, dancing and laughing. They held glasses and bottles of champagne in their hands and beckoned for Theo and his men to join them inside the cars. His men stood there, open mouthed, and then they laughed. Over the years, there hadn't been much they hadn't seen when they arrived "in country" at some broken-down, third-world airport or jungle landing strip, but this was a first.

"Our velcoming committee, Herr Leutnant?" Klaus Reimer, the German asked.

"His brother is a fine Dutch gentleman," Joost DeVries, one of his Dutch Marines replied.

"Throw the gear in the car trunks, and let's get going," Eric Smit, his First Sergeant ordered. "And with all due respect, if he was *that* fine of a gentleman, the girls would've gotten on the airplane in Bahrain or Alexandria, not here for a ten-minute ride into town."

They all laughed, and Reggie MacGregor, the Brit added, "Well, from what I've seen out of you blokes, I'm not sure those tarts would have survived the experience."

"And from what I've seen," another Dutchman, Joost DeVries, added, "I'm not sure they'll survive the ride into town."

As they laughed and piled into the two limos, three per car, Theo warned, "Mind the bubbly. This may not look like Afghanistan, but they brought us here for a reason." He got into the front passenger seat of the lead limo, leaving two of his men in the back with the three cocktail waitresses. They didn't seem to complain. On the other hand, the driver wasn't used to customers who sat in front with him. He gave Theo an odd look until the Dutchman said, "What are you waiting for? Go."

It took less than fifteen minutes for the two big limos to navigate the Expressway and the city and pull under the glittering front portico of the Bimini Bay Hotel and Casino. When the cars stopped, two doormen dressed in tuxedos, top hats, and white gloves opened the side doors of the limo. His men piled out the back doors with champagne glasses and bimbos in hand, wondering what planet they had landed on. Theo slowly emerged from the front seat into the sensory assault of colorful flashing lights and loud music. He grimaced as he looked around, finally seeing his older brother Martijn push his way through the tall floor-to-ceiling glass doors.

"Theo!" Martijn called to him. "Thank you so much for coming. I know it has been…"

Theo gave him a cold stare. "It is a job, no more and no less." He turned his eyes and saw four bellmen open the limo's trunks. They began to unload the canvas overnight bags and "equipment" cases, and stack them on two luggage carts. "No!" he snapped. He turned toward his men and told them in Dutch, "Carry your own bags and don't let them out of your sight."

"Let us get you inside and over to registration," Martijn said as he put his arm around Theo's shoulders. "I have some nice rooms reserved for you and your men."

"No registrations and no names," Theo told him. "Just get the keys, if you please. I want the rooms to remain vacant on your inventory."

"I should have anticipated that. Unfortunately, we are in different lines of work, aren't we, my brother?"

"That is why you called me, isn't it?" Theo said as he let Martijn lead them inside. "Because there are things you cannot do, or will not do."

"Of course." Martijn laughed. "But Donatello needs to speak with you. He has a few issues to discuss."

"Have my other two men, Benson and Kowalski, arrived yet?" Theo asked, looking around suspiciously, always on guard.

"Benson has, within the hour, but I have not seen a second man. Benson is in Donatello's office waiting for you. Do you mind telling me who he is?"

"The American officer I told you about. He served in their Rangers and Delta Force, so we shall see if he knows anything that can help us."

On the flying bridge of *The Enchantress*, Bob sat in the captain's chair with his bare feet propped on the top of the yacht's extensive control console and his laptop balanced on his legs. His eyes were glued to the laptop's screen as he watched the rotating camera views switch from the casino's front and rear doors. Ace was in the mate's chair next to him, scanning the Bimini Bay's entry road, the boat marina, and the rooftop through the binoculars.

"You know," Ace said. "I think Zeiss makes the best long-range optics this side of the Hubble telescope. You can count the hairs on an elephant's ass at a thousand meters with these."

"Just don't drop them. They also make the most expensive ones."

They'd been at this since 07:00, shortly after sunrise, and could already feel themselves going brain-dead. Two hours of this was the maximum anyone could take and still keep their focus, so they were due to rotate jobs in another fifteen minutes.

"Want more coffee?" Ace asked.

"No, that would make three, and I'm jumpy enough," Bob replied as the screen switched back to the casino's big front portico and he saw two black limos pull in and stop.

"Check out the front entry," he told Ace as he froze the camera rotation and watched the doormen and four bellmen with luggage carts come out and surround the two cars in an elaborate show of service. Ace focused the Zeiss binoculars on the doormen as they opened the car doors and a half dozen casino girls and casually dressed men piled out of the cars.

"Heavy hitters," Ace agreed. "They must be the characters Dorothy said she saw at the airport a little while ago. Look, the hotel even sent the bimbos to fetch them."

As Bob watched, he saw Martijn Van Gries come out and approach the lead car. "And Martijn Van Gries, too," Bob quickly told him. "Check out the other five." He watched them push the bellmen aside and unload the car trunks themselves. "Canvas gear bags, hard cases, the boots and casual clothes — they look just like us."

"What does that tell you?"

"Somebody brought in even more reinforcements, like Ernie said, but those aren't Mafia. They look like Special Ops to me, maybe not American, but somebody's."

Bob watched as Martijn Van Gries shook hands with the man who got out of the passenger seat of the lead car. They were smiling and talking. "Recognize any of them?" Bob asked.

"Didn't Van Gries tell you he had a brother?"

Bob took the binoculars and looked for himself. "A lieutenant in the Black Devils. We may have met him in Iraq, but that was a long time ago, and I'm not sure."

"Well, if that's him, it looks like he's gone over to the 'dark side,' Obi-Wan."

"Really?" Bob laughed as they watched the six men go inside.

As they entered the Bimini Bay lobby, Martijn Van Gries swung by the large, glitzy reception desk and had the front desk manager give him the keys to six empty rooms, which he quickly distributed as he led them to the casino's back service corridor and the executive elevator to the penthouse.

"Donatello has been under a lot of pressure from his New York superiors, who have sent some additional men down here, so kindly be on your best behavior."

A thin smile crossed Theo's lips as his brother pushed open the hand-carved, decorative double doors to Carbonari's penthouse suite and they all walked in. A large, olive-skinned Italian in a well-tailored suit and tie sat behind a wide antique desk. Benson sat alone in an overstuffed chair off to the side, looking bored, while four bulky middle-aged men in slacks and sports coats stood along the far wall, eyeing Theo and his men. They were obviously American Mafia, Theo thought, perhaps ten years older, twenty pounds heavier, and thirty IQ points fewer than his own professional soldiers. Including himself, there were now thirteen men in the penthouse office. Theo looked down and gave Benson a brief hard look as he turned back toward Carbonari.

Carbonari stood, walked around the desk and extended a warm smile and his hand to Theo. "Martijn's told me a lot of stories about you," Donatello told him. Theo replied with a polite nod and a firm handshake, thinking that despite his size, Carbonari had the soft grip of a woman.

"It appears you gentlemen are ready to get to work," Carbonari went on. "But before you do, there's some people I want you to meet. This is 'Cheech' Mazoulli, one of my associates from Brooklyn." He nodded toward one of them. "I lost some security people, and Cheech's boss was kind enough to loan him and some of his men to me for a few days. They'll work with my regular security guards and keep an eye on the hotel and casino for me."

Theo stared at Mazoulli and his men, noting the bulges under their arms, but he did not extend his hand to Mazoulli, any more than Mazoulli did to him. "My brother hired us to eliminate a specific problem Mister Carbonari has. I assume you and your men will handle the hotel and casino, and stay out of our hair, much as we will attend to his problem and stay out of yours. Since we are all armed, I believe that is essential. Is that agreeable?"

Mazoulli stared back at him and then turned on Carbonari. "What's this crap, Donnie? I thought Angelo put us in charge of security down here."

Theo watched Carbonari's face. When Mazoulli used Carbonari's nickname, he saw an imperceptible narrowing of Carbonari's eyes. "I'm afraid that's not quite right, Cheech. These guys are here doing some personal work for me," Carbonari told him. "You and your crew will be in charge of hotel and casino security, especially around the table games and poker rooms. But there's been some threats directed at me by some disgruntled customers, some Army types. That's why Theo and his men are here, to deal with them for me. So, as he said, you do your job, and he'll do his."

Mazoulli shrugged and motioned his men toward the door. "I got two more guys goin' through the other two hotels. You want I should introduce you to them too?"

"I think we shall recognize them," Theo answered with a thin smile.

Mazoulli looked at him and frowned. "I'll say one thing, dis guy's got balls. He any freakin' good?"

"Let me worry about that, Cheech. I wanted us all to meet, but now he and I have some details we need to talk about, if you don't mind."

Mazoulli nodded to his men and he led them out of the room.

Carbonari closed the door behind them and said, "You won't have any problems."

"I never have problems, merely interesting opportunities," Theo told him, and then turned toward Benson. "How nice that you could finally join us, Captain. Do not run away; you and I need to talk."

Benson leaned back in the overstuffed chair and nodded, but he did not reply.

Theo turned back toward Carbonari and said, "I understand this Major Burke has taken a dislike to you and some of your people?"

"Yeah, well, some things got out of hand last week," Donatello began as he walked back to his desk, and sat on the edge. "One of Burke's former sergeants lost a lot of money in the casino. He climbed out a window as he attempted to get away from my security people, but he slipped and fell off a ledge. It was an accident. Even the local police and the coroner said so, but Burke doesn't seem to agree. He holds me responsible."

Theo thought about it for a moment and asked, "Was it an accident?"

"We're a casino. Dead men don't pay off their markers, so we're the last ones who'd ever want to snuff the guy. We tried to explain that to Burke. He came here with the cash to pay off Pastorini's debt, but after Pastorini took his swan dive into the parking lot, Burke wouldn't give us the rest. Three of my men followed him back to Chicago to try to get him to change his mind."

"Really?" Benson looked up at Carbonari and chuckled. "How did that work out?"

"Not very well," Carbonari replied, visibly annoyed by Benson's flippant tone. "They got the worst of it and ended up in jail, which is why I had to bring in some help from New York to fill in for them."

"So, he took out three of your security guards?" Benson asked. "How many men did Burke have?"

Carbonari glared at him, getting visibly angrier. "They said Burke was alone, except for two women, a child... and a cat."

"A cat?" Benson shook his head and choked with laughter. "Priceless! I suspect the only reason he let your men live was the presence of the two women and the young child... or maybe the cat had a sensitive stomach."

"I don't find it very freakin' funny!" Carbonari's voice boomed. "I met Burke in Martijn's office a week or two ago. He's a little guy, a runt, how was I supposed to know?"

"You weren't," Benson said as he sat up. "He doesn't look like much, does he? But Pastorini was one of his top men, and he holds you responsible for his death, regardless."

"Yeah, he said he's coming after me now, and that ain't very freakin' funny!"

"Oh, Burke is anything but funny," Benson said as he looked across at Carbonari. "He can be like a... force of nature. Lieutenant Van Gries here is one of the most lethal men I've ever seen operate on a battlefield. His other men here are pretty damned good too," Benson said looking around at them. "For that matter, so am I. But I've never seen anyone as deadly as Burke. If he says he's coming after you, you can count on it; and you are correct to be worried... very worried."

"Sounds to me you're setting up some bullshit excuse for when you fail," Carbonari said as he turned toward Theo and glared at him. "Just tell me, can you stop the guy, or not?"

"In all likelihood, yes," Theo answered. "We know he is coming, but he does not know we are here. That is a critical edge, and we need to keep it."

"There's another bright spot too," Randy Benson said. "We know you are his target, and that makes our job a lot easier."

"All right, what do you need to stop this 'force of nature' of yours?" Carbonari demanded to know.

"I see you have security cameras throughout the hotel and casino," Benson said. "I need to watch all the footage for the last few days to see if Burke is already here and see how many of his people he brought with him."

"Do you have any idea how much footage that is?" Martijn scoffed.

"There isn't any choice. If he isn't here yet, he will be."

"Well, I guess you can watch them in my office," Martijn told him. "Theo can set up there too. That way there will be fewer New York 'distractions' for you to deal with."

"Then, if you do not mind, we shall get to work," Theo said with a curt bow.

Carbonari dismissed them with a nod. "Martijn, stay here for a moment, you and I still have a few accounting issues to resolve."

CHAPTER TWENTY-ONE

Theo, Benson, and Theo's five mercs were in the elevator on their way down to the first floor when Theo turned on Benson. His hard, cold eyes studied the American captain for a moment, and then he asked, "Where have you been? You haven't returned any of my calls."

"North Carolina, trying to track down Pastorini. As you heard, that was a waste of time. So, last night I drove up and got a room here using one of my cover IDs."

"Where is Kowalski?"

"Dead," Benson answered calmly.

Theo stared at him. "I sent you two over here to find Pastorini and the gold. Pastorini is dead, and now you tell me Kowalski is dead as well?"

"Pastorini was killed here in Atlantic City by these morons, but his girlfriend is living in their house near Fort Bragg. We figured that was where he hid the gold, so we broke in, intending to make her talk. Unfortunately, she had a gun, and Kowalski took three in the chest in the bedroom doorway. He was dead before he hit the floor. The little bitch got me too," Benson said as he opened his shirt and showed Theo the bandage on his upper arm. "But don't worry. Kowalski was clean when he went down, no markings or IDs."

"And the gold?" Theo demanded to know.

"I went back two days later, intent on cutting her heart out, but she was gone. I spent all afternoon and evening searching the place. I looked everywhere. Nothing! I figure when we're done here, we can go back down there to Fayetteville and make her talk."

"You think she knows where it is?"

"Well, if she doesn't, we're really screwed, because I don't know where else to look."

"All right. When we are done here, we shall pay her a visit... *all* of us," Theo told them, his eyes still hard and cold. "Now tell me what you know about this man Burke."

"Everyone uses code names over there. We only worked together briefly once or twice, and assignments are secret, so I really don't know much."

"But you just told Carbonari..."

"Would you rather I told him Burke was a supply clerk? How much would he pay us then?" Randy Benson told him with a knowing smile.

By late morning, the Geeks had changed into their swimsuits and were lying in the sun on the white-leather upholstered benches on the aft deck. From the periodic updates they gave Bob, he knew they had worked their way through the half-dozen passwords that Lonzo and Chester brought back from their late-night foray into the janitorial world. One by one, they were taking a run at various personnel, customer support, and accounting systems, so far without much success. Bob spent most of the morning with Ace on the flying bridge. They had extended the low awning over it, allowing them to sit relatively unseen in the shadows.

"You ready for a beer?" Bob asked as he stood and stretched.

"God, yes!" Ace answered. "And I'm glad I'm not the only one."

Bob turned in the chair and saw the Geeks were still busily working away on their laptops. He shook his head, thinking that swimming suits were like bell curves. A few people look fabulous in them, most don't, and some should never go near one. The Geeks were in the latter category. In Bob's experience, however, the all-time worst was a holiday crowd on a nude beach in southern France that was favored by large, multi-generational families — kids, teens, parents, and grandparents. They all arrived with their blankets, chairs, and baskets of food and wine, and promptly shed everything for an extended afternoon picnic. That was enough to convince him that in many instances, clothes had been invented for a very good reason.

Bob walked back to the aft railing, looked down at the Geeks, and laughed. They looked as pale as poached white fish, he thought, and had about as many muscles. What was it Koz called them? The "brainiac night-crawlers?" The benches they were lying on had pure-white, upholstered cushions, making it hard to tell where Geek began and leather bench ended. Patsy Evans was lying next to Jimmy with her body snuggled against his. She was reading a fashion magazine, while the guys were completely engrossed in their laptops. They might not look good in their swimming suits, Bob thought, but Patsy certainly did, even if the other two were too dense to understand much about the female figure.

"You know, the sun's getting higher," Bob called down to them. "If you're going to lie out there for much longer, put on some sunblock. The sun will fry your brains if you don't."

Patsy looked up at him over the top edge of her sunglasses and grinned. "Already done, Major, sir, and I've been re-basting his delicate alabaster skin every hour."

"Alabaster?" Linda called out from the galley below. "Just don't forget poor Ronald."

"Oh, don't worry, Linda. I do Ronald too... No, no, I didn't mean it that way," Patsy laughed, and Linda laughed right along with her. Jimmy and Ronald finally looked up, glanced at each other, and frowned, not having heard the conversation.

Bob raised his hands in mock surrender and said, "I'm staying out of this." He turned around, opened the small refrigerator built into the front console on the flying bridge, and pulled out two bottles of Budweiser. As he handed one to Ace, he turned back to the video feeds on his computer. Interesting, he thought. On the screen, the security guards had rotated again, as they did every two hours. Most of the regular ones were young and beefy like the twin Hulks who visited him in Arlington Heights. They were private contract hires in gray slacks, blue blazers, white shirts and ties, like he saw in and around the casino on his last trip. For the first time, however, Bob saw that the blond-haired, blue-eyed cast from Gold's Gym had been joined by the New York City lounge lizards who had arrived earlier. While the blue-blazers were posted at the doors or followed regular patrol routes around the perimeter and through the parking lots, the beer guts appeared to be roving, strolling at random through the hotel and casino entrances, through the garages, and across the parking lots.

Bob stared at the screen for a while longer, and then went back to the aft railing and called out, "Hey Jimmy, come up here for a minute." The young computer wizard quickly pried himself free from Patsy Evans and scampered up the narrow, curving staircase. "How are you coming with the passwords?" Bob asked him.

"Well, not as well as we'd like, I'm embarrassed to say," Jimmy answered, as his frustrations began to show. "The passwords the janitors brought back last night led us into a number of potentially useful areas, like personnel, the hotel and casino employment records, hotel reservations, and even their daily room charges and accounting, but they don't let us get all the way into the upper finance levels where you want us to go. But you told us not to press it, so we didn't."

"You did the right thing," Bob quickly agreed. "I don't want to trigger any alarms."

"However, I was thinking there might be another way. What we've been trying to do is break into their system remotely, using passwords from their outer office personnel where your guys are cleaning. Not knowing how Boardwalk Investments is structured, those people may not even have access to the higher-level accounting and records you want, no matter what password we use."

"What other choice is there? Break into the Business Office and use one of theirs?"

"That's an option, but there is adequate anecdotal information online to indicate that the higher up the corporate food chain you go, the more careless people get. It's the people with the corner offices who make the most mistakes with their own internet security. So, if we can get into one of those corner offices…"

" 'Adequate anecdotal information online...?' Whose office do you want to try? Carbonari's or Van Gries's?"

"Well, what if Ronald and I go down and get janitor jobs? If we could get into one of them for even a few minutes — I was thinking Van Gries's, because he's head of finance — I think I could get into the system. They might even be hiding their server or a small mainframe in there."

Bob stared at him for a moment. "That's way too risky. Look, Ernie will be back from Chicago in a few hours with his pickpocket friend, and we'll turn him loose on the casino tonight. Like you said, I had hoped we could get what we needed by cracking into their computers remotely; but if we can get our hands on their master key cards, maybe we will try doing it the old-fashioned way."

"What about going in his office window? Patsy and I were watching this Tom Cruise movie last night, and they cut their way into the window of a high-rise office building with a circular glass-cutting laser gizmo..."

Bob stared at him again. "I guess I missed that one."

As they were talking, Ronald came up the stairs behind Jimmy and looked around at all the sophisticated navigational equipment in the command console on the flying bridge. "Man," Ronald said, grinning, "this is like the bridge on the Millennium Falcon."

Ace lowered his binoculars a few inches and looked at Ronald out of the corner of his eye but didn't say anything.

"Did you tell him about our idea?" Ronald asked.

"All right, ignoring the break-in and the laser gizmo ideas," Jimmy said, "Ronald and I thought we might go back to the casino tonight. This time, instead of staying 'low key,' we could make it real obvious that we're card counting."

"Yeah, yeah, we could start winning big time!" Ronald snorted.

"And how long do you think that's going to last before their security people grab you and thump your pointy little heads?" Ace asked. "You know they don't like card counters."

"That's the whole point," Jimmy answered with an alligator smile. "When they do catch us, they'll do exactly the same thing they did at the Sun or the Bellagio. They'll drag us up to their security office, shove us around, threaten to beat the crap out of us, and take all our money away."

"I'm missing something," Ace said, shaking his head. "How is that a good thing?"

"Because we'd be inside their offices, 'behind the curtain,' as it were." Ronald snorted again. "Maybe we'll see that guy Corliss you were talking about and those two big Hulks. Most importantly, though, it'll give Jimmy and me a chance to see what kind of computer equipment and network set-up they have in there, and if there are any tech manuals lying around. Cool idea, huh?"

Bob frowned. "You're only guessing what their reaction might be."

"They can't kill us!" Ronald answered nervously. "Can they?"

"It's New Jersey," Ace answered with a shrug. "I'm just sayin'."

"Ah, you're just trying to scare us again. Card counting is legal here. We checked," Jimmy answered him.

"Like he said, 'it's New Jersey,' " Bob warned.

"They do have a point though," Ace conceded. "As much fun as it is to just sit here and drink beer, time's not on our side. We need to do something."

"I guess I agree," Bob told him. "But you guys know there are risks going in there, right? We can protect you up to a point, but you'll be on your own once they grab you."

"My assumption is we should be there when things get rocking around midnight. That's when the most people will be there," Jimmy suggested.

"I think you're right. Worst-case, they'll try to minimize the disruption when they grab you and shut you down."

"Yeah, with a big crowd, they'll have to be careful about the blood splatter," Ace said with a straight face. "Comping all those dry-cleaning bills can get excessive."

Bob gave him a look. "Then I'll put you in charge of protection. You can take The Batman, Bulldog, and Dorothy along to keep an eye on them. Just be careful."

As the men began discussing Jimmy's idea up on the flying bridge, Patsy Evans put her magazine down, checked her tan, and bounced down the stairs from the aft deck into the main lounge. She saw Linda at the sink and intended to quickly pass through and make a quick pit stop in the forward head, when Linda intercepted her and steered her into the small kitchen.

"Linda, I really have to go, and this isn't…"

"Yes, it is. I'm your best friend, and you need a little 'reality' check."

"Don't start on me again, just because you don't like Jimmy."

"I *love* Jimmy!" Linda answered. "So does Bob."

"Well, you sure have a funny way of showing it."

"You're acting like two high school kids in heat."

Patsy's eyes narrowed. "Well, maybe you forgot how it feels to be young and in love."

"Love?" she scoffed. "How old is he?"

"It may surprise you to learn that we are both twenty-one."

"No, girl. He's twenty-one going on fifteen, and you're twenty-one going on thirty."

"And Vinnie was thirty-three, going on forty-three," Patsy snapped back, crossing her arms across her chest. "That's what's been bothering you two, isn't it? You think I'm supposed to sit around moping because Vinnie's dead, but I'm not going to do that. He was a great guy and a lot of fun, when he was around. I'm not saying he wasn't. He taught me a lot, probably way too much," she said, sounding embarrassed, "but we were never in love. He was way too old for me, and the Army came first with him, anyway. I knew it, and he knew it too. So we were just having fun. Jimmy's so different. We can talk, and we like the same music, TV shows, and stuff. When I say things to him, he knows what I'm talking about. So, what's wrong with that?" she asked, and then stormed out.

Linda watched her walk away and turned back to the sink. As much s she hated to admit it, Patsy was right. She was too young to wear black.

At 3:00 p.m., Ernie and Dorothy drove into the marina parking lot and walked down the pier to the boat, escorting a short, plump man between them. He was impeccably dressed in an expensive, camel-colored mohair topcoat, gray slacks, and a white open-collared shirt. His hair was badly thinning, and he combed it straight back off his forehead. As he walked down the long pier to the boat, he looked up at the bright sun and out across the water to the numerous sail and powerboats moored in the marina and paused to take several deep breaths of the fresh, tangy sea air. Halfway up the pier, he stopped in midstride as a large, dark-gray pelican dove and hit the water in the empty boat slip next to them with a large splash and came up with a fish. The man pointed at it and laughed. It was obvious he was having the time of his life, but Dorothy and Ernie carefully kept their positions flanking him and nudging him along toward the big white powerboat at the end of the pier.

When they came aboard, Ernie steered the little man onto the aft deck. As he passed Patsy and the two Geeks, he gave her a pleasant smile and polite, old-fashioned bow. "Lovely, absolutely lovely," he said, his voice carrying a faint Eastern European accent. "Can we not stay up here, Ernest?" he pleaded with a dramatic sweeping motion of his hand. "The bright sunshine, the water, the boats, the beautiful young women…"

"Downstairs, Dimi." The big Chicago cop pointed to the narrow staircase and the main lounge below.

"You know I cannot swim, and I am getting much too old to run."

Ernie pointed to the staircase again. The little man sighed but did what he was told.

Most of the others had already gathered down there, including Bob. Ernie motioned for the little man to sit in one of the plush swivel chairs while Ernie took the one next to him.

"Oh, my!" the little man said as he ran his hands over the leather and rocked back and forth in the chair. "Can I take one of these back to my jail cell with me?" He laughed aloud.

"Ladies and gentlemen, this is Dimitri Karides. Dimi, I won't bother introducing you to everyone, since you're not going to be here all that long. Suffice it to say, Dimi is one of the world's most renowned 'hand magicians,' as he prefers to call himself. If you have something in a pocket, hanging around your neck, or fastened around your wrist that Dimi takes a fancy to, it will be gone in a matter of seconds."

"Oh, Captain Travers, you so exaggerate," Karides laughed and dismissed the thought with a wave of his hand. "I prefer to think of myself as a 'financial liberationist.' I only 'acquire' things from people who will never miss them," he said with a stern wag of his finger, "and I never, ever steal from the poor."

"Whatever." Ernie looked around the room. "Just keep your hands on your wallets."

"That won't be a problem," Bob told them. "We all fall in the poor category."

"The poor category?" Karides scoffed as he looked around. "That wonderful airplane you sent for me, and now this sailing yacht…?"

"All short-term rentals, I assure you," Bob answered as he looked at the clothes Karides was wearing. "But it looks like your business has been good."

"Oh, these?" Dimitri looked down at his topcoat and slacks. "They are nice, aren't they? I made Ernest stop at one of the finer men's clothing stores in Woodfield Mall on the way to the airport. Cook County jail managed to misplace all my clothes. No doubt, they augmented some guard's retirement fund. Anyway, I told Ernest he could either put me to work down here in one of those bright orange jumpsuits or buy me a new outfit. So I suspect I have your expense account to thank, Mister Burke. But that orange jumpsuit would never do in the casino tonight, would it?" he said with a pleased smile.

"I guess not, so long as you can get us what we want," Bob replied.

"Mister Burke," Karides smiled politely, "surely you jest. In return for these lovely clothes and a fine dinner, perhaps accompanied by one of your beautiful young ladies…"

"You'll have to settle for Ernie," Bob replied.

"Oh, let Dorothy go with them," Ace laughed. "They've been flying all day, so she deserves a good meal, too."

"Most excellent," Dimitri said with a polite bow toward both Ace and Dorothy, and then looked at his watch. "And I know exactly where we shall go. If you do not mind, though, perhaps there is a place where I can take a nap. It has been a very long day, and one should be at the top of one's game, given what I was told about tonight's opposition."

At 8:30 p.m., a car containing Dorothy and Dimitri Karides in the front and Ernie Travers in the back drove out of the marina parking lot and headed south to Atlantic Avenue, with Dorothy behind the wheel. When they reached South Albion, a small residential street, Dimitri directed her west to Chef Vola's "old school" classic Italian restaurant hidden away in the basement of a big 1920s house at the end of the block.

Two hours later, Ernie finally pushed his plate away and said, "Unbelievable. That was the best veal parmesan I've ever eaten, and believe me, I've eaten my share."

"Same for the linguine with white clam sauce," Dorothy agreed. "How did you ever find this place?"

Dimitri smiled contentedly. "When one is incarcerated twenty-four hours a day, one has ample time for every back issue of *Conde Nast* and *Gourmet Magazine.*"

"But you told me you'd been dreaming of a big steak?" Ernie asked.

"Ah, that was before you told me our destination was Atlantic City. The condemned man is entitled to a dinner of his choice, is he not?"

"Let's hope it doesn't come to that," Ernie said.

"Ernest, you forget I am the very best. It will not come to anything, I assure you. The dinner, however, is a different story. This superb restaurant has been at the top of my list for years."

Ernie looked at his watch and saw it was almost 11:00 p.m. "We need to get going. The others will be at the casino by now, and we need to allow time to look around."

"True, but we cannot leave without pie; it is the specialty of the house."

"Pie? I don't know where I'd put it," Dorothy told him.

"Then we shall order a slice of the banana cream pie, a slice of ricotta cheesecake, and three forks. I have dreamt about them for two years. Besides, it will take your friends at least an hour to sufficiently rattle the casino pit bosses so that they summon the demons to drag them away from the tables. That is the moment to strike."

"When there is a lot of movement and distraction?"

"Precisely."

CHAPTER TWENTY-TWO

More than half of the tables on the main floor were full by the time Ernie, Dorothy, and Dimitri arrived around midnight. They had come straight from the restaurant, and despite the pleasant weather, Dimitri still wore his bulky, camel-colored mohair overcoat. The other two followed him as he strolled around the interior of the casino and circled the gambling tables, which were arranged in back-to-back rows running down the center of the casino's three wings. Each table was semicircular, designed for a specific game and to accommodate up to eight players, each of them playing against the dealer, not each other.

Ernie looked at his watch. A large crowd of amused onlookers had gathered around the blackjack table at the far end of the row. They were watching two geeky young men who sat at opposite ends of the table, each with a large stack of chips in front of him. One wore a black, flat-brimmed, Chicago White Sox hat and a dark blue sweatshirt with the name "Berkeley" and the university's large, circular seal in gold on the front. The other was hatless, dressed in a red-and-blue-plaid flannel shirt and a pair of thick, black-rimmed glasses held together at the nose bridge with a thick wrap of white masking tape.

As they played, they had become the center of attention. Laughing and bantering back and forth with the crowd in loud voices, they insulted the onlookers behind them, the dealer, the other players at the table, the pit boss in his black suit, and even the security guards in their blue blazers, who had crowded around the two ends of the table. The young men were cocky to a fault, apparently competing to see who could be the louder and more obnoxious. That said, it was hard to deny the growing stacks of chips sitting in front of them.

Scanning the faces in the crowd behind them, Ernie quickly picked out The Batman, Bulldog, and Ace spaced out around the outer edge. They saw Ernie too, and quickly exchanged brief nods. Dorothy walked around to the other side of the crowd, where Ace stood and slipped her arm inside his, leaving Ernie and Dimitri alone on the dealer's side. Dimi was a foot and a half shorter than the Chicago police captain. He raised his hand and motioned for Ernie to bend down and lean closer as he whispered, "Do you see the two awkwardly dressed gentlemen behind Jimmy and Ronald? I assume those are some of your New York City adversaries?"

Ernie followed Dimitri's eyes and saw two men standing together at the rear of the crowd, conspicuous by their ill-fitting sports coats, open collared shirts, and far too much bling. Ernie sighed. "Well, I can't see the St. Anthony medals around their necks or their Knights of Columbus pins, but I'd say you're right."

Dimi scoffed. "If that is the best that the opposition has to offer, then I assure you they are schoolboys compared to the Russians and Serbs I have had to deal with. Nonetheless, they are the ones I want."

For the moment at least, it appeared as if the two Mafiosi were content to stand there with their arms crossed over their chests and stare unhappily at the two young men. However, as Ronald raked in another stack of chips, Ernie whispered to Dimi, "You'd better get ready. I don't think they're gonna wait much longer."

A scantily clad casino cocktail waitress walked by carrying a crowded tray of drinks. Dimitri looked up at her with a pleasant smile and took two of them.

"Hey!" she began to object. "Those are for…"

"Give this delightful young woman twenty dollars, Ernest, and try to keep up," Dimitri said as he slipped through the crowd like a snake through tall grass and around to the other side.

Ernie pulled a twenty-dollar bill from his pocket and dropped it on her tray, which satisfied whatever moral outrage she was having from the little guy's rudeness. Ernie turned and tried to catch up with the short Greek; but as he did, he saw the two thugs nod to each other and begin moving in on Jimmy and Ronald. They nodded to the pit boss, who stepped forward with four uniformed security guards. The dealer was about to deal the next hand, but he immediately stopped and announced, "Sorry, folks, but this table's closed for a shift change."

"Hey! What the hell, man," Ronald complained loudly. He turned toward the crowd and said, "You people don't want them to close us down, do you? Come on, give it up for keeping the table open!" He stood, raised his hands over his head, and began rhythmically clapping. As the rest of the crowd began clapping and hooting along with him, the dealer leaned forward and raked-in his stack of chips and Ronald's.

"Those are my chips!" Jimmy complained loudly as two security guards stepped in and grabbed his arms. Two more guards grabbed Ronald's and lifted him out of his chair.

"If you'll come with us, sir, we'll pay you out in the office," the pit boss said as he led the way, pushing through the crowd of onlookers and opening a path for the others toward the service corridor. As the two Gumbahs turned and began to follow, Dimitri stepped in front of them, stumbled drunkenly, and fell into them. His drinks went flying, hitting one Gumbah in the face with the ice and cold liquid, and the other in his shirt-front, with the rest running down the fronts of their suits. As he went down, Dimitri reached out and wrapped his arms around the two men to break his fall, but only succeeded in knocking them off-balance.

"Oh, my! Terribly sorry," he babbled as he danced around in a small circle with the two men. "Excuse me, I can't seem to…" he said, continuing to push, pull, and paw them, until they all fell to the floor, with Dimitri on top.

"You dumb bastard!" one of the Gumbahs swore.

"Watch out," the other one warned as Dimitri attempted to get back up at the same time the Mafioso was pushing Dimitri away. "Jeez!" the gunman said as Dimitri fell on top of him again.

"Whoa, where do I get off this ride," Dimitri continued to blubber.

"You'll have to pardon my friend," Ernie said as he stepped in and tried to help Dimitri up, but the short Greek kept tipping over and falling on top of the two mobsters.

"I'll break his freakin' neck, is what I'll do!" the first one replied as he rolled over and got to his knees, brushing the ice and drink off the front of his suit. "Jesus Christ!"

"Sorry, my friend had one too many," Ernie said. "He needs some air."

"I'm going to be sick," Dimitri mumbled as he suddenly leaned over them again and began to gag. The Gumbahs were still trying to get to their feet, and that was all it took for them to shove Dimitri away and try to crawl out of the potential blast zone.

Ernie got his arms under Dimitri and pulled him to his feet. As the little man continued to say, "Sorry, sorry," Ernie turned him around and pushed him into the crowd, which quickly opened and closed behind them as he coughed and gagged. They then ducked behind one of the bars, headed for the door to the Self-Parking ramp, and were gone in a matter of seconds. They ran up the stairs to the next level, both men laughing hysterically, and then weaved through the rows of parked cars until they reached the other side of the garage and took the stairs down to Ernie's parked car.

"That was brilliant, my friend," Ernie told him. "You had me so convinced that you were about to throw up that I wasn't sure I wanted to touch you either."

"And surrender that fine dinner? That was not going to happen, Ernest."

"You're hurting me!" Jimmy complained as the beefy security guards pulled him down the service corridor. It wasn't much of a contest, he had to admit. The guards' fingers easily circled his biceps and Ronald's, and they could probably have picked up the two Geeks and carried them down the hall one-handed if they wanted to, without even breaking a sweat.

"Easy, dude! We got rights, you know," Ronald complained.

"Yeah?" The pit boss quickly answered. "Well, they don't include card counting."

"Card counting? We didn't do anything," Jimmy said. "And you can't prove we did."

"Shut up!" the first Gumbah added as he caught up, still trying to brush the drink off his suit jacket, eager to smack something. His name was Marco Bianchi and his long-time classmate from auto shop at Thomas Edison Vocational High

School in Queens was Selmo Lombardi. Both were recent graduates of the Midstate Correctional Facility in Attica, New York. It seems that their youthful interest in automotive mechanics had blossomed into multiple counts of Grand Theft Auto, Intent to Deprive, Grand Larceny, Auto Stripping, and Possession.

"Goddamnit, I ought to break your freakin' fingers, both 'a youse," Bianchi went on until he saw the blue and gold sweatshirt and fumed, "Berkeley? I lost five hundred on you dumb bastards in dat bowl game last year. I oughta rip that out of your freakin' hides!"

In less than a minute, with more pushing and shoving, the group had continued down the corridor and around the corner, where the pit boss knocked on the last door on the left, marked Business Office. That was when Selmo finally caught up, even angrier than his pal. "Where'd that little weasel in the camel-colored coat go, Marco? I'll kill him if I catch him; I swear I will!"

Suddenly, Lombardi stopped in the center of the hallway and began patting his jacket pockets. "Ey! What the hell?" he asked, "Where's my radio? And my cell phone...?"

Marco Bianchi turned, looked back at him, and quickly felt his own pockets. "Damn, Selmo! Me, too. My wallet's gone... My keys, and my goddamn gun, too!"

The two burly, middle-aged men stopped and stared at each other, dumbfounded, until their surprised expressions were suddenly replaced by looks of angry recognition.

"That little bastard picked our pockets, didn't he?" Lombardi asked.

"You can't kill him. He's mine, and I'll kill him with my bare hands if I have to!" Bianchi growled as the office door opened and they found a puzzled Martijn Van Gries staring out at them.

"Who are you going to kill?" the Dutchman frowned.

"Nobody... nothing!" Lombardi quickly answered. "Here's dese two freakin' card counters you spotted on the blackjack table. Marco and I gotta go. There's somethin' we gotta take care of," he told Van Gries as he and Bianchi turned and ran back down the hallway toward the casino floor.

Unfortunately for the two Mafiosi, they were already far too late to catch up with Ernie and Dimitri, who were already in Ernie's rental car and exiting the parking lot into one of the side streets to the west. Ernie continued on to Pennsylvania Avenue, and turned south.

"I hate to say that looked easy," Ernie began, "but that looked easy."

"Things always do, when you are not the one who is doing them."

"Well, whatever you did, I couldn't see a thing."

"Some police detective, you are."

"Okay, I deserved that. Did you get much off them?"

Dimitri gave him an amused look and shook his head. "You have seen me work before. You are supposed to observe these things, Ernest" he said as he reached into the inside pockets of his large overcoat and began pulling out various things.

Ernie's mouth dropped open as he saw a two-way radio, two cell phones, two wallets, two plastic Bimini Bay key cards, a key chain with at least a dozen keys dangling from it, and a .38-caliber snub-nose revolver.

"Whoa!" Ernie looked down, wide-eyed. "You've got to be kidding. I didn't see you take any of this stuff, or even see your hands inside their clothes. Then again, I never saw what you did back in Chicago, either. Jeez, you are good Dimitri, I gotta give you that."

"*Good?*" the little man raised an eyebrow, clearly offended. "I am not merely *good*, Ernest; by now, you must admit I am *the best*."

Once they reached Baltic Avenue, Ernie turned west and pulled into a 7-Eleven parking lot, swinging the rental car into a space along the outside row under one of the tall pole lights. First, he picked up the small, commercial Motorola RDV two-way radio, looked at it for a moment, and then took a close look at the two iPhones.

"The guys back on the boat are going to have a lot of fun with these," he said, "and I'll bet my old pal Carmine Bonafacio with the New Jersey state police in Trenton will have even more." Ernie then looked at the key chain, which had all sorts of odd-looking keys hanging from it. "These will take a bit of research to figure out which locks they go to, but that's very doable," he said as he picked up the two plastic key cards, both of which had the words "Casino Operations" printed across the front in red letters.

"I think you hit the jackpot with these, Dimi," Ernie grinned from ear to ear. "I'll bet my pension these are masters." Finally, he picked up the two wallets and pulled out the driver's licenses. "New York, with addresses in Brooklyn. Figures," he said as he quickly poked through the rest of the wallet's contents and saw a rather mundane collection of credit cards, health club membership cards, and the like. Finally, he opened the back of each wallet, pulled out two rather thick stacks of large bills. Quickly fanning the bills, he said, "Looks like more than three grand here, maybe four, not a bad haul."

"For your retirement fund, captain?" Dimitri asked.

"You know me better than that," Ernie answered.

Dimitri turned away and looked out the window. "All right, Ernest, what now? Do I at least get to sleep in a soft bed with clean sheets and have one more good meal before you return me to that god-awful Cook County jail of yours?"

Ernie looked at him. "Tell me, where would you go if I didn't take you back?"

Dimitri's head snapped around and he gave the big cop a long, appraising look. "Me? Where would I go? Oh, abroad, definitely abroad. Paris, and the south of France, I think. I have always wanted to eat my way through the finer restaurants in Provence."

"You wouldn't stay around Philadelphia or New York? All those pockets to pick?"

"Ernest," he shook his head. "As I've told you, I think of myself as a 'liberationist Robin Hood,' " he said with a pleasant smile as he looked down at the items he took from the two hoods. "One thing is absolutely certain, you would never see me back at your O'Hare Airport or in Chicago, for that matter. No, not ever, my friend."

"Good," Ernie smiled as he picked up the radio, the telephones, the keys, the key cards, the wallets, the pistol, and jammed them in his jacket pockets. "Want some coffee?" he asked.

Dimitri looked at the 7-Eleven building and looked puzzled. "What do you purchase in a place like this? Gasoline or coffee? And why would I want to ruin the wonderfully lingering taste of that fine meal with something like that?"

Ernie laughed. "Point taken," he said as he got out of the car, paused, and looked back inside at the smaller man. "By the way, I may be in there quite a while," he added as he closed the car door and walked away.

Dimitri looked down. When he saw the big cop had left all the cash from the two wallets lying on the car seat and the car keys in the ignition, he smiled.

Twenty minutes later, Bob sat in the captain's chair on the flying bridge watching the exterior camera feeds from the Bimini Bay, when his cell phone rang.

"Burke here," he answered.

"Hey Bob, are any of your guys free at the moment?" Ernie Travers asked.

"Yeah, I think the janitors just came back."

"I'm in the parking lot of the 24-hour 7-11 over on Baltic, west of Pennsylvania. Can you send one of them over here to pick me up?"

"Something wrong?"

"No, no," he heard Ernie laugh. "I just need a ride."

"Problems with the rental car?"

"No, I think it's fine, last time I saw it."

Bob frowned, trying to make sense of what the big cop had just said. "And your Greek friend Dimitri? Is he fine too?"

"Oh, he's fine, too, the last time I saw him."

This time, it was Bob's turn to laugh. "I assume there's a story in there somewhere."

"You may so assume. But the good news is, there were a lot of pockets picked tonight, and I have an interesting collection of toys to show you when I get back to the boat."

Former U.S. Army Captain Randy Benson sat in the Bimini Bay's Risk Management office with Theo Van Gries and two of his men — Reggie MacGregor, a surly Brit who had been given the boot by the British SAS a few years before, and Eric Smit, one of Theo's former Dutch Marine NCOs, who were on their break. His other three men were patrolling the Bimini Bay and Tuscany Towers, while Benson and Theo sat at the room's two computer monitors watching live, rotating, quarter-screen video feeds from the complex's security cameras. Smit napped on the couch behind them, while MacGregor had chosen Shaka Corliss's large, over-padded desk chair. He had his feet propped on the edge of the desk as he flipped through a stack of porn magazines he found in the bottom drawer in Corliss's desk.

Theo preferred the human touch, which is why he had his men on random patrols of the casino buildings and grounds. Benson, on the other hand, preferred to systematically work the cameras. Watching the fast-moving, black-and-white video feeds was mind-numbing work, but the cameras took him places it would take a handful of mercs an hour or two to cover on foot, Benson thought. With over one hundred cameras inside the building and another thirty outside, he initially set the camera feeds on a two-second rotation, which meant it took almost two minutes. After the first thirty minutes, he began to eliminate cameras that he felt covered areas that would not be of much use. He quickly eliminated over half of them, allowing him to concentrate on the entrances and the more heavily-trafficked public areas, and to slow the rotation to four seconds. The full rotation still took two minutes. He knew he would get a migraine if he kept it up for another day or two. Theo on the other hand, did not even try. He took manual control of his video feeds and bounced around from camera to camera, based on what he thought looked interesting.

Earlier, Benson had asked Martijn how he could access the video feeds from earlier in the week. Martijn showed him where he could find them in the computer's data directories, but warned that with so many cameras, the files were huge. The recordings for the past forty-eight hours were kept in the video system itself. After that, they rotated onto the casino's main security server, where they remained for eight more days before being recorded over, one day at a time.

Ten days, Benson thought. That was cutting it close before the video would be recorded over, but he still had time. By then, he had become intimately familiar with the layout of the security cameras, the zones, and how to navigate through the system. So, when Theo left for a "walk about" floor check, Benson quickly scanned through the backup directory on the server. He found the listing for the Bimini Bay's recordings from nine nights before and queued up the video he wanted for the card tables on the casino's main gambling floor. Rotating from camera to camera, it did not take him long to find his old comrade-in-arms, Vinnie Pastorini, sitting at a high-stakes blackjack tables *that* night. He had a short stack of chips in front of him, and a cute young brunette hanging all over him, laughing, drinking, and having a great time.

Benson paused the video playback for a few moments and zoomed in on the girl's face. He had never been terribly good at names, but he never forgot a face, especially a cute one like hers. Over the years, he had met many of Vinnie's girlfriends, but he had never seen this one in the flesh. Four nights before, however, he had seen several framed photographs of her and Vinnie. They were sitting on a shelf in the living room bookcase of the house they shared in Fayetteville, North Carolina. Both photographs had been taken at a party or reception of some kind. Vinnie looked surprisingly good in his formal dress blues and the girl would look good in anything. In the first photograph, they sat cheek to cheek at a large, round-top table covered with champagne glasses and silverware.

In the other photograph, two couples stood side by side in front of an altar, laughing and smiling. Vinnie and the girl were on the left. On the right was none other than Major Robert T. Burke and a woman in a wedding dress. Benson had no doubt that it had been taken at Burke's recent wedding. That photograph was interesting, but Benson's eyes returned to the shot at the poker table. The girl looked spectacular, but the small, gold lion's head hanging around her neck at the poker table looked even more spectacular. Benson never forgot a face — same face, same girl, wearing *his* gold medallion.

The online property records of Cumberland County, North Carolina, revealed that the house had been purchased two months before, for cash, and was owned in common by U.S. Army Sergeant First Class Vincent Anthony Pastorini and a Patsy Steinhauer Evans, citing a suburban Chicago address. Vinnie paid cash for the house? Cash! Benson had been inside it twice. He was no expert on North Carolina real estate, but he guessed it had to be worth $250,000, even down there. That raised the burning question of where did Vinnie get that much goddamned cash? As everyone at Fort Bragg knew, Vinnie and money were never long-term friends. He went through it faster than he made it. So, if the money for the house hadn't come from the girl, the infinitely more troubling explanation was that Vinnie had already begun selling the gold, selling *their* gold, selling *his* gold!

Eighteen months before, when the first malodors began to emanate from the CIA's joint operation in Mosul, the Army CID questioned him and the other Army personnel assigned to that unit at least a half-dozen times. That neither surprised nor overly concerned Benson or Theo Van Gries. Theo ran the unit for the CIA, which was notoriously more understanding about trifling matters like this than the Army. So Theo was able to run interference with the uniformed branches for the time being; as long as no one found the gold, and no one talked.

Bringing Vinnie in was Benson's idea. The sergeant had not been part of the museum heist itself, but he had been shipping materiel in and out of country for Delta for months. Theo needed to get the gold out of the country before the CID found it, so they struck a deal with Vinnie. He provided the perfect cover and was able to smuggle it back to Fort Bragg. He was then to sit on it until the others were able to rotate out of the war zone, in return for a share. Unfortunately, his greed and gambling addiction must have gotten the best of him. After six months, Vinnie became very uncooperative and uncommunicative with his old partners and stopped answering Theo's phone calls. Benson and Kowalski were Americans. They already had phony IDs and phony passports, so Theo sent them back to the States to track Vinnie and the gold down, and beat it out of him, if necessary.

When he and Kowalski confronted Vinnie at Fort Bragg, the conversation proved brief and rather one-sided. Vinnie claimed that the gold had been seized by US customs, and he was now in as much trouble as the rest of them were. When he then took off to Atlantic City, Benson and Kowalski followed him to the casino and finally tracked him down at Caesars. After the three thugs from the Bimini Bay dragged Vinnie back to his own hotel and eventually up to his fifth floor room, Vinnie managed to escape out the window. Benson and Kowalski were able to corner him in the elevator lobby, and, as they say, "push came to shove." Vinnie played dumb and again refused to cooperate, which so infuriated Benson that he gave Vinnie a flying lesson out the fifth floor hallway window.

As he watched the sergeant tumble through the air toward the asphalt below, Kowalski wasn't happy with him, but Benson was not overly worried. If the gold was anywhere, it was back in Fayetteville, and his next best choice was to "discuss" it with the girl. Kowalski liked that a lot more. When the girl put three bullets in Kowalski's chest and winged Benson, the most Benson could say about the trip was that it had eliminated two shares of the loot. Other than that, it was a complete fiasco. The second visit to the house was proving to be another waste of time, until he saw the photograph of the girl wearing the gold lion's head medallion around her neck, and he knew all was not lost.

After that, it wasn't hard to put the pieces together — a girl from suburban Chicago, photographs of Burke's wedding, the dust-up between Burke and Donatello Carbonari, threats, assaults, and now, the increasing likelihood that Burke would actually be coming here to Atlantic City to take on the New Jersey mob. That seemed too good to be true, because Burke had no idea that Theo and his Black Devils were already here to stop him. In the melee that was sure to follow, all Benson needed was to get his hands on the girl and make sure that neither Burke nor Theo walked away. Given their reputations, he was fairly certain that they would take care of that themselves. He wanted the gold, *all* of it, and getting rid of both of them was essential if he wanted to keep it. At the same time, finally getting his revenge on the man who had undermined his Army career from the moment he showed up in the Unit would add whipped cream and two large cherries to the top. Gramps! he mumbled to himself. Gramps! Bob Burke would pay for that.

On several occasions over the past two days of watching videos, Benson thought he recognized some faces. Could they be Burke's men, he wondered. Unfortunately, with the long hair, hats, and constantly changing beards and mustaches, he doubted their wives or girlfriends could recognize them half the time. As Benson watched casino security gather around one of the blackjack tables to deal with two card counters, Benson's eyes focused on the crowd. He immediately recognized Ace Randall and Joe "The Batman" Hendrix. After all the nights he spent on one rocky piece of ground or another with those men, they could change their clothes, hair, and even put on hats; but they could never hide "that look." It was the way their heads and eyes never stopped moving, how they held their hands and fingers at the ready, and in the way their bodies moved, like jungle cats on the prowl. Deltas! That meant the last piece of Benson's plan was falling into place. Burke couldn't be far away. He was here!

Benson looked closer at the two loud, noxious jerks at the blackjack table. They appeared familiar. And why were Ace Randall and The Batman standing nearby, watching them? Were they their security? Or was it all some coincidence? Unfortunately, ten years in Special Ops taught Benson never to believe in coincidences.

That was when the pit boss and the uniformed casino security moved in on the two blackjack players. Benson turned toward Theo Van Gries and said, "Come over here and take a look at this, Theo," he motioned toward his screen. "I found them."

CHAPTER TWENTY-THREE

Martijn Van Gries held his office door open. With a big smile and a dramatic sweep of his arm, he motioned for the two Geeks to step inside.

"Said the spider to the fly?" Ronald asked as he stopped in the doorway and complained loudly. The big security guard behind him gave him a two-handed shove in the back and Ronald found himself lying on his face on the carpet in front of Van Gries's desk. Jimmy decided he needed no such assistance, and quickly stepped inside on his own.

The pit boss was last in, carrying two nearly full trays of chips, which he sat on the corner of Van Gries's desk. "They're all yours," he said. "I gotta get back." Van Gries nodded as the pit boss turned and left, closing the office door behind him.

"You're gonna hear from my lawyer!" Ronald picked himself off the floor and wagged a finger at Van Gries. "You can't treat us like this," he blustered.

"Of course I can," Van Gries told him, sounding surprised by the statement.

"We have rights, and…"

"Sit down," Van Gries pointed to the two chairs in front of his desk. "You were card counting. We have you on video, tonight and last night. That's stealing, plain and simple."

"Card counting is legal in New Jersey," Ronald countered.

Martijn stared at him for a moment. "It's no more legal than if I tell Robert and Anthony here to drag you out to one of our boats, break your legs, and throw you overboard in the Gulf Stream. Take your pick, because no one will ever know or care, except for the sharks, of course. Is that what you would prefer?"

"You're just trying to scare us," Jimmy told him, almost convincing himself.

"Scare you?" Van Gries answered. "Yes, that is exactly what I am trying to do, Mr. Talmadge, and I hope the lesson takes better than it did in Las Vegas or Connecticut."

Jimmy listened to what Van Gries was saying, until he saw the laptop sitting on the desk. Its top was open, and one look told him everything he needed to know. The black laptop bore the distinctive, iridescent green logo of a Razer Blade, the biggest, newest, meanest gaming machine on the market. With state-of-the-art graphics, it was the only model faster than ones he and Ronald had talked Charlie out of a few months before.

"You have a Razer? That's so sick," Jimmy said.

"You two are gamers?" Van Gries stared at him and then smiled, "I suppose that was a stupid question, wasn't it? What do you play?"

"Mostly *World of Warcraft*, but *Leagues of Legends* from time to time. And you?"

"*Leagues*, but I am into *Forge of Empires* now."

"We have EON17-SLXs, but Razers are on our shopping lists."

"Oh, you will not regret it," Van Gries said, as he looked them over again. "When do you play?"

"Every weekend. And you?"

"When I can," Van Gries answered with a thin smile. "But too much of my time is taken up dealing with *klootzakken* like you two... that means 'assholes' for those in the room who are not conversant in Dutch."

Jimmy suddenly heard a man laugh. He turned and saw a large man with a neatly trimmed beard sitting on a couch along the side wall of the office reading the morning's Daily Racing Form. He appeared to be studying the two Geeks with the same cold, analytical stare that Jimmy remembered getting from the Deltas back in North Carolina. This time, however, there was no humor behind those eyes; and it sent a shiver down his spine. There were two other men in the room too, but Jimmy could not see their faces. They sat bent over computer monitors with their backs to him.

"If you are as smart and tech savvy as you pretend," Van Gries continued, "you should know that the gaming industry maintains a national registry of cheaters; and your petulant, frowning faces have been on it from the moment you were tossed out of those other casinos. We are a good bit more sophisticated than most. We download that national data into our own facial recognition program, and it picked you out the moment you walked through the door yesterday. So welcome to the Bimini Bay, Mr. Barker... and Mr. Talmadge."

"Then why didn't you stop us?" Jimmy asked.

"Oh, last night you merely piddled about the tables, so we ignored you. Tonight, however, you crossed the threshold; and then you got quite obnoxious about it."

"We don't know what you're talking about," Ronald postured.

"Of course you do, Mr. Barker. You are stealing, and we become a tad medieval when we catch people doing things like that."

"Medieval?" Ronald snorted and nudged Jimmy. "Really? What's next? The rack? Drawing and quartering?"

While Ronald droned on with his complaints, Jimmy scanned the room. On the wall to the left of Van Gries's desk, he saw several framed photographs and a diploma from MIT in cardinal and gray, with its distinctive gold. Below it stood a bookcase, the top shelf of which contained a row of pale blue binders with yellow, red, and green multi-colored Rubik's Cube logos at the top of their spines, and the bold initials DACI. DACI? Suddenly it came to him — DACI! Digital Analytics Consultants, in Princeton. They must have been the ones who designed Van Gries's software, and Jimmy knew exactly what that meant.

"You know," the Dutchman shrugged, "for two high-end gamers, you two are not very street smart, are you?" He then turned toward the big man on the couch and said, "Herr Bakker, scheit hem, als je wilt."

"Say, what?" Ronald frowned.

"Herr Bakker is Dutch, as I am, and I told him to shoot you when he is ready."

Ronald sat up and watched the bearded man lay the *Daily Racing Form* aside, stand, and pull a small automatic pistol from his waistband. He then produced a silencer from his pocket and screwed it onto the barrel, smiling the entire time.

"More threats?" Ronald scoffed as he sat back in the chair and crossed his arms over his chest. The bearded man stepped across the room with the supple stride of a large cat. When he reached Ronald, he lowered the automatic and shot him in the foot without a second thought. With the noise suppressor attached, the sound from the small pistol was little more than a soft "Phutt!"

"Ah!" Ronald screamed as he leaped out of his chair, looked down, and saw a small, round hole in the top of his instep. "Ah, Ah!" Ronald repeated as he jumped around in front of Van Gries's desk on one leg, screaming in pain and bleeding.

"I'll bet that hurts," Van Gries commented in a pleasant voice. "Fortunately for you, Herr Bakker is carrying his small-caliber pistol today. Were he carrying his 9-millimeter handgun, you would be missing part of your foot about now. Can I now assume you got the message? Or does the lesson need repeating?"

"You son of a bitch! You son of a bitch!" Ronald screamed as he hopped around in front of his chair in a small circle.

Van Gries shrugged and motioned to the bearded man again. "Herr Bakker, once more if you please."

Ronald's eyes went wide as Bakker pointed his pistol at his good foot. Somehow, Ronald managed to levitate himself onto the chair as the man fired two more shots, "Phutt, Phutt!" They missed his foot and embedded themselves harmlessly in the carpet.

Van Gries turned toward Jimmy and asked, "Do you need a lesson as well?"

"No! No, I get the point," Jimmy quickly answered as he drew his feet under his chair.

"Excellent!" Van Gries smiled as he bent down, opened his bottom desk drawer, and pulled out a two-inch wide roll of silver duct tape. "Here, this should do the trick," he said as he tossed the roll to Jimmy. "Wrap some of this around your partner's foot a dozen times or so, Mr. Talmadge."

"Duct tape...? Around his foot?" Jimmy asked.

"It is one of the most amazing inventions of the twentieth century, and I do not want your friend bleeding all over our casino. But if you have a better suggestion?"

"Are you crazy?" Ronald complained loudly. "I need a doctor... I..."

"If you do not shut up, Mister Bakker will tape your big mouth shut and drag you out to the loading dock, where I will tell him to shoot you a few more times, in places much more painful than your foot. It is only a short distance from there to our boat in the marina."

Jimmy's mouth fell open as he stared across the desk at Van Gries.

"The tape, Mr. Talmadge," the Dutchman said as he pointed down at Ronald's foot. "Do as I told you and then get out of Atlantic City, both of you."

"What about our money?" Jimmy dared ask as he pointed to the stack of chips on Van Gries's desk. "That's ours."

"It was yours; now it is mine," Van Gries answered with a pleasant smile. "And if I ever see you two in my casino again, this little lesson will be nothing."

The two mammoth security guards shoved Jimmy and Ronald through the door and into the corridor. Jimmy had Ronald's arm draped over his shoulder as they hobbled away toward the casino as if they were running in a three-legged sack race. When they reached the main casino floor, one of the guards pointed to the door to the Self Park ramp further up on the right and said, "Go out that way, and keep going. Mr. Van Gries don't want no blood on his carpet, not unless he tells us to put it there."

Randy Benson sat up in his chair and looked even more intently at his computer screen when the camera showed the door to Martijn Van Gries's office swing open and the two Geeks go stumbling back out. One was limping badly, while the other provided support, being pushed and shoved along by two uniformed casino security guards. When they reached the main casino floor, the guards turned around and headed back to Martijn Van Gries's office. No sooner were they out of sight than "Ace" Randall, Joe "The Batman" Hendrix, and a tall blonde woman emerged from the crowd and helped the two blackjack players toward the parking garage door.

"Theo, get your men down there and stop those two," Benson ordered.

The Dutchman turned and glared at him, irritated by the American's order. "Are you coming too?" Theo asked. "Or are you staying here, above the fray again?"

"I don't want them to know I'm here, not yet; there's too much at risk. Now get out there, before they get away. We need to find out where Burke is."

189

Theo slowly rose with a barely-disguised expression of disgust and motioned for MacGregor to come along. The two mercs drew their automatic pistols and racked a round in the chamber. For an angry second, Theo considered using it on the arrogant American; but he finally turned and headed for the door.

Dorothy put her shoulder under Ronald's arm. With Jimmy on the other side, they quickly hustled Ronald out the door and into the parking garage.

"Get them in the car and wait '30.'" Ace told The Batman and he flipped him the car keys. "If I'm not out by then, take off and I'll meet you at the boat."

"Roger that," The Batman immediately replied as he headed out the door behind Dorothy. No questions passed between them, and no answers were required.

Ace followed them to the parking garage door, turned around, and scanned the hallways and aisles around him. He was about to follow them out, when two men ran out of the service corridor door and headed toward him. Ace turned and faced them, leaning against the doorframe with his arms crossed over his chest. To the uneducated, it might appear to be a relaxed, nonthreatening posture, but Ace had his weight carefully balanced on the balls of both feet, with hands, fingers, elbows, knees, and feet ready to explode into a half-dozen different martial arts moves should the situation arise. He also had a 9-millimeter Glock tucked in the rear waistband of his slacks, and a six-inch survival knife up his sleeve. As for the two men running at him? Like a heat-seeking missile, he tracked them every step of the way as they approached.

Fortunately for everyone involved, the two men stopped when they were still six feet away and carefully spaced themselves out to each side of him. He had done this before, and it appeared they had, too, showing the same athletic strides, confident body language, and wary expressions that he and his men had. They were pros, and he realized he could be looking into a mirror.

"Is there some reason why you are blocking the door?" the older of the two men asked in accented English.

"Is there some reason why you're in a hurry to get through?" Ace replied.

They stood appraising each other for a moment longer. All three men had closely cropped, tactical beards, which somewhat obscured their appearances, but the accent? At first, it sounded like German, but it was a touch harder around the edges, more likely Dutch, he thought. That was when he realized he was talking to the man who got out of the limo this morning and shook hands with Martijn Van Gries. It was his brother Theo. Like Bob Burke, Ace knew he had met the man before. Where and when, he couldn't quite remember, but he had an image of him in dusty tribal clothing, scuffed boots, and carrying a Dutch-issue, Diemaco C8 assault rifle, which had been "tricked up" with a long-range sniper scope.

"I think I know you, don't I?" Ace finally asked, continuing to eye him carefully.

"Yes, somewhere, a few years ago. You are Delta, aren't you?"

"Was," Ace lied. "Now, I'm just another wandering, out-of-work Army veteran. And you're Dutch, with the Royal Dutch Marines aren't you? Where was it? Jalalabad? Or Khost?"

"God only knows," the other man answered. "You are Randall, aren't you?"

"Yes, and you are…"

"Van Gries, Theo, and you are correct; I am late of the Korps of Mariniers."

"A couple of out-of-work guns for hire? Is that what we're becoming?"

"I believe I do remember now. But it wasn't Jalalabad or Khost, it was in a base camp up in Nuristan Province, up in the mountains near the Pakistani border. Some of my men and I were seconded to an ad hoc NATO field force. You had a small squad of men, perhaps six or eight, and there was a major in charge. You called him *De Geest*, the Spirit?" Theo asked, as he finally understood. "His name was Burke, wasn't it?"

Ace smiled, surprised Van Gries would know the name, but he didn't answer.

"Yes, a very interesting fellow. Is he here with you?"

"The major? No, no, he got out two or three years ago, and I'm not sure where he is now," Ace told him. "You said your name's 'Van Gries?' Didn't I see that on some of the casino sales material? Is this the family business, perhaps?"

"No, no," Van Gries chuckled as he looked around the gaudy casino. "That is my older brother, Martijn. I believe he is the bookkeeper here. He needed some help with a small security issue, so I brought MacGregor here and a few of my other associates to help him out. So, tell me about those two card counters your people just hustled out the door; what was that all about?"

"Oh, they're just a couple of kids we met at Harrah's down in North Carolina. They have a system for blackjack, and they're pretty damned good at it. Me and my friends bankrolled them for a few weekend trips to the casinos in the nearby states. They do their thing, and we provide them with some security. That's all."

"You are not running them?"

"No, but why's that any of your business?"

Theo shrugged. "Because it would put you in a position you would not want to be in."

"I wouldn't? Ace asked, sounding surprised.

"No, and judging from the way one of your blackjack players was limping, it does not appear that your security accomplished very much tonight, did it?"

"Every job has its occupational hazards. I didn't get a chance to talk to them, so I'm not sure what happened. I hope it wasn't you or your people, though."

"Why would you say that?"

"Because that would put *you* in a position I don't believe *you'd* want to be in."

"Perhaps we shall have the opportunity to see who is correct," Theo said as he turned away. He looked back over his shoulder and added, "But I suggest you do not come back here unless we both care to find out."

Ace walked out the doors and through the darkest parts of the parking garage. The car was gone, as he expected, so he set off jogging downhill. He ran fast enough to get him where he wanted to go, but slow enough to look as if he was merely out for the exercise, not running away from something. *The Enchantress* was moored less than two thirds of a mile south of the Bimini Bay directly across the harbor, but the shortest combination of roads that would get him there was four times that distance, taking him in a long loop to the far end of the marina. However, as he expected, by the time he got to the bottom of the casino access road, he saw Dorothy sitting in the rental car waiting for him. She flashed her headlights and he quickly jogged the rest of the way over and got in.

"What took you so long?" she asked, obviously concerned. "Problems?"

"Nothing I couldn't handle. Is Ronald okay?"

"Yeah, but not very happy," she told him. "Some big Dutch guy shot him in the foot with a small-caliber handgun, maybe it was a .22, or even a .32. The bullet went through-and-through, but I'm sure there's some broken bones in there. The Batman's running him to the hospital for x-rays."

"Yeah, by the time this thing's over, we're gonna have some serious conversations with those people."

Theo Van Gries walked into his brother's office with Reggie MacGregor tagging behind. The Scot flopped on the couch, while Theo took a seat on his brother's desk. Benson was still there, watching the security feeds on the computer as he had been.

"His name is Randall," Theo said. "I remember him from the mountains in Afghanistan. I remember Burke too. They are good, very good."

"As good as you and your men?" Martijn asked him.

Theo's head whipped around, and he turned his angry glare on Martijn. "That is a question that only dead men can answer. When you told me your friend Carbonari had a problem with an American soldier, a major named Burke, I did not make the connection and place the name with the face. I also did not know he was bringing his other men with him." He looked down at Benson and asked,

"How many Deltas did he bring with him, Captain?"

"I have no idea," Benson answered. "So far, I've only seen three of them on the videos. I doubt there's much more than that."

"You doubt it, but you don't really know, do you?" Theo nodded, thinking over the worsening situation, and becoming increasingly unhappy. Finally, he turned toward Bakker and said, "We must rethink our tactical plan, Lucas, the observation points, shifts, weapons, all of that." Finally, he looked down at his brother and told him. "I need to bring in more men, Martijn, and to do that, I need more money. The risks just increased exponentially."

"Donatello will never agree," his younger brother answered.

Theo leaned in even closer and said, "Perhaps you can whisper sweet nothings in his ear tonight and talk him into it."

"You don't understand. He'll tell me to use the men they sent down here from Brooklyn. There are a half-dozen of them. Can't you use them?"

"No, you'll just have to try a little 'harder,' if you get my meaning, *brother*."

CHAPTER TWENTY-FOUR

"**Well, that didn't** work out too well," Bob said as the group gathered around the big boat's central lounge. It was 1:30 in the morning. Chester and Lonzo had just returned from playing janitor all night. Ace and Dorothy were back from the Bimini Bay. The Batman and Bulldog were still at the hospital with Ronald, while Koz kept watch up on the flying bridge with binoculars and an automatic rifle. Patsy hung all over Jimmy, as usual, happy he wasn't the one who got hurt, while Ernie Travers went around dispensing fresh beers.

"What was it they taught you at West Point?" Ace asked. "The best plan only lasts until the first shot is fired."

"Helmuth von Moltke," Bob answered, immediately recognizing the quotation. "But I don't think the old field marshal was referring to the top of Ronald's foot."

"By the way, I think I met one of von Moltke's great-grandsons tonight, and you're not gonna like it. You remember that op we ran in Nuristan Province up near the Pakistani border three, maybe five years ago?"

"I remember those goddamn mountains," Chester chimed in.

"And a lot of snow and ice," Lonzo agreed.

"And do you remember that NATO contingent we worked with for a couple of days when we swept that valley?"

Bob frowned as he tried to remember. "Wasn't it a mixed unit of British SAS and some German Kommando Specialkrafte, the KSK, as I recall."

"You've almost got it, and there were some Dutch..." Ace led him on.

"Was that Martijn Van Gries's brother?" Bob exclaimed. "He told me his brother was in the Royal Dutch Marines, the Black Devils, but I never made the connection."

"I remember those guys," Koz agreed. "They were pretty damned squared away."

"Theo Van Gries," Bob confirmed. "Tall, quiet, and dead eyes, like a shark."

"No overweight Gumbahs from Brooklyn with .38-caliber police specials?" Ernie asked glumly. "I think Carbonari just ratcheted up the opposition again."

"The guy who shot Ronald in the foot was Dutch," Jimmy joined in. "He and Martijn Van Gries even talked to each other in Dutch. His name was Bakker."

"Like the rest of you, I'd like nothing more than to kick their butts for what they did to Vinnie," Linda finally spoke up. "After all, that's what we came here for, to bring down Donatello Carbonari; but it sounds like he brought in a half-dozen extras from *The Godfather*, plus the Dutch Foreign Legion. There comes a point when we might want to reconsider what we're doing here before things go from bad to worse."

"Point taken," Bob reluctantly admitted.

"But things *aren't* going from bad to worse!" Jimmy stood up and began pacing nervously around the room, insisting on being heard over all the "adult" chatter. "Ronald and I learned a lot in there, a lot more than you think. Sure, he got shot in the foot, but it's not like his foot is the most important part of a gamer's anatomy."

"Okay, what did you learn?" Bob asked.

"Well, first, they took us to Van Gries's office, not to the Security Office or 'Risk Management,' like we thought they would. There were some beefy guys in blue blazers who dragged us down there, but there were no black guys like that Shaka Corliss you described, or big blond football players, just three or four military types."

Bob looked at Ernie Travers and shrugged. "Maybe they *did* get rid of him."

"And I got a chance to look around his office," Jimmy said excitedly. "Van Gries has a hugely expensive gamer laptop sitting on his desk. It is big and fast, and you can run almost any financial or security system through that thing, particularly if it's connected to the mainframe we think they have in the basement. He hung his MIT degree in a big frame on the wall, and..."

"MIT versus Berkeley again? What's the point spread now?" Ace asked.

"You guys! You never take me seriously."

"Sure we do, Jimmy. They tease everybody when we stand down," Bob told him. "If they didn't like you, they'd totally ignore you."

Jimmy looked at him and frowned, still not sure. "Okay, but my point is that under that stupid MIT degree is a bookcase, and in that bookcase is a row of tech manuals from a company called DACI. That's Digital Analytics Consultants, Inc.; they're a big software development company up in Princeton. Obviously, *they're* the ones who Van Gries used to design and integrate his security and financial software. I recognized their logo from halfway across the room. They tried to hire Ronald and me."

"And we won the lottery?" Patsy asked with a big grin.

Jimmy looked at her and frowned, not quite sure if it was a compliment or more teasing. "I guess," he answered.

"Why did you turn them down?" Bob asked. "Did Charlie overpay, or did they have too many MIT guys?"

"He *definitely* did not overpay us, Mister B., and oddly enough, their Princeton office has quite a few Berkeley guys. That's what I'm getting at! One of our classmates took a job with them there. He's a cray cray Russian ex-pat named Sasha Kandarski, a *really* obnoxious knuckle dragger. He *always* needed deodorant, but he's a top gun on security systems, codes, and back doors. Almost nobody over here wants to go into that kind of 'drudge' work these days, but you can make a real bundle if you're good at it, and Sasha was very good at it. We always kidded him about how he left his KGB background off his resume. He'd laugh along with the joke but it was a strained laugh, and then he'd quickly change the subject. But those firewalls we ran into were Sasha's work, I knew it the first time I saw it. As soon as Ronald comes back, if you say DACI, he'll say Sasha Kandarski, you just watch."

"You really can tell who did the programming?" Koz asked.

"More often than not. It has to do with where they got their early training, the basic structure they use, how they sequence things, and how they handle problems. It's kind of like fingerprints; and yes, you can usually tell."

"My grandfather worked in military intelligence in London with the OSS, MI-6, MI-8, and MI-9 in the listening posts in St. James, Claxton Street, and the old Saint Ermin's Hotel," Bulldog spoke up. "He said the same thing about the Morse Code operators back in World War II. They knew the 'key stroke signatures' of all their agents in France. When they suddenly changed, they knew the Germans had caught them. I guess it's like a fingerprint."

"Exactly," Jimmy went on. "As I got into their systems the past few days, I felt little alarm bells going off in the back of my head. Ronald did too. Something looked familiar. At first, we both wrote it off to a lot of cutting, pasting, and boilerplating. Not knowing the company name, we never put it together, but it's Sasha Kandarski. I know it."

"Makes sense," Koz agreed. "The Russians don't care who they work for."

"Okay," Bob said. "But where's this taking us?"

"Where?" Jimmy asked. "To Princeton. Let's go up there and lean on the toad."

"Lean on the toad?" Ace choked on his beer and laughed. "Jeez, Ghost, we've created a monster."

"Yeah, and I think I know just how to make him talk," Jimmy beamed.

Five minutes later, Bob walked up the stairs to the flying bridge, where Ernie was on guard duty. Bob began opening the cabinet drawers, picking up the seat cushions, and looking in the side lockers. Ernie sat in the captain's chair watching him.

Bob finally stood in frustration and looked around. Hands on hips, he mumbled, "What the hell! I know I left it here somewhere."

Ernie's curiosity was sufficiently aroused that he finally asked, "All right, I give. What are you looking for?"

"That pickpocket you flew down here from Chicago. I know he has to be here somewhere."

Ernie tipped his head back and began to laugh. "Good one. You got me."

"But I haven't got Dimi. Do you?"

"Not exactly... The official answer is that he seems to have abandoned ship earlier tonight, and I didn't notice he was gone until tomorrow morning."

"And the unofficial answer?"

"He's a nice old guy. He was a big help and he put himself at risk for us so I really couldn't see sending him back to Cook County jail. Could you?"

"You gonna get any blow back over this?"

"Not really. What are they gonna do? Demote me to lieutenant and dump me out at O'Hare? Besides, Dimi was officially nonviolent, and he'd probably be eligible for an early release in a few weeks anyway. So I decided to expedite the process a little. I guess any blow back depends on where he dumps your rent-a-car."

"He has your car, too?"

"Well, technically it's your car, but how else was he going to get away. Walk?"

Princeton, New Jersey is an hour and a half northwest of Atlantic City, halfway between Philadelphia and New York City. The huge military complex of Fort Dix and McGuire Air Force Base is about two-thirds of the way there. Very convenient, Bob thought.

Sasha Kandarski was a fat, overweight Russian ex-pat who did not seem to understand the western concepts of personal hygiene, changing bedding, housekeeping, taking out the trash, or getting up before noon. When he was suddenly awoken at 6:00 a.m. that morning, he found four large men dressed in black from their black rubber-soled shoes to their black ski masks standing around his bed, pointing guns at him.

"Why take him?" one of them asked. "Why not just do him here?"

"Shto?" *What?* Kandarski asked, only half-awake as he pulled his blanket up to his chin and tried to hide. "*Do?* Do what here?"

"He's just another damned terrorist," another one grunted. "We can say he pulled a gun. Who's going to care, anyway?"

"Terrorist? Nyet! Nyet! I am not..." Kandarski screamed as one of them slapped a strip of duct tape across his mouth.

"It don't make no never mind to me what you do, but they said they wanted to talk to him first," another man said as he wrapped more duct tape around Sasha's wrists and ankles, and pulled a hood over his head. They then picked him up, and dropped him inside a thick, black-rubber body bag.

Being manhandled, carried down a flight of stairs, and tossed in the truck's rear cargo area was no way to start a day, Kandarski probably thought. The bag stunk like the inside of an old car tire, but that was nothing compared to the stark terror of a thirty-minute ride in the dark, while being bounced around inside the back of the big truck. Finally, it stopped. He heard the truck's doors open and slam shut and men laughing. Someone grabbed the body bag by its handles, pulled it out of the truck, and dropped it on the hard concrete. More hands pulled down the body bag's big zipper, reached inside, and stood him upright.

"Ah, man, he pissed himself!" he heard.

As the duct tape was ripped off his ankles, he looked around and saw he was standing in the bright sunshine outside an airplane hangar between two big, black, unmarked Chevy Suburbans with US Government license plates. Behind him, less than a hundred feet away, sat a gray executive jet with US Air Force markings. Its rear passenger door was open, and the staircase was down. A short distance away from the jet sat a matte-black, US Army stealth Blackhawk helicopter. As Kandarski looked at them, his eyes went wide.

The men still wore their black ski masks, and they were none too gentle as they grabbed his arms and dragged him through the open door into the aircraft hangar. If the fat Russian hadn't already pissed himself inside the black rubber bag, he would have done it then. They shoved him down on a rickety card table chair and suddenly ripped the duct tape off his mouth.

"Ah, Ah!" he screamed as half of his scraggly face hair came off with it. As he rubbed his cheeks and cursed under his breath in Russian, he looked up and saw he was seated six feet in front of a long folding table. Other than the table, an empty chair on the other side of it, and the four men in the ski masks, the big hangar was empty.

Long, silent minutes passed, until he finally asked, his voice croaking, "What? What you want with me?"

"Shut up!" one of the men answered.

After several more long minutes, another side door opened and an older, smaller man with short gray hair strode briskly in wearing a US Army dress green uniform. Behind him came a second man, who closed the door and stood in front of it with his arms folded across his chest. The first man walked up to the table, pulled out the other chair, sat down opposite Kandarski, and glared at him for a moment, as if the Russian were a bug under a microscope. Kandarski knew little about military uniforms, Russian or American. However, he knew if the man had a chest full of ribbons and medals, as the man in front of him had, that meant he had been in combat and killed many people. Second, the three stars on his shoulder meant he was a general. In Russia, a general, especially a general in the FSB where Sasha worked, literally held a man's life in his hands, and was someone to be truly feared. Third, there was no name tag above his pocket, as American soldiers usually wore, which meant something really bad was about to happen to him.

The general pulled a folded sheet of paper from his jacket pocket and laid it on the table. "Mr. Kandarski, this is a Rendition Order. Do you see that airplane sitting out there?"

The Russian turned his head and looked out the window at the gray passenger jet sitting on the tarmac. He already knew it was there, but he needed time to think. "Yes, yes, I see it, I see it. But what do you want of me? Please, I do nothing…"

Stansky shook his head. "We both know that's a lie, which is why that airplane is waiting to fly you down to Guantánamo Bay. You've heard of Guantánamo Bay, haven't you?" Kandarski nodded faster than a bobble-head doll in a San Francisco earthquake. He began to say something in protest but the general cut him off. "Once I sign this order, the CIA will fly you out of here and keep you there as long as they want, for aiding and abetting a terrorist organization."

"Terrorists! But I swear, I do nothing…"

Stansky simply ignored him. "And after they've squeezed out every little dark secret that's inside that ugly little head of yours, they'll toss you to their friends in the Russian FSB for whatever else they care to do with you. You *do* know what the FSB is, don't you?" the general asked, "the old KGB?"

Kandarski turned white and he nodded even faster. "Yes, yes, I know FSB, but I did not…"

"Yes you did," Stansky cut him off and raised the sheet of paper. "Remember that work you did for an outfit down in Atlantic City called…" He looked at the paper again. "Boardwalk Investments?"

"Yes, yes, of course!" Kandarski quickly admitted. "They own casino. I develop software systems, but…"

"Then you admit it?

"Yes!… Uh, no, no! No, I…" He paused, trying to think his way out of this. "Boardwalk people are not terrorists. They are…"

"They are what?" Stansky leaned forward, his eyes drilling into Kandarski.

"They are… Mafia, sir."

The general looked across at Kandarski, as one might look at a very slow third grader. "Sasha, how can someone as smart as you be so stupid? The Mafia? Really? Two years ago, the Gambinos and Luccheses worked out an arrangement with Al Qaeda to launder money through their casinos in return for weapons, bootleg oil, cocaine, stolen Middle Eastern art, women, you name it. It all gets run through the Crimea, Turkey, and Sicily. That security and financial software *you* wrote for them is at the heart of their terrorist cell."

Kandarski's mouth fell open. He stared across at the general, speechless.

"But today is your lucky day, Sasha," Stansky told him. "I was about to sign this Rendition Order, when a young analyst who works for us came to me and told me that he knows you and that you might not be a spy or a terrorist."

"No, sir, I am not!" Kandarski pleaded. "I swear. But who iz this fellow, I will..." That was when the side door opened again, and Jimmy Barker walked in. "Jimmy? Jimmy! Oh, thank God, Jimmy..." Sasha jumped out of his chair in joy, until two of the black-hooded men shoved him back down on it, hard.

"Is that the man you told me about, Jimmy?" Stansky asked.

"Yes, sir. It's been a few years. He's gotten fatter and uglier, but..."

"I can see that, but you think we can trust him, that he'll work with us?"

Jimmy stared at Sasha for a long, painful moment or two. "I think so, sir," he finally told him, not sounding completely confident in his answer.

"All right, Sasha, here's the deal," the general told him. "My men are going to drive you back to your apartment and give you one minute to grab your things. Then they'll take you to your office, where you'll copy all your programs and files, and get every single document that you have related to Boardwalk Investments. You are not to say anything to anyone about what you are doing. Do you understand me?"

"Yes, oh yes, I..."

"Good. If anyone asks, you can say you are sick. You've come down with the flu and may not be back for a few days, maybe a week. Then, you'll bring all the Boardwalk material outside, where my men will be waiting for you, understand?"

"Oh, yes. Yes, sir, anything!" Sasha babbled.

"My men will then take you to a location where you will meet with Jimmy and another of our analysts, Ronald Talmadge. I understand you know Ronald, too?"

"Oh yes, yes, Ronald! He iz good friend too, they..."

"You are to work with them and give them your full cooperation to crack into those data systems. If you don't, the jet will be sitting here waiting for you. All that Jimmy or Ronald need to do is give me the word, and you are off to Guantánamo. Clear?"

"Yes, sir. Clear, very, very clear," Sasha told him as the enormity of his situation finally weighed in on him.

"And just so you know," Stansky leaned forward and gave him his sternest expression. "We inserted a tiny GPS tracker and audio device under the skin in the center of your back, where you cannot reach it." Kandarski immediately leaned forward and tried to reach his hand up his back, but one of the masked men slapped it aside. "Do not even try, Sasha! Our people at Langley will be listening to every word you say, and know exactly where you are every minute of the day. That device in your back contains two grams of plastic explosive. If you run, or try to take it out, it will explode and cut your spine in half. Is that clear?"

Sasha's mouth dropped open again, but he quickly nodded his agreement.

"Good, because the clock's running, Sasha. Understand?" the general said as he motioned to the masked men. "Get this man out of here."

General Stansky watched two of his masked men escort Sasha Kandarski back to the black Suburban, with Jimmy close behind. They quickly got inside, slammed the doors shut, and sped away. That was when Bob Burke and Ace Randall finally pulled off their ski masks, and they, General Stansky, and Command Sergeant Major O'Connor roared with laughter.

"Goddamn, Bobby," Stansky told them, almost in tears. "I swear, that was the most fun I've had in years. When I told him I'd turn him over to the FSB, I thought that fat moron was going to crap his pants."

"From the smell of him, I'm not sure he didn't," Ace said.

"Lord, you got that right!" Stansky laughed even harder. "Your guys better run that Suburban through a carwash before they take it back to the Corrections Center."

"With the windows down?" Bob asked.

"No doubt about it," Stansky agreed.

"An exploding chip in his back?" Ace laughed. "Did I miss some new tech?"

"I think I saw that in a James Bond movie," Stansky admitted. "I'll call General Browning at McGuire and thank him for the use of the hangar and the jet, and fly you gentlemen back to Atlantic City. But do you think that Russian will be of any use to us?"

"Jimmy thinks so," Bob told him.

"That kid's pretty smart, isn't he?"

"You wouldn't believe it."

"When he said the Russian had gotten fatter and uglier, I almost lost it. How come we can't get them like that?"

"They're pretty high maintenance, sir. I'm not sure you can afford all the laptops."

"Or the cute girls," Ace added.

CHAPTER TWENTY-FIVE

By 8:00 a.m., Bob, Ace, Koz, and Ernie had returned from their early morning trip to Princeton and were huddled around the dining room table drinking coffee. Linda was putting away dishes and could never tell whether they were strategizing or telling jokes. The Batman and Bulldog had brought Ronald back from the hospital around 4:00 a.m., just after Bob and the others left, and were now sitting on the flying bridge, keeping watch on the casino. It was hard to keep things quiet on a boat, even a large one, and Linda had heard the commotion when they came in. When she saw Ronald limping, she insisted on hearing the whole story.

"A couple of the small bones in his foot are broken. Nothing critical," Bulldog told her.

"Because it's not your foot," Linda corrected him.

"I can't argue with that, but they gave him Percocet, and some other stuff."

"Percocet?" Linda said. "You guys eat that stuff like candy."

"Yes, we do, but he'll have to see a hoof surgeon after the swelling goes down, and the doc said *Dancing with the Stars* is out."

Linda turned and looked at the aft deck. The morning sun was warm, and the two Geeks were already sprawled in the sun. They were bent over their laptops, head-to-head with a very strange new creature that Koz and Ernie had dragged aboard. He was short and very overweight, with wild, unkempt curly hair, a scraggly beard, and round black eyes, which never seemed to stop moving. Before they allowed him to set foot on board, they escorted him to the Port-a-John at the end of the pier, made him change into a pair of Ernie's old swim trunks, and threw his clothes in a nearby dumpster.

"But I took shower," the Russian complained.

"Take another one," Ace told him as he tossed him a bar of soap and made him scrub from head to foot, before he hosed him down on the pier.

Watching the show, Linda thought he was the hairiest man she had ever seen. Ace must have thought so too, because he made him scrub a second time, with the threat that he'd use one of the stiff brushes they used to clean the decks if he didn't get it right this time. Now, he lay in the sun on the aft deck with the other two, looking like a big sheep dog after an unwanted bath. Chester sat in a deck chair at the top of the gangplank, obviously keeping watch on them. Odder still, Jimmy was allowing the new guy to use his prized new laptop, which Linda never thought Jimmy would allow anyone else to touch.

Finally, Bob got up from the dining room table and walked into the galley for another cup of coffee, patting Linda on the butt as he passed.

"There hasn't been much of that lately, you know," she said.

"I know. There's going to be some serious R&R when this thing's over."

Patsy nudged Dorothy and laughed. "More R&R? Those two? Now there is a shock."

"Sweet young things like you aren't supposed to know about things like that," Bob answered.

"Yeah, right," Patsy chortled. "Well, maybe I'd know more about them if you didn't keep Jimmy up all night playing with that stupid computer."

"He isn't playing, he's working, and it's important," Bob corrected her. "And maybe he wouldn't be up all night trying to get the work done if you didn't keep tiring him out on your afternoon 'breaks.' "

"It's called love." Patsy turned and looked at the aft deck. "What do we have now? The Three Geeks? Athos, Porthos, and Fatso?"

"Good one," Linda laughed. "But it's nice to hear you're reading again."

"No, only the video," Patsy answered, "but none of those three are Logan Lerman or Orlando Bloom. So who's the new guy?"

"His name's Sasha," Bob said. "He's Russian, and he went to Berkeley with Jimmy and Ronald. He's working with them on something; so don't be a pest."

"Working with them?" Linda asked. "Really? Is that why you have Chester posted at the gangplank with a scowl and a bulge under his shirt?"

Bob walked out on the aft deck and knelt between Sasha and Ronald. "How's the foot?" he asked Ronald.

"Awesome," Ronald looked up, glassy-eyed, and smiled. "What foot?"

"That's okay, you'll remember as soon as the Percocet wears off. Like the other guys, I've been shot more often than I care to think, and it's going to hurt." Bob glanced at the computer screens and asked Sasha, "Well, are you in yet?"

"Oh yes, Mister Bob." Sasha looked up at him and drooled. "These machines you buy Jimmy and Ronald are totally dope. You buy me one, I kill for you."

"Well, I don't think we need you killing anyone at the moment, so you just keep popping the top on their databases and accounts, Sasha. That's all you need to do, deal? But remember, if we don't get everything, poof!" Bob pointed at Chester. "He sends the signal, the little chip explodes, and no more Sasha."

"No, no, no poofing, Mister B. I already give Jimmy codes."

Bob turned to Jimmy and asked, "So you're in?"

"Yep. About twenty minutes ago. Using his programmer back doors, we got behind all the firewalls with no problem, and I've been prowling around in their security and financial systems ever since. What do you want to know, Boss?"

"Well, first, can you download the stuff we want without tipping off Van Gries?"

"That arrogant MIT derb!" Sasha shook his head in disgust.

"Jimmy and Ronald already told us that story."

"He tried to tell *Sasha* how to do firewalls." Sasha pointed at the laptop. "He tried to tell *me!* He is Dutch moron!"

"So I'll take that as a 'yes.' When we're ready tonight, around 7:00, I want you to download all of his bookkeeping and financial structure stuff to a couple of email addresses I'm going to give you. When that's done, stay 'under the hood.' At 8:00, I want you to start draining their accounts and transfer everything to a series of offshore accounts I'm setting up. Then we'll crash their systems and get the hell out of Dodge. You got all that?"

"Sounds like fun." Jimmy rubbed his hands together and grinned. "The WOPR's going to run Global Thermonuclear War on their asses!"

"That's exactly what I want, Professor Falken." Bob smiled.

"Totally dench!" Ronald grinned.

"Who iz diz Falken?" Sasha frowned, not understanding. "Who iz Dench?"

"Never mind," Jimmy told him. "Once the flash drives are inserted into the pedestal computers, the Trojan Horses will take some time but they'll upload automatically into the mainframe. Then, it's goodbye Martijn."

"Goodbye, Martijn! Poof!" Sasha grinned.

"Didn't you say he was running their systems off that super laptop of his?" Bob asked.

"My bad," Jimmy confessed. "Sasha showed me where I had that all wrong."

"They have big mainframe, all right, Mister B. Eet iz in basement. Eet iz big mainframe — really *big* mainframe! That was where we work."

"But once we have the Trojan horses uploaded, *we'll* control it," Jimmy said. "We can tell it to do anything we want with those accounts, even lock Van Gries out."

"Yes, Boss." Sasha grinned. "Anything."

"We'll do it then," Bob told them. "Have the flash drives ready to install by 4:00 p.m., when the janitors report in."

"Then you buy Sasha one of these," the Russian said, pointing at Jimmy's laptop and grinning. "The lovely EON17-SLX, yes?"

"Actually, if everything goes right, you can have *that* one," Bob said, pointing at Jimmy's. "As I understand it, I owe Jimmy and Ronald something even newer and bigger."

"The new green logo Razer Blade!" The two Geeks high-fived each other and grinned, so Bob told Sasha, "And you'll have something even better to work for next time."

"Ochin Khorosho! *Very good*," Sasha said as he high-fived the other two as well. "At 4:00 p.m., eef eet iz Global Thermonuclear War you want, Meester B., then eet iz Global Thermonuclear War you get."

While Bob talked to the Three Geeks on the aft deck, Linda, Patsy, and Dorothy were finishing drying the lunch dishes. "How come we get stuck with this, while they drink coffee around the table, or sit out there in the sun?" Patsy complained as she put the last plate away.

"Newbie." Dorothy looked at her and laughed.

"Definitely a Noob," Linda cackled until she noticed the warm golden glow of the medallion hanging around Patsy's neck. "Nice. I haven't seen that one before," Linda said. "Is it new?"

"Oh, not really," Patsy answered as she tried to slip it back inside her blouse.

Linda was quicker, however. She took it out of Patsy's fingers and held it up to the light. It was an animal of some sort, perhaps a lion, crouching in profile, on an ornate gold chain. "Jeez, this little sucker's heavy," Linda said.

Dorothy took it from Linda and also looked. "It's heavy because it's gold."

"Oh, no," Patsy said. "It's just some cheap costume jewelry Vinnie brought back from the desert after his last deployment. Maybe it's gold plate, but that's about it."

Dorothy gave her a skeptical look as she bounced it up and down in her hand. "Costume jewelry, my sweet patootie. This is the real stuff, girl. Look at the sheen on it, and it looks old."

"No, no." Patsy shook her head again. "He told me he bought a bunch of this stuff in the bazaar in Doha. He liked to dress me up in them at night, you know."

"His little Persian harem girl?" Linda said as she gave Patsy a tickle. "Sounds kinky."

"Hey, lady, Bob's your second time around. You're telling me you've never done a little 'role-playing' to spice things up?"

"I'm not saying anything, girlfriend." Dorothy laughed and then turned toward her and whispered, "But if you need to bring out the toys to get Jimmy turned on…"

"Jimmy?" Patsy giggled. "Not hardly. But when I put *all* of them on, it really makes me feel… sexy, you know," Patsy said as she gave the other two a very knowing look.

"What do you mean, all of them?" Linda asked as she pointed at the medallion. "You mean there's more of these?"

"Look, I shouldn't have worn it." Patsy took the medallion away and tucked it back inside her blouse. "Vinnie didn't want me wearing it around Bragg because he said the guys were already jealous enough of him. It was just for us, for our little games. But with him gone, I thought it might spice things up with Jimmy, too."

That was when Bob came back in from the aft deck and walked by. Linda grabbed his arm and pulled him into the group. "Show him," she told Patsy.

"Show me what?" Bob asked as he smiled at Patsy.

"It's nothing," Patsy answered as she shrank back and wouldn't look at him.

"Show him!" Linda told her, friendly but insistent.

"I knew I should've never worn it today," Patsy grumbled as she reached up, pulled the medallion out of her blouse, and held it up for Bob to look at. "It's nothing, really."

"May I?" Bob asked her as he raised the chain over her head, taking it off so he could take a closer look at the medallion. He looked at the lion, turned it over and examined the back, and whistled. "Where did you get this?" he asked Patsy.

"From Vinnie," she said as her shoulders slumped. "I was just telling the girls that he bought a bunch of stuff in the market in Doha on his last deployment and he... well, he liked to dress me up in them at night. I'm not in any trouble, am I?"

"You? No, I doubt it, but this isn't cheap costume jewelry, Patsy."

"I told you it wasn't," Dorothy quickly agreed. "I've done a lot of traveling around with the Air Force and bought my share of bling. This is real gold, girl."

"The question is, where did *Vinnie* get it?" Bob said. "Look, he's gone. You can't get him in any trouble, and he can't get you in any trouble, either, so just tell me."

"She says there's more," Linda told him.

Patsy put her hands to her face and started to cry.

Bob put his hand on her shoulder and quietly asked, "How much more?"

"A box. There's maybe two or three dozen pieces in there, maybe more. I've never counted it. Old stuff, big and heavy, made of gold, some with inlaid stones, and a bunch of coins, too. He just brought it out one night, and started dressing me up in it, you know." She sounded embarrassed. "We were just... playing games. He had it before I met him, I'm sure of that, and he kept the box on the top shelf of our closet, pushed to the back. I'm not tall enough to see back there, but one night he decided to show it to me in case something... well, in case something ever happened to him."

"Did he say where he got it?" Bob asked.

"He said he and some guys bought a bunch of stuff in the market in Doha.

He said it was just cheap gold plate costume jewelry, but he figured out a way to get it back into the US without going through customs and paying any taxes and duties, and all that. The other guys are still over there, and he was holding it for them. He said they're going to split it up after the rest of them rotate back."

"And the box is in the house, on your closet shelf?" Bob asked.

"It was, but he started getting phone calls and he decided to move it. He let me keep a couple of pieces out so he could, you know... dress me up in them at night. But he moved the rest of it."

"Do you know where he moved them to?"

"Well, he never told me, but after we moved into the new house, there weren't but so many places he could have put them. The big dummy, even *I* knew that!"

"So you know where they are?" Linda asked.

"When he was off on a field exercise for a couple of days and I had nothing to do, I... kind of poked around a little. I mean, if something ever *did* happen to him, well...?"

"So where are they?" Linda asked again. "You know somebody tore your house apart a couple of days ago. That had to be what they were looking for."

"That stuff? Come on," Patsy scoffed until she looked around at Bob, Linda, and Dorothy's faces, and her mouth dropped open. "He told me it was cheap costume jewelry. I thought maybe my neck would turn green. I never thought..."

"I don't think your neck's going to turn green," Bob told her. "Where's the rest of it?"

"Out in the garage, in the corner. The ceiling is made of plywood. There's a pull-down ladder so you can get up into the crawl space, where we store suitcases and stuff. But that isn't where he put the box. It's in the back-left corner where the roof comes down real low. One of those pieces of plywood isn't nailed down. It looks like all the others, but you can push it up. The box is up there behind one of the ducts. Vinnie wasn't as dumb as a lot of people thought. You could tear the whole house down and never see that box up there."

"Figures," Bob said as he looked at Ernie and motioned for him to come over. When he did, Bob handed him the medallion; he didn't need to say anything.

Ernie held it up and looked at both sides of the medallion in the chain. "Wow! I did a few years in Burglary, but fine art isn't exactly my shtick. I did make a few trips to the Art Institute downtown with the kids, and they have some stuff like this on display. I'd say this is old, very old, biblically old, and without biting into it and breaking a crown, from the patina it's probably pure gold."

"Jesus, you think it isn't just real, it's real-real?" Linda asked.

"Oh, yeah! They took their gold jewelry very seriously back then. From the luster and feel of the piece, it's maybe 20 or even 24 karats, or pretty damned close, not that it matters. This is a museum quality antique," he said as he looked around at the others.

"That's what I thought," Bob said as a puzzled expression came over his face. "But if there's more of this stuff, when Vinnie got in trouble and owed all that money to the mob, why didn't he try to sell it, or trade it to them, or even melt it down? 47th Street in Manhattan is only a couple of hours up the road."

"I asked him the same thing," Patsy said. "I didn't think it was worth very much, but we were in *real* trouble with those guys. I told him, 'Take it to a pawn shop and sell it.' "

"What did he say?" Bob asked.

"Nothing. All he said was that it belonged to the other guys, and he couldn't. For some reason, he was more scared of them than he was of Van Gries and Shaka Corliss; and that never made any sense to me."

Bob looked at her and could tell she was telling him the truth. "All right, I'm going to give General Stansky a call. Someone needs to get that stuff out of harm's way, and it will get you off the hook."

"So you think it's hot?" Linda asked.

"The truth is, I have no idea." Bob looked around at them and lied through his teeth. "There are some stories floating around that Vinnie was working with some CIA guys up in Mosul at the same time there was a burglary at the National Museum in Baghdad, but who knows? The safest thing to do is to let the authorities figure this out. Agreed?"

Patsy nodded and held her hand out. "Do you think I can keep wearing it, at least until we get back home?" she asked. "It was from Vinnie, and…"

Bob looked at her for a moment and then hung the medallion back around her neck. "I don't see what it would hurt if you wear it around here on the boat. We can tell them you found it, and after the break-in you realized it might be valuable and want to turn it all in. Just promise me one thing." He looked Patsy in the eyes and laughed. "Don't lose it."

Later, up on the flying bridge, Bob spent some time looking through the latest video feeds from the Bimini Bay casino, and then scanned the hotel, the parking lots, and the boat marina with the binoculars one more time. Satisfied that everything looked quiet, he sat down on the flying bridge with Ace, Koz and Ernie to finalize his tactical plan.

"You two are the best shots in the outfit, next to me, of course," he told Ace and Koz.

"Once upon a time, old man," Ace laughed.

"And in a galaxy far, far away," Koz added.

"So, what are we going to do?" Ernie asked.

"I'm calling it 'the Casper Plan.' The Geeks have figured out how to get into Carbonari's computers. Tonight, while Chester and Lonzo make their rounds, they're going to insert a half-dozen flash drives into some of the desktop computers in different departments and upload the Trojan Horses. That will get us into their mainframe. Around 8:00 p.m., we're going to clean them out, all their money and records. That's going to all vanish, and so will we, like a bunch of little ghosts. We'll be long gone before they ever know what hit them."

"You mean we don't get to shoot anybody?" Ace complained.

"Sometimes, that's the sweetest revenge of all, but you don't need to worry. If we take his money, his partners up in Brooklyn will do it for us.

"And the Barretts?" Koz asked. "What have we been toting those suckers around for?"

"Backup, if we have to go to Plan B... or Plan C."

"You want us to use the nests we checked out on Tuscany Towers and Siesta Cove?"

"Correct. Ace, you take the Tuscany Towers, because it has the better view of the Bimini Bay helipad and Carbonari's penthouse. Koz, you take the Siesta. It has a better view of the harbor, the side and rear of the buildings, and the access roads. Together, you'll have it in a cross-fire if it comes to that, which I doubt. But you're the last ones out. You provide any cover we need, and then rendezvous with us down the coast. Ernie, you're in charge of the boat until I get back. The rest of us fall back here, and the gangplank comes up at 9:00 p.m."

"Are we taking spotters up to the roofs?" Ace asked.

"Chester and Lonzo. They go on the clock at 4:00 p.m. They've got rounds to cover, so as soon as they finish planting the flash drives, I told them to get out. That should be by 7:00, when they can rendezvous with you in the parking lots and go up. Take the optical scopes as well as the night vision scopes but keep the Barretts in their cases until you get up there. With their janitorial uniforms and the key cards, you should be able to get up there without any problem. And take the tactical radio headsets; we need to stay in touch."

"So we're going tactical at 7:00 p.m., and beat feet at 9:15?" Koz asked.

"That's right. We're hitting their computers and bank accounts as soon as the Geeks tell me the Trojan horses are uploaded, that we've taken control of their systems. We should start downloading the files we want by 8:00. There's an FBI office over in Northfield, on the mainland. The SAC is a guy named Philip Henderson who's getting an early Christmas present. Ernie, you do the same with your pal Carmine Bonafacio with the New Jersey State Police. We're sending them all of Carbonari's financial records. As soon as that's done, we'll hit Boardwalk Investment's bank accounts. We'll clean them out, plus all the money that's supposed to be going to the Gambinos and Luccheses in New York and to the other mob families across the country. That's going to simply vanish."

"Well, that should start the pot boiling," Koz chuckled.

"Ah, the beauty of paperless, electronic banking," Ace added.

"We should have the accounts cleaned out by 9:00, and the boat underway, out of the harbor and crossing through Absecon Inlet by 9:15. That's when you guys pull out, get in your cars, and head south for the pier at Ventnor, where we'll pick you up. It's high above the water but you can rappel down, which you said you always wanted to do anyway."

"It's not going to take Van Gries or Carbonari long to figure out they have a big problem," Ernie warned. "They can't lose that much mob money and expect anyone to believe that it's not their fault."

"I'm sure they'll lash out at anyone they can get their hands on," Bob agreed. "Which is why we need to be long gone by then. When they come up empty-handed, they're going to run as far and as fast as they can away from here."

"We can put a couple of rounds into the engine of that helicopter," Ace suggested. "That'll slow them down and change their travel plans, but what if we get a shot at Carbonari or Van Gries? Should we take it?"

"Not unless things blow up. My preference is to sail quietly away with no one even knowing we were there. We can let the New York mob do the heavy lifting for us later, and there will be less chance of blow back."

"And where are you going to be until then?" Ernie asked.

"Right here with you, the girls, and the Geeks... unless I'm not." Bob smiled.

"Until it hits the fan, you mean?" Koz asked.

"It wouldn't be a Bob Burke operation unless it did," Ace laughed.

CHAPTER TWENTY-SIX

At 7:00 p.m., Cheech Mazoulli made his mandatory daily phone call to Brooklyn to his boss, Angelo Roselli. Mazoulli knew this would not be pleasant. He wasn't happy with what was going on in Atlantic City and he knew damn well that Angelo would be even less happy. Cheech left the Bimini Bay early and drove the side streets down to Caesars on the Boardwalk, where there was an old-fashioned pay phone inside near the restrooms that he could use. "Old-fashioned?" he spat out the window. When he was growing up in Queens, the neighborhood telephone was in the laundromat on the first floor of the firetrap apartment building where he and his family lived. Hell, it was the *only* freakin' phone anybody had, except the bookies in the back room of the barbershop on the corner, and everyone was glad to have it. Today, try to find a pay phone that wasn't all beat to hell, had a phone book, and was still working, he thought. There weren't any! That was why Cheech thought all this crap Angelo made him go through with pay phones and the carefully circumscribed language was a bunch of nonsense. If the FBI's gonna get you, they're gonna get you. Period! End of story. Then again, he wasn't the boss and nobody asked him what he thought. So, if Angelo wanted him to talk Pig-Latin through a tin can on a string, he guessed that was what he'd do.

At exactly 6:59, Cheech stood at the pay phone, dialed the number and began dropping quarters into the slot. When Barbara answered, he mumbled, "It's me. Da Baker in?"

Barbara had done this a million times before and needed no introduction. "Hang on. He's in the kitchen, up to his elbows in cannoli, but he said he wants to talk to you."

Barbara put him on hold, leaving Cheech to wonder. Angelo wants to talk to him? That was never good. The best time to talk to a boss was when you weren't even on his radar, and the only reason he picked up the phone was 'cause he didn't have nuthin' better to do.

Cheech kept feeding the pay phone, wondering how long his quarters would last, when Angelo suddenly picked up at the other end. "What the hell's going on down dere?"

"Uh, nuttin' dat's any good," Cheech answered. "You know, it's dat guy. He don't listen to nuttin' I say. And that Dutch freak! Tell me I can cap his sorry ass. I swear, I'll do it for free," he began his rant.

"We never got dat money da prick was supposed to send up here today by 5:00. Da eight and a quarter, it never showed up. I want you to go rattle that bastard's cage, and rattle it good, you hear me? Take Eddie and Petey wit you. And if dat Dutch prick gives you any trouble, you send him to the freakin' dentist. Bust 'im up good, you hear me?" Angelo shouted into the phone.

Cheech wanted to tell him about the other foreigners Carbonari had brought in, those Dutch and German mercenaries who worked with the Dutchman's brother. He also wanted to tell Angelo how Marco Bianchi and Selmo Lombardi had their pockets picked right on the floor of the goddamned Bimini Bay casino, for Chris' sake! Unfortunately, he never got the chance to tell him any of that. Angelo had hung up and Cheech found himself staring at the pay phone. Frustrated, he slammed his fist into the wall. He'd send dat Dutch clown to the freakin' dentist, all right. Angelo could take dat to the bank!

Sunset had always been Martijn Van Gries's favorite time of the day. After he finally managed to pry himself away from the office that afternoon, and before he would adjourn to one of the city's finer restaurants for dinner, he enjoyed retreating to the aft deck of "his" sailboat in the marina for a bottle or two of the finer wines from the Bimini Bay's collection. He found the cool ocean breeze, the sounds of the seagulls, and an hour below deck with the ever-eager and always inventive Eva Pender the perfect way to end any day.

The sailboat wasn't "his," of course. It was a luxurious oceangoing sailing yacht that belonged to Boardwalk Investments, but Donatello never used it. He could get sick in a bathtub and almost never left dry land. The same was true for most of their New York City partners. Those bozos couldn't even swim, which was astonishing to someone from a country where every child learned to swim before the age of two. When the New York crowd came to town, it was for the gambling and the women, not for a blue-water cruise. The boat was virtually his now, and that was just fine with Martijn. It was the newest, state-of-the-art Beneteau Oceanis sixty-foot long, single-masted sailboat, which Donatello named the *Prancin' and Dancin'*. Designed for the open ocean, this gorgeous blue-water yacht had a short, wide aft deck and long, triangular bow. With a 150 horsepower Volvo Penta engine, it had power when it needed it, and B&G electronics throughout. It was fully automated; one person could control its 2,000 square feet of sail from the helm station.

Martijn kept it in the end slip of the furthest pier in the Bimini Bay marina, as far away from the hotel, casino, and other boats as he could get, with the bow pointed toward the casino and the open stern facing the harbor. Eva was an excitable and very vocal lover, who got off doing it in unusual places all over the boat, any time, day or night, and then walking around naked afterward. Consequently, Martijn opted for privacy. He wasn't worried about Donatello finding out about him and the woman. Donatello already knew. As long as Martijn did not entertain other men there, and as long as he occasionally allowed Donatello to watch and join in for a threesome, the big Italian couldn't care less.

That evening, Eva was below deck singing in the shower as Martijn poured himself another glass of wine and leaned back on one of the soft cushioned chairs on the aft deck. It faced south, toward the smaller boat marinas across the open harbor. He leaned forward and pressed his eyes into the dual apertures of his tripod-mounted Oberwerk BT-100-45 long-range binoculars to see what was going on. The precision optical instrument was more like a dual-lensed telescope than a pair of binoculars, and the finest and the most powerful of its kind. In fact, the precision lenses and aluminum frame were so heavy that they came mounted on a heavy tripod base for stability.

Ever since he was ten years old, Martijn had been an unabashed voyeur. He loved watching people who did not know they were being watched, especially when they were doing things they didn't want other people to know they were doing. He found that the bigger the house and the bigger the boat, the bigger the egos and the bigger the secrets that were kept inside. And just because the house or the boat was big did not mean that they afforded their owners any privacy, not that any of them seemed to care. With its 70x to 180x magnification, the Oberwerk was powerful enough to let him see exactly what was happening on most of the boats in the harbor. He could see through their portholes, down through their gangways, and count the freckles on the naked guests sunbathing on deck.

With everything going on at the casino right now, Martijn hadn't been able to get away to the sailboat and Eva for several days now, and he was still enjoying the warm glow of the expensive wine, the red and gold sunset, and her. He could smell her all over him. He raised his hand to his face and could smell her and taste her on his fingers. Feeling quite pleased with himself, Martijn slowly scanned the Bimini Bay marina, rotating the binoculars from boat to boat. He then turned them on the rest of the harbor, eventually focusing on the public marina across the wide boat channel from the Bimini Bay. To his surprise, he saw that someone had docked a spectacular Ferrenti power yacht in one of the transient slips. He smiled. "His" Beneteau Oceanis was a beautiful, oceangoing sailboat, but the Ferrenti was in another class altogether. Even used, they must cost at least two million dollars on the open market, especially one that appeared to be in as good shape as that one.

He wondered who owned it? Maybe some billionaire on his way south to Fort Lauderdale or Fort Myers for the winter? Maybe it was headed for the regatta at Antigua, or it was swinging by St. Barts on the way to Monte Carlo? Or maybe it was another of those damned Arab princes with their entourage of arrogant men and pouty women. They usually drop a bundle in the casino and pay handsomely for the disruptions and damages they invariably create in the restaurants, hotels, and gambling tables, but sometimes they aren't worth it. He would make a few telephone calls, find out who they were, and tell Theo and his men to keep a close eye on them. No, better still, he would turn that task over to that moron Cheech Mazoulli and his Brooklyn boys. Yes, that would be perfect! When Mazoulli screwed it up, as he surely would, the Arabs would storm out and Martijn could get Donatello to complain to Angelo and blame it all on Mazoulli.

Martijn focused the binoculars on the Ferrenti. At first, there wasn't much to see. The big powerboat was parked directly across the harbor and bow-on to his Beneteau Oceanis. The Ferrenti's bow was illuminated by the full light of the setting sun, but its portholes and windows appeared to be fitted with darkened glass, and there wasn't a damned thing that Martijn could see inside. "Damn," he swore. He did see two men standing on the open bridge. One of them was big and had a can of beer in his hand. Martijn saw his face but did not recognize him. The other man had a large pair of binoculars of his own and was using them to scan the Bimini Bay marina and the waterside of the hotel and casino. Unfortunately, his pair covered most of his face. Cheeky bastard, Martijn thought. This marina is only big enough for one voyeur at a time. If you're looking for something interesting to gawk at, why don't you confine your attentions to your side of the water.

He re-focused on the man with the binoculars. The Dutchman blinked. It might be his overactive imagination, but he swore the fellow was looking at the *Prancin' and Dancin'*, looking directly at him! But what could he see? While the big Ferrenti was docked in the bright sun, it was setting directly behind Martijn's sailboat, casting him and his aft deck in deep shadow. Martijn extended the Oberwerk's lenses to their maximum magnification. The water in the harbor was very calm, but at this distance and magnification, even the slightest motion would blur the image. To their left, behind the two men, he swore he saw several more heads on the aft deck, but that was all he could see. Refocusing back on the bridge, three women in bikinis join the two men in the wheelhouse. He focused on the two men again, but still could not get a clear view of the one with binoculars. One thing for certain though, none of those people looked like Arabs.

As he focused on the smallest of the three women, a slight breeze came up. The sailboat began to gently rock, and she refused to stop moving in his lens. Still, there was something faintly familiar about her. Finally, she turned her face toward him and paused long enough for him to see it was Patsy Evans, the young woman who came to the casino with Pastorini, the soldier who took the swan dive off the fifth story ledge of the hotel tower. No doubt about it, he thought. It was her, and that could only mean one thing. The Dutchman turned the big lenses of the Oberwerk back on the man with the binoculars and waited. Thirty seconds, and then a minute later, his patience finally paid off. The man lowered them long enough for Martijn to get a good look at his face. A cold shiver ran down Van Gries's spine. It was Burke! No doubt about it, it was that bastard Burke.

Van Gries was sitting in a deepening shadow and his face was completely screened by the tripod and body of his own binoculars, but he ducked even lower anyway. He reached into his pants pocket, fumbled with his cell phone, and speed-dialed his brother.

"Theo," he said, "get Benson and come down here to the sailboat as quickly as you can... Yes, now! I have something you must see, both of you; but put on your hats, and try to stay out of sight from the harbor. Now hurry!"

Five minutes later, the other two men remained in the shadows as they approached the sailboat and slipped aboard through the forward hatch, hidden from the harbor by the bridge and the wheelhouse, and joined Martijn in the galley. "Benson," he motioned for the American to come closer and pointed at the big pair of binoculars on the tripod on the aft deck. "Go up there and take a look. They are focused on a big yacht across the harbor. Look up on the flying bridge and tell me if you recognize anyone."

Benson gave him an odd look, but he did what he was told. He crept up the stairs, slipped into the deck chair behind the tripod, and put his eyes to the twin apertures.

"You can use the dials on each side to adjust them," Martijn told him.

Benson turned his head and glared at him with barely disguised contempt. "I know how to use one. It's like a spotter scope. Do you have any idea how many times I've...?"

"Look at the damned boat!" Martijn snapped. "While they are still there, if you please!"

Benson shook his head and pressed his eyes to the apertures again. He could tolerate Theo, but some days, like today, when they got together, the Van Gries brothers reminded him of an old drinking song from his college days at Indiana. "There's the highland Dutch, and the lowland Dutch," he began to sing softly under his breath, "the Rotterdam Dutch, and the Goddamned Dutch! Singing, glorious, glorious, one keg of beer for the four of us..." and so it went. That was them, he thought, the Goddamned Dutch! He focused the big binoculars again. But Martijn was right about one thing, you can see a gnat's ass at a thousand meters with these things. First, he lessened the magnification to get a wider view of the yacht. Then, he slowly focused in on the flying bridge and the people standing there.

"Do you see them?" Martijn asked impatiently. "The two men and the women?"

Benson immediately recognized his old CO, Robert T. Burke, in the flesh.

The second man appeared to be bigger and heavier, but Benson didn't recognize him. For certain, he wasn't one of Burke's Deltas. To his surprise, seeing Burke for the first time in several years reminded Benson of better days, when he was a better man. He and Burke had worked and fought the good fight together against a lot of bad guys. Then he met Theo Van Gries and his band of CIA contractors in Mosul. Now, those good days were gone forever.

"Yes, it's Burke," Benson finally confirmed. "No doubt about it."

"Who is the other man with him? Martijn asked.

"I have no idea, but he isn't one of the Deltas, at least none that I know."

Theo Van Gries had crept up the stairs behind him and elbowed his way behind the binoculars for a quick look. "He is right. It is Burke, and I do not know the other man either."

"Why are you surprised?" Benson asked Martijn. "We knew they were coming; it's why you and Carbonari brought us here," Benson reminded him as he got behind the binoculars again. "Now the mystery's over. We know they are here, and we know where they are. That's a big advantage, and we need to use it."

"Benson is right," Theo said. "We must take them out before they come for you."

"Agreed," Benson said. "We need to hit their boat, and we need to do it before they get any more organized than they probably already are. How fast can you get your men assembled?" he asked as he continued to scan at the big Ferrenti through the long lenses.

Theo looked at his watch and picked up his phone. "Give me five minutes. We'll meet in the hotel lobby. Our cars are in the garage."

"By the way, do you know who the women are?" Martijn asked Benson.

"I'm pretty sure the one in the middle is Burke's new wife. I saw their wedding photograph online a few months ago, but I have no idea who the other two are," Benson lied, as he focused the binoculars on Patsy Evans. He knew exactly who she was. As he continued to stare at her through Martijn's powerful binoculars, the rays of the setting sun caught the unmistakably warm, deep-yellow glint of 24-karat gold hanging around the young woman's neck. Benson already knew what he was going to do. He had sold his soul to the Devil back in Mosul a year before, and now he wanted what the Devil promised him. All that was necessary was for him to get the girl alone for a few moments. He would make her talk.

Bob Burke and Ernie Travers remained up top on *The Enchantress's* flying bridge watching the video feeds from the casino's front and side doors, scanning the harbor and the Bimini Bay's perimeter with the Zeiss binoculars. Bob looked down at the face of his iPhone to make sure no text messages had come in.

The screen showed 6:40 p.m., and he should be seeing one soon from Chester and Lonzo that the last of the flash drives were installed and were uploading, and that they were now retracing their steps to retrieve them. So far, however, there was nothing.

"I'm not sure I've ever seen you this nervous," Ernie commented.

"It's the waiting. That's the way it always is. The last time you and I worked together, back in Chicago, it was different. I've probably got twice as many people involved here, including the women, the Geeks, and my men, and I still don't have a good feel for the ground. I knew Chicago, Indian Lakes, and that big park. I'd been living there, and *they* were the strangers, not me. But here? New Jersey might as well be the other side of the moon. And look at that monstrosity," Bob said as he waved his hand at the huge Bimini Bay hotel and casino complex and the other two hotels off to the left. "We'd need an infantry company to take that place."

"I know what you mean," Ernie nodded as he pulled out his Glock automatic and rechecked the load for at least the third time since he had come up to the bridge.

"Mr. B.," he heard Jimmy call to him from the aft deck. "Come here a minute. You gotta see this."

"Speaking of nervous," Bob laughed. The Geeks were still working away on the laptops, digging deeper into Martijn Van Gries's files. "Hold down the fort while I see what Jimmy wants," he told Ernie.

Bob slid down the railings of the narrow staircase and landed on the lower deck. As he did, the Geeks were pointing at Jimmy's laptop and laughing hysterically. Bob bent over and they rotated the screen so he could see, and he found himself looking at a torrid love scene featuring two men going at it on a large, round bed with silk sheets. Bob blinked. As the two men rolled over and the smaller one got on top, he immediately recognized it was none other than Donatello Carbonari and Martijn Van Gries. Bob blinked and his mouth fell open, which made the Geeks laugh even harder.

"You want to know the really good part?" Jimmy asked.

"There's a 'good' part?" Bob quickly asked.

"Iz real good, Meester B." Sasha vigorously nodded his head.

"There are dozens of videos with those two 'doing the nasty,' " Jimmy told him.

"Eef you want, I sell these for 'big money' back in Moscow," Sasha offered.

"There are hundreds more of these," Jimmy continued, "and most of the others have audio feeds, too. Most feature other people — middle-aged men with young women, boys, other men, you name it. I have no idea who any of them are, but the others appear to have been taken in hotel rooms."

Bob thought it over for a moment. "I think our boys have a little blackmail and extortion scam going here. That's what I think."

"What's so funny?" He heard Linda's voice directly behind him as she put her hands on his back and tried to look around him at the screen.

"I'm not really sure you want to do that," Bob warned, as the camera really got up close and 'personal.'

"Oh!" Linda exclaimed. "Isn't that..."

"In the flesh... so to speak," Bob chuckled.

"I can see that!" Linda also began laughing and shaking her head as Patsy and Dorothy stepped over and joined the group.

Dorothy cocked her head and looked at the screen. "Party time at the monastery?"

"Yuck! Those two? Figures!" Patsy said as she stared at the screen for a moment.

"Something tells me his Italian friends up in Brooklyn wouldn't look very kindly on a few of those videos, would they?" Jimmy said.

Bob straightened up and smiled. "You know, that's a great idea, Jimmy. We have some e-mail addresses associated with the notifications on those accounts." He looked at his watch and saw it was 6:50 now. "After the files and accounts are transferred, pick out a couple of the best ones, and do it."

CHAPTER TWENTY-SEVEN

When Bob returned to the flying bridge, he was still laughing, and Ernie cracked up laughing too. The humor break did not last very long, however. Ernie suddenly sat up and pointed at the monitor screen. "Check out those three guys headed for the rear door of the casino. Wherever they're going, they're in a hurry," he said.

Bob bent over the monitor and immediately saw trouble. Martijn Van Gries was in the lead. Behind him came his younger brother, Theo. It had been a few years since Bob met him in Afghanistan, but when the two brothers stood side by side like this, and you could see both of their faces, Bob had no doubt it was him. However, the worst news came in the shape of the third man trailing the other two. As he hurried toward the casino door, he turned his head for the briefest of instants and looked back across the water at *The Enchantress*. He could grow a beard down to his knees and wear any kind of baseball hat he wanted, but Bob immediately recognized his old executive officer, Randy "Gramps" Benson, and he felt his heart sink.

"Problems?" Ernie asked.

"Looks that way," Bob replied. That was when his cell phone finally beeped. He looked down at the screen and saw a text message from Lonzo. It was 6:50 p.m. About time, he thought. Lonzo and Chester were supposed to be wrapping things up, getting out of there, and rendezvousing with Ace and Koz at the other two hotels. That was the plan, anyway, until Bob saw Lonzo's message.

"Two Gumbahs nosing around computers," the text message said. "Already found one flash drive. Looking for more."

Ernie had seen the screen too. "Why don't you tell them to get out of there. They've already uploaded the Trojan horses. Do the flash drives even matter anymore?" he asked.

"I don't know. It isn't even 7:00 yet, and we just got into their system. There's a lot of work to do to download and clean out the accounts." Bob looked at the cell phone screen again and debated before he picked it up. "Be there in Five. Stall," he texted back and quickly sent a second text to Ace and Koz. "Go up to roofs. Lonzo and Chester delayed. Get ready."

"What are you gonna do?" Ernie asked him.

"I'm going over to the casino and get Lonzo and Chester the hell out of there," he said as he checked the magazine in his Beretta.

"Want me to drive?"

"No, I'll take the CRRC, the rubber boat, across. It'll be a lot faster. The

Batman and Bulldog are down in the lounge. I'll take them with me, too. You stay here. With the girls and the Geeks down below, I need someone here to hold down the fort."

"And miss all the fun?"

"Don't worry, you'll get your share before this is over. We're not done."

"I'd complain that you're discriminating against old farts, but you're right. Your guys can move a lot faster than I can."

"Yeah, but you can shoot just as straight."

Bob slid down the banisters to the lower deck, grabbed the CRRC, and flipped the rubber raft into the water. He called for The Batman and Bulldog to join him. Turning to the Geeks, he said, "If you guys are in the system, I need all three of you to start downloading the files and hitting the bank accounts right now. We may have problems so there's no time to waste. I'll be back as quickly as I can. Work with what you got, but get it all going, now."

When Martijn and Theo Van Gries and Eddie Benson reached the hotel lobby, Theo's two Royal Dutch Marines, Eric Smit and Lucas Baker, plus Reggie MacGregor, the lone Brit, were already there leaning against the front desk, waiting, and looking bored. Theo was in the middle of explaining the situation when his cell phone rang. He glanced at the screen and saw the call was from Joost DeVries, his third Dutch Marine. He debated for a moment, and then turned aside and answered the call. As usual, the conversation was brief, except for a series of "Ja... Ja..." and "Ja," plus several grunts and a final, "We're on our way."

When he hung up, he turned back toward Martijn. "That was Joost. He ran into several of your New York 'friends' down by the elevators several moments ago. You remember that ignorant lout Cheech Mazoulli? The one who was so impressed with himself? Joost said it was him and two of his gunmen."

"What did they want? Martijn asked. "We are a little busy right now."

"They had just come from the office wing and were waiting for the elevator to go up to Carbonari's penthouse. He said they did not look very happy, especially that Cheech fellow. As they got in, he told Joost we should start packing before they threw us out. As the door closed, he saw Mazoulli pull out his pistol."

Martijn stood there for a moment, debating what to do. "Did Joost follow them upstairs?" he asked.

"No. He is waiting for us in the elevator lobby."

"Burke will have to wait..." Martijn began to say.

"No!" Benson cut him off. "He can't wait. We may never get this opportunity again. You two go upstairs with Joost. The three of you should be able to take care of those Brooklyn greaseballs. Meanwhile, I'll take Smit, Bakker, and MacGregor with me and visit the boat across the harbor. If we move quickly,

Burke will never know what hit him."

Theo quickly nodded. "Benson is right. That is what we must do."

"Will your guys do what I tell them to do?" Benson asked.

Theo turned toward them and said in Dutch, "Doen wat hij zegt te doen," *Do what he tells you to do*, and then looked back at Benson. "Now they will, captain."

"Then let's get this done," Benson said as the group broke up. He led his three toward the parking garage while the Van Gries brothers headed for the elevators.

Even with three large men sitting in the CRRC, its powerful Yamaha 200 hp outboard didn't seem to know the job was any tougher. In less than five minutes, they had rocketed across the darkening harbor to the dock at the Bimini Bay marina. As they bumped up against the pier, Bob pulled out his cell phone and managed to type a one-handed, one-line question to Lonzo.

"Where R U?" he typed.

Ten seconds later, as Bulldog tied the boat to the first marine cleat he could find, Bob read the reply, "Business Office," and jumped out. He and the other two sprinted toward the casino's side door, ignoring the vocal complaints from the marina attendant. Boardwalk Investments' administrative offices would all be closed now. Bob had been there before, on the last trip, and knew they were located down that nondescript side corridor across from Van Gries's office, halfway around the casino toward the hotel. He knew not to run inside. That would immediately draw the attention of security, so he slowed to a long-stride walk. It would get him there almost as fast but not look dramatically different from a gambler in serious need of a restroom.

When they reached the hallway to the administrative offices, he took a quick left and continued down the corridor until he saw the small black plastic sign above one of the doors which read "Business Office." A janitorial cart was parked outside, and Lonzo had been clever enough to block the door open with a trashcan. He heard men arguing inside and stopped. He signaled for Bulldog and The Batman to remain behind him and pulled out the Beretta tucked in the rear waistband of his pants. Quickly, he screwed a silencer to the end of the barrel, and stepped through the doorway, holding the automatic down the seam of his pants leg out of sight.

He found four men standing in the center aisle of the large open office, arguing. Two of them were Chester and Lonzo, still dressed in their janitor uniforms. Lonzo had been pushing a vacuum cleaner while Chester had been emptying trash cans. He held one against his chest as they argued with the two Gumbahs standing in front of them. Bob immediately recognized them as Marco

Bianchi and Selmo Lombardi from the photographs on their New York driver's licenses. They were the two who had had their pockets picked and their other toys taken away by Ernie's fast-fingered Chicago pickpocket friend, Dimitri. Lombardi had an old Colt .45 automatic in his right hand, and he was holding it under Lonzo's nose, threatening him. In his left hand, he held up a mini-flash drive, one which looked suspiciously like the ones the two janitors had been installing in the desktop computers around the office.

Bob didn't wait. He pushed the door open and walked right in. He plucked a piece of paper off the first desk he passed and acted completely unaware that anything unusual was going on inside the office. "Maybe you can help me out," he called to them as he held up the sheet of paper. "We have a delivery of stationery and envelopes for a Mrs. Johnson," he said as he pointed back toward the lobby, continuing to walk toward them.

Bianchi turned and glared at him, irritated by the disruption, and snapped, "Get yer ass out 'a here!"

"Look, I know the office is closed, but it was a bitch to get down here from Philly with all the traffic. You don't suppose anyone would mind if we drop them off in her cubicle, would you?"

"You hear what I said? Get out 'a here, now!"

"Hey, come on, it's just stationery," Bob said, getting still closer.

"You deaf or somethin'! I ain't telling you again," Bianchi said as he swung the big Colt around toward Burke. As he did, Lombardi also turned and looked at him, which was when Lonzo grabbed Bianchi's gun arm and pushed the Colt out of the way, stepped forward and drove the palm of his hand up and under Lombardi's nose. Normally, that was sufficient to drive the cartilage in the nose up and into the brain, and prove instantly fatal. Apparently, that didn't apply to thick-skulled Sicilians, however.

Lombardi screamed and stumbled backward, bringing his hands to his face as the Colt went off with a loud Blam! Even inside an office with an acoustical tile ceiling, carpet squares, and upholstered office cubicles, the booming gunshot was loud. The bullet caught Lonzo in the thigh. Enraged, Lombardi shook his head and tried to bring his gun hand around toward Lonzo again. That was when Bulldog stepped through the office door and shot Lombardi three times in the center of his chest. His eyes rolled up in his head and he collapsed on the floor, with Lonzo falling on top of him. By that time, Marco Bianchi had drawn a long-barreled .38-caliber revolver from his shoulder holster and began turning toward Bob. Chester shoved his trashcan into Bianchi as Bob raised his own silenced Beretta and shot Bianchi twice in the forehead. The Brooklyn street soldier collapsed on the floor next to Lombardi.

Chester immediately bent down and rolled Lonzo onto his back. Bob knelt next to him and checked out the bullet wound in his leg. It appeared to have struck the thick part of his thigh and had gone completely through. Lonzo was bleeding steadily, but it did not look as if the bullet had hit bone. All in all, Bob realized it could have been a lot worse. There wasn't a man in his unit who didn't have considerable experience treating bullet wounds, often their own, himself included. Working together, he and Chester grabbed some towels and trash bags off the cart and quickly got Lonzo's leg bandaged and the bleeding stopped.

"I'll be fine, I'll be fine," Lonzo kept telling them. "We gotta get out of here." That was no doubt true, Bob thought, but first he and Bulldog dragged the two Gumbahs into one of the cubicles where they would be out of sight from the door and the main aisles. As he did, The Batman wheeled the janitorial carts inside the office and placed them, the vacuum, and some trash cans on top of the worst of the bloodstains on the carpet.

"All right," he said as he turned toward Chester, as the two men got Lonzo to his feet. "Your car is parked in the lot, isn't it?" Chester nodded. "There's an emergency exit at the end of the hall. You know where it opens out?" Chester nodded again so Bob said, "Go get your car and bring it around to that door. We'll walk Lonzo down the hall and go out there. You drive him around to the boat, and I'll call Ernie and have them meet you in the marina parking lot and get him aboard. There's a large medic first aid kit on the boat. The wound doesn't look that bad. We can get him to a doctor soon as we get down to Cape May, or we can call our friends down in North Carolina for a pickup. We can decide that later, but let's move."

"Got it," Chester answered as he got up and sprinted away.

"I'm totally copacetic," Lonzo added through clenched teeth. "Just get me the hell out of here. I've seen all the vacuum cleaners and trash cans I want to see for a long time."

"Did you manage to pick up all the flash drives?" Bob asked him as he and Batman got Lonzo to his feet and headed for the door.

"Hold up a minute," Lonzo said as he leaned up against one of the cubicle walls and rummaged through his pants pockets. "There were eight when we started. Here's three, and Chester has two more." He dropped his in Bob's hand. "They're the ones we retrieved here and in data processing, before those two morons saw two in personnel and came looking for us. I don't know what tipped them off. Maybe they saw what we were doing, or maybe they're smarter than I thought; I don't know. Whatever, the one you shot has one, and I don't know where the last one is. Maybe we can look around…"

"No. We're out of time, and I'm not worried about one. Jimmy can figure out some way to disable it remotely."

"That kid's pretty smart, isn't he?" Chester asked.

"Smarter than you or me," Bob answered. "But I guess that's why he's doing what he's doing, and why you and I ended up in the Army doing what we're doing."

"And bleeding," Lonzo managed to laugh.

"You got that right. Now let's get you to the car."

The first hint that Donatello Carbonari got that he had a problem was when Cheech Mazoulli, Eddie Costa, and Pete Moretti — three of the Lucchese goons who had driven down from Brooklyn — kicked in the front doors of his penthouse. Those twin doors were made of hand-carved teak with ornate brass hinges, locks and a large, decorative door knocker on each side. They were some of Donatello's fondest possessions. Breaking them like that, when all Mazoulli had to do was knock, really pissed Donatello off. What pissed him off worse, however, was the fact that he was a Don, albeit a minor one, and they were showing him no respect. Street soldiers, even a minor underboss like Mazoulli, weren't supposed to be rude like that to their betters, even ones from Atlantic City.

Donatello's first indignant reaction was that they should've knocked. However, if he was being completely honest with himself, he knew he never would have heard them even if they did knock. At that moment, he was on the big, round bed in the master bedroom on the far side of his townhouse apartment mounting a skinny, fifteen-year-old male prostitute who was half his size. It was a clear night outside. The master bedroom had a twelve-foot-high ceiling, a large, circular mirror over the bed, and the entire north and east walls were taken up by floor-to-ceiling windows. The drapes had been pulled open and all of the bedroom lights were on, providing a spectacular view of Atlantic City and the smaller towns and cities up the coast and halfway to Staten Island and New York City.

It was an amazing sight, as anyone who had been in Donatello's penthouse had to admit. That was pretty much what the three Gumbahs thought after they kicked in his bedroom door, marched into the brightly lit bedroom with their guns drawn, and stood at the foot of the bed, staring down in astonishment at Carbonari and the boy.

"How dare you!" Carbonari shouted as he turned his head and looked back over his shoulder at them. "Get out of here! Get out of here!"

Donatello could scream all he wanted but when the kid underneath him looked back and saw the three angry men with pistols, he screamed too, quickly disengaged himself, and bolted for the bathroom as fast as his feet would move, locking the door behind him.

"Where's da goddamned money, you freakin' pervert!" Cheech screamed as he pointed his pistol at Donatello, too flustered to keep his composure.

"What money?" Donatello screamed back and tried to cover himself with the sheet. "What are you talking about?"

"Da money, you moke, *da money*. You know exactly what I'm talkin' about!" Cheech stepped closer, cocked his pistol, and pointed it at Donatello's head. "Da money never got dere, and Angelo ain't screwing around wit you no more, you... piece of crap."

"Angelo? I sent him the money, all eight and a quarter million. It went out a couple of hours ago, so put that damned gun down."

"Bullshit! Angelo says it never got dere. Da account's empty. There ain't nuttin' in it, and I ain't puttin' nuttin' down."

"Call him! Tell him to look again. We sent it up there, I swear."

Cheech stared at him for a long moment, debating what to do, until he finally pulled out his cell phone with his free hand and began to do the unthinkable. He began to dial Angelo's office phone number in the restaurant, until a better idea suddenly popped into his head and he put his cell phone away. Keeping his pistol pointed at Carbonari, he walked to Carbonari's desk, picked up his desk phone, and dialed. He expected Barbara to answer as usual, and was surprised when Angelo himself picked up the phone.

"Yeah, what da hell do *you* want?" Angelo had Caller ID and thought it was from Carbonari. Cheech put him on speaker just as Angelo began his rant. "You son of a bitch, where's..."

"Dis ain't da guy, it's me," Cheech jumped in.

"Oh, yeah? Well, all I want to know from *you* is when's his goddamned funeral?"

"He says he sent it, all of it. I told him you said dat thing is empty, but he said to tell you that you should look again. He said he sent it. He said he sent *all* of it."

"You tell dat freak I *did* look! I looked a couple of times because I couldn't believe he was freaking stupid enough *not* to send it when I told him to. And you wanna know what we found in dere? Videos! Videos of him and dat other guy, dat Dutch freak Von Greasy, or whatever. It was da two of them, together, doing it. Dat's what's in dat account, a bunch of goddamn videos of the two of them. You know what I mean? I thought I was gonna puke."

"Yeah? Well, if you wuz here a couple minutes ago, when me and da boys walked in his penthouse, you wudda puked for sure. Guess what we found? Him and some kid doing it."

"No, wait a minute, Angelo, this is all some mistake," Carbonari pleaded as he crawled across the bed toward Cheech and the telephone. "Somebody's setting me up, I swear!"

"Take care of him. I don't ever want to see him again," Angelo screamed back.

Cheech began to say something else but realized the line had gone dead. Angelo had hung up on him again. Cheech turned, looked down at Carbonari, and pointed his pistol at Donatello's head. Cheech was old-fashioned. He had no use for those fancy semi-automatic 9-millimeter European pistols that seem to be so much the rage with the cops and even some of his own guys these days. He preferred an old-fashioned, gunmetal-blue Colt .357 Magnum Python revolver with a six-inch barrel. As his father once told him as he waved the big pistol in front of his face, "Look, bonehead, if you can't stop some moke wit' one 'a dese t'ings, right in his grill, den you can't stop him wit' nuttin'."

Cheech smiled as he watched "the Don" squirm and crawl away from him on the messed-up bed. Carbonari pulled the top sheet up to his chin, tried to cover himself with it, and began to cower.

"You freakin' coward!" Cheech leaned in closer and screamed at him. He'd always been the top enforcer within Angelo Roselli's extended crime family, and the "muscle" when the boss needed it. There wasn't much Cheech wouldn't do if the old man told him to, and there wasn't much he hadn't already done at one time or another. Most of the time, he was paid to do it. Occasionally he did it for revenge, or for spite, or for just plain orneriness, but he had never killed a man for pure pleasure before, not until now. This was one he would enjoy.

Unfortunately for him, that was when the Van Gries brothers stepped into the bedroom accompanied by Joost DeVries and Reggie MacGregor, two of Theo's mercenaries, and all the fun suddenly escaped from the room like the helium from a two-hour-old birthday balloon.

CHAPTER TWENTY-EIGHT

The marina where the big Ferrenti yacht was moored was functional, but it wasn't designed for pleasure boats. Bob had grabbed the slip because it was the only one in town that could accommodate a boat of the size of *The Enchantress*, other than the Bimini Bay marina across the harbor. The parking lot was small, made of gravel, and was dimly lit by two sodium vapor lamps on a pair of tall poles. In addition to *The Enchantress* and a handful of other smaller pleasure boats, there were a half-dozen large, unsightly work-boats that were used for dredging and towing which were docked along the quay. On the opposite side of the parking lot, three tall boat sheds effectively screened the parking lot and pier from the nearby streets and businesses, all of which were dark at this hour anyway.

It took Gramps Benson and Theo's three mercs — Eric Smit, Lucas Bakker, and the German, Klaus Reimer — less than four minutes to drive around from the Bimini Bay to the marina's parking lot. They came in two cars and parked in the shadows near the boat sheds, wasting no time moving around the edge of the lot to the quay, and up the pier to the big boat. The narrow pier itself was illuminated by a series of small, low-voltage lights set atop the knee-high utility pedestals. They were fifty feet apart and centered on each boat slip. The small lights might be useful to prevent the occasional drunk from falling off the pier as they returned from the local bars at night, but they did little else.

Benson opted to bring two cars, because he didn't know what would happen when they reached the boat, or how many people they would be bringing back with them to the Bimini Bay, if any. From the reputations of the men on each side, the last thing he wanted was to get in a protracted firefight with his former Delta comrades. Then again, it might eliminate a few more of his Iraqi Museum heist partners and increase his share, the ever-opportunistic Benson thought.

He and the other men had changed into dark shirts and sweaters in the car but in the dim light, it didn't matter. The office and nearby boats and buildings were closed for the night, and there was little traffic on the surrounding streets. He had no doubt that Burke would have posted a guard, most likely up on the flying bridge, but the bow of the big yacht pointed at the harbor and the gaudy, blinking lights on the Bimini Bay Hotel, not at the parking lot. Hopefully, all that glittering neon would distract the attention of whoever was on guard up there long enough for them to get aboard. That was Benson's primary concern, because the guard would be armed and the flying bridge would be the most difficult area of the boat to reach.

A large awning covered the flying bridge. Even at night, it cast a deep shadow, making it pitch black underneath, except for the faint glow of a handful of the dials and gauges on the instrument panel. Benson had brought a pair of night vision goggles which he slipped on halfway up the pier. Unfortunately, the interior lights in the main lounge were lit, as were the lights on the aft deck and even the small LED lights that lit up the water around the boat. All of that direct and reflected light rendered his night vision goggles almost useless. Benson squinted and tried to shade the lenses, not knowing whether there was one man or two up there. All he could make out was the dim figure of one large man sitting in the captain's chair. The good news was that he appeared to be the only one up there. The bad news was that Benson had no idea who he was.

The main lounge was another story. From a hundred feet away, he saw three very animated young men huddled around two laptop computers that were standing open on the dining room table. They were banging away on the keyboards, waving their arms back and forth, laughing and arguing with each other, and totally oblivious to whatever else might be going on around them. He recognized two of them as the young blackjack card counters he had seen on the security cameras the night before, but he didn't recognize the third one sitting with them. He was short and fat, with unkempt hair and a scraggly beard. Whoever he was, he and the other two clearly were not soldiers, and should pose little danger. Finally, he saw three women sitting on the couches at the far end of the lounge. One was definitely Burke's wife and one was definitely Patsy Evans. The third one was a mystery, but how much problem could one female cause? Still, if Burke was anything, he was very clever. As Benson knew, there was a pattern to this. Somehow, the card counters, the women, the Deltas, and the man up on the bridge all fit into Burke's plan.

As Benson and his men approached the yacht, he gave a series of quick hand signals to the others. First, he and Smit would move on the flying bridge, with Benson quickly ascending the stairs and Smit covering him from the aft deck. With that accomplished, Bakker and the German would enter the lounge, neutralize the six sitting there, and search the cabins for any others. As if the assault had been practiced for days, their moves were tight, quick, and it was over in a matter of seconds.

The first thing the man on guard up on the flying bridge heard was Benson whispering from the head of the stairs behind him. "You on the flying bridge, take off the headset and don't say a word or you're dead," he said calmly and quietly. "We have two pistols trained on you and we aren't accustomed to missing, so don't force me to shoot."

Slowly the man removed the PRC 154A Rifleman tactical headset and dropped it on the deck at his feet. "Good," Benson said. That eliminated the threat of him radioing Burke. "Now, remain facing forward, place your weapon on the deck, if you please, and stand up." Clearly, the guard had been caught by surprise and wasn't very happy about it.

"Do it!" Benson ordered. "This is the only warning you're going to get," he added, and the man finally complied. He bent over and placed what appeared to be a Glock 9 on the deck at his feet. "Thank you," Benson told him. "Needless bloodshed won't accomplish anything for any of us, so come down here."

The man carefully navigated the steep stairs from the bridge and joined Benson and Smit on the aft deck. Benson looked at him and frowned.

"Who are you?" Benson asked, more than a little curious.

"Ernie Travers, Detective Captain, Chicago Police Department."

"The Chicago police?" Benson shook his head in amazement. "My, my, the Ghost does attract an eclectic mix of friends, does he not?"

"And you?"

"Me? Oh, I'm Randy Benson, as Bob and most of the others will tell you."

"Of course, his old exec." Ernie nodded knowingly. "Well, it looks like you've been a bad boy, Captain. He's not going to take this lightly, you know."

"Unfortunately, you're probably right. Unfortunately for all of us." Benson sighed. "Now, Mister Police Captain Detective, since I hope you're the sanest and most experienced in this bunch, I have three other men with me, hard, experienced men with guns. I want you to go downstairs with me and tell your people to stay calm and not cause us any trouble. We didn't come here to hurt anyone. We came here hoping to find the Ghost and the other Deltas, but they appear to be elsewhere, don't they?"

Benson waited but Ernie only smiled, shrugged, and said nothing. "I suppose that was too much to expect, wasn't it," Benson admitted. "All right, downstairs with the others. I guess we'll have to do this the hard way, won't we?"

By the time he, Smit, and Ernie stepped inside the main lounge, Benson's other two men stood on one side of the lounge, guns drawn, and their six prisoners sat on the couch and chairs against the bulkhead on the other side. Benson gave Bakker a questioning look, but the big Dutchman could only shake his head, no. There was no one else aboard. Again, unfortunate for everyone.

As the two groups stared at each other, Jimmy got a long look at Lucas Bakker. "You! You're the son of a bitch who shot Ronald in the foot, aren't you?"

"You want one too, little man?" Bakker answered in heavily accented English as he lowered his Glock 17 automatic and pointed it at Jimmy's foot. "That was my .22. I use it on pests. This is the one I use when I want to make really big holes in someone."

"That's enough," Benson called him off. "Now tell me, where, oh where has the elusive Major Burke gone? Who's going to be the first to tell me and save the others some needless pain and anguish?" Benson asked as he looked around from face to face.

"I will. It doesn't matter anymore," Ernie Travers answered as he looked at his watch. "He and a dozen Deltas went to the casino about fifteen minutes ago. Some went by boat, some by car and some by helicopter, to take the penthouse. By now, they are no doubt in control of the place, as Carbonari, Martijn Van Gries, and the rest of your people over there can tell you, even the half-dozen Mafia thugs who came down here from New York." Ernie paused and watched them glance at each other and shift back and forth nervously.

"You have a vivid imagination, Detective. Helicopters? And a dozen Deltas?" Benson asked, trying to sound confident, but the body language on the other two was unmistakable.

Ernie didn't stop. "It's a very quiet night. I haven't heard any gunshots, so I assume it all went as planned." Finally, he looked at Benson and shrugged. "With those new stealth helicopters they have down at Fort Bragg now, what do you think happened?"

Benson looked at the others, and then at Smit. "Call Theo," he said.

Ernie continued anyway. "Your best move is to get out of here right now, and out of Atlantic City, because they'll be coming back."

Smit kept his eyes and pistol trained on the prisoners, but he pulled out his cell phone and pushed a couple of speed dial buttons. Seconds later, someone answered. A few quick sentences passed back and forth in Dutch before Smit rang off and looked back at Benson.

"He is lying," Smit said. "Everything is quiet over there."

Benson shook his head. "Nice try, Captain-Detective. I expected nothing less from one of the Ghost's friends." He turned his eyes on Patsy. "Miss Evans, I need a brief conversation with you in private, if you please." Benson motioned for her to accompany him.

She stood and took several very nervous steps toward him, until he reached out, grabbed the gold necklace, and ripped it off her neck, snapping the chain. Startled, she screamed and raised her hands to her neck. Jimmy immediately jumped to his feet and went for Benson, shoving him in the chest with both hands. The effect on Benson was minimal. He barely moved, but he raised his Beretta and brought it down hard in the center of Jimmy's forehead. The slightly built Geek collapsed on the deck like a sack of flour at Benson's feet.

Dorothy didn't appreciate that at all. She flew out of her chair and was almost on Benson before Klaus Reimer stepped forward with his pistol. Dorothy was tall, muscular, and far more powerful than she looked, and compared to calf roping or bull riding, one macho kraut didn't concern her very much, even if he had a 9-millimeter automatic in his hand. She grabbed his arm, twisted, and flipped him halfway across the room, breaking his wrist, dislocating his shoulder, and throwing him into Smit and Benson at the same time. All three of them ended up in a heap against the bulkhead with Reimer on top, screaming in pain. His automatic came to rest on the deck at Dorothy's feet. She bent down to pick it up, just as Benson's Beretta went off. He may have been trapped beneath Reimer; but his aim was unerring and the bullet caught her in the midsection. She bent over, dropped to her knees, and toppled onto the deck.

Linda rushed forward to help her, but Benson crawled out from under the other two and shoved her angrily back onto the couch.

"No more!" Benson screamed as he pointed his pistol at the others, his own men included. "I didn't want any shooting! What part of that didn't you understand?" he said as he bent down, picked up Reimer's pistol, and jammed it in his belt.

Linda got back up anyway and glared at him. "I'm helping her whether you like it or not!" she said as she knelt on the floor next to Dorothy. "Get me some towels from the kitchen and the first-aid kit!" she ordered Benson.

In frustration, Benson looked at Bakker, who was closest, and nodded. Bakker turned, grabbed three dishtowels off the rack and the big first-aid kit which was sitting on the kitchen counter, and handed them to Linda.

"You're going to regret this," Ernie warned, looking at Benson.

"Who the hell is she?" Benson angrily demanded to know.

"Ace Randall's girlfriend." Linda looked up at him, her eyes burning with rage.

"Like I said, you're going to regret this," Ernie repeated.

Benson said nothing but the expression on his face told the story. The Chicago cop was absolutely right. There were two men in this world who Gramps Benson never wanted to cross. One was Bob Burke, and the other was Ace Randall. Only the Devil knew which one was the more lethal when provoked.

"Watch them," he told Bakker, and then turned on Patsy Evans. "Come here." He glared at her, grabbed her harshly by the arm, and dragged her down the narrow corridor into the master bedroom. Out of earshot from the others in the lounge, he slammed her up against the bulkhead and held the gold medallion in front of her eyes.

"Where's the rest of it?" he demanded to know.

"I don't know what you're talking about."

"I'm talking about the gold from Baghdad, where this piece came from, so don't get cute with me, little girl. I was Vinnie's partner when we took it. So were those other guys." He nodded toward the lounge. "All we want is our share, but Vinnie wouldn't give it to us."

"I... I don't..."

"Oh, yes, you do! I tore that little cracker box house of yours in Fayetteville apart, and I couldn't find it. But you know where it is," he hissed as he dangled the medallion in front of her. She looked up at him, terrified, but didn't say anything. His eyes flared angrily as he tightened his grip on her arm and threw her on the bed. "Have it your way. I'm going to enjoy this a lot more than you will, and after I'm finished, I'll turn the others loose on you. I'm a gentleman, but they aren't, so sooner or later, you're gonna tell me what our old partner Vinnie did with the rest of it."

He grabbed the waistband of her shorts. She struggled and tried to get away, but his grip was like a vice. "All right, all right, I'll tell you." She finally gave up. "It's in the garage. He hid it in the garage."

"Don't give me that crap. I looked there," Benson shot back, but he stopped his assault. "I looked everywhere. Now where is it!"

"Up in the ceiling, in the back corner above a loose piece of plywood."

"If you're lying to me..." He glared down at her and tugged at the waistband again.

"I'm not! That's where I got that," she said as she pointed to the medallion in his hand.

He looked deep into her eyes for another long minute. He saw fear and anger, a lot of that, but he didn't see any duplicity. "All right. But for your sake that had better be the truth. And one other little thing. If you don't want them to come visit you, this stays between the two of us. Understand?"

Benson pulled her off the bed and dragged her back up the corridor to the main lounge, where he shoved her back in her chair.

Linda pointed at Dorothy. "She needs to go to the hospital," Linda told him. "She needs to go now. Let me take her. I won't say anything."

"Oh, no, you're coming with me. I know who you are and you're my 'Bob Burke Get Out of Jail Free Card.' "

"Not if Dorothy dies." Linda looked up at him with hard, angry eyes. "Then, there'll be nothing that will save you. Or any of you," she added as she looked around at the others.

Benson looked down at the woman lying on the floor and knew Linda was right. "My answer is still no. However, I'll leave the two card counters here with her. They can call the paramedics as soon as we leave, but you, the big Chicago cop, and Vinnie's squeeze Patsy are coming with us. I know Ace and the Ghost. They'd take a shot at me with a Barrett without a second's hesitation, but they wouldn't dare with you in the way."

Benson turned and looked at the three Geeks. "All right, which one of you is the smart guy who hacked into the casino's computers?"

Both Ronald and Sasha immediately raised their hands. "Me, I did it!" they said, almost in unison. "I was the one who hacked into them."

On the other hand, Jimmy sat with his head in his hands and blood running down his forehead, staring daggers through Benson.

"That's what I thought," Benson quickly answered. "You," he pointed at Jimmy. "Get your laptop. You're coming with us."

"With Patsy?" Jimmy asked.

"Yeah, her too," Benson told him with an amused smile as he looked at Reimer and shook his head. "Him and her? Man, I never saw that one coming. Let's get out of here."

As soon as Bob was able to get Lonzo into the back seat of Chester's car, he told The Batman to go with them and told Bulldog to stay with him at the casino.

"I hate to disagree with you, Ghost, but you need me here," The Batman told him.

"Since when did you start debating an order?" Bob asked.

"Since you became a civilian."

"The men come first with me, and they always have. You know that."

"No, the mission did," The Batman corrected him.

"Look, I'm not arguing with you. Go with them and help Chester get Lonzo on the boat. I'll call ahead so they'll be waiting, then you can come back here. Meanwhile, Bulldog and I will reconnoiter and meet you at the back door in ten. Good enough?"

"Good enough," The Batman said as he jumped in the rear seat with Lonzo. Chester floored it, taking most of the downhill exit road on two wheels.

Bob keyed the mic on his headset. "Ernie, this is Ghost," he said, and waited for Ernie to reply. "Ernie, Ghost, come in," he called again, but all he heard was silence. Technical problems? Or something else, he wondered. But there was no time to find out.

Bob keyed the mic again. "Ace, Ghost. We've had a few problems back here," he quickly told him, "You and Koz will have to work without spotters."

"Roger that, no problem. What's with the boat?"

"I don't know. Chester will be there soon. Then I'll know."

"Roger that. So what's Plan B?"

"You and Koz go to the Tuscany Towers roof, both of you, opposite corners. I'll try to get some people up there with you but we're running a tad short on help at the moment, so stay frosty and keep me advised."

"Roger that. Did you copy, Koz?"

"Copy. The loading dock in Two."

Ace found a parking space near the emergency stairs and grabbed his backpack and guitar case from the trunk. Inside, the guitar case was lined with hard foam and had a series of sculpted indentations to hold the major pieces of his M-107 Barrett semi-automatic .50-caliber sniper rifle. It was Ace's favorite. At four times the weight of an M-16, it was solid, very accurate, and packed enough punch to stop a charging elephant. Its bullets produced over 11,500 foot-pounds of pressure, which could punch a hole through a half-inch of plate steel; or, he figured, through three Gumbahs standing in line. He had it broken down into the upper and lower receiver assembly, the barrel, a bipod support, a Leupold Mark IV scope, its BORS scope computer, and an AN/PVS Night Vision Scope, and could have it assembled and ready to fire in thirty seconds or less.

He also carried a backpack which contained a combat medic first aid kit, three ten-round magazines for the Barrett, six more magazines for his pistol, a prying iron, a hammer, several screwdrivers, pliers, and a spotter scope. Thirty rounds from a Barrett was more than enough to send their uncles and cousins running out of Little Italy like rats leaving a sinking ship. Finally, he carried his favorite Beretta automatic with a silencer in a shoulder holster under his left arm and a six-inch tactical knife in a sheath on his belt. Bring the bastards on, he thought. Tonight, payback was going to be a bitch.

Koz arrived at the loading dock seconds after he did, carrying much the same gear. Using one of Chester's master key cards on the rear entry door, they were inside, with no guards, no alarms, no muss, no fuss… except for a security camera located fifty feet down the hallway and pointed directly at them. The emergency stairwell door was on their immediate left, and it also had a key card reader. The two men kept their faces turned away from the camera and were through the door in seconds. With everything else going on at the Bimini Bay tonight, Ace doubted anyone would be watching the camera feeds too closely. Even if they were, all they'd see was two guitar players in the band arriving early.

He and Koz jogged up the seven flights of stairs to the rooftop. This time, the fire door had a hefty Master padlock and a thick hasp, not a magnetic key card lock. Ace gave it a quick look, reached in his backpack, and pulled out his pry bar. He jammed it in behind the hasp and stopped to looked at Koz. "A little help?" Ace grinned at him.

"A big guy like you? I thought you'd be too embarrassed to ask," Koz smiled back as the two men took firm grips on the pry bar.

"One, two, now," Ace said as they dropped all their weight on it. With a splintering "Crrraaack!" the metal hasp ripped free of the metal door and hung loose down the door frame. "Piece of cake, Staff Sergeant."

Koz pushed the door open. "After you. Now let's punch some holes in those bastards."

"For Vinnie."

"For Vinnie. You set up in the left corner of the roof and I'll set up in the right, then I'll check in with the boss."

A three-foot high parapet wall ran around the perimeter of the Tuscany Towers roof. With all the bright lights and signs attached to the outside of the building, the low wall cast the roof in deep shadow, screening it from the ground and from the roof of the Bimini Bay. Ace sat in one corner and began assembling his rifle. Looking around, he saw a twelve-inch drain hole in the base of the parapet wall, which would provide a ready-made firing hole. With the M-107 assembled and a magazine loaded in its receiver, Ace assumed a prone position and took aim on the penthouse. He glanced over and saw that Koz was doing the same thing in the opposite corner. Using the BORS digital computer on the rifle's scope, he calibrated the yardage to the penthouse at 922 meters, slightly over half a mile. Carbonari's helicopter was a shade closer at 912 meters. Piece of cake, he thought, and right at the optimum distance of the rifle.

He pulled out the spotter scope and pointed it at the penthouse. The lights were on inside and he saw activity. Carbonari and three other men were having what appeared to be a heated discussion. Looking closer, one of them had a pistol pointed at the Don. Interesting, Ace thought, wondering if he could get a clearer view through the scope on the tripod-mounted rifle. As he set the sniper scope down and reached for the Barrett, he heard a loud voice call out behind him from the emergency stairwell door.

"Ey! Who's up here? What the hell's goin' on?"

Ace rolled onto his side, looked back at the doorway. He saw a big man backlit by the light from the stairwell below. From the loud sports coat and the big revolver he held in his hand, it had to be one of the Gumbahs from New York. The man stepped out on the roof and Ace a saw a second gunman coming up behind him.

"Look at dis, Nardo, somebody broke the freakin' lock off," he heard the second man say. As Ace watched, the second man pulled a large revolver out of his shoulder holster.

"I can't see a goddamn ting up here, Fabio," the first man answered as he crouched down, waving his pistol back and forth. "You see anything?"

Ace was lying in the deep shadow behind the parapet wall where it would be impossible for either man to see him or Koz before their eyes adjusted to the darkness. Unfortunately for them, Ace wasn't going to allow that to happen. He drew his silenced Beretta. In a sweeping motion, he aimed at the body mass of the second Gumbah and put three rounds into his chest. The man staggered backward and then sat down in the doorway. The one in front already had his pistol out, but that was as far as he got before Koz took him out with a single shot from his

Barrett — louder, but much more effective. As Ace expected, the .50-caliber slug blew a large hole in the big Italian. He did a cartwheel and landed in a heap on the gravel roof, several feet away.

"Two down," Koz said.

"And half 'a freakin' Sicily to go," Ace answered.

CHAPTER TWENTY-NINE

If it was easy for Cheech Mazoulli, Eddie Costa, and Pete Moretti to bust their way into Carbonari's penthouse on the top floor of the Bimini Bay, it was that much easier for Martijn and Theo Van Gries, Joost DeVries, and Reggie MacGregor to follow them inside. Donatello's prized front doors stood wide open. The decorative hinges were bent and pieces of the ornate locks lay all over the entryway carpet. That was warning enough, so the four men drew their pistols and stepped cautiously into the foyer. They immediately heard loud, angry voices coming from the master bedroom to the right and as they continued on through the great room to the bedroom doors. They too were standing wide open. When they looked around the doorframe, what they saw was utterly bizarre, even by Atlantic City standards.

Donatello Carbonari was lying near the headboard of his huge, circular bed, obviously naked, with the top sheet pulled up to his chin and his left hand raised, whimpering and begging. Standing around the bed were three of Angelo Roselli's henchmen from Brooklyn with their guns pointed down at him. Their boss, Cheech Mazoulli, had a large .357 Magnum Colt Python revolver in his hand pointed directly at Carbonari's head as he screamed, "You freakin' piece 'a crap! You freakin' coward!" And from the angry expression on Mazoulli's face, it was obvious to Martijn that he intended to shoot. It was equally obvious that the three New York hoods were so busy terrifying Carbonari that they were completely unaware that the Van Grieses and their three mercs had stepped into the bedroom behind them.

Without any further thought, Martijn raised his new Walther PPK and shot Cheech Mazoulli twice in the head. He wasn't concerned about attaching the silencer, or about any resulting noise the gunshot would create. After all, this was *his* hotel. He was standing in Carbonari's own bedroom, and he could shoot anyone he damned well pleased! Martijn finally looked down at the whimpering figure of his boss with total disdain. He gave serious thought to emptying the remainder of the magazine into the debonair "Don," but chose not to, at least for the moment. Despite Donatello's stupidity and faults, until they got their hands on the rest of his money, Carbonari could still be of some use to the Van Grieses.

Theo and Joost carried their usual Royal Dutch Marine Corps service pistols, the much more powerful semi-automatic 9-millimeter Glock 17-Ms, while MacGregor had the equally deadly SAS issue Sig Sauer P226. After Martijn fired, the three mercs promptly dispatched Mazoulli's two companions, Eddie Costa and Pete Moretti, in a hail of gunfire before Cheech Mazoulli's body even hit the carpet. All three New York gunmen now lay at the foot of Carbonari's big bed, bleeding all over his plush white carpet, and very much dead.

"Cleanup in Aisle 6," MacGregor quipped as he scanned the room to the left.

"In his line of work, the man should rethink the white carpet," Joost DeVries added, as he swept the room to the left. "Those stains will never come out."

The loud volley of gunshots did have one other consequence. It spooked the boy hiding in the bathroom. Suddenly, a skinny, naked fifteen-year-old burst through the bathroom door and dashed across the bedroom. He almost knocked Martijn down as he headed for the great room. Martijn turned and glared down at Carbonari. "You old queen!" he said as he raised his Walther, turned on the young boy, and shot him three times in the back before he reached the doorway.

At this point, Donatello completely freaked out. His legs began moving, faster and faster, as if he was pedaling backwards on a bicycle, his heels digging into the mattress, as he tried to get away. Martijn stepped over to the edge of the bed as Carbonari looked up at him, wide-eyed, terrified. The Dutchman looked down and slowly shook his head. "Donnie, Donnie, what have you been up to?" he asked him as he waved the Walther at the body. "Teenage boys, now? Look at what you made me do." Carbonari was still in a panic, and when that didn't work, Martijn took a step closer and gave the big Italian a hard, backhanded slap across his face. "Get a grip on yourself!"

Carbonari sat up and looked down around the edge of the bed, barely able to see the dead bodies of the New York gunmen. "But... but those were Angelo Roselli's men. Mazoulli is a 'made man,' you can't just kill guys like that."

Martijn laughed and turned toward Theo and Joost. "Actually, it was rather easy. Besides, I had no choice, and neither did you. In case you did not notice, Mazoulli had that very large cannon pointed at your head and was about to splatter what few brains you have all over your headboard. I am no longer certain how much that would have bothered me, but it certainly would have bothered you."

"But it's all a mistake," Carbonari tried to explain as he began to calm down. "You *did* send Roselli the money, the eight and a quarter million this afternoon, didn't you?"

"Why? Did he say I didn't?" Martijn scoffed.

"Yes! He said the money never got there. Worse, he says all of their Atlantic City accounts are empty."

"What?" Martijn asked as he looked down at him in disgust. "Get dressed," he told Carbonari, none too politely. As he did, he exchanged a quick, questioning look with Theo, and then marched past his brother into the great room. He went directly to Carbonari's corner desk and turned on his desktop computer. It was obvious to Martijn that there was a role reversal about to take place here. It was a long time coming, and would probably be terminal, but until Martijn understood what was going on, Donatello still had his uses.

"He told you he never got the money? That is not possible," Martijn muttered, mostly to himself, as the accounting software opened and he leaned closer to the screen, working the mouse and the keyboard simultaneously with lightning-quick strokes. As he did, Carbonari appeared behind him, wearing a thick, white bathrobe. He put his hand on Martijn's shoulder, but Martijn brushed it away. Rejected, the big Italian took a half-step backward. Finally, Martijn got through the numerous layers of software security that he had in part designed and reached the spreadsheet screens he wanted. Then, he froze. His eyes widened as he stared at the columns and rows in disbelief.

"It shows you sent him the money, right?" Carbonari pressed him.

"No, my 'Sicilian Adonis,' it shows we've been penetrated, but not in the way you like. The money is gone."

"You mean the money that was supposed to be sent to Roselli? The New York money, right? That's what you mean, isn't it?"

"No." Martijn slumped back in the chair. "All of it. The New York money, the bank money, our money, your money, all of it. It's gone."

"All the money?" Carbonari asked in disbelief.

"Yes, someone cleaned us out, and I think I know who. It was that bastard Burke. I knew he was out to get us, to get *you*, but he is what…? some old infantry retread. I… I never thought the fellow was half this smart."

"But… how could he?" Carbonari asked as his brain raced ahead. "We… we've got to tell Roselli what happened, that it wasn't us, that it was that guy Burke, and we got hacked."

Martijn looked up and laughed. "Do you really think that will help, Donatello? Do you think they will believe you? If you do, you are a bigger fool than I thought you were."

"But what are we going to do?"

"Burke came in here on a big boat today, perhaps yesterday. It is docked at a marina across the harbor. I saw him and so did Theo and Benson. That's where Benson is. I sent him and three of Theo's men over there to find him. He's the one who took our money, I know he did. I just don't know how he did it. But I will. And if he values any of those friends of his, he'll put it all back."

"But what if he won't? What if he can't?" Donatello asked in a panic.

"Then we are dead men, all of us."

Chester raced down Maryland Avenue in the rental car. As he blew through the intersection with Absecon Boulevard, he passed two other cars headed in the opposite direction. They had tinted window glass and he couldn't see inside even if he wanted to. He took a hard right on Melrose and soon reached the small marina across the harbor where the big Ferrenti yacht was parked. The rental car careened on two wheels as it skidded into the gravel parking lot, and he finally brought the car to a stop at the foot of the long wooden pier. The Batman was in the rear seat, continuing to hold a compression bandage on Lonzo's leg.

"How's he doing?" Chester turned his head and asked.

"Better," The Batman quickly answered. "The bleeding is largely stopped."

"Good, let's get him aboard." Chester opened the car door and paused for a second as he looked down the pier at *The Enchantress*. He was looking at the aft end of the big yacht. All of its interior and exterior lights were on. He could see the aft deck and into the main deck lounge beyond, and he didn't like what he saw. There was no one on the aft deck. He saw no one inside the big boat, either, and that wasn't right.

Chester reached back inside and turned off the car's interior dome light as The Batman got out his side. Chester opened the rear door and was helping The Batman pull Lonzo out of the back seat when he looked back at the big boat. "Wait one," Chester told them as he pulled out his Beretta automatic and chambered a round. "Stay here with Lonzo until I check out the boat."

"Roger, but be careful. Looks deserted, doesn't it?" The Batman replied as he jacked a round into his Beretta as well.

Chester walked up the side of the parking lot to the pier, staying in the shadows as best he could, and then walked up the pier to the stern of *The Enchantress*. He looked up at the flying bridge, saw no one standing guard, pulled out his pistol, and went on full alert. He finally stepped aboard the big boat with a light, soft tread, walking forward until he could look down into the main lounge. That was when he saw Dorothy lying on the deck with Ronald and Sasha kneeling on each side of her holding a bloody compress on her abdomen.

When Chester stepped inside the lounge, no one appeared happier to see him than Ronald. "She's been shot," he said as he moved aside to make room for Chester.

"Where is everyone else?" Chester asked as he knelt next to her.

"They took them. Four men with guns. They just drove away…" Chester looked under the towel. That was all it took. He keyed his tactical radio mic and said, "Ghost, Chester. I'm on the boat. The only ones here are Dorothy, Ronald, and the Russian. Everyone else is gone. Ronald says four armed men took them away. And Dorothy's been shot."

"Copy. How bad?"

"Bad enough. In the gut, and she's bleeding. She needs a doc."

"Chester, this is Ace. I'm coming down. I'll be there in Five."

"Ace, Ghost. Negative on that. I understand how you feel, but we already have two of our guys down there and one's medic qualified. Let me call our friends down south for a dust-off, ASAP. Meanwhile, I really need you and the Barrett up on that roof. Do you copy?"

"Ace, Chester. Ghost is right. We'll take care of her until the bird gets here. I'll get the bag and start saline and meds."

There was a long pause at the other end until Ace finally replied, "10-4… for now."

"Roger," Ghost answered. "You and Koz keep your scopes on that roof. In a couple of minutes, I'm gonna need you big time."

"Oh, no doubt about that," Ace answered as they heard him chamber a round in the big Barrett. "By the way, we have two Gumbahs KIA up here. They got nosy."

"Chester, Ghost. Will the parking lot work as an LZ?"

"Looks like it. When they're two minutes out, I'll illuminate with headlights and a green flare. Tell them they can pick up both packages. Copy?

"Roger that."

"Ghost, Chester. Wait where you are. The Batman and I will join you at your location after pickup. No sense you and Bulldog taking them on alone."

"Chester, Ghost. You want in, you best hurry. We aren't waiting."

"Chester, Ace. Don't worry. We got two Barretts up here and clear fields of fire. They won't be alone."

"Ghost, Chester. As I drove here, we passed two dark-colored sedans going fast up Maryland. That could be them."

"Copy. You copy, too, Ace?"

"Roger. Two cars just pulled into the garage. Couldn't tell."

"Just keep eyes on the roof while I make the call."

"Wilco," Ace answered as he pressed his eye to the scope, focusing on the brightly lit windows of the penthouse.

Bob already had Command Sergeant Major Patrick O'Connor's cell phone number in his speed dial before they left Fort Bragg. At 10:00 p.m., most senior NCOs were already in bed unless they were drunk, partying, or otherwise raising hell. In O'Connor's case, it was impossible to tell which over the phone. He always answered with the same flat, deadpan, wide-awake growl. This time, however, Bob heard the loud, rhythmic beat of a helicopter in the background.

"O'Connor, sir," the big sergeant major answered.

"Ghost here, Command Sergeant Major," he said, trying to hear him. "Are you up in in a chopper?"

"Something like that."

"We have a problem. I need a dust-off for two in Atlantic City. GSW's — one an ambulatory leg wound, the other a serious abdominal wound to a female Air Force officer. Think you can arrange that?"

After a momentary pause, O'Connor quickly replied, "10-4, Ghost. I'll reach out to Fort Dix and call you back with an ETA. I'll tell them a couple of our key operators were mugged and we'll throw a national security blanket over it."

"10-4."

"By the way, you can expect a couple of visitors shortly."

"I hear there's nothing more dangerous than a second lieutenant with a map or a general with a helicopter."

"Couldn't agree more, Ghost. We're giving a new tactical stealth bird a night test flight."

"You aren't carrying the rockets and mini-gun, are you?"

"You know old boys with new toys. What channel can we reach you on later?"

"We're using twenty-seven. 'We'? Are you along for the ride, too?"

"Wouldn't miss it. Besides, someone has to keep him out of trouble."

"Roger that. What's his call sign?"

He heard O'Connor chuckle. "You'll know it when you hear it."

"10-4," Bob sighed.

As O'Connor hung up, Gramps Benson and his strange procession reached the Bimini Bay's penthouse via the express elevator. Eric Smit led, with Ernie Travers and Linda Burke walking close behind. Patsy Evans was behind them, still helping a dazed and bleeding Jimmy Barker. Lucas Bakker followed, helping Klaus Reimer, while Gramps Benson took up the rear, with his Walther PPK hanging casually down his right pants leg. Reimer pressed his dislocated right arm and broken wrist tightly to his chest. He was sweating and pale, obviously in considerable pain and not handling it very well. From the expressions on Benson's and Bakker's faces, none of the other men had any sympathy for him. Gunshot wounds and broken bones were all-too-frequent occupational hazards for Special Ops troops in any army. One was expected to simply gnaw off the offending appendage and ignore the pain, but never ever let them see you sweat. Then again, Reimer was a German, which meant he got even less sympathy from the three Dutchmen.

As they walked through the open door of Carbonari's penthouse apartment, even Benson had to stop and gawk. Martijn Van Gries sat at the computer which rested on Donatello's antique French provincial desk. Joost DeVries and Reggie MacGregor had posted themselves in opposite corners of the room, pistols out, waiting patiently for orders from Theo. The rest of the scene was bizarre.

Sprawled on the floor in the bedroom doorway was a young, naked boy with three bullet holes in his back. Beyond him, Benson saw three more bodies lying at the foot of Carbonari's massive bed. From their clothes, he immediately recognized them as three of the gunmen who had been sent down from Brooklyn to help with security.

That was when a badly shaken Donatello Carbonari stumbled out of the bedroom, suit jacket in hand, buttoning his white shirt. He gave the boy's body a wide berth as he continued on into the living room. When he looked up and saw Benson, his men, and the others standing in the middle of the living room, Carbonari stopped dead in his tracks. His mouth opened, as if he wanted to say something, but the whole thing appeared to be too much for him to comprehend at that moment as he turned away and continued on toward Martijn Van Gries.

Interesting, Benson thought. The pot was beginning to boil.

The northwest side of the penthouse had floor-to-ceiling glass, and the drapes hung wide open. Ace continued to stare through the powerful optical scope on the Barrett. It was as if he was standing in the room next to them, providing a ringside seat for the high drama now taking place inside.

"Ghost, Ace, our missing parties just entered the penthouse — Linda, Patsy, Ernie, and Jimmy — and I see Carbonari, both Van Grieses, their five mercs, and our long-lost Exec, Gramps Benson. Copy? It's what you might call a 'target-rich environment.' I'm not sure who I want to hit first. Any suggestions?"

"Wait 'til The Batman and I get up there. Four of our people are in there, so don't fire unless things go bad."

"Roger, that. I'll hold... for now."

For the next three minutes, Ace lay motionless on the rubber pad with his eye pressed against the aperture of the Barrett's scope, looking at the Bimini Bay's roof through the small drainage hole in the parapet wall. His field of vision was narrow, but that didn't matter. The scope covered the entire rooftop and he saw all he needed to see. At a distance of a half mile, the rifle barrel barely moved as he zoomed in and tracked the sight back and forth across the penthouse windows, watching the show inside, licking his chops, and waiting for the order to fire.

That was when he heard the helicopter. Anyone who served in the Army in combat in the past fifty years knew four distinct sounds — the crack of an AK-47, the crunching Crump! of artillery and mortar rounds, the deep rumble of a flight of B-52s passing overhead, and the rhythmic Thump! Thump! Thump! of a helicopter. When you spend enough time in war zones, as Ace had, those sounds became part of you like bone and muscle. Still, not all Thumps! are the same. Like many others, Ace could tell each helicopter model by its unique rotor blade sounds. From what Ace heard in the dark sky above him, it wasn't a Blackhawk, SuperCobra, or Iroquois, as the old Huey warhorse was officially called. What he heard was a smaller bird, most likely the new Lakota light helicopter which the Army had begun buying for Medevac missions.

He looked up and saw it coming at him, sweeping in from the northwest across the marsh and turning down the Absecon channel that ran between Atlantic City and Brigantine.

"Ghost, Ace. I have the Lakota dust-off inbound from the northwest." At 140 mph, the little sucker could really move, he thought, and God, was it nimble, and quiet.

"Roger. Chester, light it up," he heard Ghost say.

The helicopter crossed directly over the Bimini Bay before it swung south toward the Gardner's Basin boat marina. Ace got to his knees and looked south over the top of the parapet wall with his spotter scope. *The Enchantress* was about a mile away, and from this height he could clearly see the car headlights and the green glow of the flares Chester set off. He could also see the Lakota as it dropped in and landed in the parking lot in a cloud of dust. The engine roar quieted down. As he waited, a timer began ticking in his head — one, one thousand; two, one thousand; three, one thousand ... When he reached twelve, the engines suddenly accelerated, there was a second cloud of dust, and the Lakota leaped into air. Its tail rose like an angry scorpion as it took off. It headed straight north over the Absecon Inlet and accelerated toward Fort Dix, some twenty minutes away.

"Ghost, Chester. Dust-off's airborne. Bulldog and I will be at the back door in Five."

"Roger that," Ace heard Ghost reply. "Make it quick. We're going up.

With a grim, angry expression, Ace resumed his position on the rubber mat, locked the Barrett against his shoulder, and pressed his eye against the scope. "Ready on the left, ready on the right, ready on the firing line," he mumbled softly to himself. It was the mantra countless Army Rifle Range instructors drilled into recruits prior to the commencement of shooting.

"What did I just hear?" he heard Koz ask from the other corner of the roof.

"Nothing, just a little wishful thinking."

CHAPTER THIRTY

Halfway across the room, Donatello Carbonari suddenly stopped as the pieces fell into place. His expression turned from dazed and confused to cold and vindictive, as his head snapped around and he glared at Ernie Travers and Jimmy Barker. "Who are these people?" he demanded to know, looking at Martijn.

The Dutchman, in turn, looked at Benson and shrugged.

"The large one is a Chicago cop," Benson answered. "A detective."

"A Chicago cop?" Carbonari stared at Benson in disbelief.

"He's Burke's friend. And this one's his wife." Benson nudged Linda.

"Where is he?" Carbonari turned on her. "He did this to me, and I want him."

"Be careful what you ask for... Donnie," she said with a thin smile.

That drove Carbonari into a rage. He drew his right arm back, intending to backhand her across her face, but Ernie Travers stepped in and caught Carbonari's arm in mid-swing.

"Try someone your own size," the big cop told him, and released his wrist.

Carbonari glared angrily at him but did not take him up on the offer. Instead, he looked down at her again. "Where is he? Tell me, or you're dead, you're all dead."

"If I had to guess, he's probably headed this way." Linda looked up at him and smiled. "In fact, you're probably standing in his crosshairs right now."

Carbonari suddenly glanced around and eyed the surrounding wall of window glass, stepped behind the big Chicago cop, and asked Martijn. "What about the money? Did you find it?"

Martijn shook his head. "It's gone, all of it, and I don't have a clue where it went. Perhaps, if I had a day or two..." he said absently, staring at the computer. "But whoever did it, did it very well."

Carbonari suddenly whipped around and stared at them. "You're the ones who did this to me, you and that bastard Burke. Aren't you?" No one answered, but slowly, Carbonari's attention turned to Jimmy Barker. "And you! You're that card counter. Your friends look too stupid to know how the machine works, but you..."

Jimmy continued to stand there, chin up, bloodied and defiant, and said nothing. Carbonari turned toward Martijn and reached for the Dutchman's automatic pistol. "I'm gonna kill them! I'm going to kill them all!" he screamed, but Martijn grabbed his wrist and wouldn't let him have the Walther.

"That would not be very prudent, Donatello," Martijn told him. "If he is the mad genius who did it, and I am beginning to think that may well be the case, we shall need him. As for the others, it is not wise to kill policemen or to 'pull on Superman's cape' as they say."

"But they took my money!" Carbonari continued trying to pull the automatic away from Van Gries, clearly becoming unhinged by everything that had happened to him in the past hour. "Make them put it back!"

"Even if he could, we would be here all night, Donatello. Besides, what would it accomplish? Angelo Roselli already thinks it is all your fault, and that is nothing compared to what he will think when he learns Mazoulli and his other two gunmen just got whacked," Martijn said as he pointed toward the bedroom.

Carbonari began looking around in a panic, realizing for the first time that he really was doomed. "My helicopter. I'm getting out of here," he said as he turned and ran back into the bedroom.

From the roof of Tuscany Towers, Ace continued to observe what was happening inside the penthouse, and finally keyed his mic.

"Ghost, Ace. I have more movement inside. Our four are still vertical and mobile."

"Copy that."

"And I count seven… no, make that eight targets," he added as he took up the slack on the trigger.

"Copy that too."

"Orders?" he asked hopefully.

"Continue to observe and report," Ghost answered. "When Chester and Bulldog get here, we'll hit them from both sides and take the penthouse."

Theo stepped over to Martijn and whispered. "I believe it is time for us to depart as well."

"Agreed," his brother answered as he turned back to the computer screen and sighed. All that money, he thought, gone. But Theo was right. This had been a good ride while it lasted, but a smart gambler knows when a hot run is over.

Theo motioned toward the helicopter sitting on the landing pad outside. "Does your 'friend' really know how to fly that thing?"

"Yes. Surprisingly well in fact."

"Good. I have no desire to talk to the New Jersey police or the American FBI, and that is a Sikorsky S-70, the civilian Blackhawk. It is quite capable of taking us to New York City, and from there we can head for Canada and back to the Emirates. Are you coming?"

"No, I believe I'll take the sailboat. I have known this would end sooner or later, and I have been planning a long, slow cruise through the eastern Caribbean.

The timing is not ideal, but it is what it is, as they say. Before I go, however, there are a few things down in my office that I would not want to leave behind."

"Like that lovely blonde fringe benefit of yours?" Theo laughed as he turned and looked at Ernie, Linda, Jimmy, and Patsy. "But what should we do with those four?"

Martijn followed his gaze and studied them for a moment, as Benson joined them. "What do you think we should do?" Martijn asked him. "Kill them?"

"Whoa! Not so fast." Benson shook his head. "In the first place, the girl is mine."

"Why?" Theo frowned. "What is she to you?"

"It's an old story. Let's say we have some unfinished business, so she's coming with me. As for the others — his wife, his friend, and the card counter... I wouldn't recommend it. Burke will never stop until he hunts you down and cuts you into little pieces."

Theo stared at Benson for a moment with a thin smile. "Someday, I would dearly love to test that hypothesis, but you are correct. This is not the time. Any other suggestions?"

"Leave them here and lock them in the coat closet. As soon as you lift off, Donatello can phone his friend, the Police Chief, and tell him they were the ones who killed Roselli's men up here. He can also tell him that they came from that big yacht across the harbor. That should keep everyone occupied for a while."

That was when Carbonari returned from the bedroom carrying a heavy briefcase. "It appears you'll have some passengers," Martijn told him. "Theo and his men need a ride, at least as far as New York."

Carbonari stared at them, not entirely certain whether he wanted to share anything with them, and began counting heads. "With me, that makes... thirteen. That's far too many. The damned thing will never get off the ground!"

"No, you misunderstand," Martijn answered with a thin smile. "Benson and I are not going, and neither are those four. That brings it down to six, plus you."

"It's still a lot of weight," Carbonari said as he gave Theo and his mercenaries a cold, appraising glance. The mercs were large, muscular men, like him. Whether the weight was the problem, or whether Carbonari simply didn't trust any of them was hard to say, but Theo Van Gries knew how to solve the problem. His Glock 17 had been casually hanging down his right leg with its silencer still attached. He brought it up in a swift motion and fired, putting three bullets into Klaus Reimer's chest. The German had been standing off to the side, leaning against one of the penthouse's expensive, overstuffed chairs. His eyes were closed, and he held his injured arm clutched tightly to his chest. He never saw it coming as the three heavy slugs blew him backwards over the chair and onto the floor.

"There." Theo turned back to Carbonari with a satisfied smile. "Now it appears we are six, Donatello. Is that more acceptable?"

"You animal!" Linda screamed at him. "Is that how you treat your men?"

"My men? We are Dutch and he was a German, who made himself a liability." Theo chuckled as he glanced around at the other four mercs. They were also smiling, all except the Scotsman, Reggie MacGregor, who stood against the near wall.

Theo turned and faced Linda. "I did not expect you to understand, Mrs. Burke," he answered. As he did, the barrel of his Glock came up again and he fired a fourth time, hitting MacGregor in the center of his forehead. The Scotsman's eyes went wide as he slowly slid down the wall and dropped to the floor. "Oops, my mistake, Donatello," Theo added, sounding embarrassed. "It now appears we are five."

Ace could only shake his head as he watched. He had received a clear order from a man he respected more than anyone else in the world to lie there and do nothing, but it really pissed him off. They shot Dorothy. He held the most powerful sniper rifle in the world in his hands, and he could do nothing. That was when he saw a series of bright, white flashes inside the penthouse. Gunshots! He was too far away to hear them from inside the closed suite of rooms, but it was four gunshots. He had seen three bright flashes, followed moments later by a fourth. He made a slight adjustment to the focus on his spotter scope, just in time to see a body fall on the floor to a join a second one already lying there.

"Ghost, Ace. I saw the flash of four gunshots inside."

"Our people?" Burke asked anxiously.

"No, it looks like Tango on Tango… and don't worry, I'm still holding."

Donatello Carbonari backed away a half step from Theo, looking very concerned now.

"What's in there, Donatello? Your lunch?" Theo asked as he pointed at the heavy briefcase the young Mafioso was carrying. "Our mother told us that a gentleman should always bring enough to share."

"Lunch is 'Dutch,' today, Theo. So if you want to go to New York, let's go," Carbonari said tersely, ignoring the implied threat.

Martijn smiled. He raised his Walther PPK and pointed it at Linda Burke as he walked toward the big Chicago policeman. "It is Captain Travers, is it not?" Martijn asked pleasantly enough. Ernie said nothing, and Martijn didn't really care if he did. "I would like for you and the others to step into that closet, if you would." Again, Travers said nothing, nor did he move. "Rest assured, I have no desire to shoot a policeman. But you will observe that while I am speaking to you, my pistol is pointed at Mrs. Burke. Do what I say or I will shoot her and the young man without a second thought."

Ernie realized that Martijn held the ace of trump, so he motioned for the other three to walk to the closet. By the time they got there, Gramps Benson had joined Van Gries and held the door open.

Like the rest of the penthouse, even the closet doors and frames were made of thick, New Jersey oak, and the hinges and hardware were solid. "Nice craftsmanship," Benson said as he tapped on the door. "That should even hold a side of beef like you, captain."

Bob entered the south emergency stairwell in the hotel's six-story tower with The Batman close on his heels. As he ran up the first set of risers, he stopped to look up and listen. He heard nothing. The building was strangely quiet, even though this was prime time in the casino. As he pulled out his Beretta and rechecked the load again, a little voice inside his head told him it was six stories straight up, plus the penthouse. Doing some quick arithmetic gymnastics, he realized that meant about one hundred and thirty steps.

"How's your legs, old man?" The Batman asked.

"I guess we'll find out," Bob answered as he set off running up the stairs, taking them two at a time. "Remember that op we ran in the mountains north of Jalalabad, where we toted two machine guns, a mortar, full packs and all that ammo?"

"I don't want to. It almost killed us."

"See? This is nothing," Bob lied, knowing that three years piddling around in suburban health clubs wasn't the same as being combat ready. Neither was he, but Linda and the others were up there, so he picked up the pace even faster. As he turned the corner at the fourth floor, he was feeling the pain and burning in his chest and legs.

That was when he heard a new voice in his tactical radio earpiece.

"Ghost, this is Dinosaur Actual, copy?" Dinosaur Actual? Bob cringed as he immediately understood O'Connor's little joke and stopped climbing in midstride. "Dinosaur" was what a handful of the more irreverent junior officers called General Stansky, but only behind his back and when they were absolutely, positively certain that neither Stansky nor Pat O'Connor could hear them. Adding the word "Actual" meant it was the general himself calling, proving that the Old Man really did have a sense of humor. The only problem, Bob thought, was he wished he didn't have it right then.

"Dinosaur Actual, this is Ghost," Bob acknowledged. The Army's Rifleman tactical radio was a great piece of equipment, but it wasn't designed to operate inside high-rise commercial buildings. "You're breaking up some. I'm inside a lot of concrete down here."

"You and Jimmy Hoffa. This is New Jersey, Bobby. What's going on down there?" Stansky asked.

"Targets are in the penthouse and on the Bimini Bay roof, we have eyes on, long guns on, are closing in from below, and are about to engage."

"Any additional casualties?"

"Negative."

"Good. You sound like you're puffing. Guess you didn't take the elevator?"

"Roger that."

"Your objective is lit up like Times Square on New Year's Eve, and there's a large bird parked on the pad. Looks like civilian Blackhawk. The Irishman and I will be loitering up here for a while. We're stealthy as hell and locked and loaded lots of ordnance, so you can make my day if you want me to take it out, or if you need anything else dented."

"Roger that," Bob said, shaking his head.

'Locked and loaded? Dented?' Bob laughed to himself. He hoped like hell that the "Irishman" would remind Stansky that this is a large civilian hotel in downtown New Jersey, not a hot LZ near Pleiku in Vietnam or the Republican Guard headquarters on the road to Baghdad. No need to inform the other guys, Bob realized. Stansky had spoken on their local, tactical net, and they had all heard.

Theo stood on the other side of the room talking with Smit, Bakker, and DeVries as Benson joined Martijn at the closet door. He allowed Ernie and Linda to pass through, but he stopped Patsy and pulled her aside. Jimmy turned and was about to go after him until Gramps raised his Beretta and pointed it at the Geek's forehead. "Don't be stupid, boy, and *do not* cause a scene. You and I went through this once before on the boat," he reminded him, speaking in a hushed voice. "You ended up with a very ugly dent in your head but you're still walking."

"You're not taking her anywhere!" Jimmy stood up straight and dared him to shoot.

Benson stepped forward and pressed his Beretta against Jimmy's forehead. "Get inside, or that talented brain of yours will be splattered all over the closet. Understand?"

"I'll be fine, Jimmy," Patsy told him. "He doesn't want me, he wants the gold Vinnie stole, that's all."

Benson's expression turned angry as he shoved Jimmy backwards into the closet. After he locked the door, he dragged a heavy dining room chair over and jammed it under the doorknob, wedging the door shut. That was when he felt the barrel of a Glock 17 press against the back of his neck, and he heard Theo Van

Gries's voice behind him.

"The gold? Did I hear that right? The girl knows where Pastorini hid the gold?" Theo asked quietly as he reached over Benson's shoulder and took the Beretta from his hand. "You knew this and you did not tell us, Benson?"

"No, no, it's nothing like that. You've got it all wrong. You see..." Benson tried to stall until he could come up with a better explanation, but he knew it had to be good. Theo Van Gries was the Devil incarnate. He could see through people, and he was almost impossible to lie to.

That was when Benson heard Martijn Van Gries's voice behind him as well. This was the perfect storm he had been trying to avoid. "Wait a minute," Martijn asked him as he began to remember. "Did you say Pastorini? Vinnie Pastorini? Tell me you don't mean that infuriating American Army Sergeant who started all this?"

Theo spun Benson around, looked him in the eyes, and said to Martijn, "We knew Pastorini in Iraq. My men and I were asked to assist Iraqi Intelligence with a little job — actually it was quite a large job — that blew back on us. We ended up holding 'the bag,' so to speak, and the investigators began watching us like hawks. We couldn't move them, but Pastorini could, by putting it in some American machinery he was shipping back to the States. We told him if he did, we'd cancel his gambling debts and cut him in for a share of the profits. Unfortunately, when he got back here, he forgot about his partners. That was why I sent Benson and another man over here. But it looks as if the captain caught the same disease Pastorini had. Tell me, Martijn, what did you mean when you said, 'He started all this?' "

Martijn stepped closer and also eyed Benson. "Several weeks ago, Pastorini lost a lot of money in the casino, three hundred, maybe four hundred thousand."

"The fool never could gamble." Theo shook his head. "He owed us a great deal, too."

"We were holding Pastorini in a fifth-floor room while Burke went to get the cash to pay off his markers, but there appears to have been some kind of an accident. Pastorini tried to get away, and he fell from a window ledge. We thought one of my security men did it, that idiot Shaka Corliss, but Corliss kept denying it. Anyway, that is what brought Burke and his Deltas into this."

Theo's eyes turned hard and cold, and he suddenly jammed his Glock hard into Benson's neck. "You told me he died in a car accident before you could get him to tell you where the gold was, didn't you? So who is this girl?"

"Oh, I can tell you that," Martijn jumped in. "She is Pastorini's girlfriend. They were living together at Fort Bragg and they came up here to Atlantic City together."

"Of course!" Theo said. "You knew Burke and all the others. You were one of them! You knew they would come up here and tear this place apart to avenge Pastorini, and you knew my brother would counter by calling in me and my Dutch Special Ops friends to stop them, didn't you?" Suddenly Theo began to laugh. "Oh, this is so very delicious! It is too bad that you and I did not compare notes earlier, Martijn. Don't you see? Benson orchestrated this little charade of his in hopes that Burke and I would kill each other off. That would leave him with all the gold, with no one chasing him, and with no need to split it with anyone."

"And you almost pulled it off, didn't you, Benson?" Theo jabbed him again with the pistol. "Something tells me that Martijn's security man had nothing to do with Pastorini falling out that window, did he? Perhaps Pastorini got you angry, perhaps he still refused to share, perhaps there was a fight, or he ran. In any event, it was *you* who killed him."

"You're out of your mind, Theo," Benson tried to argue. "Why would I do something like that? I don't have the gold. Vinnie never told me where it was."

"Perhaps not, but you know something, or you think the girl does."

That was when Eric Smit joined the conversation. "Gold?" he asked as he dug his hands into Benson's pants pockets, turning them inside out until he found the glittering lion medallion and its broken gold chain. "He tore this from the girl's neck while we were on that boat tonight. It is part of what we took from that museum in Baghdad, isn't it?" Smit glared at Benson. "Give him to me and Lucas. We will pound the truth out of him."

"There is no need for that," Theo said as he took the lion medallion from Smit's hand and held it up, admiring its rich yellow glow. He turned toward Patsy. "Where is the gold?"

"Like I told him," Patsy pointed at Benson, "it is in a box in the garage, up in the corner of the ceiling. Take it! It's all yours. I don't want it, and I never did."

Theo smiled. "From the mouths of babes."

"Gentlemen, gentlemen, this is all a misunderstanding." Benson tried to smile, but by that time Joost DeVries, Lucas Bakker and Smit had drawn in close, and they all had their Glock automatics pointed at him.

"You know, in the Dutch Army we have a term for a soldier who cheats his comrades," Bakker said to Benson. "Rarely does it end well for the fellow."

"The gold, how much are you talking about, brother?" Martijn asked, more than a little curious.

"Ten million Euro, give or take, and now we have half the number of partners to split it with as we did when we started." Theo smiled. "Are you sure you don't want to reconsider and come with us?"

"No, I have some business of my own to attend to," Martijn answered, "but we do need to get out of here."

"Yes," Theo quickly agreed. "And there will be a slight change of plans.

Now that I have lightened the load, Benson and the girl will come with us too. Donatello will make a slight detour to drop us off in North Carolina on his way to New York City."

"I'm doing what?" Carbonari whipped around and glared at the Dutchman.

By that time, however, Theo had his Glock 17 pointed at Carbonari. "Donatello, I do not really need to take Benson along and I no longer need the girl. For that matter, Sergeant Smit is quite capable of flying a Blackhawk, so I do not need you either. So, the choice is yours. You can either fly us down there and be on your way, or you can join the rest of the bodies strewn about your penthouse."

Carbonari tightened his grip on the heavy briefcase and quickly nodded. "All right, all right, then let's get out of here!" he hissed and turned toward the door to the rooftop deck.

"My point exactly, except for a slight change of plans," Theo said as he pulled the chair away from the closet door and opened it. He reached inside, grabbed a surprised Linda Burke by the upper arm, and pulled her out of the closet. Quickly he closed it again and pushed the chair back under the door lock, leaving Jimmy and Ernie inside with surprised expressions on their faces.

"My sincere apologies, Mrs. Burke," Theo said. "But travel is so much more interesting when you have someone to share it with, don't you agree? Besides, I will feel a tad safer with you by my side."

"Ghost, Ace. "They're on the move again, coming this way and going out on the roof. I think they're headed for Carbonari's helicopter."

"Ghost, Chester. We're downstairs heading for the service corridor. What's your position?"

"Halfway up the south emergency stairs. You and Bulldog use the key card and take the executive elevator to the penthouse. We'll clear the elevator lobby and meet you up top."

"Roger."

"Ace, Ghost. No need to hurry. They may be moving, but they're not going anywhere."

If nothing else, Martijn Van Gries understood timing. After watching enough gambling at the poker tables in the casino, he knew when a man should ante up, when he should double down, and when he should fold them and wait for a better hand. That time had come. He walked out of Donatello's penthouse suite with what he'd walked in with two years before — a head on his shoulders, a Walther PPK tucked behind his belt, and empty pockets; but that would not last much longer. As he strode into the penthouse elevator lobby, he pulled out his iPhone, touched Eva's speed-dial number, and pressed the elevator down button.

Before he left the boat, he had told Eva to stay there, which should make things infinitely easier.

"It is me," he said as soon as she answered. "Get dressed and start the engines. Cast off everything except the bow line and be ready to leave as soon as I jump on board."

Cell phone reception inside a steel elevator never was the best, but he heard her say, "Leave? Where are we going, Martijn? I don't have any of my things and…"

As the elevator doors closed, he swore he heard some kind of commotion and doors slamming in the emergency stairwell. Trouble? Or Burke? Tonight, they were about the same. "Listen to me!" he cut her off. "You have your getaway bag on board…"

"Yes, but the cat, the rest of my stuff, I never thought…"

"It is too late for all that. Your passport is in the safe on the boat and it is time the cat learned to fend for itself. We can buy anything you need later. Get moving, now! I'll be jumping on board in a couple of minutes."

Nine hundred and twenty-two meters away, Ace Randall watched the penthouse doors swing open and a cluster of people walked out onto the pool deck. One of the Dutch sergeants, Eric Smit, came out first, walking point, with Donatello Carbonari close behind. He was followed by Patsy Evans and Gramps Benson, side by side and arm in arm, whether she liked it or not. Theo Van Gries came next, with his left arm wrapped around Linda Burke's neck and his Glock 17 in his right. It tracked back and forth as the group moved out onto the roof. To Theo's right walked Lucas Bakker, and Joost DeVries covered the rear, walking backwards with his eyes on the inside of the penthouse and the doors to the lobby beyond. The group quickly passed between the swimming pool and the sauna and headed toward Donatello Carbonari's helicopter.

About to engage? Ace chuckled to himself. You bet your sweet ass we are, general. The show is about to start. He was almost at the same elevation as his targets, and he had estimated the wind to be a negligible two or three knots, quartering from his right. He made a very slight one click adjustment to his scope, and knew he was ready.

"Koz, see the two outriders? I'll take the one in the rear, you've got the point man. On my mark…"

CHAPTER THIRTY-ONE

Martijn Van Gries ended his phone call to Eva Pender as the first floor elevator doors opened. He leaned out and made a quick scan of the service corridor. It was empty, so he walked far enough to be able to see the hotel's reception area. Except for two desk clerks and several guests checking in, it was empty. Nothing appeared out of order. This was very late on a weeknight. Except for some scattered slot machine players and gamblers in the poker room at the far end, the casino appeared lightly populated. Satisfied, Martijn turned and was starting down the service corridor toward his office when something to his right drew his attention. It was movement. That was what always caught the eye, not shape or noise. He saw two men dressed in blue janitor's uniforms running toward him from the nearby exit door. Whether they were coming for him or just the elevator was impossible to tell but both men carried pistols in their hands. Glocks, he recognized at first glance.

"Dammit," he swore as he pulled out his Walther and fired two quick rounds in their general direction. His silencer was in his pocket, unattached, but the Walther was only a .38-caliber. Its gunshots were enough to scatter the people in the lobby but not nearly as loud as the 9-millimeter cannons the other men carried. It was unlikely that he hit either of them, but all he wanted was to slow them down and buy time while he took off down the service corridor toward his office.

He had always been more of a sprinter than a runner. With elbows and knees pumping, he even surprised himself how fast he was moving, faster than at any time since he ran track for the exclusive boys' school in Leiden where his parents interned him and eventually his younger brother, like two illegal aliens. Being small, and effete, the only good things Leiden had taught him were how to run from trouble faster than trouble was chasing him, and how to "accommodate" it if he couldn't, two lessons which proved useful in later life.

As he reached the bend in the corridor and took the sharp turn to the right, three bullets dug long gouges into the wall to his left. He heard them rip into the drywall and saw the dust, but he heard nothing, which meant they were using silencers. No matter how much he pissed off Angelo Roselli and the Brooklyn mob, they wouldn't be using silencers or Glocks. They preferred loud .357 Magnum revolvers, sawed-off shotguns, and baseball bats, and would never be caught dead dressed like a janitor. No, these were Burke's men, and it looked as if he was getting out just in time.

"3... 2... 1... Mark," Ace said into his chin mic as he ever-so-gently squeezed the trigger.

For all of the power an M-107 Barrett delivered, its heavy, 661-grain, full-metal-jacketed steel-core bullet delivered a surprisingly easy recoil. Its unique barrel assembly, receiver, and internal springs absorbed most of the rearward kick, leaving the shooter ready to fire another round almost immediately, should that prove necessary. However, when that first shot was taken by Master Sergeant Harold "Ace" Randall, Staff Sergeant Rudy "Koz" Kozlowski, or virtually anyone else in the Unit, a second shot was rarely needed.

Ace's shot struck Joost DeVries "dead-center of body mass," in the middle of his back, as described in the class, knocking him off his feet onto the blue plastic pool cover four feet to his rear. At almost the same instant, Koz took out Lucas Bakker with a headshot, painting Donatello Carbonari from the waist up with blood, bone, and bits and pieces of whatever else was inside the Dutchman. His body crumpled onto the deck as the warm, wet shower struck Carbonari in his face. He looked down at the gore splattered all over his $5,000 Savile Row suit, screamed, and dropped to his knees next to Bakker's body, shaking, and attempting to hide behind his briefcase: a physically impossible proposition for a man of his size.

Chester wanted to fire a fourth round at Martijn Van Gries, but the Dutchman suddenly cut to the right, and disappeared down the service corridor before Chester could get in the shot. He quickly keyed his chin mic and said, "Ghost, Chester. We're in the first floor service corridor. That weasel Martijn Van Gries came out of the executive elevator and took off toward the offices. He fired on us so I returned fire but missed. Should we pursue?"

"Negative," Bob told him, still breathing heavily from the run up the stairs, resorting to monosyllables. It was a bitch to get old, but he guessed it beat the alternative. "He can't get far; let him go. We need to stay focused on the roof."

"Roger that," Chester answered as he pressed the Up button on the service elevator.

Since it had just brought Van Gries down, the doors immediately opened, and Chester and Bulldog stepped inside. Chester kept his eyes on the corridor, hoping Van Gries would reappear, but that didn't happen. He quickly swiped the copy of the security master key card that Jimmy had made for them in the elevator card reader. That activated the penthouse stop and the doors immediately closed. As the elevator began to rise, both Deltas used the opportunity to check their weapons before the doors opened again.

After Martijn turned the corner, he stopped dead in his tracks and doubled back, waiting with his gun drawn, listening, but the footsteps of the two men stopped at the elevator. He heard them talking, perhaps on a radio, but they didn't try to follow. That was good, because he didn't want a gun battle, not here, not now, and certainly not with them. He had too many other things to do before he could leave this stupid city and never come back.

First, he had to go to his office. Once inside, he locked the door, went to the center of the room, and shoved aside one of the two matching armchairs that sat in front of his desk. He pulled up on the corner of the center carpet square beneath it, revealing a recessed piece of three-quarter-inch plywood set flush with the floor. He lifted it aside. Underneath lay the face of a custom steel-walled floor safe that he had installed one weekend, when Donatello went out to Vegas for a long weekend. The combination was an unusual five-number set, which made the safe virtually un-crackable. He went to all that trouble because this was where he kept his own, very private getaway bag. It did not contain underwear, socks, or toiletries, however. It was a custom-made, five-inch-deep, weapons-grade aluminum attaché case, which contained his collection of six forged passports, each in a different name and issued by a different country — the US, Canada, Ireland, the UK, Belgium, and the Netherlands — plus $200,000 in cash, $300,000 in bearer bonds, and a long metal tube with another $300,000 in gem-quality diamonds he had acquired on three trips to Amsterdam. That should be enough to tide him over for a quick getaway, until he was able to meet with his bankers in the Caymans and Switzerland.

With his attaché case in one hand and the Walther in the other, he eased open the hallway door and took a quick peek outside. The corridor was empty, so he ran to the emergency stairwell and disappeared downstairs. There was a second reinforced steel door at the bottom which was capable of withstanding anything short of a howitzer or a half-hour with a blowtorch. It had both a key card and keypad for access control. Very few people had the required card, and even fewer knew the key code.

He locked the steel door behind him and found himself inside his nearly dark Computer Operations Center. Even in the middle of the night, he always had one man on duty down here in "the dungeon," as the hired help called it. Their job was to monitor the hundreds of hotel and casino security cameras, and to note any unusual activity in his "special" suites upstairs for recording. As Martijn strode in, the duty operator was sitting in front of the tall bank of security monitors with a headset on his ears and his feet propped on the console. His name was Philip, and the last thing he expected to see at this hour was his boss coming through the door. Martijn had to smile as he watched Philip turn his head, see him, and topple onto the floor when he realized who had just walked in.

"Mister Van Gries," Philip stammered as he got back on his feet, clearly flustered. "God, I'm glad you're here. I put in some calls to you and Mr.

Carbonari, but… well, you need to see what's happening up on the roof, and in the penthouse. There are men…"

Martijn nodded. "I know all about it, Philip, everything's under control."

"Shouldn't I notify someone? I know you said we should never call…"

"The police?" Van Gries asked, with a frown. "No, you are to call no one, and certainly not the police," he reminded him as he walked to the far corner of the room and used his key card and a still different key-code to open a cabinet that held a large, secure server. Martijn opened his attaché case, reached inside the server cabinet, and began pulling out two dozen Kingston Predator one-terabyte, high-capacity flash drives, one at a time, and dropping them into his case.

"But there are men up there with guns, Mister Van Gries," Philip blathered on. "And… well, I think people have been shot up there. I… I didn't know what to do."

Several of the flash drives contained the hyper-secure backup set of his personal accounting and investment portfolio. For several years, Martijn had been using some very complicated algorithms to skim minor amounts of money from the transfers that went in and out of the hotels and casinos. The individual amounts were so small and the accounts so diverse that it would take an army of forensic accountants to figure it all out. Donatello knew nothing about it, the New York partners knew nothing about it, and he thought it highly unlikely that Burke's hackers knew anything about the money or his private accounts scattered around in Belize, Bangkok, the Caymans, and Switzerland.

The remaining thumb drives in the server cabinet contained the videos he had been using to blackmail several dozen VIPs over the past year or so. Martijn's proprietary software integrated their personal information with hotel and restaurant charges, gambling records, and carefully selected audios and video feeds from the specially outfitted hotel bedrooms they had been assigned to upstairs. His custom audiovisual software was motion activated and allowed Martijn to quickly edit everything out except the "juicy stuff." As with the account skimming, he was always careful. He only hit these people up for relatively modest amounts of money, small enough that they could afford, but not large enough to drive them into doing something stupid, like running to the police or not paying. Potentially, his little extortion scheme could provide an even greater income stream than what he had been skimming from the three casinos. Yes, he thought, it was the gift that would keep on giving.

"I… I saw you up there in the penthouse with the others, and I remembered that you said we should never call the police, so I didn't," Philip went on, further sealing his own fate. "But I couldn't get Security to answer their phones or pages, not even those new gentlemen from New York, so…"

"There is no problem, Philip. Everything is under control. It is merely a security drill. Can you come over here for a second and give me a hand with this?"

"Yes, yes, of course, Mister Van Gries." Philip quickly stepped over and knelt next to the Dutchman. Martijn picked up one of the flash drives with his left hand and showed it to Phillip to draw his attention toward the attaché case, while he pulled out the Walther PPK from his pocket with his right hand and shot Philip in the side of the head.

"No loose ends," Martijn began softly repeating his mantra. "No loose ends..."

Finished retrieving what he had come for, Martijn reached back inside the server cabinet. At the bottom, under two locked but innocuous-looking metal covers, sat two red switches with small lights above each one. He unlocked the covers, flipped them up, and pushed the two switches down. The two lights immediately came on, turned bright red, and began to flash. The switch on the left deactivated the computer room's foam fire suppression system, while the one on the right activated the timed detonators on a series of white phosphorus incendiary charges that Van Gries had placed inside the room, the servers, and control devices. There would be no explosion. The charges would ignite and burn for one minute at over 5,000 degrees, more than enough time to incinerate everything in the room and turn it into molten plastic, metal, and ash, even poor Philip. Because the ceiling and walls of the room were made of twelve inches of reinforced concrete, a fire like this would create intense heat inside like an old-fashioned tandoor cooking oven, leaving the fire department's arson inspectors scratching their heads, but it would have no effect at all on the hotel or casino.

Martijn looked at his watch. Time to go, he thought, as he picked up his attaché case and quickly climbed the metal stairs to the rear loading dock door. Provided he encountered no further interference, he would be standing at the wheel of his yacht in two minutes, and motoring toward the headland and Absecon Inlet with the ever-erotic Eva at his side when the charges went off in another five. After a leisurely sail to a private marina he knew about in Bermuda, the yacht would be given a complete cosmetic make over.

After that, he would visit his bankers in the Caymans before sailing east and island-hopping his way down the long chain along the eastern Caribbean, from the Turks and Caicos to Grenada and Trinidad and Tobago. The native populations there were a gentle and easy-going folk who spoke a lilting Dutch and French patois. They understood fine dining and civilized conversation, and Martijn could forget all about Atlantic City, its infamous New York City crime bosses, and the god-awful fractured English they spoke. More important still, he could forget all about that vengeful bastard Robert T. Burke. It was unfortunate that Martijn finally had his various operations and scams humming at full speed when Burke had to stick his nose in and ruin everything. After all, as his brother Theo amply demonstrated upstairs, in the grand scheme of things, what difference does one army sergeant make, more or less?

When Bob and The Batman finally reached the top of the emergency staircase, they paused. From the blueprints Ace photographed in the City Building Inspector's Office, Bob knew the emergency stairs terminated in the penthouse's elevator lobby at a thick steel door, a magnetic lock at the top and a key card reader on the adjacent wall. Ace said Carbonari and the others had gone outside and were on the deck, but they may have left someone behind.

He quickly keyed his chin mic and asked, "Ace, Ghost. Sit Rep?"

"We put two down. The others are in a nervous clump near the helicopter."

"And the girls?"

"They're fine, but Benson and Van Gries are using them as shields."

"Everyone's outside now?"

"As far as I can tell, but I don't see Ernie or Jimmy."

"10-4."

Bob pointed his Beretta at the magnetic lock. "Heads up," he warned The Batman as he turned his face away and fired three quick shots into the center of the lock mechanism. That was where he knew its circuitry was located. Magnetic locks were wonderful inventions, he mused. They could hold back a charging rhino, but the same 9-millimeter bullet that could put the big animal down could also render the lock useless if properly aimed.

He turned the doorknob, pulled it open, peered around the doorframe into the elevator lobby, and looked into the penthouse beyond. From the way Ace described the action on the roof, it was unlikely that anyone out there had heard him, but it paid to be careful. The penthouse's ornate floor-to-ceiling lobby doors hung askew, with bits and pieces of broken hardware strewn about the entryway floor. Obviously, someone had been in a hurry to get inside. The foyer was empty, so he and The Batman stepped inside the great room and saw the bodies of two of Theo's men on the floor. Glancing into the master bedroom to his right, he saw the body of a boy lying in the doorway and three more bodies on the floor at the foot and sides of the bed. From their gaudy jewelry and poor taste in clothing, Bob knew it had to be three of the bozos whom Carbonari's bosses had sent down from New York City.

"Someone's been cleaning house up here," The Batman said.

"A falling out of thieves," Bob answered. But why, he wondered.

They split up and worked their way along the two sidewalls, staying low behind the chairs and couches as they headed for the rear doors to the deck. As he got within three feet of the hall closet, he heard whispered arguing going on inside. He immediately recognized one of the voices as that of Ernie Travers. The CPD captain was attempting to whisper, but that wasn't working too well. It sounded as if he was arguing, teeth clenched, and he wasn't too happy with whomever it was who was locked in there with him. The other voice was louder and whinier, and Bob immediately knew it had to be Jimmy Barker. Someone had wedged a stout dining room chair under the doorknob. Given what looked like a solid core door, a thick chair, and premium door hinges, Bob doubted that even Ernie could force it open from the inside.

He knocked on the door and asked, "If I let you two out, will you stop arguing? Or should I just leave you in there for a while longer?"

That shut them up. "Is that you, Bob?" he heard Travers ask.

"You didn't answer my question," he said as he put his foot against the chair, shoved it aside, and turned the doorknob, opening the door far enough to look inside. From their embarrassed faces, he knew he had his answer.

"It wasn't me. He..." Jimmy complained as he stepped out into the room. Bob quickly grabbed him by the seat of his pants and dumped him behind the couch. "Stay down and shut up. There are five or six guys out there with guns. If they end up running back in here, they'd love nothing better than to shoot you full of holes. You got that?"

"But they've got Patsy!" Jimmy argued.

"And they've got Linda," Bob replied. "So do what I told you."

The body of one of Theo's men was lying a few feet away from the young Geek. He had been shot twice in the chest and was very much dead. Underneath him, Bob saw a Heckler and Koch P1 9-millimeter automatic. That was the standard German Army sidearm these days, so the body had to be Klaus Reimer, the Bundeswehr veteran.

"Who shot him?" Bob asked Ernie.

"Theo Van Gries. Dorothy broke Reimer's wrist and dislocated his shoulder before she got shot back on the boat. Apparently, Theo Van Gries doesn't have much use for liabilities or for Germans. He is one stone-cold killer."

"Yeah, that's what happens to you when you spend too much time in the desert fighting people who are even worse than you are," Bob told him. "Ever use one of these?" he asked the Chicago cop as he tossed him the P1.

"I'll figure it out," Ernie answered as he quickly dropped the magazine out of the receiver, checked the load, and jacked a new round into the receiver. "After twenty years working the streets of Chicago, there isn't much I haven't shot or had shot at me."

"Well, if you don't like that one, there's something else lying over there." Bob pointed to the second body. "And I think I saw a selection of revolvers in the bedroom."

"Can I have one?" Jimmy asked.

"No!" Bob and Ernie answered in unison.

"Stay behind the couch or get back in the closet," Ernie told him. "The last thing we want is you behind us with a loaded gun." Then he turned toward Bob and added, "Just so you know, I intend to empty this thing into the first one of those bastards that shows himself, so don't get in my way."

Theo Van Gries found himself in the center of the mounting chaos on the pool deck. Normally, he thrived in the quick-pulse, high-octane moments of a fast-moving firefight, when life itself was sliding down the edge of a razor blade. It made him feel alive, and he had come to love it and even crave it. In his career in the Royal Dutch Marines in Iraq and Afghanistan, he had been under fire almost as often as Bob Burke had and was every bit as much of a skilled, professional soldier. Combat! There was nothing like the sound of gunfire first thing in the morning. It was better than that first coffee to focus the mind and get the heart pumping.

As the seconds slowly ticked away, Theo's brain began to function like a ballistic computer. Triangulating the bodies of Lucas Bakker and Joost DeVries at the moment the bullets struck them, he saw how their bodies moved. He saw the directions of the blood splatters and heard the trailing, deep-throated Blam! Blam! of the gunshots as they rolled across the roof. Snipers! There were two of them using long rifles, located to his left. From the distinctive sound, he knew it had to be .50-caliber Barretts, the favorite of the Americans, and the bullets had arrived with deadly accuracy.

Two of his three remaining men, Lucas Bakker and Joost DeVries, were down. That only left his top NCO, Eric Smit, who was now lying on the deck behind one of the pump housings a few feet away; the unarmed turncoat American, Benson, who was hiding behind the girl; and Donatello Carbonari, whimpering and cowering behind his briefcase, to take on an unknown number of Deltas. They were out there in the dark waiting for clear shots to kill the rest of them.

Theo still had his arm around Linda Burke's neck. He knew she and the girl were the only two things keeping him alive. Instinctively, he pulled her closer and turned her in the direction of the shooters, moving back and forth and up and down every few seconds to throw off their aim. Still, all he could see out there was the dark night, the colorful lights of the city below, and the equally tall rooftops of Tuscany Towers and Siesta Cove beyond. That was it, he suddenly realized. The shooters were on the roof of Tuscany Towers! He could only curse his own stupidity. Burke was one clever, patient bastard. He must have placed two long rifles on the other hotel roof earlier in the evening, and they had ample time to measure, triangulate, and zero in on every square inch of the Bimini Bay's penthouse roof at their leisure. They had been lying there in the dark, waiting for him and his men to stop arguing and come strolling out toward the helicopter without a care in the world. Then they took their shots.

From the amazing accuracy, he knew it might be Burke, or perhaps Randall out there, not that it mattered. The rest of Burke's men came with excellent reputations as well, and men like that rarely missed. Like lambs to the slaughter, Theo had led his men right into their crosshairs. What a colossal blunder, he cursed himself.

"It's Burke!" Benson turned and told Van Gries as the two men huddled behind the women. "He must've put two shooters on the other hotel roof."

"Don't you think I know that, you idiot!"

Smarting from Theo's rebuke, Benson looked around and saw they were standing in the center of the roof and would already be dead without the women to hide behind. Before the first shot, he already had his arm around her waist and was holding her close. That may have caused them to look elsewhere for their first targets. When Bakker and DeVries went down, he immediately grabbed a handful of Patsy's hair and stood her up in front of him. She would keep him safe for the moment, but that was about all. Theo had taken his Beretta away, but Benson was not completely unarmed. He slipped his hand into his rear pocket and pulled out the six-inch stiletto knife he always kept hidden there. He opened the blade, pressed it against Patsy's throat and whispered to her, "Don't move a muscle. Do you hear me?"

To his left, he saw Carbonari hiding behind his briefcase. "Donatello," Benson shouted at him. "The helicopter. Get in and get it started. We've got to get out of here!"

The big Don looked over and stared back at him with vacant eyes. Benson couldn't tell if Carbonari understood anything he was saying, but he tried again. "The helicopter, start the helicopter!" Benson screamed at him again, but the man just sat there wide-eyed and unmoving. He appeared to be in shock, not that it mattered any longer.

Burke had been two steps ahead of them all night; and as if to prove the point, Benson heard three more carefully measured .50-caliber rounds. He ducked again, but it wasn't necessary. The bullets weren't aimed at him, they struck the helicopter's engine and turned it into so much scrap metal. As oil and hydraulic fluid poured out on the helipad, it was clear that Carbonari's big toy wasn't going anywhere now. That must have gotten the Don's attention too. Instead of inching toward the cockpit, he suddenly turned and scrambled away on his hands and knees, dragging his briefcase behind him, until he got behind the big bamboo-sided Tiki bar near the pool.

Like Theo Van Gries, Benson remained where he was, hiding behind the girl. "We can't stay here," he called to the Dutchman. "They're going to pick us off one by one."

"Have you reached any other brilliant tactical conclusions?" Theo called back.

"The penthouse — we've got to get back inside, it's our only chance," Benson answered as he tightened his grip on Patsy's hair. "Back up, one step at a time," he ordered as he began pulling her toward the penthouse doors, exposing as little of himself as possible.

CHAPTER THIRTY-TWO

Dutch Marine sergeant Eric Smit lay curled up in the deep shadow behind the pool pump. With a half-dozen bright floodlights on the penthouse and around the pool, the rooftop was like a shooting gallery, while their enemy remained in the dark waiting patiently for their next shot. "A hell of a mess we've gotten ourselves into, eh, Luitnant?" he called out to Theo Van Gries.

"Agreed, Sergeant. Who forgot to turn off the lights?"

Who indeed, Smit wondered? He was the senior sergeant, a tactical expert in his own right, and was supposed to think of things like that. In the end, he had failed. Well, he thought, this was probably as good a day to die as any other. As the sound of gunfire and oil and hydraulic fluid dripping beneath the helicopter faded away, the rooftop grew deathly quiet again. Smit turned his head and looked back longingly through the penthouse doors. He knew that was their only way out now, but that was when he saw that bastard Burke and another man advancing slowly across the great room floor toward him, blocking their way.

Smit swung his Glock 17 around and was about to fire at Burke when he heard an ominous sound in the dark sky above him and paused. It was a helicopter, circling the big hotel like a vulture. From his years in Iraq and Afghanistan, Smit was familiar with dozens of makes and models of helicopters from as many countries, but the rhythmic "Thump, Thump, Thump" of this one was different. The sound was in the lower registers and very quiet. While he had never seen one, he knew the Americans were developing stealth helicopters down at Fort Bragg for commando missions. That meant Burke had help, big help, and it offended Smit's sense of fairness. War was supposed to be between men, but what chance did they now stand?

He raised his pistol and tried to focus again on Burke when the black helicopter suddenly swooped down out of nowhere and roared across the roof, only a few feet above him, pounding the Sergeant with its downdraft and deafening noise. He pulled the trigger, but he knew he had been distracted and the helicopter had spoiled his shot. He looked up and cursed the phantom machine as he swung the Glock away from Burke and began firing at the black machine, over and over again, until his magazine clicked empty.

As Bob advanced slowly through the penthouse toward the doors to the outside deck, he never saw Eric Smit curled up in the shadows directly in front of him. With the bright lights all around, the small shadow behind the pump housing was like a black hole, rendering the Dutchman almost invisible until he raised his arm. Burke knew Smit had him cold. His Glock 17 was pointed straight at him and the Dutchman couldn't miss at this distance. Then the helicopter roared across the roof and threw off Smit's aim. Instinctively, Burke dived behind the couch. Had Smit remained focused, Burke knew, he would be dead. He looked back up and saw the Dutchman standing, aiming at the helicopter and firing round after round at it as it disappeared into the darkness. With no further thought, Bob pointed his Beretta at him, pulled the trigger, and put the Dutch sergeant down.

Twenty feet away from Smit, Donatello Carbonari was also hiding in the shadows, but he was behind the Tiki pool bar. With his options running out, he drew his legs underneath him as if he were in the starting blocks of the 100-yard dash, trying to summon sufficient courage to run across the open deck to the safety of the penthouse.

"Ready... set..." He rocked back and forward, filling his lungs with a last, desperate, deep breath of air. He was only a split second away from a sprinter's start when the helicopter flew directly overhead and sucked the last ounce of courage out of him. Broken, he slumped even further back into the shadows. Unfortunately, Donatello found no sanctuary back there, either. The man with the rifle knew exactly where he and all the others were. As he cowered even further back, the bastard fired another round, this time into the bar itself. The large slug barely slowed as it smashed through the bar's decorative bamboo facing. It narrowly missed Carbonari but smashed into the ample supply of liquor and wine he kept on the inside shelves, shattering a half-dozen bottles and giving him a quick shower of whiskey, bamboo splinters, wine, and broken glass. With his face stinging from the whiskey and a dozen small cuts, Carbonari screamed and bent over, whimpering, not knowing whether to throw up, stand up and run, or collapse on the deck, emotionally exhausted.

"Martijn!" he screamed in desperation. "You bastard, you got me into this. You got me into this." If that damned Dutchman hadn't tried to squeeze every last dime out of that American Army Sergeant Pastorini, Carbonari would never be in this mess to begin with. That vengeful bastard Burke would never have come here, Martijn would never have called his brother, and the Don of Atlantic City would still be sitting on top of his little world, enjoying the most delicious food, the most delicious wine, and the most delicious young men. He looked down at himself, covered with one of his best vintages and his own blood, remembering that one of his favorite young men was lying dead on his bedroom floor at that very moment, and went into a rage.

"Martijn, I'm going to kill you!" he screamed again as he felt himself sliding down the slippery slope into the flames of his own private hell.

"**Ace, Ghost.** What can you see? You got a shot?

"Negatory, Ghost. Too risky. I can get the crosshairs on bits and pieces of Van Gries and Benson, but that's about all. Koz, you got a shot?"

"Same-o, same-o here. Too risky, but don't worry. He ain't going nowhere."

"Koz, Ghost. You want to explain that to Linda?"

"Point taken."

"Ghost, Ace. If it was your head he was holding the gun against, I'd take the shot, but we like her better. Let's face it, it's a standoff. He can't move and we can't shoot."

Theo Van Gries continued shifting slightly to his left and to his right behind the woman so the riflemen had no clear shot at him. In the past three minutes, his little adventure here in New Jersey had quickly gone from bad to worse. Joost DeVries, Lucas Bakker, and now Eric Smit, his three best men, were all down, not to mention the two he had dropped inside. He was now alone, and it was time to withdraw on whatever terms he could negotiate from a far superior enemy.

Theo was a realist, and he knew he had been badly outplayed by a master. In the process, he committed the two most unforgivable cardinal sins an infantryman could commit. First, he allowed his own ego to seriously underestimate his enemy. And secondly, he painted himself into a corner up here on the roof. They were in an exposed position, six stories up, alone, and with an unseen and highly skilled enemy in front of him and behind him with superior weapons. His only allies now were a traitor, a coward, and his own wits. Marvelous!

As he thought about it, he could only laugh at himself. If there was a better definition of a hopeless military position, he couldn't think of one. His instructors at the Royal Dutch Naval Academy in Den Helder would cut off his buttons and break his sword over their knees if they could see him now. He couldn't run and he couldn't fight, so he was down to his last card: the one he was holding in his left hand. He tightened his grip around Linda Burke's throat and waited for Burke to come to him, as he knew he must.

Finally, Donatello Carbonari knew he could sink no lower. He rose to his feet, extended himself to his full height, and straightened his jacket and tie before he turned toward the penthouse door. They could kill him if they wanted but, he decided, he would go out with some measure of dignity. Unfortunately, as he took the first long, confident stride he stumbled over his briefcase and almost fell again. The briefcase skittered halfway to the pool, but he no longer cared about any of that. The sniper was still out there too, but Carbonari no longer cared about him either. If the man was going to shoot him, at least he would be properly dressed for the newspaper photographs. He left the briefcase where it fell, straightened his jacket again, and continued walking toward the penthouse. Sure enough, standing in the center of the doorway was that bastard Burke with a pistol in his hand. Carbonari didn't look at him. He raised his chin and strode past Burke as if he and the others were not even there.

"**Ghost, Ace.** Fish in a barrel, you want me to put him down?"
"Negative. Don't worry, he has worse problems than us."
Ace sighed into the open mic and said, "If you insist."

Linda Burke knew that the almost humorous distraction that Carbonari had just provided might be her last chance. Theo still had his arm around her neck and his pistol pressed against the back of her head, but his attention was everywhere except on her. Remembering bits and pieces of a half-assed Women Against Violence self-defense course her girlfriends talked her into taking one night after too much to drink, she suddenly leaned forward, dropped down, and tried to twist away from him. Her plan was to catch Theo in the groin with her elbow or forearm and break free of his grip. Unfortunately, Theo Van Gries was not a five-foot-eight, 130-pound female Recreation Department instructor. As she dropped and twisted, he did the same. The best she could do was to hit him in the hip with her elbow.

For a brief instant, Ace had a clear shot at Theo from his waist up. Unfortunately, Ace too had been as distracted by Carbonari as everyone else had been. By the time he pulled the trigger, the Dutchman had ducked, his head and shoulders were no longer in the crosshairs, and the bullet missed high by at least six inches.

Fully understanding what just happened, Theo stooped even lower, got a firmer, five-finger grip on Linda's hair, and pulled back sharply until she screamed. Slowly, he got back up, carefully keeping his head directly behind hers as he forced her to stand in front of him again.
"I am not amused, Mrs. Burke," Theo growled at her. "I swear, if you try anything like that again, I really will kill you."
With an expert sniper to his front and an even more angry Bob Burke to his rear, Theo Van Gries knew his position was hopeless. He was a realist and could see there was only one solution.
"Major Burke," he called out. "I propose a temporary cease-fire, if you will,

sir. I don't want anyone else to get hurt up here, not your wife, and certainly not me. Agreed?"

"Agreed," Bob answered as he stepped out onto the roof and walked toward Van Gries.

"Ghost, if I get another shot...?"

"No, stand down, everyone, until I hear what he has to say. Copy?"

"Copy," Ace answered, if reluctantly.

As Bob approached, Theo Van Gries straightened up and gave him the slightest nod of the head. No one else saw it, but Bob had, and understood its meaning.

"Well played, Major," Theo said as he glanced toward the Tuscany Towers building. "Master Sergeant Randall is a superior shot. Can I assume you told him not to kill me?"

"Can I assume the pistol you're holding to my wife's head is empty?"

"Touché." Theo smiled as he released his grip on Linda's hair and lowered his Glock. "I sincerely apologize for my rudeness, Mrs. Burke. My mother would not be pleased with me, but such are the fortunes of war these days." With that, he bowed to her and handed her his pistol. "I am your prisoner, madame."

She took the heavy pistol in her hands, looking down at it for a second, obviously debating whether to use it on him herself. In the end, she drew her leg back and kicked him in the groin as hard as she could. "Take your apology and shove it!" she told him.

Fortunately for Van Gries he saw it coming, turned slightly, and caught the kick in his thigh. That was painful enough, he thought as he limped around for a moment, but it could have been much worse. The woman knew how to kick. Finally, he looked up at Burke. "No doubt I deserved that, but you and I still need to talk."

"About what? Desperate men in hopeless positions?"

"No, about how much you and I have in common at the moment."

"You and I have nothing in common."

"You could not be more wrong. What we have in common is our sometime, mutual comrade-in-arms, Captain Randy Benson." Van Gries turned and pointed a long finger at Gramps, who was still hiding behind Patsy, perhaps hoping they'd forget he was there. "He is the only reason you and your men, or I and mine, came here to begin with."

"Benson? I don't think so. I came here because your brother and his mob friends killed one of my sergeants, and then you decided to get in the way."

"No, Benson killed him. Then he sucked us both in, hoping we would kill each other off before we figured it out."

Bob stared at him and then at Benson. "And why would he do that?"

"The oldest reason in the world, Major, for 'the stuff that dreams are made of,' I think Bogey called it, for the gold." Theo reached in his pocket, pulled out the ancient lion medallion, and held it up. Even at night in the dim glow of the floodlights, it hung there like liquid sunshine. "Beautiful, is it not? But do you know what it is?"

Bob turned and looked at Benson, and then at Patsy. "Not entirely, but the last time I saw it, I think it was hanging around Patsy's neck."

"She got it from your Sergeant Pastorini, but it has been through many hands over the years. It originally came from the royal Assyrian tombs, which were excavated in Nimrud and Ur over a century ago. The last time I saw it was in Baghdad. It was one of fifty-five pieces that my CIA-sponsored burglary ring were told to take into *protective custody* from the Iraqi Museum of Art before someone really did steal them, or so we were led to believe." Bob frowned and Theo laughed. "Major, I am an infantry officer, not a cat burglar or an art thief. How else do you think we pulled that assignment off? It was a CIA operation, an inside job, from Day One, or that was how it started, anyway.

"You know how things were in Iraq — how they still are — greed and corruption everywhere. Well, someone in Baghdad convinced someone in Langley that this cache of items was a national treasure which needed to disappear before the really bad people in the Iraqi government got their hands on it. They teamed us up with some Iraqi military intelligence and museum people who turned out to be only slightly less corrupt than the people we were supposedly saving these items from. It was supposed to be a simple in-and-out, but no sooner did we get in the door than things went very wrong. The Iraqi Intelligence people tried a double-cross. Shots were fired, they came out on the short end, and we ended up with the gold. Once that happened, Iraqi politics took over. They turned on us and the CIA was quick to follow. We became that 'rogue operation up in Mosul' and everyone suddenly 'disavowed' any knowledge of the operation, as they say in the movies."

"You're too tall for the Tom Cruise part," Bob told him.

Theo smiled. "You are right. Cruise is more your size. But we were on our own. We were able to hide the gold temporarily but the CIA, the Iraqis, and the CID were all over us. We became everyone's easy target."

"Why didn't you just give it all back?"

"We couldn't. No one would ever believe us and handing them the proof would simply put a noose around all of our necks. The simple solution would have been to melt them down, or throw them in the river, but I refused to do that. They were a cultural heritage. So the only choice was to get them out of the country before they caught us 'red handed,' as you call it in your movies. Fortunately or unfortunately, that was when your Sergeant Pastorini entered our desperate little drama. He smuggled the gold out for us, but then we could not get him to give it back."

"Who else knew the CIA was behind this? Anyone?" Bob asked.

"No, only me, a few people in Baghdad, the wrong ones, and supposedly their handlers back at Langley. None of my men knew. Not even Benson. They all thought we really were stealing the pieces. Like I said, you were there, you know how things worked, and down deep, you know what I am saying is the truth."

"Ghost, Ace," Bob heard in his ear. "You aren't buying this, are you?"

Van Gries saw the thin smile on Burke's face and asked, "That little bird in your ear doesn't believe me, does he?"

"You might say that."

"I'm not sure I would either, but it was your Sergeant Pastorini who double-crossed us, and it was your Captain Benson who killed him, not my brother's people. What does that make it? A triple-cross?" Theo said as he turned and glared at Benson.

Patsy had been listening to every word Theo Van Gries said. Finally, she turned and tried to push Benson away. "You bastard!" she called him, but he still had a handful of her hair and a knife at her throat.

Bob finally turned toward Benson. One look in his eyes told Bob all he needed to know, and who was telling the truth. "Let her go," he told him.

"I don't think so," Benson said as he tightened his grip.

"Ace has his Barrett lined up on your head, Ernie Travers has a H & K P1 pointed at you from the penthouse door," Bob told him as he nodded toward Ernie, "and I have my Beretta."

"And none of you will dare shoot as long as I have this blade at her throat."

At that point, Theo Van Gries stepped forward. "Pardon me for interrupting, Major, but since it appears that you may be tied up for a while dealing with him, if you have no objections, I believe I shall leave." Theo handed Bob the gold medallion. "You can add it to the rest of the pieces in Pastorini's garage in Fayetteville, and perhaps I can go visit them someday in Baghdad."

Burke looked at the medallion for a moment, and then back up at Theo.

The Dutchman shrugged and said, "Whatever grievances and honor violations you and I had between us have been resolved now. We no longer owe each other anything."

"There are six bodies inside that penthouse," Bob told him. "Who answers for them?"

"And three more out here. Smit, DeVries, and Bakker were good soldiers with at least a shred of honor before your CIA came along, but they are on your side of the ledger. I shot MacGregor and Reimer, but they were mercenaries, hard cases the world will not miss. The boy is between my brother and Carbonari. And as for the three New York gunmen lying near the bed, well, they got what they deserved and neither you nor I are the police."

"What about your brother? I'm not finished with him."

Theo smiled. "Martijn? He has always been able to weasel his way out of most problems on his own, so he is your problem now, not mine. Besides," Theo said as he looked around the roof, "he appears to have disappeared. Carbonari was neither of our concerns to begin with, and Benson is all yours. Can you think of anything else?"

Bob stared at him for a moment. "Dorothy. Someone needs to answer for Dorothy."

"Ah, the young woman on the boat who was shot. I sincerely regret that happening, but I was told that was Benson's doing, he and Reimer. Reimer is dead and you have Benson. That should be a sufficient 'mea culpa' to satisfy anyone."

Bob turned toward Linda, who he had not talked to since he left her on *The Enchantress* with the others earlier in the evening. "Is that true?" he asked her.

Linda frowned for a moment, thinking, and then she nodded. "It all happened so fast, but yes, it was Benson who shot her."

"As I said," Theo shrugged, "perhaps we shall meet again, under more pleasant circumstances, Major. Until then, if I can ever be of assistance, most evenings you can find me at the bar in the JW Marriott in Kuwait City." When Burke made no reply, the Dutchman gave him another polite nod, turned, and began walking toward the penthouse door.

"Ghost, Ace." Bob heard that voice in his ear again. "You aren't going to let him go?"

"Yeah, think I am" was all Bob could think to say as he turned and watched Theo Van Gries walk through the doors, cross the family room, and exit out the large penthouse's front door before he turned back and looked at Benson.

"Surely you don't believe that preposterous story about the gold and how I threw Vinnie out a window, do you? That never happened."

Burke looked at him. "Really? He never said you threw him out a window, he just said you killed him. If you want me to believe you, let the girl go."

"There's three of you, with guns, what chance would I have?" Benson asked.

Burke looked at him and tossed his Beretta on the deck, and then turned to Ernie Travers. "Stand down, I've got this. You hear that, Ace?"

"You drive me crazy when you pull this crap, you know," Ace said in his earpiece.

"Stand down, Ace... You too, Koz. That's an order."

"Roger that," Ace replied. "Just make him suffer before you kill him."

"Wilco."

"What did Randall just say?" Benson asked, skeptical. "I don't care what *you* say. He's always hated me, and I know he's going to shoot me anyway."

"Nope." Bob keyed the mic and said loud and clear, so all the others would hear, "He won't interfere and neither will the others. Everybody hear that? Good. So it's just you and me." Bob began to walk around as he continued to talk to Benson, feeling the old juices coming back. "That's what you always wanted, isn't it, Randy? A shot at the champ?"

"I remember when I joined the Unit," Bob said. "Richards, the old CO, had rotated out and you'd been there for what? Two years? You were a big guy, every bit as big and muscular as Ace and Koz. When they put you three together, people thought you were triplets, didn't they? Three big, old, gnarly Deltas out to kick the world's ass. The job and the promotion were supposed to be yours. It was in the bag! And then the Big Green Machine decided to screw you over and send in a new guy to take *your* job in *your* group. They passed you over for a little shrimp of a newly minted gold-leaf major. I didn't even look like a Delta, did I? I couldn't be what? 150 pounds sopping wet? And there you were, stuck saluting *me* and taking *my* orders. I'll bet that really pissed you off, didn't it, *Gramps*?"

CHAPTER THIRTY-THREE

Benson's eyes narrowed, as they darted back and forth between Burke and the others. God, he hated that guy, but he was stuck. He had dug himself a very deep hole with the gold, but it almost worked. Almost! And for ten million Euro, more than twelve million dollars split with *no one*, he would do it all over again. Benson watched Burke closely as he walked around him, watching his hands and how he moved. It had been three years since they served together. Burke spent the last three years behind a desk. That was a long time. Did he appear older, fatter, and out of shape? Maybe. He did look stockier than he used to, even a bit jowly? Maybe, but the little weasel had always been quick and lithe, and the only way to find out for sure was to accept the challenge and take him on. It was also the only ticket out of here, he knew.

Gramps! That was what they started calling him as soon as Burke arrived, because Benson was a year and a half older, and therefore the oldest man in the Unit. Gramps! It still rankled. He was the ROTC guy, the world's oldest captain, who ended up in second place to a West Point "ring knocker" who needed what they called "command time," which was a polite way of passing over Benson and saying he was second class. And what did Burke do with the opportunity? He turned in his papers, resigned his commission, pissed it all away, so two careers went down the toilet. Gramps! For the executive officer, the "Number Two," to be called "Gramps" was the kiss of death and every enlisted man in the Unit knew it.

Despite the risks of taking on Burke hand to hand, Benson knew there were two certainties. If he did nothing or tried to run, Ace Randall would gun him down, despite any assurances Burke had given. On the other hand, if he took Burke on and beat him, the Ghost would do exactly what he promised, even if it killed him.

"Come on, Gramps," Bob called him out with a slight voice inflection to needle him. "Back then, you were hard-scrabble tough. I remember you were that big nasty bastard, who could have kicked my ass any day of the week, couldn't you? Oh, I took up some martial arts stuff and even got pretty good at it myself. So, who knows? I'm a sneaky little bastard, but after three years sitting behind a desk this is your big chance to prove you are the better man and always were. It's just the two of us now, *mano a mano.*" Burke continued to circle. "Here I am, all of your frustrations wrapped up in one little package. What's it going to be? Put up or shut up. Let the girl go, beat me, and you can walk away. You can even keep the knife... Gramps!"

"All right, you bastard!" Benson finally had enough. He took the knife away from Patsy's throat and shoved her across the roof into Linda. "Put up or shut up, you said? I guess we'll see," he said as he dropped into a perfectly balanced defensive fighting position, knees bent, his hands out in front of him, knife at the ready, moving counter to wherever Burke went.

Bob smiled. Given the size difference between them, his natural advantage was being lower, lighter, and quicker. The textbook approach was for him to bob, weave, and make the occasional quick thrust, staying on the perimeter just beyond his larger opponent's reach. The goal was to tire him out and wait for him to make a mistake. That was what the textbook said, but Benson knew that too; that was why he would hold the center, wait, and cut Burke to pieces with the knife every time he came in and tried to strike. The knife was the key. Leaving Benson with it was Burke's big mistake. Since the major left the Unit, Benson had spent countless hours working with the knife until it became one of his specialties, but Burke wouldn't know that.

"Ghost, Dinosaur," Bob heard in his earpiece. "What the hell's going on down there? I see three KIA now, including the one I buzzed. You okay?"

"AOK, Dinosaur, and thanks. He almost got me."

"You're getting old, son, like me," Stansky replied.

"Who are you talking to?" Benson demanded. "I thought this was just you and me?"

"Just another bird in my ear," Bob told Benson and then keyed the mic again. "Dinosaur, can you swing over to the Tuscany roof one and a half kliks southeast of my pos and pick up Ace and Koz?"

"Ghost, Ace. You sure you want to do that right now?"

"Ace, I'm sure," Bob answered. "After that, Dinosaur, you can swing by here and pick us up."

"Ace, Dinosaur. He is one confident son of a bitch, isn't he?"

"Roger that, sir, roger that," Ace answered. "Packing up, and ready for extraction in One."

"Who was that?" Benson demanded. "A goddamned flock of birds this time?"

"No, only one. Sometimes I just hear voices, that's all."

"Voices, huh? Then you don't need that earpiece or the chin mic, do you?" Benson stated. "You were the one who said this would be *mano a mano*, remember? Just you and me, and that means no outside help."

Bob looked at him and smiled before he looked around at the others again.

Ernie Travers, Linda, Chester, The Batman, Bulldog, and even Jimmy Barker had all come out on the deck to watch. "Listen up, this is between me and him. Nobody interferes," he reminded them. "If Benson wins, he can walk out of here. Everybody got that?" Bob said as he pulled off the headset and tossed it aside.

Benson smiled too, knowing that without the earpiece, none of the other Deltas would be able to tell him how good he had gotten with the knife, either.

And so they began, exactly as Benson expected. The two men focused entirely on each other, tuning everything else out as they began to circle. Benson had watched Burke in hand-to-hand combat before, always against larger men, and this would be no different. Burke always danced his opponent on the balls of his feet, upright, making a rapid series of hand and head fakes, as Burke measured him and tried to tire him out. As time passed, he knew Burke would get bolder and bolder, so Benson held back and didn't take any of the feints. He stayed solid and frosty, bent at the knees and waist, getting a feel for his rhythm, waiting patiently for him to make that first big mistake, because it would be his last.

Unfortunately for Gramps, the slow circling, bobbing, and weaving lasted less than five seconds. That was when Bob suddenly ran straight at him in an all-out, win-or-lose, fast, Krav Maga attack, which was the last thing Gramps Benson expected. With his arms and legs churning, Bob was inside Benson's reach before the bigger man could react. He made a sweeping block of Benson's knife hand with his left forearm, pushing the knife outward, as he continued on in. As he did, he drove his right elbow into the center of Benson's face, flattening his nose, and stunning him. At the same time, Burke drove his left knee into Benson's groin. As the bigger man stumbled backwards, Burke brought that same elbow down onto the bundle of nerves in the right side of Benson's neck, temporarily paralyzing the arm. For all intents and purposes, the fight was already over. While Bob was unaware of Benson's new proficiency with a knife, Benson was equally unaware that Bob had turned away from all the conventional defensive martial arts he once was an expert in, such as Karate, Judo, Aikido, Tae Kwon Do, and had spent the past three years concentrating exclusively on Krav Maga, the lesser-known, extremely violent system of attacks and counter-attacks developed by the Israeli military.

"Look at his upper arm," Patsy screamed at Benson as she pointed at his shoulder where blood was now coming through his shirt. "I bet that's where I shot him that night in the house in Fayetteville."

"You really are a piece of work, aren't you, Gramps?" Bob said as he began to circle him again. For all the damage he had inflicted on Benson, amazingly, the bigger man was still on his feet. The knife had fallen on the deck, his right shoulder was bleeding and his arm hung numb at his side. He stood there wide-eyed, wobbling back and forth, and bleeding badly from his nose. Somehow, however, he was still standing. Finally, his eyes cleared and they focused on Burke. A loud, desperate, unearthly moan came out of him as he bent over, picked up the knife with his left hand, and looked at it for a second, and suddenly charged.

Benson may have only been moving at half his normal speed, but he still packed considerable power once he got that weight and muscle moving, too much weight, momentum, and power for Bob to match head-on. As a result, Bob did not use Krav Maga; he reverted to one of the oldest Judo moves in the books and went with the flow. He dodged the knife, pushed it aside, and took several small steps backward until he matched Gramps' speed, and grabbed the big man's shirt-front with both hands. Bending his right leg at the knee, he jammed his left foot into Benson's gut, continuing backward even faster as he sat down, bringing all of the big man's size and momentum with him. Continuing to roll backward, he kicked upward with all his strength. It is called a *Tomoe Nage* or Circle Throw, one of the "backward sacrifice throws" as they are called in Judo. Complicated and used with considerable risk, it is a thing of beauty when properly timed and executed, as this was.

Bob ended up on his back on the deck, while Benson found himself sailing high in the air, cartwheeling toward the edge of the roof. While that was not Bob's intention, Benson came down hard, headfirst on the top of the parapet wall. He seemed to stand there for an impossible moment, upside down, looking back at Burke and the others. Already stunned, it took Benson a second or two to realize what was happening, before he toppled backward over the edge and fell off the roof. Consequently, it was only when he passed the third floor that he began to scream in earnest. That, in turn, only lasted a few seconds more until he hit the concrete sidewalk below and the screaming suddenly stopped.

There was silence on the roof until Ernie Travers said, "I bet that hurt."

"Good!" Patsy Evans snapped angrily as she folded her arms across her chest. "Now he knows how Vinnie felt!"

Jimmy Barker hurried over to the side of the roof and looked down. "No, he's not feeling much of anything, now, but I wouldn't want to be the one who had to clean that up."

That was when the all-black Iroquois helicopter came in and touched down on the far side of the roof. Bob quickly got to his feet and put his headset back on.

"Ghost, Dinosaur," he heard. "There's a whole bunch of police cars and emergency vehicles converging on your position. Time to di di mau," or *run like hell*, in Vietnamese, Stansky said.

"Roger that. Sure took them long enough," Bob answered Stansky as he turned to the others. "All right, everybody get in," he said. "It may be a tight squeeze, but the bus is leaving. Jimmy, you and the girls hop on somebody's lap. We need to get out of here, and back to the boat."

Giving the roof one last look, he saw Carbonari's briefcase lying near the bar, ran over, and picked it up. After a quick head count to make sure everyone was there, he jumped through the Iroquois' rear door and had barely landed on the helicopter's deck when Stansky kicked the bird in the butt, and it took off low and fast, heading northeast toward Absecon Bay and the vast open marshes beyond.

Bob crawled to the edge of the helicopter's deck and looked down. Stansky was right; it looked as if every police car, ambulance, and fire truck in Eastern New Jersey had descended on the Bimini Bay complex. Odd, he thought, as he looked at the rear side of the building. He swore he saw smoke billowing out of the mechanical building next to the loading dock. Well, that was where they suspected Martijn Van Gries's data center was hidden, so perhaps it wasn't so odd after all.

As Stansky took the big black bird down to the deck, Bob had a beautiful view of Clam Creek as the moonlight and neon lights of the city reflected off the water of Absecon Channel. A large sailboat was motoring out and already halfway down Absecon Inlet, heading toward the Atlantic Ocean. It made a lovely sight in the moonlight, he thought, and in a few minutes, he planned to be doing exactly the same thing.

Bob rolled over onto his back and looked up. Jimmy was sitting sideways in Patsy's lap. Her arms were wrapped around his neck, and she had him in such a fierce lip-lock that he figured it would take a pry-bar to get them apart. Oh, well, they had earned it. Linda sat next to them in the front row of seats on Ace's lap, with her arms around him and Batman who had somehow squeezed in next to her. On the rear side sat Koz, Bulldog, Chester and Ernie. With General Stansky and Command Sergeant Major Pat O'Connor next to him in the co-pilot seat, that was a lot of weight for one small helicopter. No wonder the Iroquois felt sluggish.

Linda looked down at him and smiled. "This could be you, you know."

"Last man in gets the floor." Bob shrugged. "It's an old air assault rule."

"Nice moves back there, by the way," Ace said grudgingly. "Good to see you didn't let yourself go completely to hell."

"I'll be the judge of that!" Linda smiled down at him.

"If you're lucky," Bob shot back, well aware that the teasing and banter were a natural and inevitable reaction to the life-and-death tension that preceded them.

Minutes later, the stealthy black bird touched down in the parking lot near Barney's Dock and everyone piled out.

"Thanks a lot, sir." Bob reached through the pilot's window and shook Stansky's hand. "Nice ride."

"Glad to help, Major," the general quickly answered. "Over the years, you've given me more than my share of gray hair, so it was fun to watch you operate 'up close and personal,' as they say. By the way, what's that?" He motioned toward the big briefcase in Bob's hand.

Bob smiled. "The truth is I don't know, and I really don't care. It's Carbonari's. He had it clutched to his chest like a life preserver, and maybe it was. Whatever, I'll let the New Jersey State Police and the FBI figure it out." That said, Bob snapped to his parade ground-best position of attention and rendered the general a crisp salute. "Hope to see you down at Bragg in a few days, sir."

"You do that, Bobby!" Stansky saluted him back. "I've got a bottle of Jim Beam Single Barrel in my desk that O'Connor's been bugging me to open for weeks now, and I can't wait," Stansky winked. "And bring the wife. There's a lot of things I need to tell that girl. Stand clear!" he shouted as he added power and worked the Iroquois' cyclic and collective controls. Without all the weight, the black bird heaved a sigh of relief. Its nose quickly rotated to the northeast until he threw its tail in the air and the black bird shot off to the northeast.

Bob didn't have to tell anyone to get on board *The Enchantress*. The others had already run below deck, and Ace and Chester were casting off the lines as he jumped onto the stern and climbed up to the flying bridge.

"Let's get out of here," he told them as he looked across the small harbor at the flashing red lights from the fleet of emergency vehicles surrounding the Bimini Bay. He moved the engines to quarter speed ahead and powered away from the pier into the boat channel, glad to be the hell out of Atlantic City.

CHAPTER THIRTY-FOUR

The old Marine Basin marina was tucked away on the water side of the Belt Parkway in southeastern Brooklyn, hidden behind rundown warehouses, storage sheds, and parked trucks. It wasn't the kind of place where it paid to stick your nose in other people's business, see things you shouldn't see, or ask too many questions. Worn out, ground down, and beat up, the marina offered no amenities. What it offered was the quickest boat access in New York City to the ocean, the Hudson River, the East River, and Long Island Sound. The kind of boats that one saw there were not luxury yachts or sail boats. They were small to medium sized work boats, dredges, commercial fishing boats and trawlers. One example was an old forty-nine-foot O'Brien fishing boat that sat at the far end of the pier. Used and abused for over thirty years, it was functional, but in serious need of repairs, repainting, and refitting.

Three weeks after the escapades in Atlantic City, Angelo Roselli still had no idea where his money was, except that it wasn't in his accounts, where it was supposed to be. He brought in some of the best accounting and computer brains money could buy in the City, and all they could tell him was that he had been cleaned out. Where did it go? Don't know. Who took it? Don't know. Can I get it back? Don't know that either.

"Like I didn't freaking already know that?" he raged every time he thought about it. After all, twenty-seven million dollars and counting was a very big deal, but he also lost an entire crew of his best Brooklyn men — six "made" men on top of that — plus a crew chief, and all those morons could tell him was they didn't know. That didn't sit well with Angelo, it didn't sit well with the Lucchese family bosses he reported to, and worst of all, it didn't set well at all with their partners, the Genoveses over in Manhattan, either. The relationship between the Luccheses and the Genoveses had always been touchy at best, and a "thing" like this could push other "things" right over the edge. So to avoid a war, there must be answers, restitution, and blood — someone else's blood, Angelo hoped — and everyone knew it.

At 2:00 a.m., the marina was quiet and deserted. After he closed the restaurant, Angelo enjoyed a leisurely late dinner of his own scaloppini, manicotti, and a nice glass of Sangiovese, swapping stories about the old days with a few of the boys. Finally, he got in his dark gray Lincoln, put a Dean Martin CD in the player, and wound his way southeast on the dark city streets for the short drive south to Shore Parkway, and then east to the marina on 41st. He still felt full, too full, knowing it was never a good idea to eat a heavy meal like that before a long boat ride.

He drove into the marina and slowly skirted the numerous potholes as he wound his way to the end of the old pier. He parked next to the boat and got out, not even bothering to lock his car. Most people would be afraid to leave a nice car like his down here on the Brooklyn waterfront at this hour, but he wasn't. The kids down here knew who the car belonged to, and they knew that taking it or even touching it would be a "life-altering" decision, as they say. He paused and looked up. There was a thin quarter moon hanging in the sky over Staten Island, and a cold, damp breeze coming up off the water. Even with his suit, the gray fedora, and a heavy overcoat, it made him shiver. Cold? Yeah, maybe it was time for him to retire to Florida or Palm Springs after all. He was getting too old for this shit.

Angelo walked with a measured, purposeful gait to the boat, stepped over the gunnel, and came aboard. He waved to the man up on the bridge and gave a quick nod to the deckhand standing near the bow as he cast off the lines. The boat was pointed out to sea and its large engines were already warmed up and idling as he stepped around a 55-gallon oil drum, some scrap metal, a plastic drop cloth, and a chainsaw that were lying on the aft deck. He ducked his head and stepped down the narrow flight of stairs to the main cabin below. He looked around, remembering that it used to be nice down here, but that was a long time ago. They used to keep a refrigerator in the corner, some cushions on the side benches, and even a few Naugahyde lounge chairs, so the boys could relax and have a few beers after they went out to fish, or whatever; but nobody did that no more. Now, the boat was only used to haul stuff.

The soft purr of the twin diesels soon became a throaty rumble, as the boat pulled away from the pier and headed out into Gravesend Bay and the Atlantic Ocean beyond. He removed his fedora, placed it carefully on the side bench, and looked down at the prostrate figure of Donatello Carbonari lying on the deck in the center of the cabin, hog tied, gagged, and looking up at him with terrified eyes. Sitting on the hard benches across from Carbonari were two other large men in slacks, Italian leather shoes, and gaudy sports coats. They were smoking, and there were a half-dozen ground-out cigarette butts on the deck between them. Each man had a large revolver hanging indifferently in a shoulder holster, and they looked down at Carbonari with cold, pitiless eyes. They had done this before. Carbonari hadn't.

"He cause you any trouble?" Angelo looked over at them and asked.

"Him? Nah, it was almost as if he was expecting us."

Angelo shrugged. "Dat's 'cause he was; wuzn't you Donatello?" He paused, and then answered his own question. "See, Donatello's been a bad boy. He forgot that dose pleasure palaces he used to run down the coast belong to us, not to him, and dat he was responsible for what happened… for everything dat happened."

Slowly, Angelo walked around Carbonari, circling, and staring down at him as if he were a bug under a microscope. "Don't get me wrong. Nobody up here minds a little skimmin' off the top. Hell, Donnie, we're all freakin' crooks to begin wit', ain't we, boys?" He laughed. "But da penthouse, da helicopter, dat million-dollar yacht, and den da Manhattan condo — even dat's okay, so long as you're makin' your 'nut.' But when you come up short, *real short*, dere's limits, and you forgot dat, Donnie, didn't you? Now, da money's gone, the penthouse and helicopter got all shot to hell, bodies all over da freakin' place, and nobody can find dat sailboat. It's a real mess you left down dere, kid."

Carbonari began shaking his head, trying to talk, but the gag was too tight, not that it mattered. None of the other men on that boat had the slightest interest in anything he had to say anyway.

As they came around the headland and entered the broad, open bay, the water got rougher, the boat began to rock, and Angelo finally took a seat on one of the benches. "Remember when we used to go down to Atlantic City and go fishin', Donnie? Let's see, it was me, you, your old man, Freddie from Brownsville, Tony from up in Queens, Lenny, sometimes Petey from Jamaica Avenue, even Father Pat, from St. Michael's. You wuz what? Maybe seven or eight then? I remember your old man had a fishing boat he used to take us out on." Angelo stopped and looked around. "It was about like dis one, wasn't it? I don't think you liked dat boat very much back den, did you? I remember havin' to hold you over the side by your feet while you upchucked your breakfast. Remember dat? Yeah, good times back then. I wonder what happened to dat old boat?"

Carbonari began to twist and squirm again on the floor, fighting the ropes, but that was a waste of energy. The knots were tight, and he wasn't getting loose.

"What?" Angelo finally asked. "You want to know where we're goin'? Oh, I think you already know dat, don't you? You're goin' for a little swim out where you can say "Hi" to a bunch 'a our old pals — your father's, mine, and I hear some 'a yours too." The man looked at his watch. "Well, we should be down dere in… maybe another hour or so, dat's plenty 'a time for us to talk, maybe even for you to talk. You see, us and da Genoveses, we gotta know where all dat money went, Donnie. Twenty-seven mil, dat's a lotta somolians."

Carbonari began to squirm again. Finally, Angelo bent over and removed Donatello's gag. "You finally got somethin' to say? Say it."

Carbonari coughed and wheezed as he pleaded with him, "Angelo I swear I didn't do it. I don't have the money."

"Ey, between you, me, and da lamppost, kid, nobody thinks you do. Da smart money's on dat Dutch prick you hired. Von Christ? Von Grass? Or whatever da hell his name is."

"Van Gries, it's Van Gries. And maybe he did take it, I don't know."

"Well, you better know. Nobody liked him from day one. He was too slick. He wasn't 'our' kind, and you know exactly what I mean! I gotta tell ya, kid, when I saw dose videos somebody sent me 'a you and him, I about puked, but dat don't matter! It's da money, Donnie. You hired da guy. Da money's gone. He's gone. And it's on *your* freakin' head."

"I know, I know, but if you cut me loose, maybe I can find him."

"You had three weeks, Donnie. Time's up. You know how dat goes; we can't make no more excuses to da Genoveses." He shrugged. "By the way, how big are you?"

"Me?" Carbonari frowned. "I don't know, six foot three, 220 pounds. Why?"

Angelo turned and looked at the other two men. "Good thing you brought da chainsaw. It's gonna be a bitch gettin' him in dat drum."

CHAPTER THIRTY-FIVE

The **Beneteau Oceanis 60** sailboat proved to be everything Martijn Van Gries hoped for, and more. Big, powerful, and fully automated, when he unfurled all 2,000 square feet of sails, she flew across the water. In every port they stopped, the sleek white hull and tall mast turned heads, and he loved it. Sailing this million-dollar yacht around the Caribbean was like walking on the moon for a poor boy who grew up in "council housing" in Rotterdam, where the walls were paper thin, and he shared a tiny bedroom with his three brothers.

Two months before, when he jumped on board the *Prancin' and Dancin'* in the middle of the night, engaged its 150 hp Volvo Penta engine, and powered out of the Bimini Bay marina into the open Atlantic, he knew he needed to clear American waters, fast. He set course east to Bermuda, where the hired help knew how to treat wealthy visitors. He had been referred to a small marina on the seamier side of the island that specialized in giving boats a complete "makeover" by some similarly shady characters he grew up with in Holland. They painted the blue hull white, added several decorative bands around it, and bought new sets of sails with brightly colored panels and designs. With a rented high-end laser printer, he created a half-dozen new foreign registrations for the boat; and by the time he left Bermuda, any "footprints" he left behind in Atlantic City had blown away with the wind.

The first night out, he painted over Donatello's poofy *Prancin' and Dancin'* and hung a new name plate on the stern that read the *Michiel de Ruyter,* in honor of the legendary seventeenth-century Dutch admiral who fought the Corsairs, the French, the British, and even Caribbean pirates in more than forty battles over sixty years. Anticipating the eventual need to disappear, he had a half-dozen other nameplates and hull decals prepared months before. He had been in a patriotic mood when he ordered them, so after the admiral, he might try the *Hans Brinker,* the *Vincent van Gogh,* the *Arjin Robben,* the *Windmill,* or the *Pieter Bruegel,* depending on how he felt.

Too bad about Donnie, Martijn thought. He saw a small news clip in the online edition of the *New York Times* that the "Don of Atlantic City" hadn't been seen in a month and might have disappeared. With local, state, and federal police investigations still swirling about following the mob shoot-out in one of his casinos, that left many Manhattan pundits to wonder. Martijn didn't. He had a pretty good idea exactly where Donatello was: in thirty feet of water off Brigantine. Not that he really missed the big pervert. Martijn had always been bi-sexual. He figured that came from sharing a tiny bedroom with a bunch of brothers, but what the hell. He still hurt thinking about the things he had to do to keep Carbonari happy. Sometimes the corporate ladder could be a bitch, and sometimes it made you one, as he well knew.

From Bermuda, he sailed a long, looping route around the west coast of Cuba, making several stops, until he eventually reached the Caymans to visit his bankers. Over the previous three years, he had carefully skimmed over eleven million dollars from the casino and hotel operating accounts, and from the Boardwalk Investment accounts, not counting the "travelling" money he brought in the briefcase. Fortunately, he had transferred the last of it to the secret bank accounts he established in the Caymans before everything went to hell. For a price, the bankers down there were masters at evading US currency and tax laws and redirecting money into a dozen even more opaque accounts in Switzerland, Russia, Macau, and other countries.

After a leisurely stay in the Caymans, he and Eva set sail again, heading for Haiti, the Turks and Caicos, and the Dominican Republic, carefully avoiding Puerto Rico, the Virgin Islands, or any other US territory, before "island hopping" down the chain of Leeward and Windward Islands along the eastern Caribbean. With each stop, he was careful to brush away whatever new footprints he left behind, changing sails, registrations, and name plates.

Bob knew that it always took a few days to "come back down" after a quick but violent dust-up like they had in Atlantic City. His first task was to check on Dorothy and Lonzo in the joint hospital at Fort Dix and McGuire Air Force Base, where the general had arranged the medevac flight that night. They released Lonzo to the outpatient center at Fort Bragg a few days later, but the Air Force kept Dorothy in the surgery and post-op wing for almost three weeks, given the more serious nature of her wound and the fact that she was a decorated officer. With a "Three-Star" from JSOC making the calls, they were treated like foreign royalty and neither the Army nor the Air Force in New Jersey asked any questions.

Eventually, those two joined the rest of "The Ghost's merry band of modern-day Robin Hoods" in the rolling, wooded hills north of Fort Bragg and Fayetteville, in North Carolina. Within a few days of arriving, Bob turned Linda and Patsy loose. They quickly found a 600-acre farm for rent which had been a corporate training center and retreat. It featured a marvelously renovated and expanded twelve-bedroom Victorian farmhouse and series of meeting rooms, barns, and other outbuildings, including an indoor pistol range. They named the place "Sherwood Forest," and it offered perfect seclusion for the group. At Bob's insistence, Linda hired the Fort Bragg Conference Center to provide housekeeping, property management, and occasional kitchen services for his growing group of friends.

They immediately flew Ellie down from her aunt's in Chicago, buying both the little girl and Crookshanks the cat their own seats in First Class. Bob still had a business to run and was required to make frequent trips back to Arlington Heights to take care of ongoing Toler TeleCom business. Before long, he promoted his and Ed Toler's Executive Assistant, Maryanne Simpson, to President, while he remained Chairman of the Board, freeing up an already impossible schedule.

Ernie Travers returned to the Chicago Police Department's south side headquarters and his important job with their Organized Crime Task Force, while the remaining Deltas — Chester, Koz The Batman, and Bulldog — reluctantly reported back to the Unit. Bob set aside five rooms on the back of the building for Jimmy, Ronald, and Sasha, with Jimmy in charge, to set up their own "KGB Spymaster Data Center," as Sasha called it, complete with its own lounge, bar, kitchen, and unlimited budget for equipment, subject only to Linda's oversight. That made the Russian very, very happy.

Patsy never again set foot in the house she and Vinnie had bought. Instead, she moved into what they now officially called "Sherwood Forest" with Jimmy, and Bob gave them the master suite in the data center.

Everyone and everything was gradually beginning to play to form, except Ace. He took some of the ton of leave he had coming and remained up at McGuire with Dorothy until she was released, and they moved in too. That was when he shocked Bob by telling him that he had put in his papers and was retiring, that he and Dorothy had quietly gotten married in the hospital chapel up at McGuire, and that they were pooling their money for a down-payment on a horse ranch in Montana.

"Whoa, don't make any rash decisions," Bob told him. "It would be a sin to waste all that Special Op experience you have jammed inside your head. And you're seriously underestimating the adrenaline rush you're going to need as you slide into retirement. Besides, I need a new executive officer, now that Gramps made himself unavailable."

"A header off a five-story building will do that, you know."

"True, but with Jimmy's cyber magic, you can still raise horses, telecommute here, and enjoy the occasional gut-wrenching operation when you want to."

Since Dorothy couldn't travel for a few weeks anyway, Bob persuaded them to stay at the "Forest" until the dust settled, after which time they might not have to worry about that horse farm down-payment.

Before they had even moved in, Bob brought down some of his tech people from Toler TeleCom in Arlington Heights to install a state-of-the-art internet and telecommunications system. He then got some high-tech signal friends from Fort Bragg to help him design an "Embassy Level" security system. With all technology in place after the first week, Bob caucused with Jimmy and set out a work program to go after the rest of Carbonari's empire and track down Martijn Van Gries.

A month later, Bob threw an elaborate and very private dinner party at The Forest for "The Merry Band" as they had begun calling themselves. The group was now up to seventeen — Bob and Linda, Ace and Dorothy, Patsy and Jimmy, Ernie, Koz, Chester, Lonzo, The Batman, Bulldog, Ronald, Sasha, Dimitri Karides, who Ernie was able to track down in France, and by special invitation, Lieutenant General Stansky and Command Sergeant Major O'Connor. Wives were invited, where applicable, because Bob and Linda figured it wouldn't prove practical not to. With the wait staff dismissed, the doors closed, and a lot of wine flowing, Bob finally stood and addressed the group.

"We began calling ourselves Robin Hood and his Merry Band, I guess that's my fault or maybe Dimitri's, because we're getting pretty good at stealing from the bad guys and trying to do good things with it. Consider what I'm about to tell you as top-secret as anything we ever did in Delta. It has to be that way. I took the liberty of incorporating us as 'The Merry Band of Sherwood Forest,' and all seventeen of you are partners."

"I bet that raised some eyebrows down at the secretary of state's office in Raleigh," Ace laughed.

"As a few of you know, so far we've 'liberated' over thirty million from the working capital of the Atlantic City and New York mobs; and if Jimmy and his guys get lucky, I don't think we're quite finished with them yet. That leaves us two problems. First, what do we do with it? And second, how do we put a structure in place to protect ourselves, in case they ever figure out who did it, and to be able to strike at any other 'targets of opportunity' that may pop up, or anyone else who pisses us off and is in need of a little behavior modification.

"As we did last time, we're donating half the money to various veterans' charities from the DAV to AMVETS, Homes for Our Troops, the USO, Fisher House, and Thanks USA. We've had some expenses to pay out of the other half, plus the cost to set up this compound and establish some reserves; but we still have enough left for some profit sharing."

He nodded to Linda, who stood and began walking around the table handing out envelopes. "There's a check in there for each of you to augment your retirement accounts in the amount of $250,000, compliments of Lucchese and Genovese families in New York City. You all get the same amount, because you all came when needed and all took the same risks. Linda and I aren't taking any, for a variety of reasons, neither are Ellie or Crookshanks the cat, even though the cat probably played as critical of a role as anybody. We invited your wives, because they need to know that you didn't rob a bank or win the Powerball

Lottery."

"Anyway," he smiled, "this isn't a democracy. It's 'The Golden Rule.' I'm giving out the gold, and I make the rules. But, like I said before, we aren't finished yet."

When the evening was over and the Merry Band began to break up and head for home or to their beds, as the case may be, General Stansky and Pat O'Connor pulled Bob aside.

"This is damned nice of you, Ghost," Stansky told him as he looked at the check. "You didn't need to do this for us, but we appreciate it. It'll help a couple of decrepit Army retirees find some land up on a lake in Tennessee and buy a couple of bass boats."

"Oh, don't worry, General," Bob told him. "I don't think you're finished earning that money yet."

"I sure hope not." Stansky winked. "Hard to argue with having fun and doing some good at the same time. By the same token, don't think I'm finished with you either. There's no telling what might come up from time to time that could use a little 'off book' servicing."

"As always, it would be my pleasure, sir," Bob smiled.

It was a beautiful morning for sailing, Martijn thought to himself. The sun was bright, the boat handled marvelously, and the sea was just right, with gently rolling three-to five-foot swells. They could do thirteen or fourteen knots if the wind held; but it slowly backed off. Still, at 10 knots it provided enough interest to keep him busy at the helm as he continued east toward St. Martin.

Now tanned and thoroughly relaxed, he and Eva rarely wore clothes, except in port. That was her idea. "Marty, why put them on, when you'll only have to take them off to make love to me," she told him with an innocent smile that belied her thoroughly kinky sexual preferences. The girl was insatiable and being alone with her on a big boat for the past month allowed them to experiment with most of them.

He sat in the captain's chair at the ship's wheel in the cockpit while she went below and came back with another gin and tonic and a fresh bottle of suntan lotion for him to rub on her. Needless to say, he had only gotten her half covered when they were both sufficiently aroused for her to straddle him and begin making love right there in the bright sunshine on the boat's double-wide helmsman's seat. She closed her eyes and rocked back and forth on top of him, slow and easy, moving with the motion of the boat as the sweat began to pour off them. Almost in a trance, he knew she could continue at that pace for a long, long time if he let her.

Completely absorbed in each other, they were unaware that a small airplane had flown over them and come back around again. It was only when the airplane passed low overhead a second time that they became aware it was even there. Eva looked up, waved, and smiled, but she didn't stop. In fact, the awareness that someone was up there watching turned her on even more, and Martijn immediately felt her move up and down on him, faster and faster.

Unfortunately, that was when his satellite phone rang on the cushion next to him.

"No, no," she said. "Don't even think about it."

He looked down at the screen and saw it was his banker in the Caymans. "No choice, it'll only take a minute."

"It better!" she said without breaking stride.

"Yes," he quickly answered the phone.

"Herr Van den Dorp," his banker began, addressing Martijn by the alias the bank knew him by, "glad I could catch you. Dennis here. I hope I'm not disturbing you?"

"Not me, but you are catching *us* in the middle of something, Dennis."

"It better only be the beginning!" Eva said as she bit his ear.

"I see, but I thought I should give you a call," Dennis continued. "I was checking my accounts, and I noticed that all of yours suddenly showed zero balances at midmorning today."

Understandably, Martijn's mind was elsewhere until Dennis said that. "What?" the Dutchman asked. "What do you mean at zero balances? I am not understanding."

"Frankly, I didn't either," Dennis said. "I phoned several of the correspondent banks, and they all said that you transferred your funds out first thing this morning. Since we gave you a very attractive funds management and transfer rate, I was somewhat surprised that you had not worked those transactions back through us again."

"Marty, you're losing it!" Eva warned. "You've got to keep your head in the game, so to speak. You know how I hate to be disappointed."

"Uh, look, Dennis, I need to get to my computer and check my screens," Van Gries said as he broke into a cold sweat. "I'll call you right back." He rang off and stood up, completely ignoring Eva, but all too well aware that their moment had passed.

"Marty!" she complained, wrapping her arms and legs around him and hanging on, as he managed to 'walk' over to his big laptop computer sitting on the counter, reach around her, and begin typing.

General Stansky was in the pilot seat in Dorothy's temporary absence, with Pat O'Connor playing co-pilot, when they came around the third time in their

Cessna 208B turboprop. Leaving Fort Bragg before dawn, they refueled at Homestead Air Force Base in southern Florida before turning east to San Juan and the central Caribbean. Jimmy, Ronald, and the mad Russian were still back in North Carolina directing them by GPS. With Jimmy's magic bag of electronic tricks, it had taken them less than five weeks to track down Martijn Van Gries, his boat, and all of his many bank accounts. The Dutchman may have thought he was the smartest thing MIT ever produced, but Ronald's limp wasn't going away anytime soon, and the three Geeks had a major score to settle with him.

Bob and Linda had their binoculars focused on the sailboat as Stansky powered back the engines as far as he could without stalling. That allowed Ace to open the side hatch while Dorothy lay on the deck with her head and shoulders out the open doorway. Ace kept a firm grip on her thick, leather rodeo belt with one hand and on the doorframe with the other.

"You sure you want to do this?" he asked her over the roar of the engines.

She turned and glared up at him. "After all those weeks in the hospital, the IVs and feeding tubes, try to stop me."

Martijn was only halfway through the accounts at the banks, but he could already see that Dennis was right. The balances were now zero. All of his money had disappeared. But how? And by whom? He was stunned and still coming to grips with the fact he had been cleaned out when that gray turboprop passed directly over them again.

This time, the airplane flew lower still, barely clearing the mast. Looking up, he saw a package the size of a cigar box fly out of the Cessna's side door and slowly arc downward toward the big sailboat. It landed in the cockpit, bounced off the deck, then off the other helm station, and skittered to rest a few feet away from him.

That even stopped Eva. Their faces were only inches apart as he tried to drop her and reach the package, but that was easier said than done. "Marty!" she screamed as she wrapped her legs even more tightly around his waist and hung on. Somehow, he managed to bend down far enough to pick it up. It was heavy, wrapped in brown paper. On top, someone had drawn a "Smiley Face," and written a short message in thick, black marker.

It said, "Fry in Hell. Burke. Boom!"

Unlike Eva and Martijn, Dorothy's timing was perfect. With agonizing slowness, the package arced downward toward the big sailboat, landing in the center of its cockpit. Bob saw Martijn pick it up, read the message, and then try to throw it overboard, but the Dutchman was too slow. Bob pressed the call button on his cell phone and a bright flash of light and a shattering explosion ripped the sailboat apart. The small gray airplane banked and came back around for another pass as the Beneteau's fuel tanks exploded in a bright orange fireball. Within seconds, the sailboat was gone, leaving behind an oil slick, some scattered pieces of white wood and plastic, and a black cloud of smoke.

"Wow!" Linda said, "Talk about your coitus interruptus; that takes the cake."

***

If you enjoyed the read, I would appreciate
your going to the <u>Burke's Gamble</u> Kindle
Book Page and posting a rating and comment.
Just click on the gold stars and "Write a
Customer Review" of your own.

http://www.amazon.com/dp/B01AR7CP80

Also, if you'd like a FREE copy of another of my
fan-favorite thrillers, Aim True, My Brothers, with
4.6 stars on 252 Kindle Ratings, copy and paste
this link into your browser:

<u>https://dl.bookfunnel.com/3uu04iwhsd</u>

AUTHOR'S NOTE

This book is fiction. My good friends and readers in New Jersey who are familiar with Atlantic City will recognize that I took a few liberties with the geography of their fair city. My Bimini Bay, Tuscany Towers, and Siesta Cove casinos do not exist. The real-life Borgata, Harrah's, and Golden Nugget casinos are located in that general vicinity, but any similarities are purely coincidental. Most assuredly, however, Chef Vola's restaurant does exist and is one of the finest Italian restaurants on the east coast. I've also taken some artistic license with streets and marinas. It is difficult enough to navigate around Atlantic City with its one-way streets, stop signs, and a general lack of street names, without subjecting fictional characters to the same inconvenience. Lastly, if I disparaged the reputation of any business or 'family' that may or may not happen to exist in Atlantic City, Philadelphia, or various New York City neighborhoods, I could hardly have done worse than *Boardwalk Empire*, *The Godfather*, or history itself. So, I hope you enjoyed the story.

Preview and Sample Chapters of

Burke's Revenge

The third book in the Author's smash hit
domestic suspense thriller series

CHAPTER ONE

Fayetteville, North Carolina

The **Fayetteville, North Carolina,** Regional Airport isn't very large. It only has four gates and a handful of flights going in and out each night; but it's available, it's quick to get in and out of, and it sure beats flying into Charlotte, Raleigh, or Charleston, if Fayetteville is where you are trying to go. Ten minutes after his flight landed, Bob Burke was through the TSA exit, down the escalator to the ground floor, and out the front doors, where he found himself in a warm, soft, late-summer, Carolina evening. Try doing that at O'Hare, he smiled to himself, or damn near anywhere else.

It was 9:30 p.m. and the sun had already set. Without giving it any thought, he paused and looked up. Even through the bright airport lights, he could see a quarter moon and a few bright stars in the sky; causing him to take a deep breath, happy to be back home after four hectic days in Chicago. Most of the other passengers who came in on his flight had peeled off and headed for Baggage Claim, so the sidewalk was empty, as was the parking lot and the entry road beyond. Well, Bob thought, at least they hadn't rolled up the runways for the night.

He was a second-generation Army brat and Fayetteville was beginning to feel like home again. He had spent the past two years working in Chicago, putting up with O'Hare, traffic congestion, and those ugly Chicago winters; and only went back because he had a business to run up there. Teleconferences and e-mail were great, but any manager worth his salt knows he must put hands on, press the flesh, and show his smiling face around the office every few weeks. To maximize his time up there, he always booked the last flight that would get him back to Fayetteville that night. It meant changing planes in Charlotte and taking one of those tiny Dash-8 commuter jets. He hated those trips, especially when those God-awful early-evening thunderstorms blew up on that last, tiring leg home. Still, a

Dash-8 beat a three-hour drive on winding roads through the fields and farms of Carolina. As they say in Fayetteville, "You can't get there from here."

As usual, most of the passengers on his flight were Army, headed up the road to Fort Bragg. They were dressed in the latest camouflage Army Combat Uniform, beige desert boots, and a beret — maroon, tan, or green, depending on their jobs. Funny, Bob thought; he had been taking this flight once or twice each month for the past six months, and he had yet to run into a familiar face from "back in the day." True, it had been almost three years since he quit the Army and took the job in Chicago, but he used to be a fixture in Special Ops here at Bragg and in Iraq and Afghanistan for almost a decade. He knew almost everyone back then, and everyone knew him, or so he thought. Now, however, other than his own "guys" from the Rangers and Delta Force, it seemed that "the Ghost" really had vanished. He shouldn't be surprised. There were 55,000 soldiers stationed at Bragg now, and two years away from that high-energy military lifestyle seemed like a lifetime. Oh, well, he thought, time marches to its own beat, and so must he.

The Fayetteville airport was definitely "no frills," — no food, no drink at night, and no shuttle buses to the parking lots. He stepped off the curb and began to hoof it across the Short Term Lot, crossing several landscaped medians, and on into the Long Term Lot, where he had parked his new Ford 150 pickup truck. He was dressed in his usual "gone-to-the-office-and-don't-give-a-damn," casual business attire — L.L. Bean chinos, a button-down blue Oxford cloth shirt, no tie, a wrinkle-free blue blazer, and his newest country affectation: a pair of lightweight cowboy boots. He carried no luggage, only two carry-ons. Over his left shoulder hung a small, black computer bag, and in his right hand was a Halliburton high-security aluminum briefcase, which had a week's worth of homework from the Chicago office jammed inside. The Army taught him to pack light, and preferably to pack nothing at all; so he left his business suits, dress shoes, ties, and all the rest of that crap in the closet of his Chicago office. With Global Entry, he could avoid the whole TSA hassle to begin with.

Midway across the dark parking lot, he stopped and looked around. He had only been gone for five days; but it had been "O-Dark-30" when he left, and he had been in and out of way too many parking lots since then. Apparently, "no frills" also extended to parking lot lights. Half of them were out, while the other half were spaced too far apart to accomplish much of anything, leaving large, dark patches all through the large lot. Fortunately, the quarter moon gave off enough light for an old infantryman like him, so he set off walking through the rows and the median strips to his right, where he was pretty sure he had left the pickup.

As he walked, he pulled his set of keys from his pocket and looked at the "keyless entry" key fob. It had one of those little red horn buttons for dummies like him who couldn't remember where they parked. It also had a remote starter button designed for "Susie housewife," so she wouldn't need to plant her warm butt on a cold car seat on one of those nasty Chicago winter mornings. Unfortunately, the remote starter could also set off a car bomb, if the Gumbahs he crossed in Chicago and New York finally figured out who and where he was. So, all things considered, Bob usually opted for the third and somewhat safer button, which would only open the door locks and make the headlights flash.

Before he did, however, he took one more look around. Sure enough, he finally saw his white Ford 150 three vehicles down in the next row, parked in the shadow of a humongous, midnight blue Chevy Tahoe SUV. When he got within fifty feet, he pressed the button to open the electric door locks, which also triggered a quick, bright flash from the truck's headlights, revealing a cluster of men huddled between his Ford and the SUV. First impressions are usually correct 99% of the time, and what he saw in that brief flash of light was four men with long hair, blue jeans, beer guts, leather biker jackets, and some serious tattoos. In the row beyond them, his headlight beams revealed four chromed-up Harley-Davidson motorcycles. The bikers were so focused on breaking into the two trucks that the bright flash of the headlights took them by surprise.

"Turn off them goddamned lights and get yer ass outta here!" the closest biker turned and growled at Bob. He appeared to be the biggest of the bunch, perhaps six foot three and 225 pounds, probably the dumbest of the bunch too, which was why they left him standing guard. Behind him, one of the others held a "Slim Jim" in both hands, working its thin metal strip on the driver's side door of the Tahoe, pushing it up and down and trying to pop open the door lock. Another biker leaned over his shoulder, watching, and waiting, while the fourth held a ball-peen hammer at the ready, in the event the more sophisticated entry methods failed.

"Sorry, Gomer," Bob answered back, "but that's my pickup truck and I'm not leaving here without it."

"Wuddju call me?" the first biker's eyes narrowed as he straightened up and turned angrily toward the much smaller man approaching them.

The biker behind him with the ball-peen hammer wasn't nearly as shy. "Oh, this here's yer truck, boy? This piece a' crap 150?" he asked, as he swung the hammer into Bob's passenger side window, smashing it into a thousand little pieces.

Even a freshly-minted country boy like Bob Burke knew that down south here, you don't mess with a man's woman, his hunting dog, or his pickup truck, probably not in that order, and the goober with the hammer had just made a big mistake. At only five foot nine inches tall and maybe 165 pounds, Bob Burke was easy to underestimate, but people rarely did that twice. When he left active duty as a Major with twelve years and six combat tours in the Rangers and Delta Force, he walked out the door with most of the top medals the Army hands out for doing what he did. That included a Distinguished Service Cross, a couple of Silver Stars, and five Purple Hearts — plus three bullet wounds and enough shrapnel in various body parts to require "hand wanding" at TSA checkpoints. He also walked out as an expert with most things that shot bullets, from a 9-millimeter Beretta semiautomatic pistol to the M4 Assault Rifle, a 105-millimeter howitzer, when needed, and his personal favorite, the 50-caliber Barrett sniper rifle. He was even more skilled in most of the Asian martial arts.

Bob looked at the biker with the ball-peen hammer and then at his window. "You know," Bob said as he lowered his computer bag to the pavement, "you should think twice before you pull this crap around Fort Bragg. There's no telling who you might piss off."

"Yeah?" Ball-Peen eyed him up and down. "What're you, another Army puke?"

"Used to be," Bob answered as he continued walking straight at them, his steel briefcase in his right hand and his eyes scanning every angle and opportunity he saw. "Now, I'm just 'the telephone guy.' "

"The telephone guy?" The biker frowned and spat on the ground, not understanding.

"That's what I said. Don't tell me you're stupid *and* deaf? That'll be $200 for the window, you dumb grit."

"Dumb grit?" Ball-Peen seethed. "Why you little…"

"What the hell you doin'?" the third biker using the Slim Jim on the Tahoe's front door finally turned and snapped at Ball-Peen. "Go shut that guy up!"

"Yeah, come shut me up," Bob smiled. There were four of them, each at least three inches and thirty pounds bigger than he was, but four out-of-shape bikers trapped in the narrow space between the two trucks didn't concern him at all, especially not after they broke his truck window.

Once Special Ops, always Special Ops, Bob remembered someone telling him, and screw that defense stuff. The best defense is always a good offense. Of the martial arts styles he knew, his current favorite was Krav Maga, the radical fighting discipline developed by the Israeli Defense Forces. There was nothing defensive about it, and it definitely was not art. Some called Krav Maga "street fighting with an attitude." You get in the first punch, the last, and everything in between, with the intent to maim or kill.

Despite his extreme daily workouts and peak physical condition, Bob Burke had no bulging Gold's Gym muscles, and looked anything but intimidating. However, he was a man with a lot of "sharp edges," as his lead NCO, Ace Randall, once put it. Whether he was using his hands, feet, a knife, a rock, or a steel-clad briefcase, he was incredibly fast, precise, and well-practiced; and the four bikers had already made several huge tactical mistakes. In addition to having larger mouths than brains, they had bunched themselves together in the narrow, three-foot-wide gap between the Ford 150 and the big Tahoe. That alone would have flunked them out of tactics at West Point, but speed usually tops stupid, anyway.

Time to force the first biker to do something stupid, Bob thought, as he closed in. What Gomer did was to telegraph a looping round-house right at Bob's head. Too little, too late, and about what Bob expected. He shifted his weight far enough back to make the biker's fist miss. As it flashed past his nose, Bob spun and snapped a quick kick into the guy's crotch with his right cowboy boot. They were light and surprisingly flexible, but the "pointy toe" was sharp and hard. The biker never saw it coming. "Oooph!" was all he managed to get out, accompanied by a painful grunt and a burst of air. His eyes went round as hockey pucks as his hands went to his crotch and he doubled up in serious pain. Never one to risk breaking bones in his hands by punching a Neanderthal in the head, Bob let the briefcase finish off the first one, swinging it up. Its hard, reinforced steel edge caught the biker flush on the forehead and snapped him upright. As his eyes rolled back in his head, Bob knew he was out on his feet. He shoved Gomer backward into the two bikers behind him before they could react, and continued to wade into them, remembering Napoleon's old maxim, "Audacity, audacity, always audacity!"

The next one in line was the redneck with the ball-peen hammer. He found himself struggling to shove Gomer aside and stay on his feet at the same time. Still, a hammer could be an extremely nasty weapon, as Bob well knew, and he had no intention of letting him use it.

"You're the moron who broke my window, aren't you?" Bob asked. "Like I said, that'll be $200. Pay up!"

With an angry snarl, Jethro drew the ball-peen back, intending to bring it down on the top of Bob's head. Like his pal, however, he was way too slow to pull that off. He was still turned, with his arm and the hammer behind him at the end of a long back swing, which left his neck fully exposed, when Bob sprang into the air and executed a perfect "Mae Tobi Geri" karate flying kick. The hard edge of his leather boot sole caught the biker flush in the throat, ending his night. Gasping for air, his hands went to his neck and the hammer went flying as he stumbled backward into the next clown in line behind him.

So far, Bob had used a simple street fighting move followed by a high-level karate kick to disable the first two, but things were still a bit crowded between the trucks. The next in line was the big mouth who told Ball-Peen to "shut him up." He was the smallest of the bunch, and Bob figured that made him the "Leader of the Pack." Seeing what happened to the first two, at least he was smart enough to quit playing with the Tahoe's door, rip the Slim Jim out with both hands, and turn to face Bob. As he did, the flying ball-peen hammer hit him flush on the shin bone. "Ah! Ah!" he screamed, wide-eyed, grabbed his leg, and began hopping around; however, with two of his men already lying at his feet, that wasn't a good idea either.

"You bastard, you bastard!" Slim Jim screamed at Burke as it finally dawned on him that this night's hijinks weren't quite going as planned.

"Don't let your mouth get your ass in even more trouble," Bob warned.

The long, thin blade of a Slim Jim wasn't designed to cut, but in the right hands, with enough malice behind it, it probably could. Still, grimacing, the biker managed to get it in a two-handed baseball grip, regain his balance, and swing it at Burke like a scythe. Bob had continued moving forward, intending to finish this guy off, but he was quicker than Bob expected. He managed to pull back at the last second as the blade whistled past, barely missing him, but it did slice through his shirt. Bob felt a sharp stinging across his chest, but that wasn't enough to stop him. The biker's follow-through left him over-extended, so Bob stepped in, dropped his left elbow on the biker's clavicle, and snapped his collar bone. Without pausing, he drew the elbow back and smashed it into the guy's face, flattening his nose like a ripe banana and driving him backward, weak-kneed.

Three down and one to go, Bob thought as he turned on the last biker at the end of the queue. "You're next, Lem," he told him. This one appeared to be no more intelligent than the other three, but he had more time to see what was headed his way. Rather than mess around with a hammer or a blade, Lem reached behind him for a blue-steel Desert Eagle .357 Magnum semi-automatic tucked in his belt, hidden under his vest.

The Desert Eagle was a huge and very heavy handgun — the perfect choice, if you want to clear out a bar-full of Hell's Angels, stop a charging rhino, or intimidate some little guy in a dark airport parking lot. However, given what the biker was facing, a smaller and lighter pistol would have been a wiser choice. The night air was warm, Lem's hands were sweaty from trying to break into the trucks, and he snagged the tall front sight of the Desert Eagle in his underwear. Boxers or briefs? That didn't "make no never mind." His confidence soon vanished as he frantically pushed and pulled on the big handgun, finally managing to rip it free. Unfortunately, by the time he did, Bob had picked up Jethro's Slim Jim from the pavement and brought it around in a short, compact swing. The thin blade wasn't particularly sharp, but speed translates into power, like Derek Jeter punching a hard line drive into the hole between third and short. It slashed Lem across his chest, arm, and shoulder, slicing through his pectoral, deltoid, and bicep muscles, and cutting them to the bone.

The biker screamed and the muscles in his arm, hand, and fingers must have involuntarily contracted, because the .357 Magnum went off with a thundering Blam! The barrel was pointing down after he ripped it loose from his pants, and the bullet ricocheted off the concrete and caught him in his own thigh. His grip on the heavy automatic failed, and he dropped it on the pavement, where he soon joined it and his other three pals, screaming and moaning.

It's never a good idea to leave temptation lying around, Bob thought as he picked up the big automatic, bent down, and pressed it against the biker's forehead. Through the pain, the guy's eyes went wide cross-eyed as he found himself looking up the wrong end of the barrel of the Desert Eagle.

"You know, Lem," Bob spoke to him in a calm voice. "This is a pretty nasty handgun to go pulling on strangers. Nobody'd blame me very much if I put a few more holes in you, just for spite, but I'm not gonna do that. I figure the one in your leg is going to keep you limping around rehab for a good long while. When you get out, though, you might consider finding another line of work, 'cause you ain't very damned good at this one."

Looking around, Bob saw two of the others were clearly headed for the hospital with Lem. Unfortunately, Gomer, the first one he put down, was already shaking his head and trying to get back up on his hands and knees. Other than a broken nose, a badly dented forehead, and no doubt some very painful testicles, he was becoming ambulatory and a viable threat again. "Can't have that, now can we?" Bob asked as he took the .357 by the barrel and cracked Gomer on the side of the head. He went back down again like a sack of potatoes.

Not one to leave a job unfinished, and still pissed about the window of his truck, he turned back and saw their four Harleys, mostly old, heavily-chromed, chopped-down, street hogs standing in the next aisle. Two were 750s, one was a 500, and one was a big old monster with so many modifications that Bob couldn't tell what it started out as. The Desert Eagle held a nine-round magazine, which meant he had eight shots left; so, he stepped closer and fired two quick ones into the circular chrome plates that covered their carburetors. That should do it, he thought. Those hogs were now dead pigs, and the only place they were going was to the shop for an engine rebuild.

As he turned and headed back to his truck, he realized the loud cannon shots from the Desert Eagle were certain to draw some unwanted official company. Time to go. Using his shirt tail, he wiped his fingerprints off the grip and trigger of the now empty automatic and tossed it under the Tahoe, well out of the biker's reach. As he passed Lem, he tapped his bad leg with the toe of his boot. The biker groaned again as Bob said, "Next time, try Chapel Hill, or give the Dookies over in Durham a try, because you're way out of your league down here. If I ever see you again in Fayetteville, you won't even limp away. You got that?"

He retrieved his computer case and opened the driver side door of the Ford

150, knowing it was time to vanish. Brushing the broken glass off his seat, he started the engine and quickly backed out of the parking space, not particularly caring if any arms, legs, or random biker body parts were in the way. The parking lot's lone exit was at the far end. As he got closer, he could see the gate was down and the shed manned. He pulled up to the window, he reached up for his parking ticket, which he always tucked behind the visor, and handed it to the attendant with two twenty-dollar bills. As the old guy in the booth ran the ticket, he kept glancing nervously to his left, staring into the dark parking lot.

"Say," the attendant finally asked, "you didn't hear no gunshots back there, did you?"

Bob turned, followed the attendant's eyes, and shrugged. "You know, I suppose that's what it could have been. There's a bunch of bikers back there on Harleys, so I gave them a wide berth."

"Yeah, I wish I could," the attendant replied nervously as he handed Bob his change and stamped parking receipt, still not sure.

"If I were you, I'd call the cops and let them handle it," Bob advised as he drove away into the night. He didn't want this, but every now and then it was nice to know you still got it. After twelve years in the Army, he'd had enough fighting and killing to fill several lifetimes. What he wanted now more than anything else was dull, boring, peace and quiet. After all, that's why he moved back down to North Carolina in the first place.

XXX

If you enjoyed this Preview Chapter you can go to the
Burke's Gamble Kindle book page and purchase one.
Just copy and paste this link into your browser:

http://amzn.to/2lORmXJ

ABOUT THE AUTHOR
WILLIAM F. BROWN

Burke's Gamble is the second story in the Bob Burke suspense thriller series, taking its place next to *Burke's War* and this year's *Burke's Revenge* as exciting, fun reads. I'm the author of nine mystery and international suspense thrillers, exclusively available on Kindle.

A native of Chicago, I received a BA from The University of Illinois in History and Russian Area studies, and a Masters in City Planning. I served as a

Company Commander in the US Army and later became active in local and regional politics in Virginia. As a Vice President of the real estate subsidiary of a Fortune 500 corporation, I was able to travel widely in the US and now travel extensively abroad, particularly in Europe and the Middle East, locations which have featured prominently in my writing. When not writing, I play bad golf, have become a dogged runner, and paint passable landscapes in oil and acrylic. Now retired, my wife and I live in Florida.

In addition to the novels, I've written four award-winning screenplays. They've placed First in the suspense category of Final Draft, were a Finalist in Fade In, First in Screenwriter's Utopia — Screenwriter's Showcase Awards, Second in the American Screenwriter's Association, Second at Breckenridge, and others. One was optioned for film.

The best way to follow my work and learn about sales and freebees is through my website **http://billbrownthrillernovels.com,** which has Preview Chapters of each of my novels, interviews, book reviews, and other links.

DEDICATION

To the best set of proof readers a writer can
have: my wife, Elisabeth Hallett in far-away
Montana, to my friend Loren Vinson in San
Diego, and to two of my neighbors in sunny
Florida: Susan Day and Ron Klock. I also
want to thank Hitch, Barb, Indira and the staff
of Booknook Biz in Phoenix for their help
with processing and conversion of the
manuscript into Kindle-Speak. And I want to
thank Todd Hebertson at My Personal Art in
Salt Lake City for the outstanding cover art he
has provided for my recent books.

Burke's Gamble

Copyright © 2016 by William F. Brown

Cover Design by Todd Hebertson

Digital Editions produced by
Booknook.biz.

Printed in the USA
CPSIA information can be obtained
at www.ICGtesting.com
LVHW022242290823
756683LV00007B/49